FACES OF OUR YOUTH

A Novel

A. Happy Umwagarwa

To my late brothers,
Lucky JC and Touring JP:
Because You Died, I Fear Death No More.

1

When blameless boys become evil guys, all of us should worry. On September 15, 2014, when I read news on Rwanda, I could not fathom how the boy I had left in Rwanda in 1998 had become the hip-hop star who was reported to have been shot dead trying to escape prison. The photo on the article was indeed of my brother, though he looked older than his age, with a face hidden by dreadlocks. It was written that my brother, David Mukiga, identified himself as Mr. D. but was called Badguy by his friends and fans. I wanted to cry, but I could not. I felt bad and guilty for having left my siblings in Rwanda, in the aftermath of the genocide against the Tutsi, during which our mother, Kayitesi, was killed.

My siblings and I were fathered by three different men who shared nothing in common, apart from the fact that each of them shared a bed with our mother during one or more nights of her miserable life. My father was a French white man whom Mama had met in her youthful years in the late 1970s when she worked as a waitress in one of the French-owned hotels in Kigali. My younger sister, Celine Kaneza, was fathered by a man from southern Rwanda who identified as a Tutsi. Then the father of our younger brother, David, was a Hutu man who seemed to have both power and money during those years when most of our country's leaders were from the North West, where he was also from. He had changed our mother's life from miserable to comfortable, if not extravagant. Though we looked different in the eyes of those who liked to spot facial differences to support nonsense racial or ethnic theories, Celine, David, and I considered ourselves full siblings. We were Kayitesi's children and did not care much about who our fathers were, even though she had not hidden the names of those men from us.

After the genocide against the Tutsi, life separated me from my siblings. My sister, Celine, went to live with our maternal uncle Kamara, who had returned to Rwanda from Burundi. Like many other Rwandans, members of our maternal family had also fled the country in the 1960s, after the 1959 revolution. My brother, David, left me and went to live with his paternal uncle, Mr. Mukinzi. His own father had fled the country after the liberation war that lasted from 1990 to 1994. I stayed alone in our mother's house till 1998, when I won a scholarship from the Francophonie to study in France.

My mission in France was bigger than just studying. I, too, wanted to discover another part of me or another nation I could call home. The minute I boarded the plane from Kigali to Paris, I waved bye to Rwanda and reclaimed my French identity. The only thing I knew was that my father was named Jean-Paul Châteaux, but I had no idea what part of France he lived in or whether he was still alive. My mother, Kayitesi, had not told me much about my father. When I was younger, I cared less about that man who had taken advantage of Mama's misery and produced me before flying back to his comfortable life in France. If my mother had not been killed by her own compatriots, I would never have wanted to search for that father who had not come back to search for me.

I searched for my father in all books and registers in France, only to learn that he had died of cancer in 1998, the same year I boarded the plane to France. When I met his younger brother, Jean Claude Châteaux, he vomited to me all his ignorance about Africa because he thought all I wanted was to inherit my father's assets. So, I decided to forget about Papa and lived in Paris like many other Africans who aimed at nothing but living away from Africa's misery. I was African. I was Rwandan. But life in Europe seemed better, and there was no way I could go back to poor Rwanda.

France introduced me to music, and my favorite instrument was the piano. After I graduated from university with a degree in computer engineering, I secured a job as an IT engineer in one of the international logistics companies in Paris. Even though music was not my career, every evening after work I liked to visit retirement homes and play for elderly people, including a lady named Catherine. Although that lady always seemed in a bad mood, she enjoyed how I played piano. She used to tell me that she did not know Africans could also play instruments that well. She never talked about her children. She never spoke about her family.

One day, Catherine's family members had to be called because she was not breathing well. When I caught sight of my uncle Jean Claude, I could not believe my eyes. The woman I had been playing piano for was my paternal grandmother. My uncle was furious and thought that I knew who Catherine was. His mother would have breathed her last if he dared scream at me. The hug my grandmother gave me brought her back to life. She smiled, and her breathing became normal. We did not have a long conversation. In fact, we did not know where to start. At least I had learned that Catherine, to whom I had given the chance of listening to my music, was my grandmother.

Unfortunately, all days are not sunny. Some are rainy. Only a day after I had hugged my grandma, I learned about my younger brother's death. I immediately bought a flight ticket and boarded a plane to Rwanda. Eight hours of air travel elapsed as if it were just a few minutes. Then the pilot announced that we were landing in Kigali.

I took a cab at the Kigali International Airport and asked the driver to head to Nyamirambo.

When I showed him the news article I had printed, he said, "Oh, have you read about the demise of Badguy? We are all saddened by his death. He was a voice to the voiceless. Mr. D. was his stage name. But Inzuki boys called him Badguy. He was a hip-hop star loved by many trash eaters like us."

I kept silent for seconds, fighting with my ballooning chest before I said, "I am also saddened by his death. In fact, I am coming for his funeral. Was he still living in Nyamirambo?"

"I don't know," the taxi driver responded. "Maybe you can contact Inzuki boys, but I have no idea where they live.

Recently, we were all surprised to learn that Miss Celine is a sister to Mr. D. Nobody knew they were related."

"Did you say Miss Celine? What do you mean by that? I mean, why is she called Miss? "

"She was Miss Rwanda 2000. Now, she is, how do they call them again? Top models. She is a mannequin."

"I get it. I did not know she is now a model. Do you know where she stays? Maybe she is the one coordinating the funeral details of her brother."

"I know where she spends many nights, but I can't tell you."

"Why?"

"I fear for my life."

"Please tell me. I swear I won't tell anyone you have told me. I must meet Mr. D's sister."

The taxi driver insisted that he could not tell me where I could find Celine. Instead, he asked questions about why I was so concerned about David's death.

"Are you a journalist?" he asked. "Do you work for BBC or CNN? I hope you haven't come to investigate."

"No, I am not a journalist," I responded. "I am a musician and loved Mr. D's music. He was my idol."

Some minutes later, the man finally agreed to drop me at the gate where my sister, Celine, spent some nights in Nyarutarama; then he drove off.

I knocked on those scary gates in a neighborhood of European-style modern houses. A voice asked me who I was and whom I was looking for. I could not see the person talking to me, but I could see my face in something that looked like a small mirror. I guessed it was a camera. The gates opened, and I walked into a big compound with impressive greenery. A man who looked as if he were in his sixties asked me again who I was.

"My name is Carlos Châteaux," I said. "I am looking for my sister, Celine."

"Your sister?" the old man asked, with an astonished face.

Before I responded, Celine came out, and when she saw me, she fainted.

"Celine!" I screamed.

"Back off." The old man pushed me. "Please, go away."

When I insisted on approaching Celine and waking her up, the man called some guys whom I guessed were his guards. They pushed me outside the gate.

My brother David is dead, I mused, *and my sister Celine is also probably going to die.* I hated myself for having left my siblings in Rwanda. *What does our late mother think of me?* I wondered. *I have deceived her.* I walked the streets of Nyarutarama, trying to catch another taxi to take me to Nyamirambo. I believed some of our former neighbors could tell me more about the circumstances of David's death. A taxi passed by, and I stopped it. To my surprise, the taxi driver was the same man who had dropped me off where Celine lived. I entered and asked him what his name was. He was called Karekezi. I asked him to take me to Nyamirambo.

When I arrived at the Nyamirambo Stadium, I turned left to go to what used to be our house. I knocked on the gate. A man whose face I had never seen before opened.

"I am looking for the owners of this house," I said.

"What are the names of the people you are looking for?" he asked.

Before I responded to the man, a lady came out. She asked me who I was. After introducing myself to her, she told me that her husband had bought the house in 2005 but refused to tell me who he had bought it from.

Only one person could tell me what had happened. I went to the house of Habimana, the man who hid us in the kitchen of his home during the genocide against the Tutsi. Though I did not want to see the face of Mukandoli, Habimana's evil wife, I had to knock on their door because I needed to talk to her husband. When Mukandoli caught sight of me, her face became full of wrinkles. She had no strength to say a word. She looked like the night she had brought killers to take our mother. My chest swelled, but I had to control my anger. I asked her where her husband was. She looked down and pinched her nails.

"In prison," Mukandoli's daughter responded, clenching her teeth.

"In prison?" I asked. "Why?"

"Go ask your relatives who accused him of involvement in your mother's death," the girl said. "Are you coming here to take our mother as well?"

I turned into a bomb about to explode on Mukandoli and said, "Speak now, say something, tell your daughter the truth. Why did you allow them to take Habimana to jail? Why? Aren't you the one …? No. Who killed our mother? Have you forgotten? I haven't. I will make sure your husband is not punished for the crime he did not commit."

"He has already been sentenced by Gacaca courts for nineteen years in prison," the woman mumbled.

"Where is he?" I asked.

"At the Kigali General Prison."

When I was about to leave that compound, I recalled that I had come to inquire about what had happened to my mother's house. When I asked her, Mukandoli told me that my brother, David, had moved into the house together with the family of his paternal uncle, Mukinzi. They lived in the house until 2005 when Mr. Mukinzi was shot dead by unidentified people. After that incident, my maternal uncle Kamara claimed that the house belonged to his sister and added that only he had the right to his sister's assets. So he sent the police to eject Mukinzi's surviving family from the house. That's how my younger brother became a street boy and, years later, a hip-hop musician, living with those who were known as Inzuki boys.

Time was running, and I had no idea who was organizing David's funeral. The taxi driver was still waiting for me. I revealed to him that I was David and Celine's half-brother. Then, I told him our story, how our mother was killed during the genocide against the Tutsi and how life separated us after the genocide.

Karekezi bent his head on the steering wheel of his car as if fighting tears in his eyes, then he said, "Let's go. We must look for members of Inzuki boys, Badguy's friends. Maybe they are planning the funeral."

He drove to Biryogo, took the muddy road close to the market, and parked the car in front of a compound with a door made of iron sheets. A guy with dirty dreadlocks and a cigarette in his hand came out. His eyes were a mixture of red and black. Looking at the face of that Inzuki boy, I imagined the blues of my brother, David, and my whole body shivered. The taxi driver said to the guy that I was Badguy's brother.

"What? Is this *muzungu* a brother to Badguy?" the guy asked. "What kind of a brother?"

I hated to be called a muzungu, which meant a white person. It always felt like they were denying me my Rwandan heritage. But that was less important at that time. All I wanted was to bury my younger brother, David, whom I had selfishly abandoned in Rwanda for Europe, where nobody called me a white guy but another African on Paris streets.

"I am saddened by his death," I responded to the Inzuki boy. "When is the funeral?"

"The *fundis* are burying him in Gatenga cemetery tomorrow," he replied.

"At what time?" I asked.

"Nobody knows. We need to pay the hospital for the mortuary services. Come and talk to our major."

We entered a compound that smelled like roasted but rotten weed. The boys did not look like human beings I had ever seen before. Their eyes were red, their hairstyles were a diversity, and their lips and gums were all black. Some were smoking cigarettes, others were sniffing some powder, and others were downing some liquids from dirty bottles that used to contain mineral water. Apparently, everybody was shocked to see me walk in.

"Hey, Rotty, who is this muzungu? Does he need some

crocodile *dawa* to smoke?" the tallest of Inzuki boys asked the one with dreadlocks.

"He says he is Badguy's blood," Rotty responded.

I confirmed I was David's brother and told them that the last time I had seen my younger brother was in 1998. They asked me so many questions, as if they did not believe what I was saying. A minute later, Rotty confirmed that he could recall David had once mentioned that he had an elder brother who was a muzungu, though he had not believed him.

When I asked why my brother had been jailed and shot dead, the major of Inzuki boys responded, "The *fundi* was accused of ideology."

"What do you mean?" I asked.

"He had taken too much weed and insulted one of those protected chicks."

"Protected chicks? What does that mean?"

"What don't you understand? In April he said words he was not supposed to say."

"What did he say?" I asked.

"I cannot repeat it," Inzuki boys' major said. "David was high and didn't know what he was saying. The *fundi* did not have any ideology, apart from getting high on life, but he simply got high on the wrong chick."

I couldn't comprehend their language.

The major told me Inzuki boys needed money to get the corpse out of the mortuary and take my brother to his resting place. I had changed a few Euros into Rwandan francs. I gave the major some money before I left. I needed to check if my sister, Celine, had regained consciousness. Maybe she could tell me more about why David was jailed.

We headed back to Nyarutarama, but when we arrived at the place, the driver advised me to stay in the car. He went to inspect the gate of the place where my sister spent most of her nights.

After five minutes, Karekezi returned to tell me that one of the guards told him that my sister had left that place and gave him Celine's telephone number. I approached a lady standing by the petrol station and begged her to call that number and lie to my sister that she had a courier for her. The trap worked, and Celine gave that lady the address to her apartment in the new luxury estate in Kacyiru.

Karekezi pressed the accelerator, and in a few minutes, we were in Kacyiru. After he dropped me there, I got out, entered the tall building, took the staircase, and rang the bell to my sister's apartment.

She opened and stared at me for a few minutes before hugging me and bursting into tears. I could feel the sorrow drums in her chest.

"Where have you been all these years?" Celine asked, after giving me a seat. "Why did you leave me? I suffered a lot."

"I am sorry," I said. "Now I am back. Tell me, what happened to our little brother?"

"I don't want to talk about that mobster," my sister responded. "David had turned into a monster. He had nicknamed himself Badguy. That's why he is dead. He had an ideology."

"What does an ideology mean?" I asked.

"Don't you know what I mean?" Celine asked me. "David's heart was full of the genocide ideology."

"Genocide ideology? I am sorry to insist; I don't know what that means. I understand the meaning of those two words, but I don't get the combination and what it has to do with David."

Celine looked at me as if I was some sort of ignorant stranger and said, "David had become *Interahamwe*. He hated Tutsis." Tears broke again from her eyes as she added, "He hated me, his sister."

"Please wipe your tears," I said as I handed her the tissue box from the table. "Is that why our brother was jailed?"

"Yes. He said horrible words to a genocide survivor, and the girl told the police. When I read it on the news, I couldn't believe my brother could say that. David had turned into something else. He was no longer my brother."

"What did he say exactly?" I asked.

"When the girl talked about how her family was killed during the genocide against the Tutsi, David asked her to shut up and added that she should know that other people suffered too. Then, the girl asked David what he meant. To make the matter worse, he said that although the Hutus killed his mother, his life had been made more miserable by the Tutsis, who had sent him to wander in the streets, eating trash day and night."

"Poor David," I said. "Is that the reason he was jailed?"

"Yes, they did well to take him to jail," Celine responded. "How can he minimize the genocide to that extent?"

"You are right," I said. "David shouldn't have asked that lady to shut up. He should have listened to her and kept his opinions to himself."

"Did you say his opinions?" Celine asked. "What kind of opinions are those? David was living in another world. He should not have blamed his own failures on Tutsis. He had decided to be not only a Hutu but *Interahamwe*, full of hatred for Tutsis. Our brother called for his death."

"Celine, my sister, listen," I said. "Now, David, our brother, is dead. Whether Hutu or Tutsi, he was our brother. Whether good or bad, he was our brother. *Interahamwe* or not, he was our brother. Guilty or innocent, he was our brother. His body is lying in the mortuary, and tomorrow the street boys he shared life with are taking him to rest. Don't you think we should pay our last respects to our younger brother? Do you remember how Mama loved David? Do you think our mother, if she can see what happens on earth, was happy about the life David was living? Is she now happy that her son has been shot dead?"

"I had nothing to do with David when he was alive," Celine responded. "I also have nothing to do with him dead. He had chosen another family, those gangsters he lived with. In fact, I do not want to associate myself with those people."

"No, sister," I said. "Remember you are talking about your brother. Please, our mother needs to see us mourning the death of her last born, who was rejected by this world for the same reasons Mama was killed."

"What do you mean? Who rejected David? What does it have to do with how Mama was killed? Are you also going to compare genocide to that nonsense?"

"David was not born a street boy. He did not smoke weed when our mother was still alive. He was neither a mobster nor a monster—however you called him. He did not hate anybody; he did not even understand the difference between Hutus and Tutsis and why our mother was killed. I am not defending what he did and said to that genocide survivor. I simply want to think that his heart wouldn't have become that bitter if the world had been salty and sweet for him. Please, let's lay wreaths of flowers on our brother's grave tomorrow."

"I have told you I have nothing to do with David, alive or dead, and I would advise you not to mingle yourself with that mess he had created around him. Unless you also want to be labeled a genocide ideologist."

Though the time was not right for me to think about anything else but the mystery of our brother's death, I could not help but notice how even my sister Celine had changed. I had so many questions in my mind. *Where was Celine when David was a street boy?* Since she became Miss Rwanda in 2000, she had been living like a rich celebrity. *Why did she not take David in to live with her when his uncle was killed in 2005? How about her? Who was that old man I found her with in Nyarutarama?* I recalled the day in 1997 when I had visited my sister at our maternal uncle Kamara's place, a few weeks after she had been taken to live with him in Kiyovu. Her lips were painted blood red, and her eyes looked smoky. I had warned her, and she had listened. But apparently, after I left Rwanda in 1998, she had adopted worse habits. *What have I done to my siblings? I won-dered. Maybe if I had not left Rwanda, David would not have died and Celine would not have become some kind of a strumpet.*

The following morning, Karekezi was at the hotel at nine o'clock. I had to organize my younger brother's funeral in those few hours I was left with. First, I went to the national broadcaster and paid for a radio death notice. After that, I went to Last Day Funeral Services, and with the bit of money I had, I bought a modest casket and a few wreaths of flowers and rented a hearse. That's all I could afford.

When I arrived at Biryogo in the compound where Inzuki boys lived, I found them all in dark shades, wearing black T-shirts, and on them it was written: *Badguy has been swal-lowed by the bad world.*

We called a minibus that took us to the hospital mortuary.

I could not believe the corpse was of my brother, whom I had left in Kigali with innocent baby eyes, in sky blue T-shirts and clean blue jeans. David was only seven years old in 1994 when our mother was killed. In 2014, when David was assassi-nated, he was twenty-seven. As I looked at the corpse, I could see how his skin had become darker. His fingernails were a lit-tle too long and dirty, and his clothing did not portray any bit of innocence. Inzuki boys were in a hurry to take the corpse and put him in the casket, then off into the hearse. They had no time for eulogies and prayers.

From the mortuary, we headed directly to Gatenga cem-etery. Maybe no church would have opened its doors to an *Inzuki boy,* even in death.

To my surprise, we found at the cemetery many people with faces I had never seen before. They had poverty in common, read on their wrinkled faces, dry necks, and dirty clothes. Some of them had items they seemed to be selling. I could see young men with a couple of pairs of shoes in their hands. I could see women with baskets or basins of tomatoes, fruits, or other vegetables on their heads. There were many taxi-moto riders in blue and green uniform jackets. It wouldn't have been far from the truth if anybody had defined these people as "poor, dirty Kigalians." There was neither a priest nor a pastor. Nobody from our maternal family was there. Nobody from David's paternal family was there. *Inzuki boys* had no time for a requiem song. They got the casket out of the hearse and downed it in the grave. I wanted to say a eulogy, but nobody seemed to have time to listen to me.

After they filled the grave with dirt, I laid on it the flowers I had bought, all by myself with nobody else, then murmured, "Rest in peace, my brother. Say hello to our mother. Please tell her I am sorry for having not taken care of her lastborn."

A tall, dark-skinned guy in stylish and clean clothes and a young lady in a short red dress were standing a hundred meters from us as if all they wanted was to make sure David was gone and buried forever.

When I moved toward that couple, Rotty, the Inzuki boy, pulled my hand and said, "Don't talk to those people. That's the chick who sent your brother to jail. Her boyfriend was Badguy's new music manager. I don't trust him."

II

Back in my room, lying alone on a hotel bed, I mourned the death of my younger brother. I could remember how our mother used to sing love songs for David or tell him bedtime stories. The brain brought back to me all memories of my brother from the time he was a baby to April 1994, when he saw what children should never have to see. I could recall how scared he looked whenever Hutu militiamen raped our mother and the questions he asked me the day she was killed. After the genocide against the Tutsi, David and I spent days together in our Nyamirambo house before reuniting with our sister, Celine, who had seen worse. Our sister, who had gone to visit her family during the short Easter vacation right before the genocide, was found surrounded by the corpses of her entire paternal family. Though I was also still haunted by the nightmares of what I had seen during the genocide, I could not help but conclude that the aftermath was much more complicated for my little brother, David, and my sister, Celine. I hated myself for having left them alone in Rwanda. I should have been there as their elder brother to protect them and accompany them into adulthood.

When I got up from my conundrums in the morning, I made a phone call.

"Hello," Karekezi said.

"Good morning," I said. "You need to take me back to *Inzuki boys*. I have to talk to Rotty."

"Okay, I will be there in twenty minutes."

The driver dropped me off not far from Biryogo market. I told him to leave. It was high time I started walking the city by myself. The tourist days were over. I had come for my younger brother's funeral, but there was no way I could go back to France, leaving his soul claiming justice.

When I knocked on the *Inzuki boys'* compound door, Rotty came out, but I did not want to enter. So instead, I offered to share tea with him in one of the Biryogo restaurants.

Rotty ordered *asusa* beans with chapatti and invited me to taste them. Even though I was a Nyamirambo boy, I had never savored *asusa* beans. I did not know they were that tasty, but they also were a little spicy.

"Rotty, now, you have to tell me everything," I said.

"Everything?" he asked. "What do you want me to tell you exactly?"

"Everything. For example, tell me why you did not trust David's music manager. I mean the guy who came to the cemetery."

"That spear is called Martin," Rotty said. "He is the one who reported David to the police. He is one of those guys who think Rwanda belongs only to them."

"How about the girl?" I asked. "The one to whom David said bad words. What relationship does she have with Martin?"

"Do you mean Linda?" Rotty asked. "She is his sugar." He laughed, rubbed his eyes, and added, "But the chick had fallen for Badguy. He used to ride on her."

"What do you mean?"

"They used to jig-jig. The girl smokes the sacred plant, but Martin does not know. So, whenever she and David got high, they got high on each other."

"Is that the reason Martin took David to jail?"

"Maybe. But Linda also confirmed to the police that David had said bad words to her. She is the one who told her boyfriend that David had an ideology."

"Why did she do that if they were friends?"

"They weren't friends but frenemies with benefits."

I sipped my tea and asked, "Were you and David good friends?"

"Yes. Everybody in *Inzuki boys* treated us like twins. I am the one who welcomed Badguy under the bridge where we spent our nights when we were both street boys. But I always warned him about how he talked to some people. He did not know how to pretend like a *fundi*."

"How?"

"He was an angry guy who spilled it to whoever messed up with him, and *fundis* are not supposed to be like that. We normally play it cool."

"What made him that angry?"

"What are you asking? Wasn't he a trash eater? Life here is tough, dude. The people with deep pockets make it even tougher for us."

"I get it," I said. "Since David was your best friend, would you do me a favor?"

"A favor?"

"Yes. David needs us. We should make sure he gets justice. We need to find the people who got him killed. Will you help me?"

"I am sorry, I don't understand," Rotty said, looking at me as if, once again, I was exposing my ignorance. "Badguy was shot by a prison officer. Do you mean you want to take the government to court?"

"No, that's not what I mean," I said. "Do you know the officer who shot him?"

"No," he responded. "They did not mention his name. The prison director said the guy was doing his job. Maybe killing *fundis* was also part of his job."

"No, that can't be. That officer must pay for what he did. Why did he not shoot him in the legs and run to catch him?"

"Hey, don't get yourself into trouble," Rotty warned me. "Here, we don't ask those questions. You should have left your intelligence in Europe before coming here, unless you want to end your life like Badguy. Don't think they will fear you because you're a *muzungu*."

"Leave that to me." I scratched my head, wondering whether I should reveal all my intentions to Rotty, who seemed terrified by what I was saying. "Shall you at least help me find more information about Martin?"

"What kind of information?"

"Everything about him. Who is he? What does he do? What is his network? Follow him. Whenever you shall see him with another person, try to find out who that person is. I want to know if he connived in the murder of David."

"Okay, I will try. But please don't confront the government. It will get you into trouble."

"Yes, I won't, at least before I get more information to substantiate my case. I believe the government was also deceived by that prison officer. So I won't take the government to court, but the prison officer."

"Be careful," Rotty insisted.

When we got out of the restaurant, I said bye to Rotty. Then, I headed to Nyamirambo to walk around my childhood neighborhood. I mused that maybe I could find a small apartment to rent and leave the hotel.

As I walked on the road next to Club Rafiki, someone touched my shoulder from the back. The minute I turned, I was hit by the beauty of her birdy eyes. She could not utter a word with her kiss-inciting lips. Instead, she wiped imaginary sweat from her palms. Her face looked familiar, but the girl I had seen at the cemetery was not that stunning. Maybe I had not paid much attention, for my eyes were still covered by tears because of my brother's death.

"I am sorry to disturb you," she finally said. "My name is Linda. I saw you at the funeral of Mr. D. Are you ... are you his brother?"

"Why are you asking?"

"Some people told me you are his brother; are you?"

"What would you do if I told you yes?"

"Nothing," she responded. "Do you live in Nyamirambo?"

"Not yet. I am still looking for a house. I am told rent here is not that exorbitant. How about you? Where do you live?"

"Here in Nyamirambo, not far from St. Charles Lwanga Parish."

I had given Rotty the assignment to investigate Martin. Now, the opportunity to do it myself presented itself to me. I could not find a better gateway to Martin's territory than through Linda, his girlfriend.

"Are you going home?" I asked. "Maybe we can walk together, if you don't mind."

"It's okay," she responded.

We strolled together on Nyamirambo Road. Her voice dragged words like in a rap song. Whenever she turned her eyes to me, she commanded my heart to dance in my chest. I could remember that my brother David had also fallen for her and vowed it would not be the same with me. I was on a mission, and there was no way I could be trapped by the same girl who had sent my brother to jail.

"Who do you stay with?" I wondered if she lived in the same house with Martin.

"With a friend of mine," she said.

"A friend of yours? Do you mean the guy you were with at the cemetery?"

"No, how can I live with a man in the same house? I am not married."

"I thought he was your boyfriend or fiancé. Isn't he?"

"He is my ex."

"Your ex? How come? Two days ago you were together. When did you break up?"

"I have told you he is my ex-boyfriend. Don't ask me questions. You have refused to confirm you are Badguy's brother."

"Why do you think I could be his brother? Did he tell you he had a brother?"

"No, Badguy never spoke about his family. After his death, I learned he was Miss Celine's brother and that they had another brother, a *muzungu*."

"Do you think I am that *muzungu*?"

"Yes. Aren't you?"

"Maybe I am, or I am simply a person who is saddened by the death of David. I am still puzzled by why he was killed and why he was in that prison."

"Don't you know why he was jailed?" Linda asked.

"They told me he insulted a lady or a girl," I said, pretending I had no idea she was the one.

"No, he did not insult me. He … he told me … no, I can't repeat it. He said bad words."

"To you? So, are you the one who reported him to the police?"

"No, I did not have the courage to do so. I was hurt by what Badguy said. It was not the first time he had said bad words to me. He had issues, and I hated him for that, but—"

"But what?" I asked.

"I have to go," she said. "We will talk next time."

"Have you arrived at your place?" I asked. "We are not yet at the parish."

"No, I just recalled I had to pass by somewhere. Sorry. It was nice chatting with you."

Before I said anything more to her, Linda crossed the road and disappeared into one of the shops next to Amahoro hostel. Talking about David must have made her uncomfortable. *Was she telling the truth about her breakup with Martin?* I wondered. She had said she hated David, but her eyes twirled with a shyness that could only signify affection. Maybe what she felt was an intersection of fondness and hatred. I wanted to run after her, at least to get her telephone number, but I would be making a fool of myself.

Arriving at the Kivugiza petrol station, I noticed a door on which was written "Houses for rent." I approached and entered. They showed me different options, and I chose a studio apartment in Nyakabanda, not far from the open market. On that day, I paid a three-month rent and was given the key to the studio. I bought a bed and a mattress, three chairs, a small table, a stove, a few cooking pots, plates, cups, forks, spoons, and knives. I had to live low, at least before finding another job. Rwanda was promoting information technology, and IT engineers had a lot of job opportunities. The next thing I was going to do was search for a job, settle, and investigate my brother's death.

The following Friday evening, I finally went to see Uncle Kamara in Kiyovu. I was lucky to find him at home. He had been married to another wife, not the one I had found in his house in 1997. The new wife seemed more decent and cultured. She welcomed me and asked what I wanted to drink before she announced to her husband that there was a visitor.

"Eh, muzungu, how are you?" Uncle Kamara asked. "You've been in Kigali for weeks, haven't you? So why didn't you bother to come here or call me?"

"Uncle, I am sorry. I came last week. The most urgent thing was ... to ... to hold last rites for my brother. Did you know David passed?"

"Of course I did. It was announced on the radio. But I had nothing to do with David. He was never my nephew."

"Why? Do you still doubt he was Mama's son? But, Uncle, even though I was still young, I remember when Mama was pregnant with David. I remember the day he was born. Mama was so happy. We all cuddled him. David was a favorite of Mama, your sister."

"Kayitesi had no other option," Uncle Kamara said. "She was disgraced by the Hutu who impregnated her with David."

"Well, irrespective of who his father was, David was your nephew, wasn't he?"

"No, he wasn't. That boy decided to go against me. He did not respect me as his uncle. His heart was as ugly as his face. He was a Hutu in and out."

Uncle Kamara's eyes, lips, and hands spoke more than his words. It was as if he wanted to justify something. He looked as if he meant that David deserved to die.

"Uncle, please remember David is now dead," I said. "He was shot by a prison officer. Do you know why?"

"He was a crook, and this country does not tolerate criminals anymore."

"Do you mean criminals should be shot dead when Rwanda has abolished the death penalty?"

"He was shot because he wanted to escape prison. David was not just a lawbreaker but a terrorist. He was worse than *Interahamwe*."

I looked at Uncle Kamara, who had already stood up from his seat, and words failed to come out of my mouth. The man was wandering in his own living room. Maybe he did not want to talk about David, but I had to make him even more uncomfortable. I needed to know what was troubling him about David's death.

"Uncle, do you know the officer who shot David? Has he been punished for that?"

"What do I have to do with the officer who shot that bastard? I don't work in prisons."

"That's not what I mean. Most people in high levels of police are your friends. I was hoping you would check with them why David was shot."

"Why should I? I will never defend a criminal like David. He had turned against me. That is how his life was supposed to end."

"Uncle, what do you mean he had turned against you?"

"That bastard accused me of having killed his paternal uncle, Mukinzi. He did not want me to take what belonged to my sister, Kayitesi."

What belonged to your sister? Are you talking about our house? Are you the one who sold it?"

"Yes. I had the right to do so as the brother to Kayitesi, who was raising her daughter, Celine."

When he said that, I understood everything. Uncle Kamara had claimed the ownership of our house. David was angry with that. That's how they had become worst enemies. *Could uncle have had a hand in David's death?* I wondered. He would not tell me. I pondered that if I continued to bombard him with more questions, he would put me in the same pot as David.

"Uncle, I understand," I said. "At the burial of David, I felt so bad to see the people he mingled with. His friends were only drug addicts and probably some ruffians of Kigali. My brother had turned into something else. But I don't think he deserved to die. Maybe they should have taken him to a rehabilitation center."

"Rehab is for street boys," Uncle Kamara responded. "It's not for crooks like David. He was an *Interahamwe* and a genocide ideologist. He was a danger to society."

I did not respond. I finished the soda his wife had served me and told him about France and how I had met my French paternal family.

"You changed a lot," he said. "Now, you look like a true *muzungu* with your ponytail."

"Uncle, I don't like it when you call me a *muzungu*. My name is Carlos."

"So, you are now a big man to start imposing how we should call you?" Uncle Kamara asked. "Everybody has called you *muzungu* since you were a child. That's not going to change."

"It has to. *Muzungu* is not my name."

A few minutes later, I said bye to Uncle Kamara and left

his house. I had a lot to brood about. I did not feel like going immediately to my new studio apartment to lonelily talk to the ghosts of David and Mama. Instead, I decided to pass by a Nyamirambo bar, took a seat by the counter, and ordered two shots of whiskey. I swallowed them instantly and asked for more. After alcohol started swaying in my big head, I paid and left.

Outside, I caught sight of a girl lying down in the drain. She was in a deep sleep as if she were a dead person. I approached and turned her head to see the face. She was Linda, the girl who had sent my brother, David, to jail. Her brown-skinned legs were naked, but her face was covered with misery. *If I take her with me and something happens, I will be sent to jail. But if I leave her here, she might be assaulted by the wrongdoers of Nyamirambo.* My head was puzzled. I tried to wake her up, but she seemed unconscious. I called a taxi. Then I carried the girl in my arms and put her in the car. The taxi dropped us off at my studio apartment in Nyakabanda.

III

In my studio apartment, I laid Linda on my bed. Her short dress was misbehaving. I did not want my eyes to force my brain to lie to me that it would be okay to kiss her inviting legs. I moved away and lay my body on the couch.

Linda started screaming in the middle of the night, "Please don't kill me! I am not a supporter of *Inkotanyi*. Don't kill my parents too. In fact, we are not Tutsis."

Her eyes opened, but she seemed to be in another place and another period. When I approached her, she wailed more. She begged me not to kill her. She kept on repeating she was not a Tutsi. I realized Linda was having nightmares of what she had lived during the genocide against the Tutsi in 1994. I did not know how to help her. Instead, I, too, started replaying the movie of what I had experienced during the genocide. I, too, wanted to tell my mother's killers that I was not a Tutsi, as if it was a sin to be Tutsi. I could visualize those assassins and imagined they were the same people Linda was seeing in her nightmares. They were wearing scary black coats. Their eyes were as red as blood. They pulled my mother away. I screamed and told them to leave her alone. They hit me with a machete. I recalled how the Hutu militiamen used to rape my mother. I could hear her cry in my ears. Looking at Linda in front of me, I saw my mother in her. This time around, I was not going to be a coward. I had to protect Linda from the evil men she was seeing in her nightmares. I had to save her from their hands. I needed to be a man.

She pushed me away when I approached her again, but I did not move. Instead, I hugged her and said, "It's me, Linda. I am Carlos. Don't worry. It's over. I am here to make sure nobody kills you. I will protect you."

Linda tried to push me again. I took my hands off her but assured her she was safe. She stopped screaming but continued to tremble with fear. Then, I came up with an idea. I turned on my laptop and played some music. The song was "Ubupfubyi" by Cecile Kayirebwa. I had to reflect on many orphans who were suffering in Rwanda. The only thing I could offer to my late brother, David, who had had to face the world alone till the day he was assassinated, was to be there for other lost orphans like him.

When I was lost in those thoughts, Linda said, "Do you have it? Please give me some. I have to take something."

"What?" I asked her. "What do you want me to give to you?"

"Whatever you have. Don't you have a babysitter?"

"A babysitter? What do you mean?"

She looked at me as if I were some ignorant guy. She must have wondered from which planet I was. Then, she recalled she had a purse.

"Where is my purse? Where have you put my handbag?"

I had put it on the small table. I picked it up and handed it to her. Linda was not facing my eyes. She looked like an asthmatic person looking for her inhaler. When she opened the bag, I noticed that she had already rolled some joints. She took a match and lighted one. I could not believe my eyes. Linda smoked marijuana. I didn't know how to stop her. Something told me to let her do whatever she thought would calm her down. I did not judge her. Maybe she needed it to stop those nightmares.

As she was smoking, she asked me questions. "How did I get here? Why did you bring me to your room? What have you done to me?"

I told her how I had found her lying unconscious in front of a bar. Then I asked her to tell me what had happened to her.

"I don't know," she said. "Don't worry. It must have been those yobbos."

Once again, I did not understand what she meant. Finally, she told me she was with bad guys and suspected they had slipped some drugs into her drink.

After smoking marijuana, Linda went back to sleep.

When she woke up in the morning, she looked exhausted.

"Breakfast," I said. "Please have a fruit salad."

I had cut for her different types of fruits—papaya, banana, apple, mango, and pineapple. After eating the fruits, she had tea, an omelet, and bread. She looked soberer than how she was the night before. I could read shyness on her face. She did not want to look me in the eye. Apart from her bitten eyes and dry face, she looked like the beauty that had struck me the first day I had seen her.

After breakfast, she said, "I am sorry for inconveniencing you. I don't know what has come over me. I had decided to be sober. But the day I learned that Badguy was shot dead, I rolled a joint again and drank a full bottle of whiskey. The last time I had lost a person so close to me was in 1994. Now, I guess I am back in those times."

"It's okay," I said to Linda. "I sympathize with you for what you went through. Please remember we are no longer in 1994. And David is resting in peace, close to the loved ones we lost in 1994."

Linda was indeed right. The assassination of David had also taken me back to 1994. This time around, the worst of it, I felt as if it were happening only in my world, outside of which other Rwandans were celebrating political and economic recovery.

At around ten o'clock, after taking a shower and freshening up, Linda left my studio apartment. I gave her five thousand Rwandan francs before seeing her off to the bus station.

When I came back to my apartment, I threw myself on the bed and reflected on Linda. What had turned a stunning girl like her into a drug addict? What was I doing with her? Was I really going to spy on her and get more information about her ex-boyfriend, Martin? I was not sure anymore. I wanted to protect her. I wanted to do for her what I had not managed to do for my siblings. Linda needed a brother. Linda needed a family.

As I continued to think about Linda, I recalled I had not seen my sister, Celine, for days. I dialed her phone number.

She was in her apartment but feeling unwell. I got up, walked to the gate, stopped the first motorbike by the road, and headed to Kacyiru.

When I knocked on the door to my sister's apartment, she opened it. She had wrapped herself in a blue and white *kanga* cloth that revealed the beauty of her gazelle neck.

"How are you?" she asked.

"Fine," I responded.

She looked troubled, but it seemed she had no words to explain to me what was bothering her.

"I have been wondering why you did not come back to see me," she said. "Have you realized you were here last before the burial of David? How did it go?"

"Do you really want to know?" I asked. "David was buried by the street mongers, beggars, and other poor people of Kigali. However, I believe he was happy to be accompanied by the people he spent the last years of his life with."

My sister muted. I guessed she was still digesting what I had just said.

"You are unwell," I said. "What is it?"

"I have not been feeling well lately. The whole body aches, and I can't tell why. But don't worry."

I could read blues all over her face. *Is she grieving David's death?* I wondered. She did not look like the Celine I had met a few days before who seemed to be sure of herself. I could not help but wonder what could have happened to my sister.

"Celine, that's serious," I said. "You've been unwell, and I shouldn't be concerned? When did it start? Have you seen a medical doctor? What are you suffering from?"

"I have said you shouldn't worry," she said. "I have seen all the world's doctors, and nobody could come up with a diagnosis. The last doctor sent me to a psychotherapist as if I were some kind of a mentally ill person. The health system in this country is a disgrace."

Celine would have sent me to hell if I had told her that maybe her doctor was right. I needed to play the good listener. My sister and I had been away from each other for sixteen years. We needed to reconnect, even though we did not know where to start. In my mind, I deliberated that Celine had also gone through a lot in the aftermath of the genocide. In fact, I had no doubt about that. Despite the fact she pretended to be in control, my sister looked like a lost soul. I had to come up with a plan to get her out of that apartment so she may breathe fresh air.

"Why don't you put on something and take me out?" I said. "You must show me the new Kigali."

"I have told you I am not feeling well," she replied. "Besides, my car is at the mechanic's."

"We can walk while enjoying the beautiful trees of Kacyiru. Come and show me the new skyscrapers and shopping malls."

"Please, I don't want to go out. In fact, I never go out."

"You never go out? What do you mean?"

"I only go out when I have to pay a visit to a few friends or when it's work, maybe a photo shooting session, a TV or radio interview, a fashion show, etcetera. Otherwise, I spend most of my time here, in this apartment."

"Did you say your doctor sent you to a psychotherapist?

Don't mind him. He didn't know all you missed was your dear brother. Here I am. I will take good care of you. I miss my little sister. We have a lot to talk about, don't we? Do you realize we haven't had a friendly talk since I came back from France? Do you know what I went through in France? How about you? Don't you think I need to know how you've been coping with life?"

"The last time you came here, you were not interested in my story," Celine said. "All you wanted to know was about David and almost blamed me for his death."

"Please forgive me for that," I said. "I guess I was devastated. The death of David broke my heart. But now, he is gone. It's no longer about him. It's about you and me. So, please, let's take a walk. I will take you somewhere for a chapati. You used to like chapati when you were younger. I hope you still do."

"Not really," she said. "I guess my tastes have changed. Now, I don't know what I love anymore. The modeling career is too demanding, especially when it comes to diet. But offered by you, I will break the rules and eat at least a slice."

I clapped and said, "That's my sister! I wanted to see that smile. Please put on something, and let's go. Today, the whole Kigali shall know you have a brother."

Celine left me in her living room and went to freshen up and change clothes.

When she came out, she was a changed person. I hated to think that her chest-revealing top, her makeup, and her long earrings were her way of hiding the pain she felt inside. Though I found it too much, there was no way I could dare tell my sister that maybe she needed to wear a different lipstick shade. I only wondered if she would be able to walk in those high heels. I decided that perhaps it wouldn't be a good idea to walk for so long. I suggested we sit at Umugano and order a few chapati from the hotel's pastry shop.

"Now I understand why you like to stay indoors," I said.

"Why?" Celine asked.

"Because if, whenever you have to get out, you have to do that makeup and wear high heels, you must sometimes feel too tired to do it."

"Stop exaggerating. Don't I look casual in these leggings? Do you think this is the kind of makeup I take on stage or for a photography session? Here are a few photos that show you what it is to be a model."

She handed me her telephone so that I could look at those photos. In some of them, she was entirely or three-quarters naked. I couldn't believe what I was seeing. In some pictures, she looked yellow, in others, she looked black, and in some, she looked white. My sister had been turned into a chameleon by fashion photographers.

"Wow, this is interesting," I said. "Celine, please tell me how you became a model. Who introduced you to modeling?"

"It's a long story," she said as she played with one of the rings on her fingers, then she made a phony smile and added, "I was pushed into it by Uncle Kamara. He convinced me I had the body shape and the looks for it."

"Why does it seem like you don't like it?" I asked.

"No, I like it," she argued. "It's now my life. I wouldn't be who I am today if I had not been crowned Miss Rwanda 2000. I changed from a poor orphan to a well-heeled celebrity."

"Good to know you like it. But what are the challenges?"

"Enormous," my sister replied. "As a model, you feel like you are owned by the whole world. I have become an object of beauty or an ornament that everybody wants to wear or decorate their house with. It's a constant fight trying to rediscover myself only to realize I am not the same anymore."

"That reminds me," I said. "Please, sorry to ask, but I wanted to know more about your relationship with the man I found you with at that place in Nyarutarama. Is he your lover?"

"My lover? I wouldn't call him such. But from the day he started dating me, at least all other men backed off. He is a well-connected tycoon of the city."

"Do you love him?" I asked.

"Hell no. That old man? I don't. But anyway, I don't believe in love."

"Then, why are you with him? The other day, it seemed you had spent the night in his house, and you are telling me he is not your lover?"

"Please, stop asking me a lot of questions. Now that you've been to Europe, I thought you had changed. You're the same Carlos who instructed me to wash my face when you found me with funny makeup. Do you remember? I guess it was in 1997."

"Yes, I do. When I returned to check on you again, I was told Uncle Kamara had sent you to live in Butare with our grandparents. Then, a few months later, I left Rwanda. I will never forgive myself for having left you and David. When did you leave Butare?"

"Didn't you say you've brought me here so that I may feel better? Now you are talking about Butare. There, I lived in a real hell. I don't even want to remember I was ever in that city. So many horrible things that I cannot describe happened to me."

"Oh, sorry. I don't mean to make you feel bad. But we have a lot to talk about. The day I shall tell you about my life in France, you won't stop me. Please tell me what happened to you in Butare."

"I have nothing to tell you about Butare. Just forget what I have said. By the way, where are the chapati we have ordered?"

I called the waiter and asked about our chapati and drinks.

Though she did not want to talk about what she had endured in Butare, I could read from Celine's face that she was emotionally taken back to those times. She took a whole chapati and munched it like a lioness looking for what to ravenously bite. She was not facing my eyes. She seemed to be fighting with the pain that was inflating her chest. She grabbed another piece of chapati, and when she took a third, I decided to let her know I was ready to listen to her story.

"Celine, am I not your brother?" I asked her.

"Of course you are," she said. "Why are you asking?"

"I know you are a brave lady. I do not intend to pity you. But I will love to listen to your story. Please tell me what happened to you in Butare. What kind of hell did you go through?"

"Carlos, I am sorry I can't talk about it. Not now, please. Not to you. Not to anybody else."

"Were you attacked by some people? Did anybody attempt to kill you?"

"I wished they had killed me. It would have been better than what I endured."

"Please tell me. I beg you."

"I won't tell you anything. Just know that Uncle Kamara is a monster."

"Uncle Kamara?" I asked. "What did he do to you? I thought you guys got along well. Haven't you said he was the one who introduced you to modeling? Was that before or after whatever he did to you?"

"It was after," Celine responded. "I guess that when he introduced me to modeling, he thought I would be a cash cow for him, but he did not know he was sending me to fishermen who are more powerful than him."

"I am sorry, I don't understand. What did Uncle Kamara do to you? Don't tell me he … No. I would kill him. I swear, I would strangle him alive."

"Stop it," she shouted. "What did you just say? Kill who? Do you also want to end your life like David? Please, I did not say anything to you. Forget everything I have just said. We need to go. I have to take some pills."

She stood up immediately before we even finished the chapati. She removed shades from her handbag to hide her eyes, then stepped forward in her high heels, with her head up as if she were tougher than life. I wished she allowed herself to burst into tears, drop everything, and admit she was not as strong as she pretended to be.

IV

One month after I had returned to Rwanda, I started applying for different IT jobs. Luckily, after sitting for a few interviews, I got a job at Smart Telecommunications Company (STC) as an IT network engineer. The salary seemed to be competitive. My aim was not to live in Rwanda for the rest of my life, but I could not let my brother David down even after his death. I had to seek his justice. I also needed to be with my sister, Celine, and help her uncover the pain underneath her makeup and high heels. I could also not stop thinking about Linda, a girl whose background I didn't know but whose soul cried for my help. My mission in Rwanda appeared to be getting more significant and more challenging. There was no way I could allow myself to be a coward. I had to be the big brother to all the blameless young Rwandans who were turned into bad guys and girls.

Even though many people had advised me not to talk to the police or the prison, I could not get justice for my brother if I avoided going where it all happened.

I went to the prison and asked to meet with the director. After I told him who I was and what I was looking for, he said to me that David was shot dead while trying to escape from prison.

"Sir, how did David manage to get out of the compound?" I asked. "Was the gate not locked and guarded?"

"Are you asking me?" the director responded. "Only the dead prisoner could tell us how he got out, but he is no more."

"Sir, I wanted to know what the prison officers who were guarding the gates said. Did he use the gate, or did he climb the fence?"

"He must have climbed the fence. Criminals have their ways. They found roped bed sheets where he had climbed from."

"And the officer who shot him? Did he also climb, or did he use the gates?"

The director stood up from his chair, shook his hands left and right, and asked, "Hey, are you carrying out investigations? Why do you want to know the tactics of our officers?"

"I am sorry, sir. I only wanted to know how my brother died."

He moved toward the window, hid his face from me, and said, "No criminal can ever escape from our prisons. Those who try to do so get the same fate your brother got. We always catch them."

"Sir, you've just said you catch prisoners, right? So why didn't the officer catch David instead of shooting him?"

"You know what?" the director said. "Get out. I have other things to do. I can't be spending my precious time discussing why we killed a criminal who was trying to escape from prison."

"I understand, sir. Once again, I am sorry. One last question: was that officer punished for his offense?"

"What offense? Doing his job? Please get out before I call one of my officers for another job here. I guess you need to be forced out of my office."

I got out with so many riddles zipping in my head. Why did it sound like a creak in the director's voice? Why did he stare at me for one minute and look away for another, as if he were thinking about what to say next? Why did he raise his voice so loud and use gestures with his hands while talking to me, as if he struggled to convince me? I could not help but think the director could be hiding something.

When I got out of the director's office, heading to the gates, I caught sight of Habimana, our former neighbor, among other prisoners who expected visits. I approached one of the prison officers and told him I wanted to talk to Habimana.

"Are you related to him?" the officer asked.

"Yes, he is my uncle," I said, thinking they would not have allowed me to talk to him if I had said we were not related. Little did I know that by saying that I could be a relative to a genocide convict, I would be regarded as adherent to those who made me an orphan.

"What do you mean he is your uncle? Aren't you a muzungu?"

"I'm mixed. He is from my mother's side."

"So, you are a nephew to a genocide perpetrator. Where is your father from? Is he from France? No other muzungu could be related to genocide perpetrators but a French."

"Sir, I don't know my father. I was born in Rwanda. Mr. Habimana is a cousin to my mother, and he did not commit the genocide. He is innocent."

"If he is not guilty, what is he doing here?" the officer asked before telling me to go and write my names in the register and wait for Habimana on one of the benches in the tent where prisoners received their visitors.

When Habimana caught sight of me, he tried to run away.

I smiled, stood up, and invited him for a hug.

He sat down on the bench but muffled his mouth.

"I am sorry for what happened to you," I said to Habimana. "I will never forget how you hid my mother, David, and me in your kitchen. You are innocent. Someone else should be here, but not you."

"It's okay," he said. "This is life. I have accepted it."

"No, you shouldn't. I will make sure you get out of this prison. Your wife is the one who brought the killers, not you."

"Carlos, I beg you. Do never say that. Mukandoli did the unspeakable, but she is the mother of my children. Let me pay for having married a wicked woman."

"If she was indeed a mother, she would not have brought the militiamen to kill our mother. But please, tell me, how did you come here? Who accused you of having killed our mother?"

"That's not important. All I know is that your younger brother, David, tried to tell them I was innocent, but they did not listen. Apparently, your uncle Kamara wanted to get rid of me. He believed I was the one who had turned David against him."

"So, you mean it's Uncle Kamara who accused you of having killed our mother?"

"He was one of the accusers. Many survivors of the genocide against the Tutsi in my neighborhood considered me one of them. They knew I was against the killings. Nobody was aware that the killers of your mother were called by Mukandoli, my wife. Everything changed in 2005 after the assassination of Mukinzi, David's paternal uncle. Rumors about me started to spread. Some neighbors started calling me Interahamwe, but nobody dared to report me to the police. Then, when Gacaca proceedings started, I was accused of having killed your mother. Those who accused me were prisoners among the militiamen who killed her. They stated I was the one who called them. Some survivors said they knew I was hiding something, though they could not put their finger on it. That's how I was sentenced to nineteen years in prison."

"Oh, no, people can be wicked. How about Uncle Kamara? Why do you say he was one of those who accused you?"

"He attended the Gacaca meetings but never said anything. He used to call me like three times a day. He made my life a real hell. In fact, I had reached the point where I wanted the Gacaca court to sentence me and send me to prison. I could not take anymore the blackmails and threats of your uncle Kamara."

"What did he say to you?"

"Your brother, David, wanted to claim the house of your mother. I accompanied him to the sector bureau and testified that the house belonged to his parents. Your uncle was not happy with that."

"Did he not want you to testify that the house belonged to Mama and David's father?"

"No. Your uncle wanted me to say it only belonged to your mother, his sister, and that David was mentally deranged and could not inherit it."

"That's stupid," I said. "Who told Uncle Kamara that a person with a mental problem, if he even had one, cannot inherit a house?"

"Kamara repeated to me that if I did not want to be assassinated like David's uncle, Mukinzi, I should change my testimony. I refused. The day Gacaca condemned me and sent me to jail, he came to the police custody where I was and said that I shouldn't have messed with him."

Although Habimana was trying to hold himself together, I could read blues from his face.

He pinched his nails, wiped imaginary tears from his face, and searched for my hands to comfort me. "I am very sorry for David. I feel so guilty for his death. He must have been killed because of me."

"What do you mean David was killed because of you?" I asked.

"Please lower your voice," Habimana said. "We can't talk about David and how he was killed here."

"Why?" I asked. "Do you know who killed David?"

"I have told you we can't talk about that. I will never forgive myself for your brother's death. What a coward and a horrible person I am! I was not able to save your mother from the killers, and now, I can't protect her sons. Please go, do never come back to the prison."

Habimana tried to stand up and leave me there. He shivered when he talked about David. I wondered if he was somehow involved in the death of my brother.

"It's okay, sit down," I said. "Let's talk about other things."

"Carlos, I'm sorry. Please forgive me."

"Forgive you for what? How can I forgive you when you can't tell me what you did?"

Habimana muted.

After about five minutes of staring at each other, the prison officer approached.

"Have you realized I have given you more minutes than I give to other visitors?" the officer asked. "Now, it's over. But remember to say bye to me before you leave."

"Okay, sir," I said. "I'm coming."

"He means you have to give him some money," Habimana murmured. "Don't mind those who say there is no corruption in this country."

"How much should I give him?"

"Five thousand should be enough."

After saying goodbye to Habimana, I shook the officer's hands with a five thousand note before leaving the prison with a head full of chanting beetles.

From the prison, I took the bus to Nyamirambo. I needed to talk to Mukandoli, Habimana's wife. Maybe she could tell me more about the circumstances of the death of Mukinzi, David's uncle, and what her husband could have revealed to her about David's death.

I knocked on the gates, and Mukondoli's daughter opened. She invited me into the house, where her mother was seated on the couch.

"Hello," I said, "I am sorry to drop by unannounced. The last time I was here, I was in a hurry. So I thought I needed to come back for a proper visit."

"A visit? Or you are coming back to accuse me of your mother's death?" Mukandoli responded.

I wanted to shout, but I decided to hold myself together. How can this evil woman dare talk about my mother's death when she knew well that I was there the night she brought in the killers? I wondered. I concluded she was as wicked as she had always been.

"No, that's not the reason why I am here. I am coming for peace."

"Okay," she said as she lifted her legs and crossed them on the small table in front of the couch.

We stayed muted for minutes before I said, "Last time I was here, you told me about the assassination of Mukinzi. I wanted to know more about his death. Who killed Mukinzi? How was he killed? Did the police identify and arrest his assassins?"

Mukandoli gave me a questioning look and said, "Why do you think I know how Mukinzi was murdered? Please, I have enough trouble already. Please don't add to it the death of Mukinzi. I have nothing to do with it."

"I am sorry. I didn't mean to say you have something to do with his death. I only thought that maybe the people who killed him may also have orchestrated the murder of David."

"No, it's different," Mukandoli said. "David wasn't murdered. He was shot by a prison officer when he was trying to escape from prison."

"Isn't that a murder?" I asked.

"No. The officer had no other option. Why did David want to escape from prison?"

I could not tell whether Mukandoli believed what she was saying or if she was simply exposing the insensitive woman she was. I mused that probably she did not have enough information on the circumstances of David's death.

"Okay, I get it. Let's talk about the death of Mukinzi. How was he killed?"

"Mukinzi's body was found in a ditch with many injuries," Mukandoli said. "The police confirmed he had been shot dead by unidentified people."

"Oh, that's sad," I said. "Mukinzi was your neighbor, right? Do you know if he had any problems with anybody? Was he a good person? Tell me everything you know about him."

"He seemed to be a good person, but he was not on good terms with your uncle, Kamara. Mukinzi claimed that your mother's house was built by his brother. He wanted to put it under his name."

"What? Don't tell me Mukinzi also wanted that house. Was David aware of that plan?"

"I don't think so," Mukandoli said. "David trusted his paternal uncle so much. He believed he could never betray him. But in David's mind, the house belonged to his parents and not to anybody else."

"Then what happened? Did Mukinzi manage to claim the ownership of the house?"

"He started the process, but I think he was killed before it was transferred from his brother's name to his. He had told the authorities that the whole family of his brother, David's father, died during the wars in Congo. He stated he was the only person who had the right to inherit the house."

"Why? How about David? Was he not his brother's son?"

"He said to me that Mukiga had never acknowledged David as his son."

"That's not true," I said. "Mukiga took care of David and our mother; he took care of all of us. He was a good man and wanted the best for David."

"Was David registered as his son?" Mukandoli asked me. "Wasn't he rather in your mother's identification card?"

"All our names were written in our mother's ID," I responded. "But that does not mean we did not have fathers."

"Carlos, in Rwanda, children's names appeared in their fathers' IDs and not their mothers. Only those whose fathers were unknown could be written in their mothers' IDs. That means your mother was a single woman."

"What?" I asked. I couldn't believe what Mukandoli was telling me.

"Yes, that's how Mukinzi could claim the ownership of his brother's house. It could have been a different story only if Mukiga had put the house under your mother's name. Then, it would be recognized as your mother's house, and Mukinzi would not have any right to claim it."

"Okay, I get it," I said. "Then, how did the house end up being taken by our mother's brother, Uncle Kamara, if it was not owned by our mother?"

Mukandoli pretended to rearrange her loincloth, hid her eyes from me, and said, "That, I can't tell you. It's a long story."

"Longer than what you have just told me?" I asked.

"No, I mean … Carlos, please don't tell your uncle anything. He might kill me."

"Kill you for what?"

Mukandoli kept quiet for a few seconds, rubbed her hands, looked down at her feet, and said, "Please forgive me for what I did. Your uncle Kamara threatened to kill me."

"What? Why did he threaten to kill you? What did you do? What should I forgive you for?"

"I am sorry, Carlos, I can't tell you."

"Okay, are you sure you can't tell me? Maybe you want to add more to what you did to my mother in 1994. Can't you at once do something right? I am not interested in the house. But I believe that story might help me know why and how my brother was killed. You did not care for our mother's life, but at least please have the courage to help me get justice for my brother, David. Don't worry; I'm good at keeping secrets."

"Carlos, I was forced to do it. Your uncle forced me to steal the house papers from Mukinzi's house, which showed that it was owned by his brother, Mukiga. I gave them to your uncle Kamara. Then, after the death of Mukinzi, your uncle asked me to—"

Mukandoli went silent again. Though she was a wicked

woman, I couldn't help but notice how she was shivering at that moment. She seemed terrified.

"What did Uncle Kamara ask you to do?" I asked her.

"He asked us to testify that David was mentally deranged and could not inherit the house. My husband refused. I also refused, but I later accepted when he threatened to kill my family."

"Do you mean you testified David was mentally ill?"

"Yes. I also testified that the house belonged to your mother."

"And Habimana, your husband, what did he say?"

"He did not know the house was not under your mother's name. I never told him about the papers I stole from Mukinzi's house. So he went to the authorities to testify that it was your mother's house and added that only you, David, and Celine had the right to inherit it. Your uncle Kamara was not happy with what Habimana did, and that's how he shifted the blackmail from me to Habimana."

"What do you mean he shifted the blackmail?"

"Before I testified against David, your uncle used to say he would kill my whole family and accuse us of having killed your mother. But after I did what he wanted me to do, he decided to use Gacaca courts to charge Habimana for your mother's death. Habimana decided to plead guilty."

I scratched my head and moved away from that woman. I wished I could slap her. I wished I could catch her immediately and take her to prison myself. But instead, I decided to hold myself together. Those who said it's essential to keep enemies closer were right. So that's what I did with Mukandoli. First, I thanked her for having told me everything. Then, I reassured her that I did not hold any grudges against her for my mother's death and for having betrayed my brother, David.

"But you will also have to promise me something," I added. "Don't tell anybody what we have discussed. You should also keep in contact with Uncle Kamara. He must never suspect that you are no longer in his camp."

"Did you say I should keep in contact with Kamara?" Mukandoli asked. "Since the house was sold, he does not speak to me."

"Please find a way to talk to him again, as long as you promise me you will never tell him I know what you said to me. I hope you understand that he is still my uncle despite what he did."

Mukandoli remained silent.

I did not tell her that I had met her husband, Habimana, at the central prison.

From Mukandoli's house, I called Rotty and asked if we could meet in Biryogo and share lunch. He agreed, and in a few minutes, we were together eating asusa beans and ugali.

"I have some news for you," Rotty said. "About Martin. Now, I think he must have something to do with the death of Badguy."

"Do you mean Martin is the one who killed David?"

"Sorry, I am used to calling him Badguy," Rotty said. "No, I don't know if he killed him, but he might have hired people to kill him."

"Hired people? Wasn't David killed by a prison officer?"

"Yes, that's what the prison director said. But who knows? Maybe Martin bribed that officer to kill David."

"Is that possible? Can the officers be hired by a civilian to kill an innocent citizen?"

"Please, keep your voice down. Let's stop mentioning the word 'officer.' All I have discovered is that there was a big grumble between Badguy and Martin."

"Was it about Linda?" I asked. "Apparently, Linda was in love with David."

"How do you know that?" Rotty asked. "Who told you she was in love with him?"

"Hmm? No … I meant … Didn't you tell me they used to jig-jig?"

"Yes, I did, but you wanted to say something else. Have you ever talked to Linda?"

"I once met her on one of Nyamirambo streets, but we did not talk."

"Did she recognize you?" Rotty asked, looking as if something told him I was not telling the truth.

"Yes, she did. She asked me if I was David's brother. But Rotty, please tell me about the beef Martin had with David."

"It was about money. Apparently, Martin embezzled money paid to Badguy when they went to a concert in Uganda. The fundi fumed and started a fight with Martin. I wished he had told me about it, but he didn't. Maybe he knew I would tell him to let it go."

"What did David do to Martin?"

"Badguy was crazy," Rotty said. "He never knew how to walk away from trouble. My friend has told me that Badguy reported Martin to the police."

"That was good. What did the police do about it?"

"Nothing. Then, Badguy decided to resolve the matter himself. He gave good punches to Martin. The fundi would have destroyed Martin if nobody was there to stop him."

"Did Martin report it to the police?"

"No, he didn't. Maybe he was afraid they would want to follow up on the case of the money he had embezzled from Badguy."

"So, how is that linked to the death of David?" I asked.

"I don't know," Rotty said. "I only think that maybe Martin planned his revenge. So, when he heard that Badguy had thrown ideology words at Linda, he persuaded her to report him to the police."

"That could be possible," I said. "But it does not mean Martin also had a hand in my brother's assassination."

"Why not? Martin is a demobilized soldier, and many of those prison officers were formerly in the army. They are his friends."

"Rotty, thanks for the info. I believe it might guide us to more clues. May I ask you for another favor?"

"Yes, go ahead."

"I want you to befriend Martin. Maybe he can reveal more to you."

"No, that I can't. There are people I only talk to from afar. Martin is not the type of those who can be my friend. He is one of those spears who might be spying on me."

"What do you mean?"

"What don't you understand? Carlos, I keep explaining things to you, but you are like your brother. You don't get it. I am the only survivor of my family. I have no parents, no siblings, no uncles, no aunts, and no extended family. So if anything happens to me, that shall be the end of my whole family."

"Oh, sorry," I said. "I didn't know you were also a survivor."

"No, I'm not," Rotty argued. "I am not allowed to consider myself as one."

"What? Seconds ago, you said you were. Now, you are saying you are not. What do you mean? How did your family members die?"

"Carlos, I never talk about how they died, and I have no intention of doing so now. You should just understand I can't mingle with spears like Martin."

"What do you mean by 'spears'?"

"Those tall guys who think Rwanda belongs only to them."

I looked at Rotty and wondered what he was thinking. Is he possibly referring to Tutsis as spears? That scared me a bit. I was taller than Martin, and though my father was French, I was a Tutsi, as far as my Rwandan identity was concerned. *Now I understand what an ideology means,* I mused.

"Rotty, Martin might be a bad guy, but that does not have anything to do with his looks or whatever you call him. Why do you call tall guys spears?"

He looked at me for a second, scratched his head, and rubbed his hands as if he wanted to retract his words.

"I'm sorry, I didn't mean anything harmful," Rotty said. "It's just that … No … I shouldn't have said what I have just said."

"It's okay," I said. "But you did not tell me how your family members died."

"I said I can't talk about their death. But if you want to

know, I'm from Ruhengeri, and my whole family was killed in 1997."

"In 1997? Who killed them?"

"I don't know," Rotty said before standing up and adding, "I have to go. It's okay. I will try to befriend Martin if that shall help us seek justice for Badguy."

"Thanks, Rotty. I will be guiding you on what to say to him and the kind of questions to ask him. Don't worry. We shall do everything tactfully."

V

Since I had returned to Rwanda, my life was so dull. When I was not at work, I would be thinking about finding justice for my brother, David, and being there for my troubled sister, Celine, and my new friend, Linda. I needed a piano if I did not want to run mad. I searched in all the shops in Kigali, but I could not find where to buy a simple keyboard.

I approached one of the workmates who seemed friendly to me. His name was James. He was the company's chief IT designer. He appeared to be interested in everything creative. Like me, he had a ponytail, but his bun was of dreadlocks. Looking at James, you could think he smoked many cigarettes, but James neither smoked nor touched anything alcohol. He was simply a cool guy who believed nature was the best gift of life. His camera studied human beauty with fascination. Whenever he showed me the pictures he had taken with his camera, he came up with fictional stories about those faces.

"James, I have been meaning to ask you something," I said to him. "Do you know where I can buy a piano from in this city? You take pictures of beauty, and I compose its praises."

"You're like my girlfriend. She is a musician. But I am not

sure you will get a piano here. She bought hers from Spain. Don't worry. Before you get your own piano, you can always come to my apartment and play hers."

"Oh, thank you, James," I said, before asking, "You mean I can't get a good piano here in Kigali?"

"I doubt," he said, before adding, "Hey, dude, it's already lunchtime. Let me go show you somewhere you will eat a good meal."

"Where?"

"Just follow me. At Mary's restaurant. I'm sure you will love the food."

James invited me to sit in his sports car, the model of a unique Ford in Kigali. He drove toward Muhima.

Even though I pretended to like the food, it was not the kind that a Nyamirambo born would want to eat. Nothing was fried. Even meat was boiled. The restaurant was full of tall guys, whom maybe Rotty liked to call spears. Most of those guys spoke English and some languages of Uganda. Looking at their suits and ties, I wondered why they loved boiled food.

"I didn't know there were restaurants like this in Kigali," I said.

"There are not many," James responded, before adding, "Most people from Uganda are used to this kind of cuisine. I don't like frying everything."

"Did you also grow up in Uganda?" I asked.

"Yes, I was born in Uganda. In fact, many members of my family are still in Uganda."

"Does that mean you are not Rwandan?"

"Of course I am Rwandan. My parents left Rwanda in the

sixties because of the bloody revolution when many Tutsis were killed and their houses burnt by Hutus who wanted change."

"Oh, sorry for that. Glad you are back to the country of milk and honey."

"Milk and honey? That's what our parents used to say, but I have not yet found what they were talking about."

"It was a metaphor. Rwanda is a beautiful country with nice people."

"That's why I keep my camera with me," James responded with a smile. "How about you? Were you born in Kinshasa? Among your parents, who is a muzungu?"

"Kinshasa? Why do you think I was born in Zaire? I mean Congo."

"Because of your fluency in French. Even though I don't know French, I can spot that the accent of people who grew up in Rwanda might not be the correct one. Some of them tremble at the idea of speaking French."

"I was born here, in Kigali," I said. "Does that surprise you?"

"Yes, but not much because of your looks, but your ways. I'm right to guess one of your parents is either French or Belgian?"

"Yes, my father was French, but I have never met him. I guess I perfected my French when I went to live in France. I have lived there for over sixteen years."

James asked me more questions about my family. I told him about my mother and how she was killed during the genocide against the Tutsi.

"Oh, sorry for that. Were your siblings also killed during the genocide?"

"No, I survived, together with my sister. You will love to meet her. She is a fashion model."

"What? Don't tell me you are a brother to Sonia Rolland?"

"No, I'm not. Celine is not mixed. She is actually my half-sister. Same mother, different fathers."

"Do you mean Miss Celine? I didn't know she had a half-white sibling. I was also born into a big family. My father married different women of different nationalities. So I grew up with all sorts of beauties. Maybe that's why I am interested in human faces."

"That's funny and interesting," I said.

James seemed to be a nice guy. On that day, he told me more about his family, those in Rwanda, those in Uganda, and others in different other countries and continents. It was my first time chatting with a Rwandan who was fascinated by diversity.

He invited me to his home to play piano the following Saturday. He added, "You should come with an empty stomach. My girlfriend shall cook Japanese food for you."

"Japanese?" I asked.

"Yes. My girlfriend is from Japan. Why are you surprised?"

"Eh? No, I'm not. I simply don't know many Rwandans who are married to Asians."

"I'm not yet married, but I'm madly in love with her. She is a true beauty. You'll tell me when you will see her."

"I'm sure you can only choose the best."

After the meal, we went back to the office. I had finally

found a friend in James. However, I was still reluctant to tell him about my brother, David, and how he was assassinated.

On that evening, I gave a call to Linda; I needed to check on her. She agreed to meet me at Ituze Club Bar for a drink. I arrived there before her, and when she walked in, my maleness quivered. Her moon eyes and biscuit lips made me forget her name. I stood up to rearrange my pants before inviting her to sit on the chair opposite mine.

"How are you, Linda?" I said. "It's been long."

"Fine," Linda responded. "You've forgotten about me."

"No, that's not true. I can't forget you. I have been busy lately. Don't you know I found a job?"

"Wow, congratulations! Does it mean you won't go back to France?"

"No. Not until I get justice for my brother, David."

"What do you mean by justice for your brother?" Linda asked.

How stupid of me, I said to myself. *What am I talking about?*

"Justice? I meant I'm still mourning him. I need to stay in Rwanda and grieve his death. There is no other way I can seek his justice. He is gone and resting in peace."

"Yeah, it's difficult," Linda said. "If he was not killed by a prison officer, it would be easier. But, unfortunately, we can't sue the government. But if I had the means, I would make sure the person who killed Mr. D. gets punished. I feel so bad that he was jailed because of me."

Her voice creaked when she spoke about David. Her chicks developed wrinkles. Her hands shivered. The death of

David must have revived death nightmares in Linda's body. I wondered if it was grief or remorse.

"Linda, David was jailed because of what he said to you, and if the law stipulates it's a crime, he had to pay for it. You did not cause his death. Please, don't inculpate yourself for that."

"Yes, but he did not deserve to die. They should not have killed him."

"You are right. Nobody should be killed for whatever reasons."

"What shall we do about it?" Linda asked. "David was sad and angry, but he was not bad. I can't believe he's gone. No. After how my whole family was decimated in the genocide against the Tutsi in 1994, I didn't know I would experience this again. The death of David has taken me back to those times. I don't sleep. I tremble with fear for the whole night. I see men in military uniforms shooting my father and all of us."

Linda could not stop tears from flowing on her cheeks. I didn't know how to help her. I pushed my chair next to hers, but my hand trembled when I attempted to wipe her tears.

When I approached her, shyness gave her the courage to dry her tears and say, "I am sorry. I shouldn't be weeping. Unfortunately, there is nothing we can do about David's death."

"Linda, may I ask you a question?" I said, and before she responded, I added, "Did David tell you he was a Hutu?"

"No, he didn't. Was he a Hutu? How about Celine? Is she

also a Hutu? And you? Tell me. I need to know. Yes, I also used to think David was a Hutu because of his flat nose. But that changed the day I was told he was Celine's brother. Then, I hated myself for having accused a survivor of the Tutsi genocide of having a genocidal ideology. Now he is dead. If I had not reported him, he would not have been killed trying to escape jail."

When Linda said that, a punch hit my heart. I wondered if the remorse was only because she thought David was a Tutsi.

"David, Celine, and I came from the same womb," I said. "Our mother was brutally tortured and killed during the genocide because she was Tutsi. We were born of different fathers, but our mother raised us not as half but full siblings."

I wished I could let tears out, but instead, my chest swelled, and my back ached. I wanted to get angry with Linda, but I had no reason to. She had liked David even when she knew he was a Hutu, but she was convinced she would not have the same remorse for David's death if she knew he was a Hutu.

"Carlos, I am sorry for your mother," Linda said.

"It's okay," I said, "David experienced what children should never have to experience. We were hiding together for all the three dark months of 1994. He was indeed a survivor of the genocide against the Tutsi."

"No, he wasn't," Linda argued. "Yes, it's sad you lost your mother, but that does not make you genocide survivors."

"Why not?" I asked.

"Because you and David were not Tutsi," she said. "How about Celine? Is she a Tutsi?"

"What do you mean? I have told you we are siblings."

"Yes, but born of different fathers, right? Was her father a Tutsi?"

"Yes," I said. "Whatever that means."

"Then, she is a genocide survivor, but not you and David."

I was shocked by how Linda's tears dried out immediately after I revealed to her that David was a Hutu.

"Linda, you don't know what you are talking about," I said. "But tell me something—"

"Tell you what?" she asked.

"Whether he was a genocide survivor or not, do you think David deserved to be killed?"

"No, he did not," Linda responded. "But I understand why he had an ideology."

"No. You don't understand anything," I said with a louder tone. "Linda, you have no idea what David endured in life. I won't talk about it now. I guess we have to go. I'm tired."

"Carlos, what is it? Please don't be angry. I didn't mean to say—"

"Please, let's discuss this another time. If you really cared for David, you should think of him as a human being, not a Hutu. David was only seven in 1994 when the Hutus you're associating him with killed his mother. And ... and years later ... no, let's not talk about this. Whatever you call ideology, David must have learned it from this unfair world he grew up in."

"What do you mean?" Linda asked.

"Nothing," I said. "I'm sorry, I have to go."

I stood up, and Linda followed me. After we reached

the gates of the bar, I kissed her goodbye and jumped on a motorbike.

As I had promised James, the following Saturday I went to his apartment in Kacyiru. It was on the third floor of the building next to the Umugano Hotel. When his girlfriend opened the door with a smile on her face, I felt the presence of her heart.

Before I wondered what language to greet her in, she said, "Hello! Welcome to our house! Please come in."

Her gestures were more formal than her hello. She bowed her head before she finally noticed I was inviting her for a handshake.

James came to also welcome me in and said, "I hope it wasn't difficult to find the address. These street and house numbers they recently introduced are confusing. For example, a street numbered 300 might be followed by a street numbered 815. You can easily get lost."

The ambiance in their living room was of serenity and tranquility with furniture in modest sizes and numbers and green plants and bamboos that communicated the couple's love and respect for nature. In the corner next to an aquarium, there was a big piano.

"What would you like to drink?" James' girlfriend asked. "We have cognac, red wine, white wine, and different types of juice."

"Apple juice, please," I said.

I had a habit of drinking alcoholic beverages only in bars or in my apartment, but never in other people's homes.

"Carlos, meet my girlfriend, Harumi," James said, before reminding her that he had told her about me.

After about half an hour, Harumi invited us to the dining table.

"In this bowl, you have miso soup," she said. "Here, this is tempura. It's a dish made of battered and fried fish, seafood, and vegetables. It's eaten with this dipping sauce."

"Do you know what?" I said. "This is the first time I'm going to eat a proper meal since I came back to Rwanda. Oh my goodness, there are even chicken brochettes—"

"Yes, we call it yakitori. We just thought that you may like chicken if you don't like fish. The rest, you have here the Japanese noodles we call udon and our healthy tsukemono pickles."

"I guess I need a pen and a paper," I said. "I should write down all these recipes."

Both James and Harumi laughed.

The food was tasty, and although it wasn't like what James had introduced me to at Mary's restaurant a few days before, Japanese food was also easy on the tongue.

After lunch, James pointed to the piano and said, "Drawing will be my dessert. You may also be playing the piano. You music it, I paint it."

"What do you mean by drawing?" I asked. "Do you also draw in addition to photography?"

"My friend, have you forgotten I'm also an IT designer? I do everything creative." Then he turned to his girlfriend and said, "Carlos is also from a family of creatives. Did I tell you Miss Celine is his sister?"

"Wow, your sister is a real beauty," Harumi said, before asking me, "Do you have other siblings?"

"No, I don't."

"Were you born only two in your family?"

"No," I responded.

"Carlos, I didn't know your mother was killed together with your other siblings," James said. "Oh, sorry for that."

"No. My brother, David, was killed a few months ago."

Both James and Harumi stared at me as if they expected me to tell them more about the death of my younger brother.

"Apparently, he wanted to escape from prison," I said.

"Oh no," James said, placing his hands on his head. "Don't tell me he is one of those prisoners they have been shooting. I never believe that story of wanting to escape. It's all staged. I am sorry to say, but your brother was murdered, and like all murder victims, he needs justice."

I stared at James in awe. My eyes could not move away from his face.

He stood up from his seat, approached me, laid his hands on my shoulders, and said, "So sorry for your loss. Carlos, I want you to know you have a brother in me. Yes, I have a big family. But I shall never forget my brothers who sacrificed their lives for this country. It hurts me so much that their blood was spilled in vain. My mother gave birth to only four sons. I am the only one alive today, even though I have many half-siblings from my father's side. My two elder brothers died in the 1990–1994 civil war. I never call it a liberation struggle. Liberation from what? If everything they fought against is still apparent even today? My other brother did not survive the war in Congo. Nobody talks about them. They are remembered as unknown soldiers."

When James said that, I removed his hands from my shoulders, stood up from my seat, and hugged him. I did not know what to say to him. I had always thought that only those who were in Rwanda in the 1990s had wounded hearts. Why had I never thought about the boys who lost their lives in the struggle? Why had I not thought about the parents who lost their sons in the Rwanda struggle and the Congo wars? I was crying for my one brother, but James, whom I thought was okay, had not lost one but three brothers.

"I have no words to express how I feel now after listening to your story," I said to James. "May the souls of your brothers rest in peace."

"Carlos, what hurts me the most is that nobody has ever told me how they died. In Uganda, some families were given the corpses of their loved ones for their decent burial and funeral. But for my family, that never happened. It's only in 1994 that we were told unofficially by their friends that they died. There was never an official communication from either the party or the army. A few years ago, I wanted to know more about their death. I approached different people who told me contradicting stories, making me even more worried and suspicious. Some said they got sick and died. Others said they were hit by bombs sent by the enemy, and others told me that they were at the frontline of the battle and the enemy shot at them. Many of their friends said they had no idea how my brothers were killed and avoided talking to me. The biggest shock was when my uncle, a retired soldier, called me to his house to warn me."

"To warn you about what?" I asked. "But you were not doing anything wrong."

"He said I should forget about my brothers and count them among many heroes who sacrificed their blood to bring us back to our homeland. I told him that was exactly why I wanted to learn more about their death. All I wanted was to write their story. The story of their heroism. How did they do it? In what circumstances did they die? Were they so brave that they accepted the frontline? Why them and not the others?"

After he said that, James ran away to his bedroom to hide the tears starting to dance in his eyes. I guessed he did not want to burst in front of me. Harumi, James's girlfriend, was already in tears. I was left alone in their living room. I could not help James because I knew nothing about the war and the soldiers. What I had lived was the genocide against the Tutsi and its aftermath. A voice in my head told me that maybe I should also forget about David. Many other Rwandans had also lost their siblings in different circumstances. My family was not particular. I moved back to the piano and played a melancholy. That's the only thing I could offer to James.

James and Harumi came back to the living room a few minutes later.

"Carlos, thanks for the music. You play so well. Don't worry, I am fine. I see my brothers in all the boys, men, girls, and women whose faces I steal with my camera. Can we go out to take some shots? We shall go by car. I like to go to the city center. That's where I find more interesting faces."

We jumped in his car and headed to Matheus shopping center.

James was known by all sorts of people in town. He had envelopes full of pictures he had previously taken in his backpack. It was amazing how he recalled where to locate the people in those pictures. He gave them the copies. They thanked and hugged him.

When we were chatting with a lady who was selling the tiny fish known as isambaza in a dirty basin while fighting with flies, we heard some noise. Street sellers were running away from the parapolice who chased them away. Some were arrested and put in a van. The parapolice said to those captured, "*Panda gari,*" a Swahili sentence that means, "Jump into the car." When the lady we were chatting with saw the parapolice, she tried to run away, but they were already in front of her. James took the basin and started speaking Kinyarwanda mixed with English and Luganda, one of the languages of Uganda.

"Please, leave this mukazi alone," he said. "I was actually telling her that street trading is not good. She has promised she won't do it again."

"Yes, boss," the parapolice guy responded. "Madam, how many times have I told you that what you do is against the law? Look at those fish in that mucky basin. Don't you know we should keep Kigali clean? Street mongers are not allowed in our city."

After the parapolice left, the lady stood up and said to

James, "Thank you so much. If you were not foreigners, they would not have forgiven me."

"No, we are not foreigners," James responded. "Both Carlos and I are Rwandans."

"Yes, I know," the lady said. "I mean because you were not born in Rwanda. The parapolice did not take me because I was defended by people who speak English and Luganda. Maybe he thinks you are a soldier. Aren't you?"

"No, I'm not," James responded, before giving some money to the lady and saying bye to her.

"Wait," he said to me after a few steps. "Look at where they are hiding. I have to go and take photos of their gray faces, the stories told by their wrinkles and their beaten-up cheeks. Look at how resentfully they look at the new Kigali skyscrapers. It is as if they feel like they do not belong."

The street mongers were hiding in the corridors between the timeworn short buildings of Matheus shopping center. James approached them. Apparently, he was a friend to many of them. They knew what he wanted. He also knew what they wanted. So he gave them money in exchange for the facial photos.

On that day, James told me many stories about those people. Some of them were survivors of the genocide against the Tutsi, who seemed to have missed their way to the Support Fund for Survivors. Others were survivors of the 1990—1994 war. Many of them were just the poor Rwandans who did not regard themselves as survivors of anything but victims of poverty and capitalism.

In the evening, my most incredible day since I had

returned to Rwanda ended. I said bye to my new friends James and Harumi.

On my way back to the apartment, I bumped into Mukandoli. She told me that the last time she had gone to the prison, her husband Habimana said he needed to talk to me urgently.

"Did you tell him about our conversation?" I asked.

"No, I didn't," Mukandoli responded. "I only told him you came to visit us, but when he asked what we talked about, I said it was simply the usual conversation about rain and seasons."

"Thanks. Do you have any idea why Habimana wants to talk to me? Is anything wrong?"

"No, my husband never tells me anything. He wouldn't even have told me he wanted to talk to you if I had not said you came to our house. He is upset with me. He has not forgiven me for the betrayal."

"Don't worry. He will get over it someday. Okay, I will go to the prison one of these days."

I said bye to Mukandoli and crossed the road toward the bus station. The idea that Habimana wanted to talk to me scared me a bit. *Does he want to make some revelations about the death of my brother, David?* I wondered. What if he'd had a hand in my brother's assassination and planned to eliminate me? Why should I trust him simply because he saved us in 1994? What if he changed to a bitter person because of what he experienced? I had no answers to those questions.

VI

On Monday, I went to the prison to hear from Habimana. When I arrived at the gate, the prison officers told me it wasn't a day for visits. I told them I urgently needed to talk to a prisoner named Habimana. They instructed me to go to the director's office and tell him what I wanted.

The prison officer I had bribed the last time I had come to the prison was with the director.

"Come in," the officer said. "Why did you tell me lies the last time you came here?"

"What lies?" I asked.

"That you are Habimana's nephew. Didn't you tell the director that you were a brother to David, who called himself Mr. D.? You must also be a genocide ideologue, aren't you?"

"Sir, I don't know what you are talking about. What does it mean to be a genocide ideologue? Yes, David was my brother, and he could never condone the genocide that made him an orphan. You should do research about people before you start accusing them of that nonsense."

"What have you just said, you young man?" the director asked. "So, you're here to insult us. Maybe you think that your skin color gives you permission to disrespect us. Okay, tell me, what relationship did a tall muzungu like you have with that ugly boy David? Unless you are French, I don't see why you would be related to Habimana, who is a genocide perpetrator, and David, who was a genocide ideologue."

"Sir, I'm sorry for my tone. David was my brother. We came from the same womb. That's verifiable information. Our brotherhood has nothing to do with our looks or skin colors."

"That's of no importance. Maybe your mother had some magic. So tell us, what did you discuss with Habimana about the death of David?"

"Nothing. He didn't tell me anything about it."

"Are you sure?" The prison officer asked. "Didn't he tell you he is the one who caused your brother's death?"

"What? What do you mean? What did Habimana do to my brother?'

"He is the one who advised him to escape prison. If he had not done so, your brother would still be alive today. Isn't Habimana the one who killed your mother during the genocide? Maybe he wanted to finish the work he had started."

"I don't understand," I said. "Besides, Habimana did not kill our mother. He is innocent."

The prison officer made a sickly laugh before saying, "Are you for real? Don't tell me you are now defending a genocide perpetrator." He moved as if he were about to get out of the director's office, but after making two steps toward the door, he turned back and asked, "Is Mr. Kamara related to you?"

"Yes, he is my uncle," I responded. "Do you know each other?"

"No, not really. Yes, I know Kamara, but not that much. But I guess you need to have a conversation with him. He will tell you more about David you call your brother and Habimana you consider innocent. Apparently, you have no idea whom you're mingling with."

"Hey, Bosco, don't go before you escort this guy back to the gate," the director said to the officer, before turning to me and saying, "I understand you had come to talk to Habimana, right? I wanted to tell you that you are no longer allowed to talk to him."

"Why, sir? Please allow me to talk to him just for five minutes."

"No. You can't, and that's final."

"Please, let me tell him that I know what he did. I must tell him I know he caused my brother's death."

Bosco made a nodding gesture to the director.

"Okay," the director said to me. "The officer must accompany you. Don't say anything else to Habimana. I hope you're aware of the consequences if you try to."

"Thank you, sir," I said. "I only want to confront him about my brother's death."

Bosco accompanied me to the waiting room and showed me the bench to sit on before he went to call Habimana. My heart jumped out of my chest at the sight of the scars on Habimana's face. He tried to vanish from the space, but Bosco pushed his shoulder and ordered him to move toward me. I could read dejection and antagonism on his face. Apparently, Habimana did not want to talk to me.

"I know why you don't want to talk to me," I said to Habimana. "Bosco, the prison officer, has told me everything. You are responsible for the death of my brother."

"Yes, he is," Bosco said. "He is the one who persuaded David to escape prison."

"That's not true," Habimana argued. "Why don't you ask this Bosco the name of the officer who shot David?"

"Don't play dumb," Bosco responded. "What else would the officers have done to the prisoner who was trying to escape? Was David in his cell when he was shot dead?"

"This officer knows more about your brother's death than what he has told you," Habimana said. "He knows well who persuaded David to escape prison. He knows who shot David and why he wanted him dead. He even knows why I have these bruises on my face."

"Talking about the bruises," I said, "what happened to you? The last time I was here, you had no scrapes on your face. I can see they are still fresh. Who did this to you?"

"The person who did this to me would kill me if I revealed his name to you."

"Five minutes are over," Bosco said to me. 'You've already said what you had to say. Don't allow yourself to be manipulated by this criminal you call Habimana."

"I'm a prisoner, not a criminal," Habimana said to Bosco, before turning to me to say, "Maybe since this prison officer has volunteered to tell you everything, he should also tell you more about what happens to some prisoners in this jail, those tortured like me or murdered like David."

"Let's go," the officer said to me. "Time's up."

He escorted me to the gate. We were silent. I didn't know what to think about the director, the prison officer named Bosco, and Habimana. Something seemed to be odd. Who told Mukandoli that I needed to urgently come to the prison? Why did Habimana not want to talk to me? Is it true he could have had a hand in my brother's death? But why didn't the officer Bosco and the prison director want me to talk to Habimana privately? What did Habimana mean when he said the officer knows much more about the death of David? I had responses to none of those questions.

When I took back the phone I had left at the prison gate, I noticed my sister Celine had sent me a short message, "I'm hospitalized." She did not specify the hospital at which she was, nor why she had to be hospitalized. I dialed her number, but she did not pick up the call.

I dialed again, no response.

Then, she sent another message: "I'm in Kanyinya Mental Hospital, room 357."

When I read *mental*, flies floated in my little head as if I were going mad. I immediately thought about the psychological effects of the genocide against the Tutsi on the survivors. In 1994, the neighbor who took Celine to the Red Cross had found her surrounded by dozens of dead bodies of her paternal family. My sister was one of those people who were killed but miraculously did not breathe their last. She never talked about what she experienced during the genocide against the Tutsi. Maybe we never gave her the chance to narrate it. We considered her to be the strongest of all of us. Her wounds had never healed. Everything she experienced during the years that followed the genocide had kept her wounds fresh, even though she pretended to cover them with red lipstick and high heels. The last time I was with her, she swallowed many tablets and told me that Uncle Kamara was a monster. She neither told me what he did to her nor what she had endured in Butare, where Uncle Kamara had sent her to live with our maternal grandparents.

I jumped on a motorbike and headed to Kanyinya Mental Hospital.

When I attempted to enter her room, a nurse stopped and said, "Wait, she is with the doctor. You cannot see her now. Go and wait over there."

I went to sit down on the waiting bench in the hallway.

"What's wrong with my sister?" I asked the nurse when she passed by.

"She has fallen down on the stairs of her apartment."

"Fallen down?" I asked. "Did she bump her head on something? I mean, why is she in a mental hospital?"

"That, I can't tell you. I am bound by confidentiality."

I waited for over thirty minutes before they allowed me to see her. She was in a deep sleep. I looked at my sister from toe to hair. Her feet reached the bottom of the bed. Her head on the headboard of that bed seemed to have longed for that sleep.

Thinking about myself, my brother, David, who had been

murdered mysteriously, and my sister, Celine, who was lying on a sickbed in a mental hospital, I looked up to the sky. I said to Mama, "Now, I need your guidance. Please tell me what I should do. Mama, I was not there to save your last-born, David. But now I'm here. Please, tell me where to touch Celine's body so that she might get up from this bed, with feet on the ground and smiles on her face. I believe you are now an angel in heaven. You see what I don't see. Please, tell me what I should do."

I laid my hand on Celine's cool cheeks, rearranged her eyebrows, and caressed her hair for minutes I did not count. I wished my eyes could let the tears out, but I had learned to control my emotions since I was a little boy. In my culture, men do not cry.

Celine slowly opened her eyes and faced the ceiling. I removed my hand from her hair. She neither looked at me nor talked to me.

"Celine," I said, "are you okay? What happened to you?"

"I'm okay," she said, "don't worry." Then, she turned to the other side of the bed and hid her face from my eyes.

"No, Celine, tell me, what's wrong?'

I moved to the side she was facing. Tears flew on her cheeks. I pulled up a chair and sat next to her. I laid my hand on hers. No word could come out of my mouth. Maybe we did not need to say anything.

"Carlos," Celine said after minutes of silence, "I've gone mad. I'm officially insane."

"What do you mean?"

"I'm mentally deranged," Celine responded. "Can't you see I'm in a mental hospital? I have been hallucinating."

"Hallucinations?"

"Yes."

"That must be the trauma caused by what you experienced during the genocide against the Tutsi.'

"No, what I saw has nothing to do with the genocide. I'm worried. I have seen people I have never met in my life. I guess they were demons."

"Demons? Do you believe in those things?"

"No, of course I don't. That's why I think I have gone mad."

"What did you see exactly?" I asked.

"After I opened my eyes this morning," she said, "I realized everything in the house had turned red and black. Groups of girls in red dresses were seated on the black chairs in my living room. One group was of girls with ugly faces. The second group was of girls with beautiful faces. The ugly girls seemed mean and irritated. They shouted that I was a bitch who sold my beauty for riches. On the other hand, the beautiful girls were cool and friendly. They called me stunning and said beauty is the wealth I did not have to work for. There was another girl whose face was also considered ugly. Unlike her lookalikes, the girl in the corner was not mean to me. She ordered the other girls to stop insulting me, but they disobeyed. She ambled toward where I was standing like a shivering, cold chick and begged me to stop crying. She promised that she shall always be by my side to protect me from this hostile world. When she came even closer, my legs trembled; I had to save myself. Instead of taking the elevator, I took the stairs. I must have fallen down on the first step. The nurse has told me that my neighbor is the one who dropped me here."

"It's strange what happened to you," I said. "What did the doctor say?"

"He has said that it happens. So they have given me an injection and said they will continue to observe me for about three days."

"What did he mean by it happens?"

"Hallucinations," Celine responded. "The doctor said they receive many patients who experience the same. Apparently, acute depression is one of the possible causes. I have suffered depression before, but it's my first time to hallucinate."

"Sorry, you will be okay," I said. "Have you eaten anything?"

"No. I'm not hungry. In fact, I haven't eaten anything since yesterday morning."

"Oh no, that's not good. I should go get you something."

"No need. I believe this drip is helping me. At least I won't be dehydrated."

"No, you should eat something. Let me ask if the hospital has a canteen."

I went outside to buy some food and drinks for Celine. I managed to get milk, juice, and some snacks.

When I came back, Celine said, "Carlos, there is something that has been bothering my mind."

"What is it?" I asked.

"I have a friend named Ingabire. We went to the same secondary school in Butare. When uncle Kamara persuaded me to enter the competition for Miss Rwanda, I encouraged Ingabire to also try her luck. She loved everything to do with beauty. I heard for the first time the word *cat-walking* from her. Ingabire is not long-legged, but she meets the height requirements for beauty pageants. The day we went for the first auditions, as soon as she entered the hall, the audience chuckled as if they found her funny. We could see them murmuring and pointing fingers at her. She must have felt noticeable for every bad reason."

"Oh, that's bad," I said. "What had your friend done wrong?"

"Nothing," Celine responded. "Ingabire's face is plain-featured. She is not the beauty that is often associated with Rwandan women."

"What do you mean?"

"She looks like the ugly girls I have seen in my hallucinations. She has a square-shaped face, a flat nose with widely opened nostrils, and big and full lips. The people thought she was too ugly to even think of competing in Rwanda beauty pageants."

"Whatever the shape of her face or nose," I said, "I don't understand why they thought she did not qualify for the auditions. Did she not fulfill the requirements?"

"Of course she did," Celine responded.

"I hope she was selected and allowed to participate in the beauty pageants. In Europe, I see models of African descent whose faces are like what you describe. Although I don't support the idea of beauty pageants, I think what they look at is the body silhouette and how the person uses that body to portray her uniqueness, confidence, and class."

"Exactly!" Celine said. "Unfortunately, Ingabire sniveled and decided to leave the scene.

"Why? She shouldn't have given up. I'm sure the judges wouldn't have minded her looks. So what does she now do in life?"

"That's actually why I can't stop thinking about her. Even though there are things she disagrees with me on, she is still the friend I call whenever I want to vent my fury to somebody. She allows me to scream and tell this world how unfair it is. But after I calm down, I think of myself as a selfish person."

"Why?" I asked.

"Because the world has been unfairer to her than it has been to me. Ingabire is an orphan like me, but she could not go to college because there was nobody to finance her studies. Whenever I ask her how her parents died, she says she is not yet ready to talk about it. But that's not the only thing that bothers me. Ingabire is a single mother whose child was fathered by the man who used to call her savage. They were never in a relationship. The man raped her before he spat on her with both saliva and insults. My friend, Ingabire, is a street monger. She sells secondhand clothes, but she does not earn enough from that risky business. I support her financially, but I never think about the wounds of her heart."

"I understand," I said. "But I guess Kigali has many more people like Ingabire."

"Yes, but she is special. Though I have not been a good

friend to her, she has always been there whenever I needed to talk to someone. I feel like a changed person after what I saw in the spiritual vision or what the doctor called hallucination. It is as if God wanted to reveal something to me. When I get off this sickbed, there are decisions I will have to make."

"What decisions?" I asked. "Tell me, please."

"No," Celine responded. "I can't tell you anything now. Just know that my life is going to completely change. I can't allow myself to go mad. There are things I should put in better shape. The doctor has recommended a psychologist who shall have more time to listen to me and guide me in the decisions I want to make. Now, it's not yet clear in my mind, but I'm sure I shall find the way."

I insisted that she tell me what she wanted to do, but she refused.

Four days later, Celine was released from the mental hospital. That day, her face was as calm as a green apple, her smile was as serene as an ocean, and her feet were not in high heels but in ballerina shoes. She seemed to be lighter than how she looked before.

During the following days and weeks, I continued to visit Celine. She was a changed person. One thing was clear: she spent more time in her apartment than she used to.

On a Saturday when I went to her place, I found a lady in the living room. Looking at her, I immediately guessed she was Ingabire, the friend Celine had told me about. Her face was adorable and wide enough to accommodate her enormous eyes, big nose, and generous lips. Her smile was glorious. You could think she had more than forty teeth.

"Carlos," Celine said, "meet my friend Ingabire."

Ingabire stood up to greet me but waited for me to invite her for a handshake. In the Rwandan culture, the elder is the one who invites the younger for a shake.

"Hello, Ingabire," I said, giving her my hand. "Nice meeting you."

"Hello," she responded. "Nice meeting you too.

Although she looked clean and well composed, her cut-short hairstyle and village-like clothing did not match the Kigali standards. The conversation between the two ladies did not sound like what you would expect girlfriends to talk about. It was not about fashion. It was not about makeup. It was not about the latest music hits. It was not about boyfriends. Celine played the listener as Ingabire told her why she had decided to stop selling secondhand clothes on the Kigali streets. The business was too risky. Whenever she was caught by the parapolice, who took away her merchandise as a punishment, she always returned to Celine to beg for some more money to restart the business.

"Have you ever thought of other income-generating activities you could start?" I asked.

"Yes, but it's complicated," She responded. "I wanted to be a tailor, but I did not manage to buy a tailoring machine and rent a shop space in town."

"That's why I have called Ingabire here," Celine said. "I'm quitting modeling. I want to nurture a new generation of models. My aim is bigger than just earning a living. We must change the status quo. Our society needs some kind of cultural evolution."

"That's impressive," I said. "But I don't get it. What status quo do you want to change? What do you mean by cultural evolution?"

"You will see," she said. "Don't you remember the vision I had a few days ago? The doctor called it hallucinations, but it was a calling as far as I'm concerned."

"Tell me more about what you're going to do."

"Ingabire and I will design clothes for all those girls, tall and short, thick and thin, round- and oval-shaped faces, those with flat noses, and those with lean noses. In short, we will showcase the beauty of all Rwandan girls."

"That sounds good," I said. "But you have to be careful. I don't know about faces, but I know models must be tall and slender. Are you sure the society is ready for that cultural evolution you suggest?"

"That's what I have been telling Celine," Ingabire said. "She thinks it's all about modeling. She has no idea that anything that touches on the differences between Rwandan silhouettes and faces may be misinterpreted. Nobody shall ever come to a fashion show of short, fat models with faces as wide as mine."

"Don't worry," Celine replied to Ingabire. "I won't be targeting only those girls. I want to showcase the diversity of all the Rwandan beauties. If anybody has a problem with that, they will have to explain why some girls cannot be models. I have gone through so much in life that nothing can scare me anymore. I don't know how long I'm left to live, but I'm glad I finally know what to do with my short life on earth."

"What do you mean by short life on earth?" I asked her. "Don't talk as if you were dying tomorrow."

"Yes, my brother," she responded. "There is a lot you don't know."

"Like what?"

"That I might be dying soon."

"Stop it. You're not going anywhere."

Before Celine responded, my phone rang.

"Hello," I said to the caller.

"I'm in trouble," Rotty said. "Under arrest."

"You're under arrest?" I asked. "Who is arresting you? What have you done?"

"I can't give you any details on the phone. It's because of Martin. He has accused me of being a thief."

When he mentioned Martin, my heart cracked at the idea that maybe he was caught trying to spy on Martin.

I turned to my sister and said, "Celine, I'm sorry. I have to go. We'll talk later."

"What is it?" Celine asked. "Who is under arrest?"

"You don't know him," I said. "His name is Rotty. He was a friend to David. I hope it's not what I'm thinking."

"What do you mean?"

"You cannot understand. Let me go. I promise I'll be right back."

"Okay, please make sure you come back."

I jumped on a motorbike and asked the rider to take me to the Inzuki boys' house. But seconds later, Rotty sent a short message to inform me they were taking him to Nyami-rambo police custody. We headed there.

"I've told them everything," Rotty said, after they gave him permission to talk to me.

"What do you mean by everything?" I asked.

"About Martin," he said. "I can't tell you more. That policeman is snooping."

"But I need to know what you've said. Have you talked about me?"

"No. I've told them I was working on my own. But now they know I have details on who Martin is and who he was working for. Were you aware he was hired by your sister's lover?"

"Hired by who?" I asked. "To do what?"

"Time is up," the policeman said. "The visit is over. "Please, go and bring clothes, bedsheets, and a blanket for him."

"Officer," I said, "Rotty is innocent. Why has he been arrested?"

"He is a suspect. You'll have the chance to prove his inno-cence in court. For now, we are still investigating his case."

"If the investigations are not over, why have you arrested him then?"

"Because as a thief, he is a danger to society."

"No, officer, Rotty is not a thief."

"Go, please. Your time here is up."

VII

I jumped on another taxi moto and went back to Celine's place. She needed to explain what she knew about Martin and his relationship with the man she used to spend nights with. My head was breaking into pieces. I could not imagine that my sister Celine could be involved with those who could be the masterminds of our brother's detention and death.

Knocking on the door to Celine's apartment, I took a deep breath. I had to calm down. She opened and stared at my face for a few seconds before sitting on the couch as if she were ready to listen. She must have wanted to know more about the person who had called me a few hours earlier and why that person had been arrested.

"Brother, what is it?" Celine asked. "What's bothering you?"

"Tell me," I said. "Do you know Martin?"

"Which Martin?" she asked.

"The one who was hired by your lover to be the music manager of David."

"That one? I met him a couple of times. He's one of Kananga's guys."

"Who is Kananga? What do you mean by 'one of his guys'?"

"Kananga is the man I was in a relationship with. Martin is one of the guys who run errands for him."

"Do you mean you no longer see the old man?"

"No, it's over. That's one of the decisions I made after the experience of hallucinations. When I was still at the hospital, I ignored Kananga's calls. Then, the day I was discharged, I went to his place at Nyarutarama to pack my stuff and leave him forever. He initially thought I was throwing a tantrum. But when he realized it wasn't a joke, he pulled my T-shirt, spat abuse at my face, and said that I was nothing without him. He threatened to stop paying rent for this apartment. He couldn't understand that his sex plaything had finally responded to the call for freedom. That man had sucked dignity out of me. Uncle Kamara had made me his puppet, but Kananga made me feel like a reusable toilet paper."

"It's good you ended the relationship. That man you call Kananga must be dangerous."

With tears wetting her eyes, Celine dabbed my shoulder. "Brother, yes, Martin was hired by Kananga to be David's music manager. The aim was to keep David in control."

I could not believe my ears. Some dots were starting to connect, but I couldn't make anything out of it.

"Martin is the one who accused David of genocide ideology," I said to Celine. "He is the one who reported him to the police. David would not have been jailed and died if the guy your lover hired had not turned him in."

"No," my sister argued. "David was jailed because of what

he had said to a girl called Linda. She is the one who reported him to the police. Martin was saddened by what Linda had done. He was not in agreement with her."

"Is that what Martin told you?" I asked.

"He didn't say it to me but to Kananga. I never speak to Martin. Kananga never allowed me to speak to any other man."

"Sister, I think Martin and your lover hid from you their plan. They must have wanted to get rid of David."

"Why would my lover want to get rid of my brother? He cared for him. When David used to portend that he would reveal to Kananga's wife and children that I was his side chick, Kananga took it lightly. He believed David was simply blackmailing us to get my financial and moral support. He hired Martin to help David take his music to another level. Kananga believed that success would make David realize that there was more to life than policing what I did with my own life. Kananga did not want David to be jailed or killed. He was also deceived by what my brother did."

"There is a lot you don't understand," I said.

"Like what?" Celine asked.

"Our brother David was murdered. That's the first thing you need to comprehend before we may discuss who might have played a role in that murder. So please stop justifying David's death."

"No, I don't justify his death. But I can't ignore that he was jailed because of what he had said and was killed because he tried to escape prison. I don't think we should blame other people for David's own blunders."

"You don't know what David went through in life," I said to Celine. "He experienced more than what your friend Ingabire might have experienced. All because his looks were different. His face was as ugly as those of the girls you saw in your vision. Do you realize that?"

"No, I don't get it," she responded. "David was a boy, and nobody cares about boys' looks."

I narrated to Celine what David had endured when we lived together in our Nyamirambo house. I told her how strangers constantly picked on David because of his looks. I told her the story of a time a man called David a Hutu and threatened to kill him."

"What?" Celine asked. "I have never heard of any person killed because of being a Hutu. Are you sure that happened?"

"Do you mean you don't believe what I'm telling you?"

"No, I trust you. I simply don't believe my ears. Why didn't you tell me? That man should have been punished for that."

"There is a lot I haven't told you. For example, you have no idea what David and I endured during the genocide against the Tutsi. Do you remember how old David was in 1994? Seven. Our mother was raped many times in front of our eyes. She screamed. The Hutu militiamen slapped her. They tortured her. David was there, sobbing and wondering what was happening. He knew it was all happening because Mama was a Tutsi, though he did not understand the meaning of that word. We hated those Hutu militiamen. We hated the Hutus who hurt and killed our mother. David was traumatized. Imagine how he felt when some men put him in the same basket as the Hutus who killed our mother. Do you understand how wounding it was for David?"

Tears flew on Celine's cheeks. She crossed her arms around her chest and pinched herself as if she wanted to calm the beetles in her body.

"Mama ..." she mumbled, "Mama ... No, Carlos, don't say they did it to Mama."

I approached my sister and covered her with my arms. I allowed her to burst into tears. I gave her all the time she needed to cry.

"Yes, sister, the Hutu militiamen raped our mother. They slapped her. They spat their smelly saliva in her face. They killed her."

"It's over now," Celine said. "I'm okay. I have no reason to be sad. I can't compare what I experienced with the pain Mama endured."

"What do you mean?" I asked. "Were you also raped?"

"Yes, but at least my rapist did not kill me. Yes, it was a horrible experience that I lived through for many years. I was raped till I stopped thinking it was rape. I have been replaying the movie of my own experiences these last few days. I look at myself and feel pity for the girl I was. Now ... to learn that Mama experienced the same, I no longer feel sad but angry. I'm irritated by the world. I'm angry with men. I'm upset."

"Who raped you?" I asked.

"No, that I can't tell you. You might hate him. You might attack him. I don't want to turn you into another David."

"Had you ever told David?"

"No, but he always told me that men had turned me into

their puppet. He hated Uncle Kamara. He disapproved of my relationship with Kananga. I did not listen to him. I thought it was because he hated Tutsis. I believed David had become like those Hutus who hate Tutsis."

"Celine, David did not hate anybody. Even the girl to whom he said bad words was his friend. Have you ever talked to her? She was also hurt by David's death, but ..."

"But what?" Celine asked.

"She told me David was a good person and that she was hurt by his death. But when I revealed to her that David's father was Hutu, she seemed to conclude that maybe it was true that David had an ideology."

"How do you mean? Do you mean she did not think it was a genocide ideology until you told him David was a Hutu?"

"Exactly. Although Linda was not happy with what David said to her, she did not think it was a big deal. Martin decided to report it to the police, then convinced the girl to give her testimony. When Linda learned that David was your brother, she concluded he was probably a Tutsi and regretted having sent a Tutsi genocide survivor to jail. So, the day I told her that David's father was a Hutu, the tears on her cheeks immediately dried, and her remorse faded away."

"What David said to her was off the beam and punishable by the law," Celine said. "But he did not say it because he was a Hutu. Not all Hutus support genocide ideology."

"Though I can't justify what David said to Linda, there is a lot of coincidence that makes me think everything was preplanned. Linda was Martin's girlfriend, and that's how she met David. Martin was hired by Kananga, your lover. I need to find the link between them and the prison officer, Bosco, whom I met at the prison, who seemed to know much about how David was shot dead. Maybe he was hired by either Martin or Kananga."

"Did you say you met that prison officer at the prison? What took you to that place?"

"I went there to visit our former neighbor, Habimana."

"Who?" Celine asked. "Don't tell me you are talking about the man who killed our mother during the genocide against the Tutsi."

"Yes, I'm talking about Habimana, who hid us in his kitchen in 1994 during the genocide against the Tutsi. He is not responsible for our mother's death. His wife should be the one in jail, not him. She is the one who brought the killers to the kitchen where we were hiding with Mama."

"Now I'm lost," my sister said. "I can't follow you anymore. I need to take some tablets."

She pulled the drawer underneath her bookshelf and grabbed a pack of painkillers. I wanted to stop her but did not know what else I would give to her. Maybe she would end up again in a mental hospital if she did not calm her discomfort.

"Celine, we need to pack this conversation for another day. It seems we have a lot to tell each other. I still haven't told you what I endured in France, and you've not told me about your experiences during all the years I was away. May I make a suggestion?"

"What suggestion?"

"What plans do you have for next weekend? I want to take you upcountry, maybe in Kibuye around Lake Kivu. We may go there on Friday and come back to Kigali on Sunday. How about that?"

"It sounds like a good idea, but I'm scared of what more you have to reveal to me."

"Don't worry. I will be more of a listener than a talker. I hope you won't have any excuses for not telling me about every bit of what you went through."

"No, Carlos. There are things I'm not yet ready to talk about. It's not because I want to hide anything from you. It's simply because I'm incapable of formulating sentences to express what I endured. It has to be clear in my mind before I can share it with anybody."

"It's all right. My ears shall listen to the silence of your voice, while my soul shall be listening to the beating of your heart. That shall communicate more than what you can say with words."

"Thanks, brother."

On the following Friday, Celine and I went to Kibuye. We had booked rooms in the Ituze Hotel.

After freshening up, we sat by the Lake Kivu for an evening tea before supper.

"I have been to this place before," Celine said. "But I was always with my nightmares."

"What do you mean?"

"It's my first time to come here alone."

"Alone?"

"No. That's not what I mean. I wanted to say that I always came with a boyfriend or one of those men."

"I get it. Today, you are with a special man, your brother. I won't touch you. I won't make you feel uncomfortable. I will just show you how brotherly love is more powerful than any other sort of love. Celine, do you remember how we used to be friends? You used to keep secrets for me. But I paid for it, didn't I?"

"Yes. Carlos, you used to steal from Mama. That wasn't good."

"You should be blamed for that. When you asked me to buy candies for you, where did you think I got the money?"

"I don't know. You simply had to buy me candies, or I would report to Mama that you had gone out without her permission."

Celine's eyes bubbled as she smiled with delight. It was as if she missed those innocent days of our childhood. I did not know how to start talking about Butare, Kamara, modeling, men, and lifestyle. We needed to continue chatting about nice things: the Kibuye sky blue, the lake, and the beautiful silhouettes of the women swimming in the lake. I had to play more the role of a girlfriend than of an elder brother.

After sharing dinner, we said good night to each other and went to our separate bedrooms.

The following morning, we jogged under the shades of the air-soothing trees of Kibuye. Then, we had a late breakfast, or maybe a brunch, at around eleven, after which I invited Celine for a boat tour of the lake.

"Sister, tell me what I should do for you to keep a smile on your face," I said. "You've experienced a lot in life. The death of your father and all the members of your paternal family.

The death of our mother. The days, months, and years that followed the genocide against the Tutsi, when you were alone in Butare without your brothers. Those experiences you are still reluctant to narrate to me. My sister, I know it's not easy. Life has not been easy for me either. Our brother David is no more. We have each other. You have me; I have you."

"I can't find words to express my feelings," Celine said. "The air feels less charged. Finally, I'm not afraid to break. I'm stronger than my demons. I can confront all of them one by one. But brother, Carlos, whenever I go to bed, I'm scared it could smell like Butare. That bed at our grandparents' house, in the room next to the living room, can tell you more than what I will ever be able to narrate. That room smelled ignominy, iniquity, and inhumanity. In that room, the devil came to my bed every night. He stole my childhood. He shamed my body. He … he is … a monster."

Celine burst into tears.

I held her in my arms and asked, "Who? Who did that to you?"

"Uncle Kamara," Celine responded. "He took me to Butare because he wanted to make me his sex toy."

"Did you tell Grandma?"

"Yes."

"Then?"

"She tsked and begged me not to say it to Grandpa. I wished they were still alive. I would confront them now. Nobody cared about what I was going through. I was on my own and at the mercy of my rapist. Kamara was like the head of that family. He even verbally abused his own parents. They could never say anything to him."

"Oh, sorry, sister. Uncle Kamara should be punished. I was told our grandparents died mysteriously in the same week. I hope that the monster we call our uncle did not have a hand in their death. Were you still living with them?"

"No, I was in Kigali. I didn't even go to their burial. When they died, I also suspected Uncle Kamara. Maybe he hit them as he used to do."

"Oh, that man is a walking devil. He should be punished for what he did."

"Please, Carlos, I beg you. Do never make me regret what I have said to you. Uncle Kamara is one of the omnipotent businessmen in Kigali. He has connections in both the military and the police. I suspect he engages in some dark businesses."

"What dark businesses?" I asked.

"Who knows? Maybe drug dealings. Maybe some mercenary executions. Maybe some secret operations. Please don't call his attention to you. Pretend you don't know anything about what he did."

"Celine, do you know our uncle Kamara might also be the one who was behind the assassination of Mr. Mukinzi, the paternal uncle of our brother, David?"

"That I know. Kamara himself confessed it to me. He said Mukinzi had taken our house and that all he wanted was to save our mother's house. It was a total shock to me when I found out that after Mukinzi's death, Kamara managed to get our mother's house papers under his name. I learned that the house was neither in my name nor David's name the day Kamara sold it to other people. That's what angered David the most. I warned him, but he did not listen. He confronted

Uncle Kamara about the house. He confronted my sex partners. David was big-headed."

"Don't say that about David. Sometimes, it's not right to use the verb 'to be' as if you want to put a label on a person's forehead to justify the injustices he suffered. David was not big-headed. He wanted to defend the dignity of his family, our family. Even though David has been muted forever, please, listen to his soul. He has a lot to tell you. He must have wanted your attention. He did not know that you also longed for a brother's shoulder to lean on."

"Yes, you are right. But I wished he had listened to me. He didn't know those people's power in this country. Or is it just me who was still enslaved by them? I'm afraid I'm going to be the one confronting them now. My freedom days are here."

Celine continued to narrate to me how Uncle Kamara exploited her beauty in addition to raping her. My sister had engaged in all sorts of jobs for Uncle Kamara. Sometimes, she was sent to spy on some people. Sometimes, she was trapped and raped by some men whom Uncle Kamara wanted to blackmail. In 2000, when Uncle Kamara persuaded Celine to compete in the Miss Rwanda beauty pageants, he had discovered another way to exploit her beauty. When Kananga, another tycoon, started dating Celine, Uncle Kamara disapproved. That was because Kananga was more powerful and feared than Kamara. It was as if his sex slave was being taken away. From the day she became Kananga's sex partner, Kamara could no longer rape Celine or use her. She became the property of Kananga, who did not allow her to speak to any other man. She moved from one master to another.

"Brother, whenever I reflect on my life," Celine said, "I hate whoever tells me I'm attractive. It's a heavy burden to be regarded as beautiful in a society that treats girls like toys. That's why I want to change how beauty is perceived in Rwanda."

"How do you intend to do it?" I asked.

"I have already told you. It will be a cultural revolution in the beauty and fashion industry. I will touch Rwandans where they shall feel it the most; their so-called Rwandan beauty."

"Yes, you told me that before. But I still don't get how it will contribute to the change this country needs. Celine, those men did not rape you because they found you attractive. You told me that even your friend Ingabire, who is considered ugly, was raped. Right? The problems we have in this country are two: The Hutu–Tutsi conflict and the culture of violence. I don't see how you will be solving those problems with modeling and beauty pageants."

"Don't you see it? Me, yes. I see the link between the two. Can you imagine Tutsi, Hutu, Twa, and naturalized Rwandan ladies cat-walking together in front of those men and women who ignored the diversity that makes up the Rwandan population?"

"Yeah, that shall be interesting to see," I said.

"In this Rwanda, some women have been made to believe that their beauty is the only thing that gives them value. Some others, considered ugly, have been made to believe that even greeting them is a favor they do not deserve. Imagine if, in beauty pageants, the only qualities that contestants needed to prove to be crowned Miss Rwanda or Miss anything were self-worth and self-expression."

"Then it would not be a beauty pageant," I said. "But maybe a confidence competition."

"Yes, it would be a beauty pageant in which girls would be confidently showcasing their beauty. Do you get it? All girls would be considered beautiful. But only the self-confident girls who can express themselves in a way that showcases better their beauty would have the chance to win."

"That's interesting."

"I will need a photographer. Someone who knows how to spot unique beauty from far and who is fascinated by diversity. I'm a model, and I know that it's one thing to be attractive and another thing to have the kind of photos that pull people into your unique beauty. For example, nobody knew Lupita Nyong'o was a beauty until they brought her closer to our eyes on TV and magazine covers."

"That beauty, modeling, fashion, and TV world is not mine," I said, "but you have my full support. I know someone who would love to be your photographer. His name is James. He's my workmate. He says he's fascinated by faces. He walks around Kigali city with a camera taking photos of Kigalians. If you want to see the diversity of Rwandan faces, all you have to do is check James's albums."

"Wow! That's the guy I'm looking for. I hope he is not one of those Kigalian men I no longer want to mingle with."

"No, he is not. He is a down-on-earth guy in a relationship with a Japanese lady. He is not searching."

"Stop it! What are you talking about? Do you think I'm scared of the singles? Maybe you don't know that the most scaring Kigalians are actually older and married men."

"James is probably the only Kigalian I trust. Don't worry."

The conversation was not only about Celine's life. I also told her about my experience in France, including how I met my paternal family.

"This world has gone crazy," Celine said. "So, do you mean you were also rejected by your paternal family? I thought Europeans had reached some other levels of understanding."

"No, it's all the same everywhere," I said. "In Rwanda, everybody calls me a muzungu because, to them, I'm noticeably white. But when I was in France, I was a black guy like any other African. On my maternal side, I'm white to Rwandans, and that feels as if I'm not one of them. To the French, on my paternal side, I'm black and not fully theirs. That's the world we live in, with these so-called ethnicities or races. Sister, it's the same experience our brother, David, lived in Rwanda. To the Hutu extremists, he was the son of our Tutsi mother, and nobody cared who his father was. Otherwise, he would not have experienced what he endured during the genocide against the Tutsi. But on the other hand, the same way I was rejected by my French paternal uncle, David was also rejected by his Tutsi maternal uncle."

"That's sadly true," Celine said. "I also did not condone how Uncle Kamara rejected David and said he should not be considered as our mother's son."

"You've got it," I said. "I'm glad you can now realize that David was more of a victim of hatred and not a perpetrator."

"But, brother, the same way we shouldn't condone how Uncle Kamara rejected David, we should also not condone how David had become hateful. Do you hate all French people or white people because your French paternal uncle rejected you?"

"No. I don't. But I'm also not convinced David hated Tutsis."

"I guess I cannot convince you about David," Celine said. "Anyway, now I understand what had made him bitter. I only wished he did not take out his rage on me. I wished he had approached me and told me all he was going through."

"Yeah," I said. "Unfortunately, David is no more to tell us why he did not discuss with you everything. Haven't you said he used to urge you to leave those men? Maybe he felt that you were too busy to listen to him. My aim is not to blame you, far from that. I just want us to understand our brother, David. If he were still alive, I would also apologize to him. I will never forgive myself for having left both of you alone to experience this world's hostility. David must have felt rejected even by his siblings."

After saying that, I bent my head between my legs. I did not want Celine to see my eyes.

To change the topic, Celine said, "You told me your grandma was sick when you left France. Do you have any news, now?"

"My dear, I have no news of them. The phone line I used to call grandma on does not go through. I lost my uncle's number, and when I tried to search for him on the internet, there were more than five people with the same name in France, and none had his picture on their profile. Maybe, one day, I shall contact the retirement home and ask for the news about my grandma. I'm terrified at the idea that maybe she passed away. She found out we were related the day before I traveled back to Rwanda."

"No, don't think like that. Let's hope she is still alive. How old is she?"

"She is eighty-nine," I responded.

After our conversation by the lake beach, Celine and I went to the restaurant to have a roasted tilapia fish.

On Sunday afternoon, we drove back to Kigali.

My routine was the same from Monday to Friday of the following week. After office work, I called Celine every evening before taking a shower, eating, watching the news, and going to bed.

VIII

On Friday, James invited me for an evening to celebrate life, despite its thorns. We met at Soso Club Bar. James never touched anything alcohol, but he was the most jokey guy in a bar.

"Carlos, tonight, I'm introducing you to another side of the city. In fact, no need to remain seated in this bar. Instead, let's do a Kigali city tour. This city has everything. You'll see both sticks and chicks.

"Sticks and chicks?"

"Yes. Don't be surprised to see some fighting and others kissing."

"Even though I still don't get it, I'm ready for the adventure. Maybe I can fall in love again with the city I was born in. Otherwise, after the death of my brother, David, and the conversation I had with my sister Celine, it feels as if I'm in a dangerous zone."

"I hear you, my friend. I have been there, and I know how it feels. The best coping mechanism is to think of life as a dangerous adventure. Let's enjoy the risks that go with this life.

One day, things shall take their own course. I remain optimistic."

"Optimistic? How?"

"Just get in the car; you'll understand where I get my optimism. You got to be observant. You'll read it on the faces of the young Rwandans in this city. The cultural revolution shall precede whatever revolution the politicians talk about. I'm only interested in the former."

I entered the car, and James drove toward Gitega on the way to Nyamirambo. In the car, he played hip-hop music of some groups that called themselves gangs or boys. Some were tough gangs, and others were dogged boys.

"James, did I tell you that my brother was also a musician?"

"No, you didn't," James responded. "Do you mean the one who was shot dead by a prison officer?"

"Yes. I had only one brother. He also played hip-hop."

"What are you talking about?" James asked. "Do you mean your brother was Mr. D.? Don't say it. Oh my! You told me your brother's name was David, and I could not connect. I loved his music. He was a member of the Inzuki boys, and they called him Badguy. Let me play his songs."

He changed the CD to one of Mr. D's. The first song went like this:

To trash eaters, smoking is our breathing,
Flying is the way we do sleeping
Beds are not meant for the bad guys
Food on plates is for the blessed.

Mother is gone forever.
No Food
No bed
Only we have is junk and gear
Big boys trade
Bad boys smoke.

"James," I said, "I'm sorry. I can't listen to these songs. Not now. Not tonight. I have already had my dose from my conversation with my sister Celine a few days ago. Haven't you promised a night to celebrate life? So change the music to something toastier."

"It's okay. Now I don't know what to do or say. I had no idea Mr. D was the brother you told me about. Now I understand his music. Have you ever listened to his songs?"

"No, I haven't. When I was still in France, I didn't know David had become a musician. After returning to Kigali, I searched for his tracks online but could not find them. So I concluded he was probably an amateur with only a few songs."

"Do you mean you didn't find them online? They are there. What name were you searching for? I hope you weren't typing in David, because he never used that name."

"No. I was generally searching for the playlists of Rwandan songs, hoping that I would find one of his audios or videos."

"Oh, I get it. But, Bro, those playlists are created by people who don't play Mr. D's songs. You should have precisely typed in *Mr. D.* or the song title. He did not have promoters, but those who understood the value of his songs knew how to find them either online or on CDs. His songs contain the prophecy that is much needed by all hapless sons and daughters of this nation."

"I'll take time to listen to his songs. I'm not a fan of hip-hop. In fact, I hardly listen to hip-hop. But I will love to understand the lyrics of David's songs. Maybe there are messages he was addressing to me. Maybe it will give me more clues about what was going on in his life that might have contributed to his death."

"Hey, Carlos, look there," James said. "This is the Nyamirambo I was talking about. Let's park the car and enter."

"Enter where?" I asked. "I don't see any door, even though I see many people in dark clothes. How about those taxi motos? Oh my! Look at that girl. Is she drunk? This must be the Sodom we read in the Bible."

"Stop judging them. I did not see that coming from you. These people simply cope with life the best way they know how to. When they are happy, they drink and kiss. When they get upset, they sink and fight. Then, the following morning, it is simply another day for them to hustle with life. Come on, let's enter and shake our bodies. The door is that big black gate with some graffiti artworks."

"No, James," I said. "I'm not judging them. But I can't enter this place. It seems it's full of drunkards and drug users."

"I know," he responded. "Carlos, you know I neither drink nor smoke. This is not my world. But you shall never understand Kigali if you don't visit all its corners."

"James, I'm very sorry. I don't feel like going in. Please, let's find a quieter place where we can talk. Something tells me you're the elder brother I never had. Even though I'm not sure I'll find words, I need to speak to someone, and you're that person."

"Okay, brother Carlos. Let's go to the rooftop of the Blues Hotel. There, we can talk calmly."

"Thanks."

When we arrived at that rooftop, we both ordered water bottles before I started narrating my story to James. It was as if I were reading the novel of my life from the beginning. My childhood and the confusion created by those who called me muzungu before realizing my hair was different and my skin lighter than the light-skinned known as *inzobe*. I talked about Mr. Mukiga, David's father, and how he treated us like his own children even though he did not live in our house. Then, I narrated to James all we endured during the genocide against the Tutsi and how our mother was killed. I also told him about how in the aftermath, some people picked on David's looks and how Uncle Kamara refused to take him and said he could not be Mama's son.

James scratched his head.

"What a story!" he said. "I wonder how many young Rwandans have experienced what you guys went through. First, they picked on you because you're of mixed race. Then, they picked on your brother because his parents were of two different ethnic groups, whatever that means. I get the meaning of Mr. D's songs. So, how about your sister?"

"My sister was taken in by our maternal uncle. Even though I did not like that he did not want to take David, who was the youngest, I thought Celine, as a girl, more needed to live in a family setting. That was because Uncle Kamara had a wife, although they were not legally married. If I could only turn back the clock and recreate the past, I would never allow that monster I call my uncle to take away my only sister."

"Sorry, Carlos," James said, putting his arm around my neck. "Why would you have not allowed your uncle to take your sister?"

I gathered more strength and told James that Uncle Kamara mistreated my sister.

"How?" he asked.

"I can't tell you more because I have no permission from my sister. But if it wasn't because of Uncle Kamara, maybe my sister would not have been crowned Miss Rwanda or become a model."

"I don't get it. Your sister is a beauty, and it's not a surprise she was crowned Miss Rwanda. Are you not happy about that?"

"Bro, if it was Celine's choice, I wouldn't mind. But apparently she feels as if she has been turned into a symbol of beauty and an object of men's pleasure. She blames it on Uncle Kamara. But please don't ask me to explain."

"It's okay. I have heard similar stories about girls who feel bad about being turned into symbols of beauty. Have you listened to the new song by Beyoncé? It's titled "Pretty Hurts" and shows how some ladies suffer because of beauty expectations."

"No, I don't know the song. But the problem is bigger than that. On top of making them symbols of beauty, some powerful men turn those girls into objects of their pleasure. My sister is one of those, and Uncle Kamara did not only encourage it but made it happen."

"Oh, I see. Sorry for that. You don't need to give me details. I understand."

"Now, my sister wants to reclaim her dignity," I said. "But I'm scared she might put herself into another danger."

"Why?" James asked.

"She has a project with details I have failed to understand. You know she is a model, right? Now, she wants to recruit all types of beauties into modeling."

"I don't understand."

"It's an inspiration she got from her recent dream or vision; I don't know. The doctor called it hallucinations. Apparently, in that dream or nightmare, she saw girls with square-shaped faces and others with oval-shaped faces."

"Hmm? So?"

"She wants to give all those girls the opportunity to showcase their diverse beauty. She wants to break the silence on beauty in Rwanda. She thinks that both the opportunities life gave her and the misfortunes she endured are somehow linked to how beauty is perceived in Rwanda."

"I guess I understand now where she's coming from. It sounds like an interesting project that I would love to be part of. How does she want to proceed?"

"My friend, I have told you I don't know. She said she needs someone who is good at photography and who is fond of diversity. I thought you were the person she was looking for. If you allow, I will give her your telephone number."

"No problem. I will love to chat more with her about it."

"Thanks."

"Carlos, I have another concern," James said.

"What concern?"

"It's about your brother, David. From what you've just told me, I don't think he was killed out of the carelessness of the prison officer who shot him."

"No, it wasn't out of carelessness. I was told it was because he wanted to escape prison. But there seem to be some details in the story that can't just be a mere coincidence."

"Which details?" James asked.

"Like the fact that his former music manager was hired by Celine's ex-partner, Mr. Kananga. David was incarcerated because he had said to Martin's girlfriend words that were later interpreted as genocide ideology. It's Martin who encouraged the girl to report David to the police."

"That's exactly what I'm talking about. Your uncle, Martin, your sister's boyfriend, whoever may have been involved in your brother's misery and death should be investigated. Then, if guilty, pay for what they did."

"James, when I try to untangle that mystery, all I get is a headache. There are two more other people in the story I haven't told you about."

"Who?"

"One of them is Habimana, who is in jail because he was accused of having killed our mother during the genocide against the Tutsi."

"Glad he's in prison," James said. "Those genocide perpetrators should be punished severely. Do you think that Habimana could have killed David to finish the job he started during the genocide against the Tutsi? Then, why would the police report that David was shot dead by a prison officer? I don't see why they would cover up for a genocide perpetrator."

"The other person I suspect is called Bosco. He is a prison officer who told me that Habimana was the one who encouraged David to escape jail. He seemed to insinuate that it was Habimana's trap to get David killed."

"Maybe. But who shot David?"

"The prison officers," I said. "But it's all confusing. When I wanted to ask more questions to Habimana, the prison officer, Bosco, did not allow it. His gestures and everything he said made me think he was also hiding something."

"Yeah, it is indeed confusing," James said. "Brother, don't worry. I'm sure we shall know the masterminds of your brother's death one day."

After that conversation, we decided to call it a night, took the lift, and went to the parking lot.

As we drove toward Nyakabanda to my apartment, I caught sight of a young lady in a short red dress, surrounded by scary-looking men who seemed to be smoking.

"James, please stop," I said. "That must be Linda. She might be in trouble."

"Who is Linda?" James asked.

"I will tell you," I said as I jumped out of the car.

After parking the car, James followed me.

"Linda, what are you doing here?" I asked.

"I'm … I am … having fun. Who are you?"

"It's me, Carlos. Linda, you're drunk. You should go home."

"Home? Me? Who told you I have a home? Do orphans

have homes? I'm a butterfly, and all we do is swing with life. I have no home."

"Please leave alone our bitty," said one of the men she was with. "She doesn't bob up with abazungu. She prefers trash eaters."

"Linda is my sister," I said. "She needs to come with me."

"No, I'm not your sister. You're a brother to Badguy. But guys, did you know Badguy was a Kambari?"

"Kambari?" one of the guys asked. He seemed to be shocked by what Linda had just said. The guy turned to his friends and said, "Do you hear what this hussy is saying? She is one of those who call some of us bad names. Let's go."

"No, please, don't leave me," Linda said to the guys.

One of them pushed her toward me and said, "Stay with that muzungu, and explain to him why you're calling a Kambari the person you say was his brother."

"Please, Linda, come to the car. I can't leave you here alone on these streets. Those guys might harm you."

James had kept quiet, wondering who Linda was to me and why I cared so much about her. He moved back to the car and opened it. Linda and I jumped in.

"Where to?" James asked.

"Please, direct him to your address," I said to Linda.

"I have told you I have no home. Orphans don't have homes, don't you get it? Take me wherever you want to take me, or take me back to the bar where you found me."

"Please drive to my studio apartment," I said to James.

"Are you sure?" he asked.

"Yes."

When we arrived at my studio apartment, I gave Linda some water to drink and invited her to lie down on my bed before seeing James off back to his car.

"Carlos, who is that girl, and how do you know her?"

"Her name is Linda. She is the girl I told you about. The girlfriend of David's former music manager, Martin. It's because of her that my brother David was sent to prison. But apparently, they were friends, if not lovers."

"What are you talking about? Do you mean this girl, who is calling your deceased brother a Kambari, is the one who sent him to jail? And she is the girlfriend of the music manager who seems to be linked somehow to David's death? So then, what are you doing with the girl? Why are you keeping her in your bedroom and on your bed? Please, let me know what's going on. I'm lost."

"James, please listen to me. It's not what you're thinking. Linda is visibly troubled. Whenever I see her or talk to her, I can't help but feel the pain of all young Rwandans orphaned by the genocide against the Tutsi. She has a good heart, but she is confused. She doesn't know whom to trust. I want to think of her as a victim."

"You have to be careful. You shouldn't trust her that much. So, please keep a distance."

"Initially, I wanted to spy on her and find more about Martin and whether or not he had a hand in my brother's death. But the more I talk to Linda, the more I feel as if she were crying for help. This is the second time she's spending a night in my room. I have never touched her. I cannot. In fact, the first night she slept in my room, I spent that night weeping. She was having nightmares of the time the Hutu militants killed her family. It was so heartbreaking to see the state she was in. It also brought back the memories of the genocide, and I simply felt connected to her. To me, Linda is another Celine, my sister."

"This Rwanda has many girls like Linda and Celine. But, unfortunately, men add to their pain by either manipulating them or abusing them."

"Yes, it's so sad," I said, before asking, "By the way, what does a Kambari mean?"

"Kambari people are a primitive tribe in Nigeria. I don't know how some Rwandans started to call Kambari those they consider Hutu. I guess the intention is to insinuate Hutus are as primitive as Kambari people."

"What?" I asked. "That's stupid. It's my first time hearing that. I knew about spears but not Kambari."

"Spears are those considered to be Tutsi," James said. "But I don't know why they call them spears. I guess it is meant to insinuate they are sharp and smart."

"Oh, Rwanda, in fact, what is even more primitive is grouping Rwandans according to the so-called ethnic groups, which seem to be in the minds of those who want to perpetuate ignorance, hatred, and division. Somebody should tell Rwandans they should level up their mentality and widen their horizons."

"Please, let me go," James said. "Harumi may be wondering where I am. You also have to go and check on the girl in your house. I hope she catches some sleep."

"Thanks, brother, I don't know what I would have done if I had not found you in this Kigali. Good night. Please say hi to Harumi."

IX

On my bed, Linda was already asleep. I did not disturb her. I slept on the couch.

When she woke up, she seemed to be sober, though she did not remember how she had gotten into my room.

"You again?" she asked. "How did I get here? Why did you bring me to your apartment? What do you want from me?"

"Linda, good morning. Don't worry, I will tell you the whole story. Do you remember the bar at which you were last night and the guys you were with?"

"A bar? Yes, I remember. They call it Ku Gicupa. It was full of people."

"Last night, when I passed by, you were outside that bar, surrounded by many men in the middle of the road. Do you know them?"

Linda scratched her head as if she were trying to remember. "Yes, they were in white clothes," she said. "No. One of them was in a blue shirt. They wanted to take me to a night-club. Then, what happened? Did we go to the party? How did I get here?"

I told Linda everything and how the guys got angry when she called my late brother, David, a Kambari. Then, I said, "Linda, those guys could have hurt you. Please be careful with the people you mingle with. What if they identify with those you call Kambari?"

"Oh no. I guess I had drunk more than enough. Sorry that I called you a Kambari."

"No, you did not. You said my brother David was a Kambari."

"Please don't take it personally," Linda said. "It's what we call Hutus."

"May I know why?" I asked.

"I don't know what it means," she said. "It's just how we call them. But it doesn't mean anything wrong."

"Linda, that's not good. You should learn the meaning of words before you pronounce them. How can you call David something you don't know the meaning of?"

"I'm sorry."

"All right," I said. "Do never repeat it."

I mused that probably what was interpreted as an ideology of genocide was David's response to those bad names she used to call him. I did not know what to take of her behavior. Was she hateful or just confused? As I reflected on how I should help Linda regain her senses, stop drinking and smoking, and rebuild her life, I thought of Celine's project. I thought she could make a good model. Even though Celine wanted to give a chance to the girls who usually are left out in the fashion industry, she also needed a mixture of all Rwandan beauties.

"I would like to introduce you to someone," I said to Linda.

"Who?" she asked.

"My sister, Celine. You told me you know her, right?"

"Yes, I do. But just on TV and in magazines. She is a celebrity. Every girl in this Rwanda wants to be like Celine. David never talked about her. In fact, I didn't even know they were related till the day David died. I will be glad to meet her, just stare at her as she walks and talks. She is a real beauty."

"Okay, let me prepare for you something to eat. You must be hungry. After taking our breakfast, we're going there, if that's all right with you."

"Perfect."

After breakfast, we headed to Kacyiru at Celine's apartment. She had received my SMS and was waiting for us.

"Hello, brother Carlos," Celine said, before turning to Linda and saying, "You must be Linda! Welcome."

After inviting us to take seats, Celine asked if we wanted some tea, but we said we had just taken our breakfast and preferred to wait for lunch.

"Lunch?" Celine asked. "Do you want me to cook for you?"

"If you like," I said. "But if you allow, I may cook for you. You tasted my food almost twenty years ago when I simply had to get you and David something to eat. Now, I'm a great cook."

"Great," Celine said. "The kitchen is all yours."

"Celine, I have told you about Linda. Despite what

happened between them, she was a good friend to our brother, David."

"Nice meeting you," Celine said to Linda. "Sorry for what our brother, David, said to you. We don't know what had come over him."

"Please, don't talk about that," Linda said. "Badguy was a good person … He was my friend. We used to tease each other and sometimes with bad words. I was hurt by what he said, but I never wanted him to be jailed."

"But you reported him, didn't you?" Celine asked.

"It was all done by Martin. He forced me to report Badguy to the police. He said if I had covered up for a genocide ideologue, I would also face the consequences."

"What?" Celine asked. "Do you mean Martin, the one I know? The music manager of David?"

"Yes, he was David's music manager," Linda said. "Please forgive me. I did not want anything bad to happen to Badguy."

"Please, stop calling him Badguy," Celine said.

"Hey, girls," I said, "can we change the topic, please? Our David is gone, though not forgotten. But we are still there, facing the challenges of this world." Then, I looked at Celine and said, "Linda is an orphan like us. She has nobody in this world. She needs you! Please accept to be her elder sister."

"Come, please," Celine said to me as she stood up and headed to the kitchen. "Haven't you said you're cooking for us today? I want to show you something."

"Yes, I'm cooking, but I still have like an hour before starting. What is it you want to show me?"

"Just come and see."

We left Linda alone in the living room.

"Brother," Celine said, "did you say I should consider Linda for my project?"

"Yes," I said. "She can make a good model, and I guess you need all different beauties, don't you? Linda has a miserable life. She needs both psychological and social support. She needs a family."

"I don't trust her," Celine said. "Something in her eyes tells me she is not trustworthy. Does she smoke?"

"Smoke what?" I asked.

"Does she take weed or some other drugs?"

"I won't tell you lies," I said. "Yes, Linda takes weed. Rotty, the Inzuki boy, told me that Linda and David used to smoke together. Whatever they did or said to each other was in that context. They were simply two drug addicts without the sense of what was happening around them."

"You should be careful with girls like Linda," she said. "In their naivety or lack of self-command, they are often used or teleguided by some big powers. I have been there, and I know what I'm talking about. If we take Linda in our project, we may be taking a bomb that might explode tomorrow."

"I understand what you mean," I said. "But I thought Linda would just be a model. We might not give her access to complete information. Just give her a chance to showcase her beauty and earn a living."

"I'm reluctant to consider her," Celine said, placing her hand on her eyes as if she wanted to think through my suggestion.

I decided to let her take some time to think about it.

When we went back to the living room, Celine turned on the fashion channel on TV. She and Linda started chatting about fashion. After a few minutes, I went back to the kitchen to cook lunch.

"Wow," Celine said as she savored my food. "I didn't know you could cook this well. Were all these ingredients in my kitchen? What spice did you add to these dodo and egg-plants?"

"I'm glad you like it," I said. "The only thing I have added to the vegetables is the red onions. In the mashed Irish pota-toes, I have simply added butter."

"That simple?" Linda asked.

"Yes," I said. "Cooking is all about simplicity."

After lunch, Celine prepared for us some coffee. We drank it before we called it a day and said bye to her.

On our way back to Nyamirambo, Linda seemed shy and quiet.

"Are you with me?" I asked her. "You're not talking to me."

"Is it because she thinks I caused Badguy's death?" Linda asked.

"What do you mean?"

"I'm not a child. Celine doesn't like me. I could read it from her eyes. She was staring at me as if I were a thing."

"Don't mind her," I said. "Maybe that's how celebrities work. It's hard to read their emotions."

"Tell me, why did you want to introduce me to her?" Linda asked.

"I thought you could connect because you're both

beautiful ladies. But anyway, don't worry, I'm sure you will soon team up. Maybe she should introduce you to modeling. Is it something you would love doing?"

"Modeling? Yes, I would love to. But I'm not sure I would be a good fit. They pick only ravishing girls."

"Is your mirror broken?" I asked. "Who is prettier than you in this Kigali?"

Linda looked down and scratched her hands as if my words made her shy.

"Carlos, I guess I now have to go home. Thank you for everything."

"Home? You've never wanted to show me your house. Who do you stay with?"

"I told you I'm staying with a friend of mine. She must be worried now."

"May I know more about that friend? How old is she? What does she do? How did you meet?"

"Why do you want to know all that?"

"Because I care," I responded. "Linda, yesterday was the second time I had brought you to my house after finding you in some dangerous situation. Don't you understand why I should be worried about you?"

"Carlos, I have no parents. My whole family was exterminated during the genocide against the Tutsi. So whenever a friend offers me a place to lay my head and call it home, I simply go. I can't count how many houses have so far sheltered me. Friends come and go, and I stay in this world, pretending to live or survive."

It was the first time Linda had spoken to me that deeply. *Maybe she is not as naïve as I thought*, I mused.

"Sorry for what you endured in life," I said. "I can only imagine how hard life has been for you. May I ask you for a favor? Please don't take it in a bad way."

"What favor?" she asked.

"Would you please allow me to be your elder brother?"

"Elder brother? How?"

"Just accept, and I will show you what an elder brother is. As silly as it sounds, I feel I'm being called by the power above to care for you. I don't know why I feel this way, but I know that I need to be there for you."

"Thank you. But since the day Hutus killed all my three elder brothers, my parents, and my two younger sisters, I no longer understand the concept of a family. You can never be my elder brother. You can't replace those I lost."

"I know," I said. "My aim is not to replace the dear siblings and parents you lost. I simply want to be there for you, either as a brother or a friend."

"Okay, you're my friend. Is that okay?"

"It's all right. Since I'm your friend, can you now show me where you stay?"

"Since you insist," Linda said.

Linda had said to me she stayed in Nyamirambo, not far from Charles Lwanga Parish. But after we took the road to Mumena, I was surprised to see us going down to a place known as Cyumbati. It looked like the countryside in the middle of the city. After entering a big compound full of timeworn uncemented houses, she pushed open one of the doors and invited me in. Her friend was there. She seemed to be in her late forties, too old to be Linda's friend. Her skin was as colorful as that of those who used chemicals to fight the effects of melanin in their skin. Her eyes were like burning charcoal. As if that was not enough to scare me, the lady had a burning cigarette in her hand.

When she saw me, even before greeting me, she winked at Linda as if she were congratulating her for bringing a man in.

"Tamari, meet my new friend, Carlos," Linda said, before turning to me to say, "Carlos, Tamari is my friend. I thank her for having given me a place to stay."

I gave a handshake to Tamari and said, "Nice meeting you."

She did not respond.

Linda showed me where to sit before she left through one of the two doors from the living room to other rooms of that small house.

"Where did you learn Kinyarwanda from?" Tamari asked.

"I'm Rwandan," I said.

"Rwandan? From where? You don't look Rwandan."

"My father was European, but my mother was Rwandan."

"Does that mean you live here in Rwanda? Have you been to Europe?"

"Yes, I live now in my country, Rwanda. May I know why you want to know if I have been to Europe?"

"I was just asking," she said.

When Linda came back from the room, she said, "Carlos insisted he wanted to know where I stayed, and that's why I have brought him here. I guess he may now leave. I will see him off."

"Okay," Tamari said, and did not add any other word.

"Are you now happy you've seen where I stay and whom I stay with?" Linda asked after we reached the street.

"Tell me, where did you meet Tamari?" I asked. "Does she have children? What does she do?"

"Those are so many questions," Linda said. "I met Tamari the same way I met Badguy. If not in the streets, I must have been in a bar when I met her for the first time, and before I knew it, I was in her house."

"So, you mean you met her on the streets or in a bar?"

"Yes. Isn't it the same with you? Did we not meet on the street and later in a bar before I slept on your bed?"

"Yes, that's true," I said. "What does Tamari do for a living?"

"Nothing."

"What do you mean nothing? Does she not have children? Where does she get money to pay rent and feed her kids?"

"From men," Linda said. "Have I answered your question?"

I did not respond.

When we reached the main road, I said, "There is something I have always meant to ask you. Do you have a telephone number?"

"Yes, I do."

She agreed to give me her number before she waved bye and returned to Tamari's house.

I jumped on a motorbike and went back to my studio

apartment. I had not slept well the previous night. I longed for a rest.

When I was lying down on my bed, my phone rang. It was a call from Rotty.

"Hello," I said.

"Hi, Carlos," he replied. "I wanted to inform you that I have been released."

"Oh, that's good news. How did it happen? What have they said to you?"

"Nothing. They simply opened the door and told me to take my stuff and go out. Then, I did as I was told."

"Please come to my apartment," I said. "You need to tell me everything. Take a bike; I will pay as soon as you arrive."

In a few minutes, Rotty was in my room.

"Now, tell me. Here, we can freely talk. What do you know about Martin? Did he have a hand in David's assassination?"

"That, I don't know yet. But I'm sure he knows something about it. So let me tell you how I managed to talk to him."

"Tell me," I said.

"One day, I saw him at Tarinyota, where he had come to see a mechanic. Then, I approached, greeted him, and asked him to buy me a joint. He smiled and gave me a 5K note. That's how it all started. I talked about his fancy car and told him some funny stories. When he was about to leave, I asked him to give me his business card. To my surprise, he gave it to me without asking why I wanted it."

"Interesting! Did you later call him? How did you manage to talk to him about the death of David?"

"A few days later," Rotty continued, "I called him and said I was hungry. I asked him to invite me to his place for lunch. He did. I rushed there. During our conversation, I asked Martin if, after the death of Badguy, he had found other musicians to manage. He responded no, before adding, 'I'm normally not into music. I was only hired by a powerful person to manage David, your friend, but now he is gone; my job is done.'"

I knew it, I mused quietly. Martin was not an ordinary music manager. He was simply on a mission to get my brother dead.

"Then, what did you say next?" I asked Rotty.

"Instead of asking him what he meant, I said, 'Badguy was a fundi, like me, but not really my friend. You know us fundis, we play it cool with each other, but that does not mean we are best friends. Badguy was a bad guy, as his name suggested. He snatched my chick, and I hated him for that. Maybe his death was the work of karma.' Martin seemed surprised by what I had just said, then he asked, 'Did you say David took your girlfriend? Wasn't he satisfied with Linda? Many people thought Linda was my girlfriend, but she wasn't.'"

"Stop there," I said. "Did Martin say Linda was never his girlfriend?"

"Yes," Rotty responded. "When I asked Martin what he meant, he said Linda was a chick he used to get into Badguy's world and complete the job his boss had hired him for. I asked him who his boss was. He responded that he couldn't tell me his name. Then, he looked at me and said, 'Just know that the guy you called a fundi was getting himself in trouble by opposing the powerful who was juicing his sister.'"

"Oh, my ear! What else did Martin tell you?"

"Before I asked Martin more questions, my phone rang. He grabbed it from my hands before I could take the call."

"Why did he grab your phone? Did he suspect you were recording the conversation?"

"Yes, he did, but I had not recorded it. The call was from the major. One of our Inzuki boys had been caught by the beasts. They took him to the shelters."

"What do you mean? I guess you should give me your slang dictionary. Who are the beasts? What shelters?"

"I mean, the police took him to the centers or stations; I don't know the difference. The major wanted to warn me to hide for a few days. That's how I asked Martin to give me a corner for a few days. Surprisingly, he accepted."

"So, you stayed in his house for a few more days?"

"Yes. Martin told me so many terrifying stories. The guy is an abuser. He treats chicks as objects. He abuses the girls of this Kigali. He also told me about some other dirty jobs he did, including shattering lives. He seemed to be convinced I knew the world he was talking about and that, probably, he could hire me to be a member of his squad. I praised him and pretended I admired his heroism."

"Then, how did he know you spied on him?"

"One day, he received a visit from someone named Bosco. When the guy said he was a prison officer, I paid attention. I went to my corner and left them in the living room to have their conversation in private."

"Did you say Bosco?"

"Yes."

"Did you manage to listen to their conversation? What did they talk about?"

"I hid behind the door from my bedroom to the living room and eavesdropped on their conversation. They talked about their scary, dirty games. It wasn't about Badguy. I gave up and decided to stop listening. But when I was about to move away, I heard the mention of your uncle's name, Kamara. Bosco was shouting, saying that Kamara should die. Badguy used to tell me your uncle was evil, but to hear that Martin and Bosco, who seemed to be eviler than him, were planning to get him killed made me hate them more."

"What? Do you mean those guys want to kill our uncle too? Why? Now I'm lost. I thought Uncle Kamara was in their camp."

"Unfortunately, I couldn't hear more. Martin did not want Bosco to continue talking about their plan. He must have suspected I was eavesdropping on their conversation. He immediately pushed the door to the bedroom and caught me with a phone, trying to record. I had not even started. Even though he found no recording on my phone, he slapped me and instructed me to pack my stuff and go. As soon as I got to the bus station, I was arrested by the police, accused of having stolen money from Martin."

"Sorry for what happened. I was scared they would keep you in custody for long. But I was prepared to get you a good lawyer."

"They interrogated me. It wasn't about the theft. They asked me why I eavesdropped on Martin and Bosco's conversation. I wondered what that had to do with the crime I was accused of. I told them it was only out of curiosity. They did not believe me. Then I said that when they mentioned the name of my friend's uncle, I wanted to know if it had something to do with my friend's death. The interrogation went on for the whole night till I admitted that I had befriended Martin with the intention to spy on him."

"Oh, why did you say it? Wouldn't it put you in more danger? Tell me you haven't mentioned my name."

"I said what they wanted to hear because I avoided more hours of interrogation, which was mixed with slaps. When they asked if I was working on my own, I said yes. They insisted, but I kept telling them I was a friend of Badguy and wanted to know if Martin was not the one who caused his death by sending him to jail. I can't repeat all the questions they asked me. They even asked what I thought about the genocide ideology of Badguy and took their time to explain to me how only Badguy should be blamed for his death. Then, after ten days in police custody, they have released me without telling me whether they have found me innocent or guilty."

"The good news is that they have released you."

"Yes, I'm glad I'm out of that place. But please, Carlos, listen to me. You should stop whatever you're wanting to do. We're playing with fire. Those powerful people can make you disappear forever. Let it go, please. Badguy, my friend, is gone forever. He is not the first or the last person I have lost because of this wicked world. Why don't I ever talk about my parents and siblings? Do you think it's because I did not love them? No. It's not even because I fear death. It's simply because there is no such thing as justice in this world. There are only three stages of life: birth, struggle, then death. I was born to struggle, and one day, my body shall get tired and push me to die. So please, accept that Badguy is gone and wait for your own day to leave. In between, enjoy the struggle."

"Rotty," I said, "I get where you're coming from. Nothing shall bring back my dear brother. But I will make sure those responsible for his death are arrested and punished. Perhaps, they are not as powerful as we think, and the little power they enjoy is from our unwillingness to confront them. Why should I let them get away with the murder of my brother?"

"Because you don't want to also risk your life," Rotty responded.

"Haven't you said we all die someday?" I asked him. "I will do what I have to do before my day comes. If I get killed, somebody else shall do the needful. But nobody should take another person's life and get away with it. No. It should be condemned. Our society is not of evil people. We should stop being frightened by a few who think they have the right to decide who should live and who should leave this world. I believe when the assassins of David shall be brought to justice, Rwanda, our beloved country, shall have proven to care for all her sons and daughters."

"Brother, I'm frightened. I no longer want to be involved in this. Please forgive me for being a coward. I can't help you. All I want is to live, however bitter life has been to me. That's why I'm a fundi. I smoke the sacred plant to soothe my brain and swing with whatever direction this life takes me."

"I understand. Don't worry. You've been kind to me.

You're like a younger brother to me. You've been a good friend to Badguy, and I shall forever be grateful. Now, I want to suggest something to you. Do you want to go out for a drink?"

"I don't drink. I only take water and juice. My sin is to smoke weed and sometimes sniff mugo."

"Oh, you don't take beer? What's mugo?"

"You call it heroin. In Kigali, we call it mugo. I don't take much. It makes fundis go crazy. I stay on weed. It's only when I want to forget I'm on planet earth that I take mugo."

"I can't offer drugs to you. Let's go to a café and have some soft drinks, right?"

"No. I would prefer food and water, if available."

"Okay. Let me get in the kitchen and prepare something for you."

X

Two days later, I called my sister, Celine. I needed to talk to her about Linda. She had a lot of updates about her projects.

"Hi, Carlos, I have so much good news. First, I have found another apartment to move into. Second, a friend of mine has offered a place for my project. She owns a hotel."

"Wow! That's good news. Apparently, you're so determined. When did you do all that? How shall you be paying for the apartment and the business location?"

"The other day, after you and Linda left my apartment, I immediately went out. I had an appointment with my agent. He showed me a few options before I settled for one apartment in Gacuriro. Then, I went to see that friend of mine who owns a hotel. When I told her that I needed office space for my project, she did not hesitate to suggest some office rooms in her hotel. Are you asking where I shall get money from? Nobody else knows but Ingabire. I managed to buy two residential houses from the little money I earned in this modeling career. I have not yet officially transferred the ownership to my name because I did not want Kananga to find out. Ingabire was the one who always collected rent for me. I believe I'm now ready to finalize the paperwork and have all my properties registered under my name. As a starting point, I will be financing the project from the rent collected from those two houses and the few moto-taxis I have in circulation. So don't worry about me."

"Two residential houses? Did you say you also have a few moto-taxis in circulation? I'm impressed. You are as business-minded as our mother. You remind me of her. Though life was bitter to her, she always found ways to sweeten it. She knew what she wanted in life."

"Thank you, brother. I wish Mama was here. She is the only person who would understand me. She wouldn't judge me."

"I also don't judge you, sister."

"Sure? Thank you."

"Listen, sister, I wanted us to discuss Linda. Please allow me to beg you to help her. Linda and Ingabire may have not been orphaned by the same tragedies, but they faced the same consequences. I have gone to the house Linda stays in. She lives with an older woman who does prostitution for a living. I am not sure, but I think ladies like that are the ones that introduced Linda to smoking and to surrendering her body to men. She is a captive who needs nothing but freedom."

"Brother, I get what you're saying. I have seen the younger me in Linda. She is pretty and naïve. She looks troubled. I'm simply reluctant to take on more burdens when I have not yet managed to stand firm on my own. But anyway, all right, I will consider her."

"Thank you so much, sister. I knew it. You can never say no to your dear brother."

"Tell me, have you talked to the friend you told me about? The photographer?"

"Yes, I have. He is so excited about the project. The guy is fascinated by the diversity of facial beauties. I never understand what it is James reads on people's faces that I don't see. He can look at a person and tell you their story."

"That's the guy I'm looking for. Good photographers can trigger emotions in both the photographed person and the person who shall look at the photograph. You shall see when the beauty of those girls, considered in our society as ugly, shall be showcased. My aim is two-fold: to empower the girls and, more important, to lock horns with the beauty bias in this country we call our land."

"Won't you need other people in your project? When do you intend to start?"

"Brother, I would like to start as soon as possible. I will first register the business because I don't want to be in trouble with the law. Then, I will start with a few models, a photographer, and a makeup artist. I have already contacted four girls who did not make it at some of the Miss Rwanda competitions where I was hired as an assessor. Ingabire has also recommended two girls. Plus Linda. Seven girls are more than enough. It will not be an easy task to train them and, later, find deals for them. Ingabire shall be our tailor, though she might sometimes subcontract other tailors."

"Wow! Apparently, it's all set. Aren't you afraid Uncle

Kamara or your ex, Kananga, might do whatever they can to sabotage your project?"

"That's for sure. They will. In fact, yesterday Kananga called me."

"What did he say?"

"The old man has not yet realized his captive is now freer than a bird. He threatened to kick me out of this apartment if I do not go to his place. I told him I am moving out before the end of next week. He asked where to, and I told him there was no need for him to know. Then, he hung up the phone. When I was wondering what Kananga was planning to do, Uncle Kamara gave me a call and invited me to go to his place tomorrow. I have accepted."

"Are you going to Uncle Kamara's house tomorrow?" I asked.

"Yes," Celine responded. "Don't worry. He won't hurt me."

"Are you sure?" I asked.

"Yes, brother. Uncle Kamara's sins are money and sex. He can do anything to get those two. But he is our uncle. We can't erase him from our lives."

"Celine, that man ... he... you told me he used to..."

"Yes, he did. I will never forgive him for that. But I have had to learn to manage him. He can never dare touch me again. He knows I'm no longer his sex slave."

"Sister, you have to be careful. Some strange things are going on. I don't know how to say this to you, but those who might have had a hand in the assassination of David are apparently planning to eliminate Uncle Kamara. Unfortunately, I have no full details and can't tell you more about it."

"Carlos, what are you talking about? I don't get it. Who wants to kill Uncle Kamara? Where did you get that information from?"

"It's just that … some people … someone has told me he overheard some people talking about getting rid of our uncle."

"Some people … someone … he told you … he overhead—what are you talking about?"

"Sister, please let me not say more about this," I said. "All I wanted was more information about the circumstances that surrounded our brother's death. But instead of learning more about David and his last days, I was told some people were plotting to kill Uncle Kamara. Maybe it's not true and we have no reason to worry. You should just be careful with Kamara. I think he mingles with not-so-good people."

"Brother, how about you? Who is giving you that kind of information? Aren't you probably the one who is rather mingling with some dangerous people? Last time, you received a call from a person who was arrested by the police. You told me he was David's friend. When you came back from the station, you had a thousand questions about Martin and Kananga. Now, you're saying you were searching for information about the death of David but found something about Uncle Kamara instead. What are you up to, brother?"

"My dear sister, do you have a watch? Look, we've talked for over three hours. It's now eleven. Let me go to sleep. I will tell you everything tomorrow."

"Please, don't hide from me whatever you're doing. This Kigali is not so safe. Be mindful of the people you talk to. Our brother was killed a few months ago. I have ended my relationship with a powerful man in the country. Everybody knows there is a muzungu in town who happens to be my half-brother. We are being watched. You need to be super careful. Tomorrow, on my way back from Uncle Kamara's place, I will come to see you. Please, promise you shall tell me everything."

"Yes, sister, I will tell you everything. But for now, good night. Please, don't think it over. Just have a nice sleep and sweet dreams. I love you."

"Love you too."

The whole night I was pondering on whether I should reveal to Celine everything about my plan to seek justice for our brother David. *Is she ready?* I wondered.

The following day, I went to the market and bought good food. The visit of my sister Celine called for a well-prepared healthy dinner.

At two o'clock, Celine gave me a call and told me that she was on her way to Uncle Kamara's place.

"Dinner shall be served at six," I said. "Please make sure you're here to gorge on the broccoli salad I'm making."

"I have budgeted only half an hour for Uncle Kamara," Celine said. "You and I need the rest of the afternoon. We have a lot to talk about. Please, make sure the salad is served cold because I will need something to calm me down after our conversation. Something tells me you're playing with fire."

"No, I'm not. Don't worry. I will tell you everything."

"Okay. See you soon."

"Sister, please be careful. Remember to keep some distance between you and Uncle Kamara."

"Don't worry. If I encounter any problem, I will call you."

"Please do. I don't trust Uncle Kamara."

"I have asked you not to worry. I will be fine."

After that call, I put on my apron and prepared the broccoli salad. It was complemented with chewy dried cranberries, flecks of red onion, and crispy, smoky nuts & seeds on top. The dressing was a mixture of olive oil, vinegar, a little honey, and a few teaspoons of Dijon mustard, which gave the salad a sweet-salty flavor. When ready, I put it in the refrigerator and went to take a shower.

I had left my phone on the table in my bedroom, and when Celine called me, I did not hear it ringing.

After the shower, I tried to call my sister back, but it did not go through. It seemed her phone was off. Even though my heart was beating so fast, I convinced myself that it was probably a network problem or that my sister's phone was out of battery.

I redialed her number thirty minutes later, but it was still unreachable. I was worried. *What happened to her?* I wondered. *I hope she is not in danger.*

At 5:20 p.m., I decided to call Uncle Kamara.

"Hello," Uncle said.

"Uncle, where is Celine?"

"What? Why do you think I would know? She must be at her apartment."

"No, Uncle, Celine has come to your house. Are you there?"

"No, I'm not. I'm in Kibuye."

"How? Have you not invited Celine to your house?"

"No, I haven't. I have not seen your sister for weeks. What happened to her?"

"Her phone is off. I think Celine could be in danger."

"Why? Maybe she turned her phone off because she was busy. Carlos, you must remember Celine is an adult. You're not her guardian. What if she is having a good time with one of her boyfriends?"

"Uncle, you can't say that about your niece. Celine has promised to come to my place on her way back from your house. She has tried to reach me on the phone but in vain. Now, her phone is off. I'm worried. Uncle, I hope you're not involved in my sister's disappearance. I swear, I won't take it. After the assassination of my brother, David, I can't deal with the disappearance of Celine. Please, help me search for her."

"Carlos, what are you accusing me of? Why do you think I should know the whereabouts of your sister? As if that was not enough, you're again talking about the death of that mugger you called your brother who was shot dead trying to escape prison. Just try any silly move; you shall see. If you mess with those men your sister shares life with, you won't be shot dead; you will be cut into pieces."

I did not know what to do or where to start searching for my sister. I decided to call James.

After about ten minutes, I heard him knock on my door.

"Tell me," James said, "where did your sister say she was going? Who took her there? Has she driven to the place, or did she take a taxi?"

"She told me she was going to see our uncle Kamara. I don't know if she drove her car or not. I haven't asked her."

"Come. Let's go to Celine's place."

"No, James, Celine could not have gone there. She has promised to share dinner with me at six. Now, it's already six fifteen."

"I understand. But we can't report your sister's disappearance to the police before confirming she is not at her place."

"Report to the police? Do you think it will be necessary?"

"Yes, it's better to inform the police before we can do anything else."

"Why?"

"Because when we shall have to make any other move, we may be questioned why her disappearance was not reported to the police."

"James, we need to be careful. I'm afraid her kidnappers might harm her if they find out it has been reported to the police."

"I think the opposite. If we don't report it, Celine may disappear for good. She wouldn't be the first or the last. A friend of mine went missing in 2011. Till now, we don't know his whereabouts. Some people told me he was killed and thrown into a river."

"Oh, so sorry to hear that. Do you mean it's common for people to just disappear like that?"

"Yes, it is. The fishy thing is that some people don't find it alarming. You will never hear radio announcements or see posters circulated with the missing person's details. It's as if it's not allowed to do the search. That's why I'm advising that we report it to the police first."

"I get it," I said. "Please, let's go. Where is my key? I was going to forget to lock the door."

"Yeah, let's rush to her place," James responded.

When we arrived at Celine's apartment, we knocked on her door till the neighbors came to complain about the noise. But, unfortunately, my sister was not there.

"Hello," I said to the neighbors. "We are looking for the lady who stays in this apartment. Have you seen her?"

"No," one neighbor said.

"Yes, in the morning," the other neighbor said. "She was standing by her balcony."

"How about the afternoon?" I asked. "Has anybody seen her?"

"No," the neighbors responded. "But who are you, and why are you looking for her?" one of the neighbors asked.

"I am—" I said before James interrupted.

"We are her business partners," he said. "We wanted to propose a modeling contract to her."

"Okay. You may probably need to check at her second home in Nyarutarama."

"Yeah, that's true," James said. "She once directed me to the place, but I forgot. Do you know the address?"

"No, I don't," the neighbor said. "But even if I did, I wouldn't give it to you without her permission."

"Thank you," I said to the neighbors. "Bro, let's go. I have an idea."

After we got down the stairs, I suggested checking if Celine's car was in the parking area. The car was not there.

"It means that wherever we shall find her car shall give us a hint of her whereabouts," James said, before asking if I had a picture of Celine's car.

"No, I don't. But it's a red Nissan, the new model."

"Okay. I see. It would be good to have the picture. Do you know the second home of Celine those neighbors are referring to?"

"That reminds me," I said. "How did you know my sister has a second home? You've just told those people she once directed you there."

"Carlos, have you forgotten I have never met your sister, except seeing her on TV? That was a lie to them so that they would feel comfortable giving me the address."

"I get it. I think I know the place they were talking about. But I'm afraid it's not safe to go there."

"Why?" James asked.

"Brother, I don't know how to say this to you. That place belongs to Celine's ex, the powerful man I told you about, the one who hired Martin to become the music manager of our late brother, David. Celine recently dumped the old man. It's dangerous to go there. One day, a taxi driver took me there. The man did not even let me speak to my sister. His security guards pushed me back to the street."

"What's that old man's name?"

"Kananga," I said.

"Kananga who?" James asked.

"I don't know. I was told he is among the powerful people in this country."

"But Kananga, I know, is married with grown-up kids. Is there any other powerful Kananga in this country? The one I'm talking about stays in Rebero, not Nyarutarama."

"Maybe they are two different people," I said to James, though I knew we could be talking about the same man.

"Carlos, it doesn't matter. Whoever that Kananga is, he should be our first suspect. Did you say Celine dumped him? Maybe he kidnapped her because he could not handle the breakup."

"That's a possibility," I said. "It will be tough to enter the old man's compound and search for Celine. The security guards won't let us in. Oh God! What can we do? I can't even imagine what whoever kidnapped my sister is doing to her. Celine has endured a lot in life; she can't take more. James, did you say you know Kananga?"

"Yes. But the one I know is married and lives in Rebero. He is a tall, dark-skinned man in his early sixties. His wife is a good friend to my maternal aunt."

"Brother, I can't hide anything from you. I believe we are talking about the same person. Celine told me her Kananga is also married. She was his side chick, if that's how they call it, or maybe his sex partner. He is the one who was paying for the apartment in Kacyiru as well. Recently, he threatened to cut his financial support and kick her out of the apartment. Celine told him she had already found another place to move into, and that made the man even more furious."

"Carlos, I can't believe we are talking about the same

Kananga. I thought he was not like the other powerful men in this country, who treat women as objects and use them for their selfish desires and interests. I can only imagine how his wife and children shall be affected by this if the news goes out that Kananga had an affair with Celine."

"I wished I knew what to say," I responded. "James, please, help me find my sister. What does our mother think of me? I was not there to save her youngest son, who had become a street boy, a drug addict, and a prisoner before he was murdered mysteriously. Now, my sister, Celine, who endured what no other young girl should ever experience in life, has gone missing. Please, help me save Celine. She needs me. She counts on me. Please, tell me what we should do now."

"My friend, I don't know what we should do. If Kananga, I know, is involved, this is more complicated than I thought. Let's report the disappearance of your sister to the police. We shouldn't tell them anything except that Celine is nowhere to be found and her phones are off. Don't talk about Kananga. We should pretend we have no single clue about who might be involved in her disappearance."

"I thought it could be useful to tell them that Celine had gone to see Uncle Kamara and that she had a relationship with Kananga. Then, maybe they would immediately search the houses of both Kamara and Kananga. I'm afraid they may not quickly rescue Celine if we don't give them some traces of where they should start."

"No, Carlos. It's too early to reveal everything to the police because we don't know what they would do with that information. We will give them the details when we have connected all the dots. The kidnappers of Celine, whoever they are, should be caught red-handed. I must see my maternal auntie and find out more about Kananga. We also need to find somebody who can inspect that Nyarutarama house. Sooner or later, we shall confirm whether Celine is kept in."

"I know who can help us," I said. "A taxi driver who once took me to that place. His name is Karekezi. He seems to be discreet and self-contained. I'm sure he can help us."

"That's fine if you trust him. But we should tell him only the minimum. His job is to keep an eye on that compound and inform us of any signal Celine could be there. We will pay him for the hours and the fuel he will spend on our job."

"Yes. I will also ask the driver to take notes of who enters or leaves the compound and sometimes follow Kananga to see who he meets."

"Indeed! That might link us to some other people who could be involved. One more thing, please," James said. "If your uncle, Kamara, calls you, please don't say anything that could make him understand you have some suspects."

"Shall I tell him about reporting the case to the police?"

"No. Say you decided not to report it to the police because you did not want Celine's kidnappers to harm her. I will make sure I sign on the police incident report so that when it is discovered, you will tell your uncle you did not know the case was reported."

"Thank you, James. Without you, I don't know what I would do in this Kigali."

"Do you know what?" James said. "Maybe we are not in the right mood to reflect well on the issue. In French, they say, *'La nuit porte conseil.'* Let's go and sleep on it. Tomorrow morning, we shall draw our mind map. I must go now. Harumi must be worried. We will do everything tomorrow: report the case to the police, talk to the taxi driver, and collect more information about Kananga and his family from my aunt. Carlos, don't worry; God is going to protect your sister. It's better to think through our plan than making a silly move that could put not only her but all of us in danger."

"James, if it could save my sister, I'm ready to go on a mountain and make noise. I feel like shouting to the world and telling everybody to stop whatever they are doing and help me find my sister. But anyway, I hear you. Let me go to my room. The night will be too long, and I'm not sure I will be able to catch sleep. No, I can't sleep when my sister could be enduring torture. Oh God! This is too much. No. Not after the death of my brother, David. Not after what we endured during the genocide against the Tutsi and its aftermath. James, it hurts to think that this is just because Rwanda treats her people differently. David, our younger brother, was a victim of hatred because of his so-called ethnicity. Celine, who lost her entire paternal family during the genocide, is now one of the victims of abuse toward women and their objectification as symbols of beauty and toys for men's pleasure. My friend, I can't take it anymore."

"Carlos, I have another idea," James said. "What if you spend the night in my apartment instead of going to yours? Come. Let's go to my place. You need a shoulder to lean on and talk to. I will lend you my listening ear. Come and play on the piano, your therapy."

I kept silent for a few minutes before I accepted James's invitation.

When we arrived at his place, Harumi served us hot Japanese soup. Then, I approached the piano to play a melancholy. James did not leave me in the living room. We talked about Rwanda, our families, and our past. I told him how our mother was raped before she was killed during the genocide against the Tutsi and how Uncle Kamara killed David's paternal uncle because he wanted our mother's house. James could not believe his ears when I told him that our uncle, Kamara, used to rape my sister, Celine, when he had taken her to live with our grandparents.

"Carlos, this is too much to chew," James said. "I knew genocide survivors have gone through a lot. I knew some families of those called Hutus have had their share of Rwanda's darkness. But I had never thought about children with mixed heritages. The story of David needs to be told. A Hutu child whose Tutsi mother was killed during the genocide but whose pain was ignored because some people chose to equate him to the assassins of his mother. Then as if that were not enough, when he dared to open his mouth about his experience, he was accused of a genocide ideology, jailed, and later assassinated in prison. Oh God! What is Rwanda doing to her youth?"

"Brother, I blame myself for everything. I should not have left my siblings. I should not have gone to France. I thought it was time for me to search for my second heritage, my father's family. That was selfish. I should not have left Celine after her entire paternal family was exterminated in the genocide against the Tutsi. I should not have left David, who did not know his father's whereabouts. Mama had raised us as full siblings, despite our different so-called races or ethnicities. She counted on me as her firstborn to be there for my younger ones. I deceived her."

"No, brother, don't blame yourself," James said, before hugging me a long one.

We went to sleep at two o'clock.

In the morning, after taking breakfast, we headed to the police station of Kacyiru to report the disappearance of Celine.

When we arrived there, James asked me to wait in the car. He did not want me to report the case to the police because he feared the information could be leaked to either Uncle Kamara or Mr. Kananga.

After about ten minutes, James came back with a piece of paper in his hands.

"Please, help me fill out this form," he said. "The officer said I should be as thorough as possible. However, there are some details I don't know, for example, your sister's birth date."

"Tell me, how did it go?" I asked.

"I told him I was reporting the disappearance of a friend of mine. He asked if she does not have any family members. I said they were all killed during the genocide against the Tutsi."

"Then?"

"He gave me this form. I told him that I needed to check with my friends about some details and asked him if I could take the form with me to my car. He said yes. So tell me, what's Celine's birthday?"

"She was born on June nineth, 1980. She lives in apartment 53, Kacyiru Luxury Estates. Let's check other details on Google Maps."

"Right. If we manage to locate Kacyiru Luxury Estates on the map, we will be able to get the names of the village and the cell."

After James completed the incident report form and submitted it to the police, we drove toward the street.

When we arrived at Gishushu junction, I got out of James's car and waited for Karekezi by the bus stop. James headed to Kimironko to his aunt's place.

It did not take long before Karekezi appeared. I entered his taxi and asked him to take me to my place in Nyakabanda. I did not want us to discuss the matter in a different environment.

When we arrived at my studio apartment, I invited Karekezi in for a drink. I told him I needed to ask him for a favor.

"My sister is missing," I said. "Please help me search for her."

"Who? Do you mean Miss Celine? How?"

I told him how I had waited in vain for Celine the previous day, who had promised to share dinner with me. I also told Karekezi that I suspected Kananga could have organized my sister's kidnapping because she had dumped him.

"That's why I thought you could help me spy on Kananga's place," I said. "And check if Celine could be there."

"That won't be easy," Karekezi said. "The entire security

team at that compound was changed, and my friend who used to work there was deployed somewhere else."

"If the security company was not changed, maybe your friend knows those deployed to that Nyarutarama compound. What if you talk to him? I will compensate for the services. I actually thought that if you continued to drive around that area, sooner or later, you will notice some clues about whether Celine is in or not."

"Carlos, I'm sorry. I can't do what you're asking me to do. I have a young family, children who need me. I do not want to take risks that could cost my life. Please, understand me. I'm sorry for your sister's disappearance, but I cannot help. Did she break up with Mr. Kananga after she learned that the man was involved in the assassination of Mr. D., your younger brother? This is political, and I don't want to be involved. Please, forgive me."

"It's okay," I said, before asking, "but tell me why you think Celine's break up with Kananga could be linked to David's assassination? Do you know something I don't know?"

"No. I don't know who killed Mr. D., but there are a lot of unconfirmed rumors I do not want to repeat."

"What rumors?"

"No, Carlos, I can't repeat rumors. Who am I to know the people who masterminded the assassination of your brother? Please don't force me to say what I might regret. In this country, the rule is don't ask, don't tell. I overheard some rumors but did not ask questions to get more details or test the veracity of those rumors, and I am not allowed to repeat them."

"Don't worry," I said. "Karekezi, you were the first person

who welcomed me back to Kigali. I will never forget how you helped me find my sister, Celine, and the corpse of my brother, David. I can never betray you. I won't force you to tell me what you don't want to say. But you should know that the only reason I did not go back to France is to find the assassins of my brother and make sure, one day, they appear in the courts of law. It's risky. If I did not trust you, I wouldn't be revealing my plan to you. You told me you loved the music of Mr. D., didn't you? Please help me seek his justice. Now, after my brother's death, we are also talking about my sister, Celine, who has gone missing. Karekezi, please help me."

Karekezi took another sip of the apple juice I had served him, scratched his forehead, but did not say any word.

"It's all right," I said. "I understand you don't want to be involved. That's okay. Forget it. Please keep what we've discussed between us. Nobody should know Celine is missing. If you reveal to anybody my plans, you know well what they will do to me, don't you? I hope you do not want to suffer the guilt of betraying our friendship."

"No, please. Don't take it that way. The thing is ... I have also suffered in this country. Carlos, I spent five years in jail, from 1999 to 2004, convicted of a crime I did not commit. When I was released, I experienced discrimination and rejection. I could not go back to my job in a bank. I was unemployed for five years until I forgot about blue-collar jobs and decided to be a taxi driver."

"Oh no. Sorry for what happened to you. What were you accused of?"

"It's a long story that I can't tell now. I was convicted of treason because I was accused of having helped my younger brother to desert the army and go into exile. My case was linked to the cases of other people who were accused of having political agendas I was not aware of, simply because some of them were from the same village I grew up in."

"Rwanda, Rwanda!" I said. "I guess I should forget my own pain and start realizing that the smiling faces of many Rwandans cover their bleeding souls. I did not know you also experienced jail. Now I understand why you sympathized with me when I told you that David, whom you called Mr. D., was my younger brother."

"Yes, whenever a prisoner is killed, my memory plays back what I lived during the five years I spent in prison. I visualize all the scenarios. I see what others can't see." Karekezi scratched his head again and said, "Listen, Carlos, yes, I will do whatever possible to help you find your sister. Tell me what you want me to do."

"Thank you so much, Karekezi. We will do it tactfully. We should avoid any unnecessary risks."

"About your brother's death," Karekezi said, "the rumor in town is that he was killed to protect the image of Celine. Some even implicate Celine in the murder of Mr. D. They say that she did not want people to know she was linked to a Hutu who was accused of having a genocide ideology."

"What?" I said. "That's cruel. There is no way Celine could have planned to liquidate her own brother. My sister has her own unhealed wounds, but she is not a murderer or a criminal. The people who spread those rumors are insensitive."

"Carlos, do you see why I did not want to repeat the

rumors? Please don't mind them. Sooner or later, you shall know who killed your brother. The most urgent thing now to do is to find your sister. You are right that maybe the rumors are spread by the people who want Celine to vanish from the scene so that she does not do or say anything that could reveal the real culprit."

"Oh God! This is too much."

XI

I spent almost two hours with Karekezi, listening to how he wanted to go about the spying assignment. He told me he would ask his cousin, a motorbike rider, to do the inspection for him. Since motorbike riders wore face masks and jackets, it would be less likely to realize that it was the same motorbike that rode around the area. The only way to distinguish them was by reading their identification numbers or the motorbike's plate numbers. But Karekezi's cousin would borrow bikes and jackets from other motorbike riders;, a practice known in Kigali as *kuroba*. Karekezi would only ask his cousin to keep an eye on the compound and report back to him all his observations. He promised he would not give any detail to his cousin, including that Celine was missing.

Thirty minutes after Karekezi had left, James called and said he was on his way to my apartment.

In about ten minutes, I heard him knock on the door.

"Hi, James," I said. "What is it? Haven't you gone to see your aunt?"

"I'm coming from her place. That's why we need to talk. I have confirmed we were talking about the same Kananga. Yes, he has a house in Nyarutarama but told his wife it's rented to some expatriates. That's what my aunt has told me."

"What? Some men can be big liars. What does he say to his wife about the nights he spends in Nyarutarama?"

"Please, Carlos, don't repeat this to anyone. We have another suspect, Kananga's eldest son. I don't know if he knows that the house has no other tenants but Celine. All I know is that he told his mother that his father, Kananga, is involved with Celine, the former Miss Rwanda. The boy has promised to catch his dad red-handed and teach Celine a lesson she will never forget."

"Oh, poor Celine, my sister!" I said. "She is in a big mess. But how do you think Kananga's son could be involved in the disappearance of Celine?"

"I don't know. But I think the boy could probably do anything to avenge his father's betrayal."

"What else has your aunt told you?" I asked.

"The minute I mentioned the name Kananga, my aunt gave me a worrying look as if her heart had jumped out of her chest. She asked me why I was asking for information about Kananga. I told her that it was because I had heard some rumors about him. She insisted that I should tell her if I am not involved anyhow in some politics. I said no and asked her why she thought so. Finally, after so much hesitance, she told me everything Kananga's wife has told her about her husband."

"Like what?" I asked.

"Carlos, please, I have begged you not to say anything to anybody. My aunt could be killed the next day."

"James, please stop reminding me that I should not repeat

to anyone what you're telling me. Have I not told you much about Kananga and my uncle Kamara, simply because I trust you? So why do you think I should be the one to betray that trust?"

"Sorry," James responded. "It's just because I'm frightened. I couldn't believe what my aunt was telling me. She was shaking as she narrated those horrible stories about some people whose deaths were planned and executed by Kananga himself. The man we are talking about is a serial killer or an executioner. This is firsthand information. He brags about it to his wife, who often comes to cry on my aunt's shoulder. Most of the mysterious murders we read in the newspapers were masterminded by Kananga."

I did not know what to say to James. I stood up from the living room and went to the kitchen to make coffee. When I came back, James listed the names of all the people who were killed by Kananga. Some I had heard of, others I did not know.

"James, do you know why those people were killed?"

"No, I wouldn't say I know. I guess it's for different reasons, political, business, or other conflicts. Now, I have no doubt Kananga could have organized the assassination of your younger brother, David. Maybe he killed him because he knew about his relationship with Celine."

"James, there is something I have not told you. Karekezi, the taxi driver, has said that some people implicate Celine in the assassination of David. They say that she got rid of him because she did not want people to know that she had a Hutu brother."

"What?"

"James, it's not true. Celine can be anything but not a murderer. She did not understand David, but there was no way she could have wanted him dead. No, my sister was not involved in the assassination of our younger brother."

"Who told those rumors to Karekezi?" James asked.

"He did not tell me where he heard those rumors from. He said that when you hear some rumors in this country, you do not ask for details."

"Anyway, I can't say anything about whether or not Celine was involved in the assassination of David," James said. "In this Rwanda, I have concluded that anything is possible. But that's not our worry for now. The most important plan we should stick to is to find your sister. Maybe, if we manage to save her from whatever she is going through now, she might reveal things she never shared with you. Tell me, has Karekezi accepted to inspect the Nyarutarama compound? Do you really trust him? We should be careful."

"Yes, he has accepted but suggested using a motorbike rider, his cousin, because it would be more difficult to realize the same bike rides around the area."

"Do you mean we are adding a fourth person to our plan? Carlos, that's trouble. Please, if Karekezi does not want to do it himself, thank him and tell him you're dropping the plan and putting everything in the hands of the Lord. The more people we involve in our plan, the more risks we take."

"Don't worry," I said. "First, I haven't said everything to Karekezi except what he already knew. Second, he promised all he shall ask his cousin is to keep an eye on that compound and take notes of his observations. He will not tell him about Celine or Kananga."

"How sure are you that Karekezi won't say more than that? What if the cousin gets caught? Won't he reveal the name of Karekezi, who will also reveal yours?"

"That's possible. But, brother, how else do you want us to find Celine? We decided not to reveal to the police our suspects because we wanted to collect info ourselves, right? Tell me how we would do it without involving other people. We should understand we can't eradicate all risks. We should attempt to minimize them or manage them. I'm sorry I'm putting you into all this. Please understand that I will make sure it doesn't put us into trouble. Karekezi does not know about you, and that has to remain like that."

"Yes, Karekezi does not know about me, but the police do. I'm sure if Kananga is involved in the case, he already knows it has been reported to the police."

Before I responded to James, Uncle Kamara gave me a phone call. It was as if he were listening to our conversation.

"Hey, Carlos," Uncle said. "What have you done? Why do you do things without consulting me? This is not Europe or the USA, where people call nine-one-one even for minor incidents. Who advised you to report the disappearance of Celine to the police?"

"Uncle, how did you know?" I said as I wrote on a piece of paper what the call was about and showed it to James. He reminded me to say I did not know it was reported. Then, I asked Uncle Kamara, "Who reported it to the police? I haven't discussed Celine's disappearance with anybody."

"If you did not report it," Uncle said, "who did then? Who else knew Celine was missing? Carlos, you're playing with fire."

"I have told you I did not report the disappearance of Celine to the police. But why would it be a problem if the police know we don't know her whereabouts? Don't you want them to help us find my sister?"

"The problem is that Celine is not missing," Uncle Kamara said. "She must be somewhere in this Kigali. Do you know all her friends and boyfriends? Have you checked with them before reporting the case to the police?"

"No, I don't know them. The only person I checked with is you. Celine had told me she was coming to your place because you had invited her. Now she is missing. I have told you I haven't reported the case to the police. But I would be grateful if you could help me search for her."

"I won't search for her. She is an adult who knows what she is doing. Just bear in mind that she mingles with men who have the right, the authority, and the means to make you completely forget you once had a sister named Celine. You have been warned."

Uncle Kamara hung up the phone after saying that to me.

"James, I don't get the game Uncle Kamara is playing. How did he know the disappearance of Celine was reported to the police? Maybe my sister is nowhere else but at our uncle's house. What if Kananga is not involved at all? Could we be searching for Celine from the wrong place? Please, tell me what we should do."

"I guess we need to take our time," James said. "Maybe we shouldn't rush things. Listen, Carlos, we have reported the case to the police, right? Second, yes, let the cousin of Karekezi inspect the Nyarutarama compound. We should refrain from making any other move. Don't worry, your sister shall be all right. Let's wait for a week or two and see how things evolve."

"Yes, you're right. But I don't know if and when I will ever be able to sleep in this Rwanda without both my brother and my sister. Anyway, I have no other option. Maybe I should start a prayer, I mean, a novena."

"What's a novena?" James asked.

"A prayer for nine days. Most Catholics do it whenever they need answers from God."

"Are you a believer? That's surprising. I don't believe in the existence of God as some people describe him. When I have a problem, I think of how to solve it. I don't pray."

"Same here, brother," I said. "I can't say I'm a Christian. I never go to church. But there are times I turn to prayers the same way my mother used to do whenever she faced challenges. She was not the best Christian. She was considered a sinner, a Madeleine if you like. But I remember how she recited rosaries during the genocide against the Tutsi before she was killed. So I guess in some situations, faith is the only thing that can keep us moving, even if it would be in a deity we have never seen."

"I get you," James said, before adding, "Carlos, let me go home now. I also need to take time to meditate. I want to draw down all these feelings of sadness, fear, doubt, and confusion on paper, as Harumi shall be playing piano with calm melodies. That's my way of praying."

"Thanks, brother," I said. "James, please remember that I'm so grateful. I don't know how I would have survived in this Rwanda if I had not met you."

"It's okay. Don't start again. Bye for now."

"Bye."

The following Friday, Karekezi gave me a call and asked if I was at my place. I said yes. He told me he was coming to give me some news.

When he arrived, after giving him a seat and a glass of water, he said, "Carlos, please remind me, what's the model of Celine's car? Is it a red Nissan?"

"Yes, it is. Why?"

"Last night, at around o'clock, the car was driven out of the Nyarutarama compound. My cousin told me that there were about three people in it, but he could not identify who they were. If it was indeed Celine's car, I'm afraid they could have taken her to only God knows where."

"Oh no," I said, putting my hands on top of my head. "But how did your cousin know it was Celine's car?"

"He didn't. All he did was report to me what he saw. He said that nobody except the security guards entered or came out of that compound for all the days he had been wandering around the area. When he saw a car coming out in the middle of the night, he decided to inform me. He said it was the new model of Nissan."

My brain could not advise me on what to make of that piece of information. *Was Celine in that car?* I mused. *What if the vehicle was simply used in the other dirty games Kananga is involved in? Oh no, what if that criminal has finished my sister?*

"Can we conclude with certainty that Celine was in that car?" I asked Karekezi. "What if they were just using the car for other errands?"

"Errands in the middle of the night?" Karekezi asked. "Celine has been missing for days now. Maybe some people have started suspecting Kananga, which could be why he decided to take her to another house."

"That's a possibility," I said, "but could there not be other possible scenarios?"

Karekezi put his hand on his forehead, covering a part of his eyes as if he wanted to reflect on something. Then he said, "No, that can't be. No, he cannot … no."

"What do you mean?" I asked. "What are you talking about? Who can't do what?"

"Never mind," Karekezi said. "It's just that this country has become unpredictable. Even what you might think to be impossible, sooner or later, you get shocked to hear that it has indeed happened."

"I don't get what you mean," I insisted. "Please, tell me, what else do you think Kananga could have done to my sister?"

"Carlos, please don't mind my troubled thoughts. Maybe your sister is in Kananga's house. Maybe he took her to another house. Or, maybe something more horrible has happened."

"Something like what?" I asked. "Do you mean Kananga could have killed my sister?"

"Please, let's not even think about that possibility now," Karekezi said. "We should remain focused. Celine is missing, and our immediate goal now is to find her, dead or alive. I will ask my cousin to keep an eye on Kananga's compound and shall keep you posted if he notices anything else. Now, I have to go. Please, take care and stay calm."

"Thanks," I said. "I was short of words and could not think straight anymore."

After Karekezi left, I gave a call to James.

"Hello, brother," I said.

"Hey, Carlos. What's up?"

"I was wondering if I could come to your place with the new report?"

"What report?" he asked.

"You will see it," I said. "Tell me when you will be home."

"Not today, unfortunately. Harumi and I are heading to Gisenyi this afternoon, and we shall come back on Monday morning. Is it urgent? If it's about the other dossier, please let me know."

"Yes, it is, but I don't know how to say this to you on the phone. It's all right. I will tell you on Monday. Don't worry, it's not that urgent. It's just that the cousin has seen the red boat getting out of the lake, but we are not sure the rose flower was in it."

"What? I don't understand."

"Please, don't ask me to explain," I said. "I'm sure you will understand."

"Let me think," James said. "The red boat ... the lake ... the rose flower ..."

"The red boat has four legs," I said. "The lake is like a fenced garden, and the rose flower is the most beautiful of all flowers. Do you now get it?"

"Wait," James said. "When did the red boat get out of the lake? How?"

"Brother, that's all. Let's discuss it when you are incognito on that application."

"Yeah, I will call you as soon as I get in the hotel room."

In the evening, when James reached Gisenyi, he called me. I told him about Celine's car being driven out of Kananga's compound. He stated that maybe they were taking her to another safe house. When I asked what he meant by a safe house, he said he would tell me face to face the following Monday and not on the application but added there was no need to worry. I concluded that he probably meant a house in a less busy neighborhood. Sometimes, it was hard to understand the jargon of Kigalians.

I started my novena prayers that evening, guided by the book I picked from a few of Mama's belongings.

The following day, at around two o'clock, my phone rang. It was a call from a number I did not recognize.

"Hello," the caller said. Her voice was familiar. "It's me, Ingabire, Celine's friend. I needed to talk to you. Please let me know where I can find you."

"Do you want me to come to your place?" I asked.

"Not necessarily. Maybe we can meet somewhere, but where there are not many people. I live in Karabaye. If you come to my place, you will have to climb Mount Kigali on foot."

"That shouldn't be a problem. I'm strong enough to climb the same hill you climb every day."

"Okay, when you get to Nyakabanda Bar, call me so that I may direct you to my place."

"All right. I'll be there in less than an hour."

I immediately got out and jumped on a motorbike to Karabaye. When we reached Nyakabanda Bar, I gave a call to

Ingabire, who directed me to her place. The biker tried to ride on the hill until I told him to park. I was afraid the motorcycle could throw us down the hill. The neighborhood was one of those they called amanegeka. What seemed to have once been a road had many parallel waterways that transported rainwater from Mount Kigali to the main canals that flowed into the Mpazi River. Sometimes, the impromptu waterways could not contain the heavy rainwater, which often found its way into the neighborhood's timeworn houses and caused deadly corrosions. The people in the community stared at me as if I were a stranger. Many children stopped whatever they were doing and accompanied me to Ingabire's place, as they repeated, umuzungu. When I reached Ingabire's place, I gave the kids a few coins for buying candies. They happily left to go to the small shop across the pathway.

Ingabire welcomed me to the compound where she stayed and asked me to enter, not the main house, but the annexed studio.

"Thank you so much," she said. "I could not believe you when you said you could come to Karabaye."

"Why?" I asked.

"Because it's far from the main road and even the motorcycles can't reach here. It's a lot of climbing. Besides, most wealthy people fear neighborhoods like this one. They think it's not safe to come here."

"The climbing is not a problem for me. It's an opportunity to exercise. But I felt uncomfortable because your neighbors were staring at me, and their kids were calling me muzungu. Thank you for welcoming me to your house."

"My pleasure," Ingabire said. "I'm worried. I wanted to ask you if you know the whereabouts of Celine. I have been trying to call her number for days now but without success. She was driving to your uncle's place the last time we talked. A few minutes after that call, she tried to call me again, but we could not talk. It sounded as if somebody had snatched the phone from her hands. I could hear noise in the background as if Celine were being forced to enter a room or jump in a car. Then, the call ended. I don't know if she had reached your uncle's place or not."

"Did you say she called you when she was being kidnapped?" I asked. "Why didn't you immediately call me?"

"I did not have your number. I don't know where you live. After days of wondering how to reach you, I recalled Celine told me that Linda is your friend. That's how I decided to call her and ask for your number. She refused because she knew me only as a tailor and not Celine's friend. When I lied to her that you promised me a job to sew a suit for you, she laughed at me, gave me your number, and wished me good luck."

"Okay, I get it. Sorry that I had not given you my number. Did you tell Linda that Celine is missing?"

"No, I did not."

"It's better that way. Please don't tell her anything. I will talk to her myself. Now tell me, were you able to identify the voices of the people who kidnapped my sister?"

"No, I wasn't. The only thing I know is that they were men unknown to Celine because she kept asking them who they were."

I kept silent for seconds, covered my lips with my hands,

and faced the ceiling before asking, "Ingabire, would you accept if I asked you to testify to the police what you heard the day my sister was kidnapped?"

"To the police?" Ingabire asked. "No, I can't go to the police. No, I can't. I have never been to the police. Please, don't ask me to go there."

"Why can't you? We need to find Celine. She counts on us. She must be waiting for us to rescue her. Please, Ingabire, help me save my sister. She told me you're the only person she trusts."

I couldn't imagine the scene when Celine was surrounded by her kidnappers. I couldn't imagine the fear, the torture, the trauma. I couldn't imagine what my sister had been going through for days. James was not in Kigali to advise me. I had to take the matter into my own hands. I mused that there was nothing we could achieve by keeping the police in the dark. Maybe Ingabire's testimony could push the police to deploy more efforts to Celine's search.

After moments of silence, Ingabire said, "I have an idea."

"Tell me," I said.

"I know the place where Celine used to spend some days, but she had stopped going there. It's in Nyarutarama. I suspect the man she was dating could have taken her back there by force."

"Are you talking about Kananga? Do you know him? Have you met him before?"

"Celine showed him to me on TV. I have never met him in person. I went to his house a couple of times when I had to take something to Celine. But I never entered the compound.

There was a security guard whom Celine trusted. He is the one to whom I used to give Celine's medications ... No, I mean, Celine's message. Maybe he can tell us if Celine is in that compound. I did not want to call him before talking to Celine and tell her that I have the message she had sent me to get for her."

"Ingabire," I said. "I beg you. Please, tell me everything you know. All those bits of info can help us find Celine. What's the name of that security guard? Do you have his telephone number? What did you say you used to take to Celine? Did you say medications? What kind of medications? Please don't hide any detail."

"Yes, Carlos. Celine takes a tablet every day. Please don't force me to give you the details. All I can say to you is that I'm worried she hasn't taken her tablets for a week. Every month, she sends me to a King Faysal hospital nurse who gives me the medications. It's a secret between the three of us. Nobody else knows about Celine's condition and that she is under treatment. She will be upset with me if she finds out I told you. Please never say that I revealed it to you. It's just because I wanted to tell you that we must find Celine as soon as possible. The security guard, who served as a messenger between Celine and me whenever she was at Kananga's place, is named Kalimunda. I can call him and ask if Celine is in that compound if you allow."

"Yes," I said, "please call him but don't tell him Celine is missing. Just say you have a message for Celine, and you were wondering if Kalimunda can deliver it for you. Even if you have refused to tell me more about the medications, don't you think Celine could be lying in a hospital somewhere if she is sick? How long hasn't she taken those medications for?"

"No, Celine is not sick at all," Ingabire said. "She simply has a condition, and she knows how to manage it. Please, accept that I won't say more about it than I already have. All we need to do is to search for her. Let me call the security guard Kalimunda."

Ingabire gave a call to Kalimunda and turned on the loudspeaker so that I could hear his responses. The security guard was surprised by the call because he wondered if Ingabire did not know that Celine broke up with Kananga. He told Ingabire that he had not seen Celine for weeks before Kananga requested his company to change all the security guards. Ingabire asked him when that happened. The guy responded that a week had elapsed; it was actually the morning of the Saturday on which Celine was kidnapped. Ingabire thanked Kalimunda and ended the call.

"This is complicated," Ingabire said to me. "Kalimunda has been deployed to another place. I understand Kananga changed the entire security team, and surprisingly, he did that on the day Celine was kidnapped. There is no doubt Celine is in that compound. I can only imagine what she is going through. That man is violent. He claims that he loves Celine and can't live without her, but he hits her whenever she does something he does not like. He must be punishing her for having dared to break up with him. Now I don't know what else we should do."

"What?" I asked. "Do you mean that man hits my sister? Ingabire, I can't imagine the kind of torture my sister is enduring if she is still alive. I'm afraid of the worst. We need to rescue Celine before it's too late. Please, accept to testify at the police station. We reported the disappearance, but maybe they haven't made any move because they have no clue where Celine could be. Your testimony shall not only confirm she was indeed kidnapped but also give them some clues as to where they could start their search."

"How? I have told you I only heard some voices. I don't think that would help the police identify Celine's kidnappers."

"You're right. But you may also tell the police that Celine had broken up with Kananga and that she was going to our uncle's place on the day she was kidnapped. I believe you know Uncle Kamara is a friend to Kananga, right?"

"Yes, I know. But I also recall Celine telling me how powerful and dangerous both men are. Please allow me to remain invisible. In this Rwanda, I have neither a parent nor a sibling. I never talk about how my whole family was murdered. I have survived to this date because I have learned to keep my mouth shut. I'm sorry, Carlos, I won't go to the police."

"It's okay," I said. "But at least, please help me search for Celine. If there is any useful piece of information, please don't hide it from me. I will see what I can do."

"Please, don't take it in the wrong way," Ingabire said. "But you should keep in mind how discreet Celine is. What shall she think of me if I reveal her secrets to anyone? Maybe she will forgive me for disclosing some information to you, but not to strangers. Besides, Kananga is one of the most powerful men in this country. He probably has his people in the police, who will report to him whatever I will have said.

By mentioning the name Kananga to the police, I'm afraid we would be putting Celine in more danger. This is complicated. Carlos, please give me a few days to ponder what we should do. I will call you next week."

"All right," I said.

When I was about to stand up and leave Ingabire's house, she said, "Carlos, I have another idea."

"Tell me," I said.

"What if I ask Kalimunda if he knows any of the new security guards at Kananga's place? Maybe they might tell him if they saw any lady in the compound. If yes, that shall mean Celine is at Kananga's."

"How will that help us if we don't want to report Kananga to the police?" I asked.

Even though I felt the urge to reveal to Ingabire that I had someone inspecting Kananga's compound, I recalled James had advised against informing many people of our plan.

"At least we will be sure she wasn't kidnapped by other wrongdoers," Ingabire replied. "Then, we will think about how to bribe the security guards and manage to talk to Celine."

"Okay. Please make sure you don't reveal any information to Kalimunda. Tell him you have been trying to reach Celine on the phone but in vain. Don't mention my name, the police, or talk about our suspicions."

"You can trust me on that," Ingabire said.

"Please allow me to take my leave, now," I said.

Ingabire saw me off to the gate of the compound she stayed in. I descended the hill, and when I reached Nyakabanda Bar,

I jumped on a motorbike and headed to my place. I guess I also needed to use the weekend for mediation and prayer. I had to trust God, who had protected my sister during all the years I was in France.

XII

On Monday, I woke up early because I had to go to the office after two weeks of leave, during which I had not rested at all. At ten o'clock, James came and invited me for coffee in our office's canteen. I told him about my conversation with Ingabire.

"I think Ingabire should accept to report what she heard to the police," James said. "Even if she chooses not to, the police may contact her, as one of the people who spoke to Celine on that day."

"How would the police find out?" I asked.

"The last time I checked, you were an IT engineer in a telecommunications company, weren't you?" James said, smiling. "All they have to do is to make a request to the legal department of Celine's phone service provider."

"I had forgotten about that," I said. "Wait ... Celine has an STC phone. So if they want that info, they shall make the request to our company, right?"

"I don't know how it works. In Rwanda, things are

sometimes done differently. I heard from some colleagues that a few members of the police have direct access to the register. But I'm not sure about that."

"James, I have an idea. Why don't we check the register ourselves? Maybe we will find the telephone numbers of Celine's kidnappers."

"Who will give you access to the register?" James asked. "Even if you did, daring to call those numbers would cost your job and freedom because you would be jailed for many years."

"I get it," I said. "It's just that I'm short of ideas. I don't know how to force Ingabire to report what she heard to the police. She has promised to call me this week after reflecting on what she should do."

Before James responded, my phone rang. It was a call from Karekezi.

"Where are you?" he said, without even a greeting. "Have you read the news?"

"What news?" I asked.

"Check on Isaha.com," Karekezi said. "Let me send the link to you on WhatsApp. We urgently need to talk. I don't know what he said to them before they finished him. I can't say more on the phone. Please, tell me where I can meet you. I need to save myself as soon as the roads are still clear."

"Let me call you back after reading the news," I said.

The news was shocking. It was about a motor-taxi rider who had been shot dead in Nyarutarama, precisely in front of Kananga's compound. I immediately understood the victim was Karekezi's cousin. The newspaper reported that the victim had tried to snatch the policeman's handgun—one of the usual stories every time the police shot dead a citizen.

"James, look at this," I said. "They have killed him."

"Who?" James asked.

"Read the news. The guy who was spying on Kananga's compound has been eliminated. Is this how it happens? Is this how a person's life ends? Tell me it's not true because I will not forgive myself for having caused his death. He was only helping us to find Celine. Now, how am I going to face Karekezi? He has just lost a cousin because of me."

"Carlos, I had warned you," James said as he stood up from his chair. "We're in trouble." He scratched his head, moved around, then added, "Let's get out of this canteen. Please do not speak to Karekezi. Don't tell him your whereabouts. You don't know who he could be with."

"What? How can't I talk to Karekezi, who is mourning his cousin, killed, trying to help me find my sister? James, please calm down. Please tell me what to do now."

"Carlos, now you have to listen to me. Remember, it's not only your sister's life at risk but yours and mine too. So come, let's go to my office."

In his office, James told me that we needed to leave the country. I thought he was exaggerating.

"James, please don't panic. I don't see why we should go into exile simply because some criminals kidnapped my sister. We have no problems with the state."

"How about the policeman who shot the motor-taxi rider? Or the prison officer who killed your brother, David?

Are they also random criminals? Carlos, there are people in this Rwanda who finish whoever messes with them. Unfortunately, we have now invaded their territory. They would not have killed the motor taxi rider if they didn't have all details about what he was up to and who sent him. They never act hastily. Everything is premeditated."

"So, do you think they know I'm searching for my sister? How would that be the police's problem? Have we not reported her disappearance to the police? James, please calm down. I feel so sad for Karekezi's cousin. But I'm now more worried than before about my sister's fate. If, as you're saying, that policeman was acting on behalf of Celine's kidnappers, then I can't imagine what my sister might be going through. Maybe she is also paying for what I have done. Do you know what? I have to go to the police and tell them everything. If I can't do it my way, the police should do their job and search for my sister."

"You have gone insane," James said. "How did I get myself into this? Carlos, please don't make any other move. Don't call anyone. Don't talk to anyone. In fact, we have to switch off our phones now, and after work, go to our homes, and stay in quietly."

"James, I'm sorry I dragged you into my family drama and troubles. Now, I feel guilty about everything. I don't want to betray your trust. I can't imagine what Karekezi shall think of me if I decide to cut off communication on the day of his cousin's death. And my sister, Celine, please don't ask me to stop searching for her. If I have to die, at least I will die trying to save my sister. I have not forgiven myself for having abandoned my younger brother, David. I don't think I shall ever be able to bear the guilt if anything happens to my sister. Brother, please understand me."

I broke into tears and ran to the bathrooms to hide my eyes. James stayed in his office, looking at the window as if he wanted to ask for answers.

When I came back from the bathroom, James said, "I'm taking ten days off. The manager has just approved my leave request. Carlos, please forgive me. I need to go somewhere and reflect."

"Where are you going to?" I asked.

"I don't know yet. For now, I'm going to my apartment. I can't tell you what my next move is going to be. Please don't tell anybody I have gone on leave or anything else."

James got out of his office, and I followed him so he could lock the door. As I watched him leave me, tears wet my eyes again. My chest was heavy. I rushed to my own office but failed to sit on the chair. Despite the potential consequences, I wondered if I should take James's advice or do what I thought was right. What if James is right? I mused. What if calling Karekezi could put me in danger? Despite the conundrums, I decided to call Karekezi but not to accept to meet him.

"Hello, Karekezi," I said with a shy voice. "I have just read the news. My condolences. I'm really sorry for what happened."

"Is that all you have to say?" Karekezi asked. "We can't talk on the phone. Please, tell me where I can meet you. I'm afraid I could be the next. I need your help."

"The thing is ... I'm afraid it won't be possible to meet

now. I have so much work and don't know what time I'm leaving the office today."

"Carlos, don't tell me you're avoiding me? Don't tell me you have no time to meet me now when you seemed to have plenty of time the day you implicated me in your affairs. Are you leaving me to face these people alone?"

"No, please, don't take it that way. It's just that I'm busy with work. I will call you tomorrow or the day after tomorrow. In fact … Karekezi, I think we should be careful. Maybe it's not a good idea for us to meet. I believe you understand why, don't you?"

"No, I don't. All I understand is that when chewing gum has no sugar anymore, it has to be rejected. Okay, that's clear. I had forgotten who you are, a supremacist. You are a product of Rwanda supremacism and white supremacism. Thanks for opening my eyes. I'm going to bury my cousin, a chance I did not have for all my other loved ones whose remains are still crying for justice. Goodbye for now. Time shall be the judge."

"Karekezi, please listen to me. Don't get angry. I … listen … maybe. No. Please, understand why we can't meet. It's for the safety of both of us."

"The safety of both of us? Am I safe? Have I ever been safe in this Rwanda? Don't worry; your Rwandan uncles won't do any harm to you. If they ever try, don't hesitate to take the next plane to France, your other country. Don't worry about me. This is my fate. I should have known better and avoided putting myself in your family drama. Please, goodbye. Forget my name."

Karekezi hung up on me. I had nothing else to do but lay

my head on the table and let the tears out. They refused. My chest was bloating. My head was about to explode. James had gone; I didn't know where. Karekezi had said goodbye. What were they going to do? I had no idea. My sister, Celine, was still missing. I had come back to Rwanda because my younger brother had been shot dead by a prison officer. I stayed because I wanted to seek justice for his death. Now, it was no longer about my brother's death but also about my sister's disappearance and my own safety. I was powerless, helpless, hopeless, alone, and out of control of anything. I decided to just vanish from my office without asking for permission because I had just returned from leave.

The streets of Kigali, despite the greenery and the fresh air, smelled death the same way they used to smell in the '90s. Finally, I was able to read melancholy and antagonism on the faces of the Rwandans on the streets, despite their beautiful but plastic smiles. I wanted to call James and tell him that I understood what he used to read on those faces he liked to photograph. I was walking without any specific destination. I did not want to go to my apartment. I was afraid somebody could come to hunt me there, or that loneliness would kill me in that room. I thought of two people: Rotty and Linda. They were the only Kigalians I seemed to know, though I was born and grew up in that city. I dialed Rotty's number; it was off. That made me a little worried, but I had already enough to worry about and no place for more worries.

I decided to call Linda. She had once or twice found calm

in my shelter. Now, it was her turn to calm down my heart and mind, though I didn't know how she would do it.

"Hello, long time," Linda said. "How are you?"

"I'm fine," I said before adding, "Linda, I need to talk to you."

"Is it about Celine?" she asked. "I know what happened, though you did not tell me."

"No, it's not about her," I said, without adding details. I did not feel like talking about Celine's disappearance or David's death. I wasn't looking for Linda for any useful advice or talk, but maybe to help me feel the same way she felt whenever she smoked a joint. That's all I was looking for, that world of Rotty and Linda. So I said to her, "I only want to be with you. I miss you."

"Okay," Linda said. "I'm in Nyamirambo at a friend's house. Another friend, not Tamari. I left her house. You can come. I'm alone. My friend went to Zanzibar with her sugarcane. Call me when you get to Club Rafiki. I will come and direct you to the place."

"Perfect. I'll be there in twenty minutes."

I jumped on a motorbike and asked the rider to take me to Club Rafiki.

Arrived at Rafiki, I called Linda, and in less than five minutes, she was there.

"This is a surprise," she said. "Did you say you missed me? You, Carlos? Maybe I'm dreaming."

"Why do you say so, Linda?" I asked. "I thought we were friends, aren't we?"

"Of course, we are just friends. How do they call it again? Friend zone? Friends don't miss each other. When they meet, they chill, and that's all. When they don't meet, they go on with their lives. That's how life is. I have so many friends, but I know they don't care about me as much. I also don't care about them. We simply swing with life in whatever direction it takes us. You never seemed that kind of a person. You're like those guys who have everything in control. What happened to you? Is it because of what happened to your sister, Celine? Don't worry about her. She masters the game. She must have made a wrong move and is being grounded for that. They will release her the day they will be convinced she got the message. Please, don't get in a flap about it. Everything will be fine."

As Linda talked nonstop, I stared at her, wondering if I had made the right decision to come to her. The way she talked about friendships and my sister's disappearance sounded uncompassionate and somehow hardhearted, but I wanted to know what she knew about what had happened to Celine and why she believed her kidnappers would eventually release her. Unfortunately, I had no strength to engage in that conversation at that moment.

"My dear," I said to Linda, "I don't know about your other friends. All I know is that you're my friend and I missed you. I have come to spend some time with you. It has nothing to do with Celine. Shall you please take me to your house?"

"That scares me a bit," Linda said. "I hope nobody sent you to me. But anyway, you're most welcome. This way, please."

We took the small way behind Club Rafiki, then down to the second street of Rwezamenyo. A small yellow fence could be seen next to the ill-kept garden. There were about five small studio apartments in that compound, and Linda stayed in door number 3.

"Beautiful place," I said, after entering the living room, decorated with a small table and three armchairs.

"You're welcome. It's better than where I used to stay with Tamari. At least here, I feel at home. My friend is young and nice, not like that old bitch who used to take advantage of me."

"What's the name of your friend? What does she do?"

"Her name is Fofo. She does almost everything—modeling, acting, dancing, and every other job that pays money, including entertaining those who need some sweet care."

"What do you mean? Does she also do prostitution, like Tamari?"

"Not really. Fofo is not that cheap. She does it clean and smart. Like now, as I have told you, she is in Zanzibar, sucking her sugarcane."

"Please," I said, "try to speak the language I understand. What do you mean by sugarcane? Does it take a person to go to Zanzibar to suck sugarcane?"

She laughed before replying, "I mean the sugar-man, one of Fofo's high-class clients. They are not like the poor men who visited Tamari every night for just a few minutes or hours. Fofo has sponsors who are ready to invest in her. She actually knows your sister, Celine, though she told me they are not friends but may be competitors. Unlike your sister,

Fofo does not serve politicians and those linked to them, but foreigners and ordinary businesspeople."

"Linda, may I please ask you for a favor?"

"Yes," she replied.

"Please, stop talking about Celine. She is my sister, and I love her so much. I'm not only worried she could be in danger, but I'm also puzzled by what's happening, where she could be, and why. If you don't want me to run mad, please, let's chill and forget about everything else. I need a drink, maybe a cold beer."

"Okay. Sorry for what happened to your sister. Let me get a drink for us. I also have a nice movie we could watch on Fofo's laptop if that's okay with you."

"That's a brilliant idea," I said. "You've finally got it; I have come here to relax and forget every trouble of this life."

After emptying many beer bottles, I fell asleep without finishing the romantic movie Linda had put on. She must have hated me for being so unromantic.

After midnight, I woke up and couldn't catch sleep anymore. The whole second half of the night till morning, I reflected on my family and wondered about the fate of Rwanda. Was being half European, and not just Tutsi or Hutu, a privilege I had over my siblings? Would David not have died if he had not experienced discrimination after the 1994 genocide, somehow because he was associated with his paternal so-called ethnic identity? The storyline of everything my younger brother had gone through seemed as if it could have taken a different direction if he was not identified as a Hutu. How about my sister, Celine, whose beauty had ended up being like a curse? What direction could her life have taken if she had not lost her entire paternal family during the genocide against the Tutsi and later searched for warmth within the community of those she considered her people, whom she thought were noble and powerful? Finally, if I weren't half-French, would I have ever left Rwanda for France to search for my second heritage, leaving my siblings to experience the genocide aftermath in solos without the support of each other? Attempting to find answers to these questions gave me nothing but a headache.

When she was still alive, our mother had raised us as if we were full siblings and not half-siblings. I was the eldest. After the genocide that took our mother's life, I should not have allowed Uncle Kamara to take Celine alone and leave behind David simply because he did not want to acknowledge he was also his nephew. I should also not have allowed David's paternal uncle, Mukinzi, to take him away from me. I shouldn't have accepted to be separated from my siblings. I should have stayed there, with them, three of us, like the traditional stone stove. As the eldest of the family, I should have protected my sister, Celine, and our younger brother, David. Was it too late? I wondered. Yes, David was already dead, and I did not know the whereabouts of Celine. But no, it was not too late; David was still begging for justice, and Celine was waiting for me to go and save her from the hands of her kidnappers. This time around, I had to do what was right, even if it meant losing my life.

"Hey, Carlos," Linda said, after she woke up and stretched her hands to touch me on the bed, but in vain. "Where are you? When did you get up? I had not realized you were no longer lying beside me. Last night, you fell asleep like a baby before the movie's end. You didn't even kiss me goodbye. And now, when I was hoping for a morning cuddle, you're there, on the chair, deep in thoughts, as if you're planning an attack on the world. Please, come back in bed."

"No, Linda, I need to take a shower and go."

"No way. You're going nowhere at this hour of the morning. Just come to bed for another few minutes. You will go after taking breakfast. Please, don't say no."

Before I responded, Linda got up and pulled me to fall on the bed. She wrapped both her arms and legs around me and asked me to relax. I indeed felt somehow exhausted and weak. As I was falling into a deep sleep again, I could hear Linda complaining and murmuring that I was a disappointment. She was angry with me for not touching her.

When I woke up at around midday, Linda had already prepared an excellent breakfast, or maybe brunch. It was what Kigalians called a special omelet, comparable to a Spanish omelet. There was also bread and African tea.

"Carlos, may I say something to you?" Linda asked.

"Do you need to ask for permission to talk?" I asked.

"I was wondering if you're normal," she said. "Are you a real man? But, please, don't take it the wrong way. It's just that … I don't know how to say this."

"What do you mean? Of course, I'm normal. I don't get the meaning of your question."

"I'm asking because it's the third time you and I have spent a night together in the same room, and you've never touched me or tried to do sex with me. I had always thought that when it comes to sex, men are always moved by instinct. Why are you different?"

"Linda, I'm not different from other men. You're a beautiful girl, and not so many men can resist your beauty. But as I said to you, you're my friend, and I respect you. I value more lovemaking than sex. So, if anything has to happen, it should be for love, not because my body is aroused by your warmth."

"Did you say you value more lovemaking than sex? How are the two different? Does it mean you don't love me?"

"No, dear. I don't hate you. But, though I wouldn't mind falling in love with you, we are not there yet. And even if we were lovers, we would make love only when it's right and feels good for both of us. It shouldn't be only for my pleasure. Do you get it?"

"I don't. But anyway, I'm not complaining. It feels good to have at least one guy who likes me as a person and not as a toy for his pleasure. May I ask you something else?"

"Go ahead, please."

"Why don't you want me to tell you about Celine? Please, listen to me. It's not that I don't care about her. It's just because I know where she is."

"Where? Where is my sister? How did you know?"

"Calm down, please. Nobody should know I told you this. It's a weird coincidence. Celine is in Rebero in a house that belongs to one of Fofo's men, a businessman. That's where Kananga is keeping her because he thought some people were already suspecting Celine was in his Nyarutarama house. Look at the message Fofo sent to me a few days ago:

'The missing miss is at Kido's house entertaining the old man not far from family.'"

"What? Yes, Kananga's wife and kids are indeed in Rebero. Oh my! That man is something else. Linda, do you know the address? We should talk to the police."

"Stop it. Talk to who? Please, don't say it to the police. Fofo will kill me. Those men are dangerous. I only said it to you so you may calm down, because Celine is still alive. She has no issues with the state. It's just that when you get involved with people like Kananga, they make you their property and take your freedom away. That's what is happening to Celine. Kananga wants her all to himself. He won't kill her. All she has to do is apologize and say that she is back with him."

I wanted to tell Linda that freedom was indeed something Celine deserved and needed to fight for. But unfortunately, she had also surrendered her own freedom to whoever wanted to have her in his hands. Yes, indeed, Celine wanted to reclaim her freedom. I could not help but recall how happy she was when she had finally waved goodbye to her master, Kananga. After that, all she looked forward to was starting her fashion business and using her modeling career to build a legacy she would be proud of.

"Okay," I said to Linda. "I guess, since you don't want me to report it to the police, I should just thank you for the info and continue to pray for my sister. At least, as you said, I'm glad she is still alive. Is it okay if I spend another night here? Maybe we should drink more to kill the hangover. What do you think?'

Linda smiled and said, "You can stay here forever if you

want, or until next week when Fofo shall return from her trip. Something stronger? I have a whiskey."

"Yes, let me have a few shots to burn all the bottles of beer I drank yesterday."

Linda and I continued to drink as we watched TV and talked about everything and nothing, till around six o'clock when she received a message from her friend, Fofo. It was a link to a long Facebook post.

"Carlos, look at this," she said. "Now this is trouble. How did these people know about the disappearance of Celine? They are saying Kananga killed her. That's not true. But, surprisingly, they seemed to have a lot more details. Who leaked this info to them?"

"What are you talking about? Is my sister dead? Didn't you say you know where she is? Who wrote it on Facebook? Who are those people?"

"I'm also reading it here. Apparently, it's a copy-paste of an article from a newspaper that supports the opposition groups operating outside the country. I normally don't read what these people post on social media. I guess Fofo has sent it to me because it was about Celine. Please, don't take it as truth. Your sister is all right."

"You can't be sure about that, Linda. Let me read the article."

Linda handed me her phone. I couldn't believe what I was reading. The article reported the assassination of Karekezi's cousin. They stated that the motorbike rider was killed because he saw a car taking the corpse of Celine from Kananga's house in Nyarutarama to an unknown place.

They declared that Kananga had killed Celine because she had ended their sexual affair. According to the newspaper, my sister was aware of the many murders masterminded by Kananga, including the assassination of her own brother, Mr. D.—David. The journalist wrote that Kananga feared Celine could make everything public if she was not neutralized.

"This is serious," I said to Linda. "What if what they are saying is true? What if Kananga killed both my siblings? Oh God, please guide me. This is evidence I should take to the police. They should go after the people who wrote this article and investigate the information."

"The police?" Linda asked. "Carlos, I know nothing about politics, but I feel you shouldn't tell the police you've read an article from a newspaper of the opposition groups."

"Why? Linda, you should remember we are talking about my sister's life. Is reading a newspaper or a social media post a crime?"

"It's not a crime, but you should wonder why that newspaper is banned and can't be accessed here in Rwanda unless the content is copied on social media."

"Then, what should I do? Whether true or untrue, the article is pointing fingers at the suspect. All I need to do is to show it to the police."

"Don't worry about that. The police know already or shall know. They monitor everything that is posted on social media. But listen, Celine is a celebrity. Now that her disappearance is in the news, Celine's fans will start asking about her whereabouts. Often, when that happens, the police react. Maybe this is to our advantage. If she is still alive, and I believe she is, her kidnappers shall have no option but release her before they are caught."

"I wish I could have the same hope. But I am afraid that in an attempt to hide all evidence and avoid being caught, Celine's kidnappers may kill and bury her where she shall never be found. Linda, I need to do something, though I don't know what. Let me call someone."

"Call who?"

"Uncle Kamara. I want to know what he thinks of this article."

"I don't know," Linda said. "I really don't know how to advise you. It seems now it's politics, and all I know is that it's dangerous. Sorry to say, but your uncle is one of those people in dirty games. Maybe he is also involved in what happened to your sister."

"Do you know Uncle Kamara? Why do you think he could be involved?"

"Eh, have you forgotten how we met? Don't you remember I used to go out with someone called Martin? He knew too well your uncle, and they were both members of the same club; of those Kigalians who execute some dirty deals, I have no details about. Please do not discuss the article with your uncle on the phone. If you want to talk to him about it, go to his place for a face-to-face conversation."

As I listened to Linda, I decided to wait and see what the following day would bring.

The following morning, I thanked Linda for having hosted me for two days and told her I had to go back to my apartment.

But before leaving, when I switched back on my phone, I noticed that the day before, I had received many calls from Karekezi, who, when he could not reach me, sent an SMS, "Don't be surprised by what I'm about to do. The world needs to know that my cousin was killed trying to help your family."

"What a bastard!" I said. "Now I know where it all came from. I screwed up. James had warned me about involving those people."

"Do you also say bad words?" Linda asked. "I did not see that coming from you. Who is a bastard? Who is James? Who sent you a message?"

"It's okay," I said. "It's just that I now can guess where the leaked information came from. James is a friend of mine."

"Is he the one who leaked the info?"

"No. He can never do that. It's another crazy guy. But never mind. I can't give you more details now."

"Why? Weren't you saying we were friends? Now, you're acting like other men who think women can't keep secrets. Anyway, don't tell me whatever you're not comfortable telling me."

"Don't take it the wrong way, Linda. I will tell you everything once I shall have connected all the dots. But for now I have to go. Once again, thanks for having sheltered me.

Linda saw me off to the main road, where I jumped on the next bike and asked the rider to take me to my apartment.

XIII

In my room, I surfed the internet to see if the news about my sister was already trending. It was an awful experience, and I hated every bit of what I was seeing and reading. Rwandans had learned nothing from history. My compatriots could not care less for the pain of others.

Some social media users who claimed to want justice for my sister were the same people circulating her photos and calling her nasty names. They accused her of having been an agent for the misdeeds of Kananga, whom they blamed for her death. They accused my sister of having despised our younger brother because he was a Hutu and later participated in his arrest and assassination. I wondered how they could claim to seek justice for the person they demonized and dehumanized heartlessly.

Then, there was a group of those who stated that Celine's life did not matter more than the lives of other Rwandans who deserved more the protection of the police. Like the first group, these defenders of Kananga also circulated photos of Celine. They wrote that she was not worth the worries of anybody because, according to them, she was nothing but a courtesan to entertain rich men.

The third group, which seemed to have not lost the salt of humanity in them, was made of those labeled as feminists, who liked Celine as a model or a beautiful lady. This group also included Rwandans who cared for any human being and all sons and daughters of Rwanda. These people were calling on the police to search for Celine and bring those who could have kidnapped or killed her to justice.

As I read everything written on social media by both Rwandans and non-Rwandans, looking at pictures and videos of Celine as a beauty and fashion icon, including those on which some people had already written Rest in Peace, I wanted to burst and cry it all out. But my chest was too heavy, and I was afraid it could explode if I didn't hold everything in.

When I was still asking the four walls of my bedroom to advise me on what I should do, I received a call. It was from a journalist.

"Hello," he said. "My name is Ndahiro. I work for Ukuri Radio. I understand you're Celine's brother. Please tell us when you saw her last and what you think about her disappearance?"

"May I know first who gave you my number?" I asked.

"No. That's not important. We got it from one of your contacts. Tell me, are you Celine's brother? Is it true that you had hired a motorbike rider to inspect Kananga's compound? Why did you suspect Kananga? There are rumors that Celine had an affair with Kananga; is that true? Shall you also tell us about the death of David, whom many people knew as Mr. D. or Badguy? Was he also related to you?"

"Hey, how long is the list of your questions?" I asked.

Though I didn't know who that person was and his real intentions, I knew I wasn't going to respond to his questions.

"Just a few questions," the journalist replied. "Tell me, are you Celine's brother? Was Mr. D. also related to you? Can you tell us what you know about Celine's disappearance and Mr. D.'s death?"

"Yes, Celine is my sister, and David was our younger brother," I said to the journalist. "We are siblings who loved and still love each other very much. That's all I can tell you now. Nothing more, nothing less."

"Is there any link between Celine's disappearance and Mr. D.'s death? Do you think Kananga could have killed both your younger brother and your sister?"

"I have told you I won't respond to those questions. Please, I have some other things to do."

"That's all right," he said. "Just tell me what you think about Celine's disappearance. Where could she be?"

"No comment, and goodbye," I said, before ending the call.

For the whole day, many other journalists, and those who claimed to be journalists, called and sent messages, until I got tired of answering "no comment" to their questions. I decided to ignore their calls and messages. I did not want to switch off the phone. Somehow, I believed somebody would call me, not with questions but valuable information about my sister's whereabouts.

As I continued to painfully surf the internet and social media, my eyes and ears were also on the radio and TV, hoping to hear somebody reporting on the case. The day was agonizingly long. I wanted to fall asleep, but I could not. James's phone number was still inaccessible. I thought of calling Ingabire but didn't know what to say to her. *No, Celine is not dead,* I mused. *No, God cannot do this to me.* The Almighty had not saved our mother when Hutu militants came to hunt her in 1994. God had not stopped the assassination of my brother, David, twenty years after our mother's death. *Has he taken away my sister as well?* I questioned. Six months had elapsed since the death of David, and I had not yet figured out how to identify and bring to justice his assassins. *How on earth shall I be able to uncover the kidnappers and killers of my sister, Celine?* I wondered. What if the criminals' aim is to finish all Kayitesi's children? Am I going to be the next? *If I don't find Celine or it's confirmed she is dead, I guess I should give up on this myth they call justice and go back to France,* I murmured to myself.

A flash of thought reminded me of Rotty. We had not talked for weeks, if not months. I dialed his number but in vain. It was off, like last time. *What happened to Rotty?* I wondered. Could he also have been kidnapped? By whom? If yes, then it means Martin, Bosco, Kamara, and Kananga are members of one criminal gang. No, I shouldn't come to conclusions. I needed to go to the ghetto of Inzuki boys and check if other fundis were aware of Rotty's whereabouts. But the idea of getting out scared me. *What if I meet those journalists or the paparazzi outside?* I wondered.

The whole day and night of Wednesday and the morning of Thursday, I was emersed in deep thoughts and self-interrogations that did not take me from one point to another. Then, at around two o'clock in the afternoon, my phone rang. To my surprise, it was James. He said he wanted to come to my place and that it was urgent. He had taught me to be suspicious of everyone and everything, and I wondered if I shouldn't apply it to him. What if he is also up to something? What if he wants to save himself and sacrifice me? I decided not to invite him into my room.

"Is it possible for us to meet in Biryogo?" I asked James. "I'm going to see someone there."

"Where in Biryogo?" he asked. "I wanted us to meet somewhere without any evil eyes. I thought your place, in Nyakabanda, is a little far from them."

"I get it," I said, "but their cameras may actually be facing the gate to my apartment. Don't you think so?"

"You're right. Okay. Let's meet in front of the Biryogo open market. I know some corners bad eyes do never reach."

I put on clothes quickly and headed to Biryogo. Before meeting James, I went to the ghetto of Inzuki boys to ask about Rotty. For the first time in many days, there was good news. Rotty had voluntarily gone to a rehabilitation center. Other fundis were mocking him, but I was so happy for him. I said bye to them and headed to the market to meet James.

"Hey, Carlos," James said.

He was wearing brown shorts and a black T-shirt and hiding his eyes with shades and his head with a cap. It was clear he did not want to be identified by anybody.

"Hi," I said. "How are you surviving hell? Bro, I'm so sorry. I didn't expect things to turn out this messy."

"No need to say sorry," he replied. "This way, please. Let's take a walk for a chat. It's better than entering any house. In this Rwanda, walls do not have only ears; they also have recorders."

We took the streets below the market and walked down as if we were heading to Rugunga. As we passed through the paths between modest houses of one of the Kigali neighborhoods that are never shown on TV, I wondered what James was up to but decided to surrender. James had proven to be a good person, a brother I could always count on. That's why I felt somehow guilty to even doubt his intentions.

"James, tell me, where have you been?" I asked him. "Your phone was off. I tried to reach you in vain till I decided to also switch my phone off."

"After I left the office," he said, "I went to my apartment and switched off the phone till yesterday, when a friend of mine, who is a soldier, called Harumi and said he needed to urgently talk to me. I did not know he now works with intelligence services. Carlos, we are in trouble. Have you seen what's trending on social media?"

"Yes, I have. Brother, you had warned me about involving other people in the search for my sister. I suspect Karekezi is the one who leaked the info to those political opposition groups. They are declaring that my sister is dead. Please, tell me it's not true. Tell me my sister is not gone."

"Listen, I understand you're worried about your sister. She could be still alive or already dead. But that's not why I'm here. I did not help you find justice for your younger brother. Your sister is still missing despite our attempts to search for her. But please help me save at least your life. Don't you have a French passport? Please buy a ticket as soon as possible, then take the next flight to France."

"Yes, I have a French passport. But why should I leave the country? Please, tell me what's going on. Am I being tracked to be also kidnaped or killed? By whom?"

"Carlos, I'm only saying to you the same thing I have been told. The soldier who called me did not tell me who was after us. When I said I have no issues with the state, he said the people hunting us, though powerful and connected, act in their personal capacities and not for the state. I guess he was referring to Kananga and his gangs of criminals."

I kept silent for minutes before saying, "I can't."

"You can't do what?" James asked.

"I can't leave my sister, Celine, whether alive or dead. Let them kill me the same way my mother was killed. Let them kill me the same way my brother was killed. Maybe Celine is already dead, and all of us can finally reunite in the invisible world. James, I have made that selfish mistake once; I can't do it again. If I had not left my sister and brother in Rwanda in 1998, maybe David would not have died and Celine would not be missing now. Let me do what's right. I have to take responsibility. I have to be there for our mother. Celine needs me now more than ever. How about David, whose soul continues to cry for justice? No, James. Please try to understand me."

"Okay," James said, seemingly disappointed by my thinking. "God knows I have done what I had to do. Sorry, I have no time to go into a philosophical debate about this. Just know your life is in danger. I have warned you. Now I have to go. Harumi is waiting for me. Please take this paper. These are my new names on social media. You can always send me a DM. I will check on you tomorrow as soon as Harumi and I reach our destination."

"New names? Why? Where are you going to?"

"I can't tell you now. Yes, the only way to contact me shall be via social media, mainly Facebook and Twitter. Those are the names I will be using. Brother, goodbye … I … no … everything will be fine. Be strong. As you once told me, sometimes all we can rely on is prayer. I'll keep you in my thoughts."

James hugged me tightly as his chest beat so fast.

I felt both love and abandonment. I was left alone to die, die for my siblings, die for my sister.

Though I wished I could just close my eyes and magically find myself surrounded by the four walls of my bedroom, it was not possible. I had to take a motorbike back to my place. Every turn the rider made, my heart jumped out of my chest at the thought that he could be delivering me to my killers. Any stop in a traffic jam meant a conspiracy to arrest me.

Arriving at my apartment was a miracle I thanked God for.

The whole night, I could not sleep. Any sound was as if somebody were trying to forcibly open my door. I was scared of the light because I thought it would reveal the corner I was hiding in. But I was also scared of the darkness because I thought it would cover the corner my hunter would be hiding in. I played hide-and-seek with death for the whole night, and somehow, I won.

The following morning, I made sure no sound came out of my room. No radio. No TV. No music. No sound of pots or plates. I wanted to convince everybody who could pass by that I was not in; I was nowhere to be found. Time was so slow. An hour felt like a whole day. I was in bed, hiding from the hunter who had not communicated when he would come hunting for me.

At eleven o'clock, my phone rang. I did not want to even look at who was calling. Maybe the journalists, I mused. Maybe my killers wish to locate my whereabouts. Perhaps someone wants to announce the death of my sister. I did not want to take that call.

The person on the line wasn't giving up. The phone rang again.

I took a peek at the phone screen as if I were afraid the caller could notice me from the camera lens. I could not believe my eyes. *These people are heartless,* I mused. How can they be calling me with Celine's phone number? Once again, I decided not to take the call.

The caller sent an SMS: "Carlos, it's me, Celine. Please call me back as soon as you can."

I looked at the message and read it like five times to convince myself I didn't imagine things. My heart was beating so fast. Anybody could be using Celine's phone, I mused. But what if it's indeed Celine? What if Linda was right that the drama on social media would push my sister's kidnappers to release her?

I dialed back the number.

"Hello, Carlos," the person on the line said, "how are you?" Her voice was not just familiar, but indeed Celine's.

"Sister," I said, "where are you? Where have you been? They said you were dead. Are you okay?"

"Don't worry," she responded. "I just wanted to let you know that I'm fine. I'm alive and safe."

"Where are you?" I asked again. "We searched for you everywhere. Celine, my sister, what happened to you?"

"Listen," she said. "I will give you answers to all those questions."

"When?"

"Tonight, if possible. I will tell you as soon as I'm in my apartment so you may come over."

"To your apartment? I mean ... Who will you be with? Why don't we meet somewhere out?"

"What do you mean by out?"

"On the street or on a restaurant terrace somewhere," I said. "The thing is ... I have been wondering what happened to you."

"Please, you have no reason to worry," Celine replied. "It's me, your sister. Can't you recognize my voice? If you want proof I'm safe and kicking, please tune in to KTV at two o'clock; I'm invited for an interview. After that, I will go to my apartment. You can come over at around five."

"Okay," I coyly said. "I will be there."

Now I was flummoxed. My sister had disappeared for two weeks. How could she reappear like that, claiming to be all right? Something in her voice sounded deceptive. It was as if Celine were acting in the movie of her own story. Maybe there were people behind her who had dictated everything she said to me. But I guess I had to take the risk of going to her place. If it was a trap, so be it. I deliberated.

As Celine advised, I turned on the TV and waited for the show she was going to appear on. I was wondering what she would talk about.

"Hello," the TV show host said to Celine. "Welcome to KTV. Thanks for having decided to come clear the rumors about your death."

"Thanks for having me," Celine replied.

Though she was wearing her exaggerated makeup with smoky eyes and a ruby-red lipstick, I could read wearisomeness on Celine's face. She was trying hard to appear on the top of whatever game she was involved in.

"Have you seen your own death announcements?" the TV host asked. "Some enemies of the state are claiming that you were kidnapped and killed. Please, tell Rwandans the truth."

"Haven't you said they are the enemies of the state?" Celine asked. "What else would you expect from them, except their usual unfounded rumors? It would help them to just drink water and relax. I'm fine and have no problems with anybody."

I couldn't believe Celine was the one talking. But indeed, yes, those words had just come from my sister's mouth. She said the news about her disappearance was rumors. *Where has she been? I* wondered. *Was the whole nightmare I have lived for weeks just a bad dream?*

"Do you mean nothing happened to you at all?" the TV Show host asked my sister. "Some people were accused of having masterminded your disappearance and later your assassination. Please, tell the world those people are innocent."

"Yes, of course. Mr. Kananga, and anybody else who has been cyberbullied for no reason, are innocent. I had gone somewhere in the countryside to take some time for meditation and rest. That's something I do very often. Those haters have no other agenda but to use my name to tarnish the image of my country leaders, whom I owe much respect and loyalty."

"Thank you so much. You're a true patriot. They also linked you to Mr. D. His real names were David Mukiga. They said he was your brother and that you accused state agents of his assassination."

"Me? No. David and I indeed came from the same womb. But he ceased to be my brother the day he went to live with his paternal family, which turned him into a genocide ideologist. He died when he was trying to escape prison. The officer who killed him was just doing his job."

When Celine said that about our younger brother, David, I felt disgusted with the person my sister had become. I wondered if I should ever trust her again. It's true she had been a victim of the world's madness, but I could not accept that she had allowed the world to turn her against her own brother. *Why does she hate David that much?* I questioned.

"Now people know the truth about your supposed disappearance," the TV show said to Celine. "Shame to the enemies of Rwanda."

"Shame to them, indeed," my sister responded. "I'm here, alive, and safe. My fans should not believe the rumors circulated on social media by those enemies of the state."

When I wanted to turn off the TV and stop listening to

the hurtful words of my sister, the TV show host said, "I have one last question. What projects are you currently working on?"

"Now, you're talking," Celine replied. "That's the conversation I enjoy the most. I have a big project I'm working on and can't wait to present it to Rwandans."

"Do you mind giving us just a glance of it?"

I waited to hear what Celine was about to say. I hoped what she told me about her project of recruiting all beauties into modeling was genuine and not a lie. *If she says the contrary, I will give up on her,* I weighed.

"I can't give all details now," Celine replied to the TV show host. "All I can say is that I would like to change Rwandans' view of the modeling career. It's not about being pretty. It's about mastering the art of showcasing one's beauty. Many of our girls don't know that modeling is an art like any other, and I believe that's what leads to their poor performance in international beauty pageants."

"What do you mean?"

"I guess it would take me a full day to explain what I mean. Let me try. You know that when we participate in international beauty pageants, we compete with those from other parts of Africa and girls from Asia, Europe, Australia, North America, and other places, right?"

"That's right," the host said.

"If that's the case, and considering the fact that some competitions no longer have the height requirement, what beauty standards do you think they base judgement on?"

"I don't know. Tell me."

"Here in Rwanda, most people judge beauty based on the facial features they culturally associate with prettiness. That's fine. But no Rwandan girl shall ever get crowned Miss World, Miss Universe, or even Miss Africa if we continue to choose them based only on our beauty standards without ensuring they have the right skills to showcase their beauty.

"That's interesting! But don't they learn cat-walking and other skills in boot camp? Isn't that what you're referring to as the art of showcasing beauty?"

"Yes, they do. But that's not enough. We need to select our models based on their talent and not their looks. That's what I would like to introduce. Modeling is an art, and only those who are creative and talented in that art can succeed in the modeling career."

"Do you mean you can pick even the ugliest girl in Rwanda to be a model?"

"Yes, you've got it. Those girls you call ugly may not meet what we perceive as Rwandan beauty but have features that are regarded as attractive in other cultures. But when they compete in international beauty pageants, with a diversity of beauty standards, what shall matter more is their ability to use their unique loveliness to attract the attention of whoever sees them or whomever they interact with."

"I wished we had more time for this interesting conversation," the TV host said. "To recap, let me remind our viewers that the rumors about your disappearance or death were baseless. It was just another miscalculated attempt by enemies to tarnish the image of the state. We also thank you for having told us about the new projects you are working on in your modeling career. Upcoming models can learn a lot from a legend like you. Have a nice evening. We look forward to welcoming you again to KTV in the near future."

Then they put on commercials, and I turned off the TV. I did not know if I wanted to meet my sister, Celine, or not. I was scared of the person she was or had become. How could she say she had gone to the countryside to meditate when the day she disappeared I was waiting for her at my apartment? Ingabire had also told me she heard the voices of people who kidnapped Celine. What kind of a dirty game was my sister playing? I wondered if what she had said about David was her own thoughts or part of whatever plan she was executing. She had invited me to her apartment. Should I really go there? Could I trust Celine? I had no answers.

I freshened up, wore blue jeans, a gray T-shirt, and a black cardigan, but decided to wait for Celine's call before taking the trip to her place in Kacyiru. I wanted her to be the first to start the conversation. I was sure she knew I had a lot of questions about her disappearance and what she had said on that TV show.

XIV

After thirty minutes, my phone rang. I took the call.

"Hi, Carlos," Celine said. "I'm at my apartment. You can come now if that's okay with you."

"Okay," I coolly responded before adding, "Celine, I have watched your TV interview and heard everything you said."

"I know," she responded. "I'm the one who asked you to tune to KTV. But please, let's not talk about that. All I wanted was to see you. Haven't you missed me?"

"Are you asking if I missed you? You can't be serious. Please don't tell me all you want is to repeat to me everything you've said on TV. I need to know the whole truth. You can fool others, but not me."

"Just come to my place," she said. "I may not say to you everything you expect to hear. But at least be assured that I will tell you where I was, and I hope that's what matters."

"Okay. I'm coming."

I decided not to take a motorbike but a cab.

Arriving at Celine's place, I looked at the building as if I were about to face doom. Nothing easy to chew would come out of my conversation with my sister. Whatever had happened to her or made her vanish would definitely be hard for me to stomach.

In the lobby, I pressed the elevator button. When it opened, I entered after checking if nobody else was inside.

On the fifth floor, I got out and headed to Celine's apartment, then rang the bell.

After checking through the peephole, my sister opened the door and welcomed me in.

When I entered, she immediately fell on my chest and said, "Thank you for coming. Brother, in this world, you're all I'm left with. I'm sorry for everything. Please find the strength in your heart to forgive me."

Her eyes were wet, but I didn't know how to console her. She did not look like the stony person I had watched talking on TV a few minutes earlier.

I held her hands as we walked to sit on the couch.

"Tell me everything," I said. "Where were you? Who did it? Please tell me. I'm listening."

"I was in hell," she said. "The devils … I was surrounded by all the devils of this Kigali. I had seen the faces of some of them before. Others, I didn't know them. Brother, I'm afraid. But at the same time, I feel stronger than ever. I have lost it all. I have nothing more to lose. I'm ready for the fight. It's a promise to myself and to my late mother. If it's a game, I'm ready to play. I know all their tactics, and I will apply them better than they can."

"You still haven't told me where you were," I reminded her. "What did they do to you? Who did it?"

"The thing is … I signed a pact with them that I shall

never tell anybody. They sold me my own freedom, and I accepted to buy it, paying a part of it."

"What do you mean?" I asked.

"If I had not accepted to play their game, I would be dead by now. I had to accept to say what you heard me saying on TV and be used as their shield or else they would have ended my life and told their own version of the story."

"Do you mean everything you said on TV is not a true reflection of your thoughts and feelings?"

"Have I ever cared about politics before? Do I even know what enemies of Rwanda they were referring to? The only thing that was genuine in what I said was about the modeling project. I am more determined than ever to implement it. But I shall have to apply smart tactics and make sure nobody wakes up before I reach the heights of what I'm up to."

"How about what you said about David? Sister, that hurt my heart more than anything else. You shouldn't have said on TV that your brother was a genocide ideologist, whatever that means. Did you think about his supporters and fans, who are now going to think of him as a bad person?"

"Carlos, I'm sorry. It's true that I did not have the best relationship with David because we were separated by how the history of Rwanda affected our paternal families. You know well that my entire paternal family was exterminated during the genocide against the Tutsis, when most of David's paternal family may have been among those who committed the genocide."

"That's true. But you should have kept in mind that David was the youngest son of our mother, Kayitesi. During the genocide, David and I were hiding in the same kitchen with Mama before she was killed. Whenever the militiamen came to torture her, David, who was only seven years old, saw everything. He remembered the day Mama was killed. Mama had never talked about the so-called ethnicities. He never associated any of us with our fathers' race or ethnicity. We were simply her children. That's what should have kept the bond between you and David."

"Carlos, you don't know what you're talking about. You were not in Rwanda to witness how David changed after he went to live with his paternal uncle. He had become another person. I could not recognize him anymore. I was also still traumatized by what I had seen during the genocide and mourning the death of my family members and of our mother. I needed my brothers. You had gone to France. Then, David, the only brother I was left with, cared only for his paternal family."

"I thought we already discussed this," I reminded Celine. "Didn't we both conclude that David was troubled by what he had experienced during his tender age? So why are you talking badly of him again? Please listen. I'm sure David loved you and longed to be with you. Maybe he also felt rejected by his maternal family and his own siblings. What made you feel he only cared for his paternal family?"

"Whenever we met, all David told me was about his father's death. When his uncle, Mukinzi, was killed, David accused me of being an ally to his worst enemy, the devil, Kamara. He used words I cannot repeat. He said I hated him because he was a Hutu and accused me of being evil. Then, whenever I talked to Kamara about David, he convinced me that my brother had become as bad as his Hutu relatives who committed the genocide."

"Did you believe Uncle Kamara? What else do you think he would have said to you? Wasn't he the one who had refused to take David to his house because of the ethnicity he associated him with? Who masterminded the assassination of Mukinzi, David's paternal uncle? Do you still have any doubts Uncle Kamara is a criminal? How about our mother's house? Wasn't Uncle Kamara interested in making the house his and selling it for money?"

"Carlos, I have a lot in my mind now and don't think I have the strength to talk about the difficult relationship I had with my dear younger brother. I'm so sorry for what I said about our brother, David. Despite all those misunderstandings, I loved him and miss him so dearly. Yes, I have always known that Uncle Kamara was evil. But now I know for sure he is a devil in a human body. Our uncle is a monster. He is a bloodsucker. He can do anything, including eating a human body."

"The day you disappeared, you were going to see Uncle Kamara, right? Please tell me what happened after that."

"Brother, please forgive me for not giving you all details now. It's not that I don't trust you. It's just that I have signed a pact of silence with those devils. I'm afraid of the consequences of breaking the pact. The devils I'm referring to seem to have eyes and ears everywhere, including under our beds. But I can promise you something: I'm ready for their game."

"You must tell me everything," I insisted. "I need to know

what happened to you. A few minutes ago, you seemed broken and ready to burst into tears. Now, you're acting again like the person I saw on my TV screen. I don't get you."

"I'm coming," Celine said as she walked to her bedroom. "You're my brother. If it's to die, I will be glad to die in your hands."

I wondered what she was going to bring and what she meant by dying in my hands.

When she returned from her bedroom, she was in an East African traditional long dress. She had also covered her head with a scarf as if she wanted to disguise herself as another person.

"Let's go down to the poolside," she said.

"Why?" I asked, wondering what Celine was up to.

"I want the fresh air," she replied. "Let's go out to see the sunset."

"At this time of the evening?" I asked. "Can't you see it's already dark?"

"Don't worry, there are enough lights. You will like it. You will see the reason why these apartments are expensive."

"All right," I said as I followed my sister to the elevator.

Arrived at the poolside, we took seats on one of the benches. My eyes and ears were all my sister's.

"The day I was kidnapped was the second-worst of my life," Celine said. The first was the day I survived death in 1994 when I was lying in the blood of my relatives. My kidnappers looked like the militiamen who killed my entire family during the genocide against the Tutsi. I had never been humiliated to that extent. They spat on me. They slapped me. That was before they injected in me something that put me into total sleep. When I woke up, I was naked and in a big empty room, all walls painted black. I was alone. I could not talk because I had a black piece of cloth in my mouth, knotted at the back of my head. Both my hands and legs were tied. Nobody came to that room for many hours. It was so totally dark that I couldn't tell the day from the night."

Celine went silent as if she were fighting with tears that wet her eyes.

"Did anybody later come to the room?" I asked. "Did they keep you there, hungry and thirsty for days?"

"I don't know how many hours or days had elapsed before he entered. I immediately recognized the sound of his steps and the perfume of his body. He kept on making moves in that room without uttering any word. You remember that I was fully naked. It was so scary. Because of how dark the room was, I could only see his silhouette and the white vest he was wearing but couldn't see what he was holding in his hands. After a few minutes, he left the room."

"You still haven't told me who that person was," I said.

Celine looked left and right to check if nobody else could hear us. Then, she said, "Kananga. He is the one who ordered my kidnapping. Martin, our brother's former music manager, was also among the guys who had executed the kidnap. However, I had not recognized him because the kidnappers were wearing masks. After Kananga left the room I was in, he sent Martin to bring me food. That's the time he whispered to me that I should behave well if I wanted not to be finished and forgotten. Those are the exact words he used."

"I can't even find words to say," I said. "Sorry would not be enough. My sister, I can only imagine what you went through. You're a strong woman. Tell me, were you still naked when Martin brought you food?"

"Yes. I guess their main aim was to humiliate me. He had a torch in his hands and scrutinized my body as if he wanted to show me that he could do anything he wanted with it. I refused the food. Martin told me that I was making a big mistake because, according to him, I needed to be strong enough for what he called a challenge. He pretended he was on my side and that all he was doing was giving me pieces of advice on the ways to appease the anger of Kananga. He advised me to apologize to Kananga and tell him that I will never dare again break up with him."

"Did you do that? I mean, have they released you because you apologized to Kananga?"

"No, I did not. Instead, I made the matter even worse. I told Kananga everything I thought about him, including that I suspected he had a hand in the death of our brother, David. That's the day my real calvary started. Now I know the meaning of the word torture. He did not do it himself. He went out of the room. After a few minutes, I saw a silhouette of another man entering the room I was in. He poured a full bucket of water on me and thumped me with a stick. I couldn't believe that was happening to me. I was still naked. I will never heal from that humiliation."

"Sorry, my sister," I said to Celine. "Those people are indeed devils. When you told Kananga you suspected he was behind the death of our brother, David, did he confess to you that he indeed did it?"

"No, our brother was not killed by Kananga," my sister responded. "Bosco, the prison officer who shot David dead, had been paid by no one else but our maternal uncle. Yes, the assassin of our brother is Uncle Kamara."

"What? Do you mean our own uncle killed our brother?"

"Yes," Celine replied.

I had always suspected Kamara but wanted to convince my mind he could not go as far as killing his sister's son. Since Kananga was the one who had hired Martin as David's music manager, I wanted to believe that he was the one who was behind the death of our brother.

"Did Kananga tell you that David was killed by Uncle Kamara?" I asked, before saying, "That monster shall pay for the blood of my brother. I will not go back to France before he is put behind bars."

"Stop it," Celine said. "Please, listen to me till the end. Don't rush anything. I have a plan. I have told you those people are devils, and unfortunately, we are somehow in hell with them. So we have to master the game before starting to strike. I will also not leave this world before Kananga and Kamara are punished by either this world's justice or God's justice.

"How did you know Kamara is the one who masterminded the assassination of David?"

"After days of torturing me because of everything I had said to him, Kananga apologized for the anger. That's the day he told me that he was also saddened by the death of David. He said that he could never have planned to kill a blood brother of the person he loved, referring to me. He added that he had believed the story of the prison services before Martin revealed to him that Bosco, the prison officer who shot David, was paid by Kamara."

"So you got the information from Kananga," I said. "What made you think he was telling the truth?"

"I have lived in the same house with that old man for many years. I know all his quirks and can tell when he tells the truth or lies. Yes, brother, our own uncle, Kamara, is the one behind the death of our younger brother, David."

"We should report him to the police," I said.

"Report who? Where? We are reporting nobody to the police. I have another plan. I haven't finished telling you the whole story. After Kananga apologized for the beatings, he continued to beg me to revisit my decision to end our relationship. I told him that I was prepared to die instead of being an eternal slave for his sexual desires. He did not utter a word. He went out and left me alone in that dark and empty room. That's the time, after many days, my head managed to let tears out. I cried for many hours until midnight, when Martin brought me a long dress and a wrapper and asked me to put on those clothes quickly because they were taking me to another place. I initially refused because I thought they were going to kill me. But Martin said nothing would happen to me and persuaded me to believe him."

"Where did they take you to?" I asked.

"At the time, I didn't know where they were taking me

to because they had covered my eyes. At least they had not given me the sleeping injection as they had done the day I was kidnapped. Now I know I was in Rebero. I was put in a better room with a private bathroom and had everything I needed—toiletries, clothes, food, and drinks. The only thing they could never allow me to touch was a phone. Though I was not allowed to get out of that room, I still have nightmares of the voices I heard in that house. What was happening in the other rooms must have been indescribable."

"What do you mean?"

"I don't even know how to describe it because I saw nothing and nobody. Every night, I could hear the voices of people shrieking and moaning. Some of them yelled that they were innocent. Brother, I'm sure some people were being executed. I could recall that Kananga used to tell me that he had eliminated some people. However, I had never cared to know how and where he performed those criminal acts. Every night in that room at Rebero, I prayed to God, thinking that somebody would come and tell me I was the next to be slaughtered."

"It's as if you're narrating a horror movie," I said to Celine. "Did you know I was searching for you? I had reported your disappearance to the police. But when I realized they were not doing much to find you, I decided to hire a motorbike taxi rider to inspect Kananga's compound. That motorbike rider saw you the night you were moved from the first place to the second. That was a few days before he was shot dead by a policeman. His death is what caused the chaos on the internet."

"What are you talking about?" Celine asked. "Did you know where I was? I don't think it was at Kananga's place because I had not seen that big dark room before. Who was that motorbike rider? You shouldn't have taken the risk. Some motorbike riders are actually agents of those high-class criminal gangs who seem to be connected to the rulers of this country. I'm sure they killed him after getting the information he was spying on them. Brother, you should be careful. This Kigali has become like those world cities where the rich and powerful are able and ready to eliminate everybody in their way. What did the motorbike rider tell you before he was killed?"

"Nothing useful," I said. "All I was told is that one day, after midnight, the motorbike rider saw your car being driven out of Kananga's compound. Tell me how they reacted when the news about your disappearance was trending on social media. Is that what made them decide to release you?"

"Yes, I guess. Yesterday morning, nobody was talking to me. The whole house was quiet. I could hear neither the voice of Kananga nor that of Martin. Last night, there was no sound in the house. The silence was scary. I wanted to get out, but the door to my room was locked from behind. Imagine being in a locked room without knowing its location and having no phone to call for help. I was convinced that's how they had decided to kill me: by hunger and thirst. I decided to sing so that somebody could come to my rescue. In the morning, I was surprised to see Uncle Kamara. He is the one who came to tell me that I should go to KTV and say what you heard me saying."

"Uncle Kamara? Was he also involved in your kidnap? How about Kananga? Where is he now?"

"I don't know where Kananga is. Uncle Kamara has told me that I needed to save my life and that of Kananga. So he made me sign a paper, a pact with the devil."

When Celine said, "a pact with the devil," she burst into tears, and all I understood was that it was serious.

"What are the terms of that agreement you signed with them? How did Uncle Kamara come into the picture?"

"Brother, don't ask me. I have signed that I shall never reveal to anyone that Kananga was my sexual partner. I will never say I was kidnapped and kept secretly somewhere. Surprisingly, the agreement includes that I shall never ask questions about the arrest and the assassination of my brother, David."

"Did you have to sign it?"

"Yes. I signed it because there were consequences for not signing that pact or breaking it after signature: death. I would not have gotten out of that house if I had not accepted to sign the damn paper."

"Was your appearance on TV also part of the deal?"

"No," she responded. "It wasn't written on that paper. But Uncle Kamara persuaded me to do it to save Kananga."

"What do you mean?"

"Apparently, Kananga was summoned by some people from the president's office."

"Did you say the president's office?" I asked. "Is Kananga that connected? Why would the president get involved in the story of your disappearance?"

"I'm not sure he was summoned by the president himself," Celine said. "Uncle Kamara said he was called by the president's office. Kananga is one of the most influential people in the ruling political party. His reputation is somehow tied to that of the party. It seems like when a situation gets too political, all government institutions, from top to bottom, get involved. Didn't you say you had reported my disappearance to the police? What had they done? I believe I now know where to touch to get those criminals finished, and that should be the stone on which we should base our plan for revenge. The keyword is politics. I'm now going to be a master of it."

"What was Kananga summoned for? Had those people in the president's office believed what was circulated on social media, or did they already have some reliable information?"

"He was questioned about our relationship, my disappearance, and the motorbike rider's death. I believe that, after the story trended on social media, the police immediately started to search for me, and sooner or later, they would have found me. That's why Uncle Kamara told me that I needed to testify publicly that Kananga was innocent. He added that if I had refused to do it, they would have had no choice but to kill me and bury the corpse where it would never be found."

"Did Uncle say that to you? Was he the one who was tasked to kill you? That man must be a real devil."

"He said he was only there to warn me and persuade me to sign the paper and go to the TV station. He continued to repeat that he was doing everything out of love because he did not want me to die like my brother, David."

"Did he dare to mention the name David? You should have told him you know he is the one who got our brother killed."

"I wanted to slap him for daring to mention my brother's name after I learned that he was the one who got him killed. But I recalled I was in an unknown place and with that wickedest person I have ever met in my life. I had to swallow my anger and show him I was glad he wanted to save my life."

"Then what did you do?"

"After taking a shower, I put on clothes and wore the makeup they had brought to me. Uncle Kamara gave me back my phone, but I decided to call you when he walked out for a few minutes before deleting the call history again. That's it. That was my calvary. I'm glad I am back to life, physically safe but emotionally torn apart. However, I need to stand on my feet and pretend I'm strong till the day I will have fully executed my revenge plan. Both Kananga and Kamara shall have to pay for all the years I have been their sex slave. Kananga will be punished for the kidnap and the torture I endured. Kamara shall not leave this world before paying for having assassinated our brother, David."

"What's your plan? Why don't you want us to report them to the police? I mean, now that we know the high-level authorities do not condone what they did to you. Sister, I think we should use the judiciary system instead. I have now learned my lesson. If I had not tried to solve the issue by myself, that motorbike rider would still be alive, and—"

"Yes, the motorbike rider would still be alive," Celine interrupted. "But I, your sister, would be dead or still tortured by my kidnappers. Brother, though I would not advise you to take similar risks in the future, I thank you for your bravery. You saved my life. The police would have never found me, not because they did not want to search for me but because there are gates they never open. When climbing a mountain to the top is not feasible, the best option is to go around it, so nobody realizes you're moving up. That's what I'm going to do. They won't see me moving. They won't even know I have any intention to move. That is, till the day they will open their eyes and find themselves in my vengeful hands."

"You haven't told me how you intend to do it," I said.

"Brother, do you know why those devils kill and save whoever they want without being caught or punished for their crimes?"

"I don't know," I said.

"It's important to know where they get that power from. The keywords are *politics, money,* and *fame.* That's what I'm going to search for. When I shall get them, I will have acquired the power to change the course of their game. Wait and see. Just, as my brother, promise you will be by my side."

"How can I be on your side when I don't get what you're planning to do?" I asked. "Are you going to play politics?"

"No. Politics shall just be useful to deviate their attention so that they won't notice what I will be up to until I have reached the top of the mountain. The most important steppingstones shall be money and fame."

"Aren't you famous already? Haven't you told me you have enough money to sustain yourself?"

"No, brother, my fame does not reach all corners of the

world, and the money I have is not yet enough to earn a *Forbes* mention. But when I will have reached the mountain-top, everything I shall say will reach the entire world. Then, if anybody ever dares to touch me again, the whole world shall interrogate him. You can't imagine how I felt like a little nothing when nobody was coming to my rescue. I felt as if I could vanish from the scene without anybody's notice. But when the news of my disappearance hit social media, my kidnappers had to change their plans. Kananga, who had vowed to make me his lifetime sex slave, agreed to set me free, and till now, I don't know in what hole he was hiding. Could the president's office people have cared if my story had not trended on social media because of the little fame I gained as Miss Rwanda 2000? Imagine if my fame were a little global; believe me, even the masters of diplomacy and geopolitics could have been involved."

"Maybe you're right," I said. "But I need to understand the entire plan."

"Don't worry," she said. "I will tell you. Look at the time. It's already nine o'clock. Are you staying for the night? Let's go inside."

For the whole night, Celine explained to me what she intended to do. It sounded in my eyes like a mathematical equation with many unknown variables. All I understood was that she needed money and fame if she wanted to have the same influence Kamara and Kananga had and be able to change the game. I told her politics was not a safe ground to play on, but she seemed unstoppable.

I said good night to her, walked to the guestroom, then lay down on the bed, my head on the pillow, eyes facing the ceiling. Though I had found my sister, who had disappeared for weeks, I was more troubled. Whatever the future held for us terrified me.

XV

In the morning, my phone rang. The caller's phone number belonged to Mukandoli. I took the call.

"Hi, Carlos. It's me, Habimana. I was released from jail yesterday."

"Habimana!" I shouted. "What a big surprise! Are you in Nyamirambo? I will come to see you today or tomorrow. But first, tell me, have you finished your sentence?"

"No. Haven't you watched the news? I'm among the prisoners who have been pardoned by the president. I'm so grateful."

"All right. I'm now far from Nyamirambo. I will call you as soon as I reach the area."

"Was that the man who killed our mother?" Celine asked. "Why have they released him? I wonder why this government decides to release those genocide perpetrators before they even finish their short sentences, which can never compare to their crimes."

"Have you forgotten?" I asked. "I told you that Habimana did not kill our mother. Our mother was delivered to the killers by Mukandoli. That man was jailed only because he had wanted to save our house from being taken and sold by Uncle Kamara."

"Ah, sorry. Yes, you told me that Habimana's wife is the one who killed our mother. But I don't see any difference between a wife and a husband. As far as I'm concerned, they are both Interahamwe. Did I hear you saying you're going to meet the man? Please don't. Carlos, you should remember that all eyes are now on us. What shall people think if they see you with somebody convicted for having committed the genocide? Our plan will be destroyed before we even start to implement it. Imagine news that Celine and his brother now work with genocidaires?"

"No, Celine. You can't ask me not to talk to him. Now that Habimana is free, he is the only person who can tell me what happened the night our younger brother was killed."

"Please don't go to see him now. It's not yet time to ask more questions about David. We have to show everybody that we have no problem in this Rwanda. We only need to ally ourselves with the powerful; I mean those who can push us to the mountain. Habimana is not one of them but a Hutu who was jailed because of his involvement in the genocide. So please, stop any contact you have with that man."

"How often do I have to repeat that Habimana did not involve himself in the killings? He is the man I owe my life to. If he had not hid us in his kitchen, we would not have survived the genocide against the Tutsi."

"If he is that good and innocent, why did he not save our mother? If it's true that his wife is the real culprit, why did Habimana not report her or at least divorce her? Carlos, the man you're going to see lives in the same bedroom with the woman who delivered our mother to the killers, and you're telling me that man is innocent? No. Please, don't go there."

"Okay, I won't," I said to Celine.

"Thanks," she said. "Brother, it's not that I'm a bad person. No. It's just that I don't trust those people. What they did to our Tutsi families is indescribable. Sorry to say, but sometimes I think that you act as if you're detached from these realities. Maybe it's because you went to France and feel now distanced from the issues of Rwandans."

"Celine," I said with a louder voice. "What are you talking about? Do you now see me as a French, the same way you saw David as a Hutu? What did you see in this Rwanda that David and I did not experience? Haven't I told you what we endured during the genocide against the Tutsi? Or do you think you're now more Tutsi than we are? I'm surprised at you."

"No, brother," she said. "I'm sorry. Please, don't get me wrong. I did not mean to say you're not Rwandan or that you did not experience the genocide. I was just wondering why it's easy for you to talk to those people."

"Which people?" I asked. "Do you mean I shouldn't speak to Hutus?"

"No. I meant those who were involved in the genocide against the Tutsi. Haven't you forgotten that my best friend, Ingabire, is also a Hutu? I don't hate all Hutus. No, I cannot hate anybody for who they are. But here we are talking about Habimana, a genocide convict who is married to the woman responsible for our mother's death."

"I have told you Habimana is innocent. I wish I had been there during Gacaca courts; I would have defended him in public. Suppose his sin is that he is married to Mukandoli. Will you also tell me that you would end your friendship with Ingabire if you had learned that her parents were involved in the genocide?"

"Ingabire told me her parents died. She is an orphan. I don't think her parents committed the genocide."

"Do you know the circumstances of their death? Have you ever wanted to know? I am not insinuating she could be the daughter of a genocide perpetrator. I simply would like to show you that even if she was, it wouldn't have made any difference to the good person she is."

"What a coincidence!" Celine said as she was getting her ringing phone from the table. "Can you imagine she is calling me?"

"Who?" I asked.

"Ingabire," Celine responded before adding, "Listen, Carlos. Maybe you need to make yourself a cup of tea and grab something to eat for breakfast before leaving. I need to speak to Ingabire in private. She is coming."

Before I responded, Celine accepted the phone call and started talking to Ingabire. After the greetings, she invited her to come to her place in Kacyiru. Celine had no idea I knew what Ingabire was bringing to her. I wanted to ask her what the medicine was about. But if I did, I would have ended the relationship with the only person my sister apparently trusted. Ingabire was maybe not a friend in the correct terms of that word but the kind of friend Celine needed, a friend who listens without questioning and a friend who gives love without expecting to be loved back.

"Breakfast is ready," I said to Celine, after making the tea and putting butter spread on our bread.

"I'm coming," Celine said.

At the breakfast table, I said to my sister, "Dear, I'm going back to my apartment. Don't worry; I will not go to see Habimana today. Not because he was involved in the genocide, for I know he wasn't. I won't see him only because you said it might jeopardize your plan, though I don't see the link. From now on, I will follow your rules and won't make any move before seeking your approval."

"Thanks, brother," she said. "We need to be super careful. Otherwise, we might end up dead like our brother, David."

I did not say anything more. Celine had believed my lie. All I wanted was to leave her apartment on a good note. She had failed to convince me that her revenge plan, as she called it, included seeking justice for David, and I knew I could not count on her for that.

After breakfast, I said bye to Celine, took the way to the bus stop, then headed straight to Nyamirambo to see Habimana. Now that he was free, I was looking forward to what he had to say to me.

Before I arrived at his house, Habimana sent me a message and suggested that it was better to meet at a bar not far from his home. I immediately understood he did not want his wife Mukandoli to eavesdrop on our conversation. But I thought of what Celine had warned me about. Is it safe to be seen in a public place with a genocide convict? I wondered before inviting Habimana to come to my apartment instead. Even though he could be seen entering the house, I wanted to believe that since my neighbors did not know him, they would just take him as a random visitor.

At my place, Habimana knocked on the door. He looked right and left as if he wanted me to immediately welcome him in. He told me it was his first time leaving his house after getting out of prison.

"Kigali has changed into a more developed city," Habimana said after taking a seat in my living room. "I could not recognize some of the buildings and the streets. Though it's a walking distance from my place to here, I was afraid I could get lost."

"Yeah, things change," I said. "Remind me, how many years were you wrongly incarcerated for?"

"Half the sentence, eight years. I'm grateful to the president."

"You shouldn't have been sent to prison, even for one day. I understand your decision, but I wished your wife had paid for her crimes, not you."

"She will face God's judgment," Habimana said. "I have heard about your sister. Is it true she was not kidnapped as she said on TV?"

"I think so," I said, before adding, "She has said she had gone somewhere for meditation. So I guess I have no reason to doubt her."

"Okay. The good thing is that she is all right. Rwandan women seem unpredictable."

"Yes," I replied. I did not want that conversation about

Celine to go on because I would not tell Habimana the truth about my sister's disappearance.

I stood up to check if I could find some fruits in my fridge. There were only apples. I cut them and served Habimana.

After two apple bites, Habimana said, "I wanted us to talk about David. He left me with a big task, and I don't know how to accomplish it."

"Yes," I said. "Now we can talk about my brother. Tell me, was he killed by the prison officer, Bosco?"

"How did you know?" Habimana asked, astonished.

"Hmm? No. Nobody told me Bosco was the assassin of my brother. It's just that he was acting weird the last time I was at the prison. Do you know he told me you were the culprit?"

"Yes. You can't imagine how sad and angry that made me. How could that criminal dare say that I caused the death of David, whom I considered my son? Bosco wanted both of us dead, but God saved me. I will never forget that night."

"Were you also going to escape from prison?" I asked.

"No. None of us had any plan to escape. It was all make-believe."

"What happened then?"

"I was in my corner when another prisoner called David and said some prison officers wanted him out. Then, when they headed to the place where the officers were standing, not far from the south fence, I tiptoed behind them because I did not understand why they would call him in the middle of the night. As soon David approached the officers, all I saw was that David was down, and I heard him moaning that he had been shot. I guess they used a silent gun. Though I immediately ran from the scene, one of the officers saw me and called my name. I recognized his voice. It was Bosco, the officer you met at the prison. The following morning, David was reported to have been shot trying to escape prison."

"Oh, my! Do you know the name of the other prison officer?"

"No, unfortunately, I don't."

"Why didn't you report the truth to the authorities? Maybe they would have made those officers accountable for my brother's death."

"In what court of law?" Habimana asked. "The story plot seemed complete. Journalists even came to photograph the rope David was purportedly planning to use to escape. It was tied to the fence, and they concluded that somebody outside the prison was an accomplice. They would have finished me before that truth could reach this country's high-level decision-makers. At least I am still alive to fulfill the promise I made to David."

"What task did David assign to you?" I asked. "I mean, what did you promise to do for him? Are you now ready to report the truth to the courts, should the case be opened?"

"Yes. I'm now ready, though I think we should plan it carefully and gather more evidence. First, we need to know why Bosco wanted David dead. Sorry to say, but I suspect your uncle, Kamara."

"Why do you suspect Uncle Kamara was involved?" I asked, pretending I did not know Habimana could be telling the truth.

"Never mind," he said. "Maybe Bosco was acting on his own. It's just that David did not have the best relationship with your uncle. But the most important thing is to search for more hard evidence that can be accepted in court. I don't think my testimony would suffice."

"You may be right," I said. "You still haven't told me what David tasked you to do for him."

Habimana reached for the bag he had placed on the chair next to the one he was seated on. He took a hard disk drive from that bag and then handed it to me.

"Connect this drive to the computer. It contains songs David wrote and recorded a few months before he was jailed. It was as if he could sense his days were numbered. He instructed me to keep the disk out of reach of anybody so that, should he die before publishing the songs, I should put them out for him. I remember how happy he was whenever he told me that he wanted those songs to be hits even after his death. He said it was the truth he wanted to tell this mad world."

I trembled as I held the HDD in my hands. I was not ready to listen to David's songs. I needed to be alone and have a brother-to-brother conversation with him. I needed to hear him sing his questions to me so that I could sing my answers to his resting soul. Receiving that HDD felt like receiving a precious gift from the younger brother I had abandoned.

"Thank you," I said to Habimana. "I will not listen to them now. I want to save them on my computer and my HDD and give you back the one David left in your hands. After that, I will think about how we can publish his songs. Please, give me some time to explore options."

"I also have some of David's clothes with me at home. I did not want to take them out of our bedroom because Mukandoli would have asked questions. Though it seems as if she had repented, my trust is still broken."

"I can imagine. I wonder how you manage to live in the same house with the woman who betrayed you to that extent."

"You will understand when you have children. Some people think only women get trapped in an unhappy marriage because of children. But when their mother is a woman like Mukandoli, the husband has to take responsibility. As long as she continues to cook my food and lay in my bed for the sake of our children and everything else we have built together, I will stay in that marriage."

"Who am I to judge you?" I asked. "As you said, maybe I will understand when I get married."

Habimana and I continued to chat about his family, the past, and the direction our country was heading into. He seemed to be more optimistic than I was. He was amazed by how the city had changed and grateful to the president who had pardoned him. He thought highly of Rwanda's leaders, which made me wonder why before I asked myself why not. He was probably one of the many Rwandans who praised the new leaders for having ended the war without involving the country in other endless armed conflicts. Contrary to Habimana, after everything that had happened to my siblings, I was one of the pessimistic Rwandans who wanted peace beyond not being in a war.

After more than two hours of conversation, I saw Habimana

off to the gate and came back into the room to play David's songs.

Usually, I did not like hip-hop because it did not sound as musical as the songs I loved, blues and jazz. But since I was more listening to the words than the beat, I found the music in the rhymes and the poetic language my brother used. I could not imagine I was listening to the boy I had left in Rwanda in 1998 when he was only eleven. *David was super intelligent*, I pondered. As I listened, trying to decipher the metaphors in the lyrics, I heard one song with the word *muzungu*. I thought David must have been referring to me. I replayed it four times, writing the few words I could catch. It was something like:

> Pigs had eaten Mama, but I was scared for dogs. Muzungu left me in the jungle; he ran away from the animals 'cause he believed he was more human. Who am I? A pig? A dog? I am a fundi. Eeeh! Eeeh! Eeeh! Don't be dogs. Don't be pigs. They eat, eat, eat, and die like pork, I mean hot dogs. A fundi eats trash but dies like a king. Eeeh! Eeeh! Eeeh! Don't be dogs. Don't be pigs.

It was not easy to decode all the song's lyrics. I understood that David thought I had left him in the jungle because I wanted to run from the animals. By the jungle, he must have meant Rwanda and compared Rwandans to animals, some as pigs and others as dogs. He also dedicated many songs to a girl named Bwiza, which means "beauty." Initially, I thought

David had something about women because his songs were full of misogynistic language. But as I continued to listen to those songs, I had a feeling that he was probably talking either about Celine or Linda. Among the songs, there were also those that sounded political and seemed less charged with figurative language than others. One of them went like this:

Waifs and strays are not counted as orphans. They are rejected by the society that schools real orphans, those whose names are on the lists. Let me dance to the song of streets. Rulers don't see all the angles. Protractors are treated as rebels because they see all angles. I hate rulers. If they knew how to measure all angles, they would measure my corner and tell me the angle degree of my orphanhood.

I continued to reflect on how to publish my brother's songs. I knew Celine was not going to approve it. Maybe she could even do whatever possible to prevent the songs' publication.

After a few seconds, I thought about James. Without him, I felt so lonely. I needed a brother to run to whenever I needed some guidance. The day James left Rwanda, he had told me that the only way to contact him was via social media and gave me the pseudonym he would be using.

Since the day the news about my sister's disappearance was trending on social media, I had not opened my Facebook account. In fact, I had realized social media was a world I did not want to live in. It was a place where all madness was exposed and a forum in which all fools had the chance to express their simplistic opinions on the most complex societal issues.

Now I had no other option but to search for James on Facebook, which I did. I had dozens of notifications, and when I clicked to check, I was shocked to see that some people knew I was a brother to Celine. They had tagged me on the insulting posts they had written about her. It seemed the members of the opposition groups who had called for my sister's release were disappointed after she said she was never kidnapped. They claimed to have credible information about what had happened to her. They accused her of having sold her soul to save her brother, who was allegedly persecuted after the news of her disappearance trended on social media. By her brother, they were referring to me. That was not true. Nobody had harassed me, and Celine could not even have known if anybody bothered me. I decided to stop reading those social media posts because the insulting language they were loaded with made me feel sick.

James's pseudonym on Facebook was Angelas Umutoni. Umutoni is a common female name in Rwanda. He had probably picked Angelas instead of Ange or Angela because he wanted to be distinguished from many Rwandan ladies with that name combination on social media. After finding him on Facebook, I opened the messenger to write to him, only to see that he had tried to communicate with me in vain.

In his first message, he had written, "Carlos, I watched your sister's interview and was shocked to read that she was never kidnapped. What's going on? Please let me know.

Harumi and I are doing well. Since last Wednesday, after spending days in Uganda, we are now in London. It was a miracle to get the visas. Please tell me, how are you doing? I'm reading social media and feel lost with everything going on."

I never replied to the message.

Since I did not reply to his first message, it was clear that James had taken my silence as a refusal to communicate with him. In his second message, he wrote, "I can't believe you've decided not to talk to me. You're one of the few people I trusted in that Rwanda. But I shouldn't be surprised. Maybe you've been coerced to play the same game your sister is playing, though I don't get it. But, brother, if it's for your survival, that's all right. I don't want to be the cause of anything that could happen to you. Take care."

"It's not that I did not want to write to you," I responded. "It's just that a lot has been happening that I did not get time to check messages on social media. In fact, I wanted to talk to you, but I'm not sure if it's safe to write down everything here."

Luckily, James was online and responded immediately.

"Carlos, don't you know you can now call via messenger? It's safer. If my laptop ends up in the hands of anybody, they will be able to read these messages but won't have access to the content of our calls. So tell me, what's up there?"

I briefly told James that my sister did not want to expose her kidnappers because that was her promise to them before they released her. However, I did not tell James everything Celine had told me, for I was not sure how James could use that information. When I told him about publishing David's songs, James immediately suggested that he could do it. He said that he would do it as if the songs were released by David himself. Though his stage name was Mr. D., James suggested adding Badguy, the nickname my brother was known for among Inzuki boys. So, he decided to make it "Mr. D. the Badguy." Unfortunately, he could not use the same channel David had created on YouTube because he had no access to the account. James gave me an email address to which I could send the recordings via Google drive, and I did. I must have trusted James a little too much. In life, I believe we all have that one person we tell everything on our mind, then leave it to the fate to decide whether or not they shall betray us.

XVI

The following weekend, I decided to call Habimana because I wanted to inform him that I had found someone who was going to publish David's songs. So we agreed to meet at one of the cabarets in his neighborhood.

"I have found a person who shall publish David's songs on all major music platforms," I said after we ordered soft drinks. "He will not put them only on YouTube but on different other sites."

"That's good news," Habimana replied. "I trust you for having checked the integrity of that person."

"Yes. He is a friend of mine. But I'm not allowed to reveal his names to anybody. The songs shall be published as if it's Mr. D. himself uploading them, at least for what the public shall see. He said he will use Mr. D. the Badguy as the artist's name to attract the attention of all David's fans."

"That's settled," Habimana said, before he scratched his head, pretended to adjust the seat, and added, "but I don't think it's all we have to do for David. His spirit has been visiting me in my dreams, and though he did not say it, I felt as if he were asking me to seek his justice. Carlos, I have an idea …"

"Tell me," I said. "Is there any way you can help me get evidence that Bosco killed David?"

"Bosco? No. That would be difficult. I can't think of anyone who can get words out of their mouth. But, please, don't take it the wrong way. I suspect Bosco was acting on your uncle's account. That prison officer threatened to kill me one day and said I shouldn't have messed with Kamara. When I asked him what he meant by that, he walked away and left me wondering if he was talking about a different Kamara."

"Do you mean we should rather find evidence about the involvement of Uncle Kamara in the assassination of David? How? Do you want to spy on him?"

"Yes. I actually already discussed it with Mukandoli. I did not tell her it was about the death of David. She has agreed to befriend Kamara and take recordings of whatever he says, including how he had sent me to prison. I have told her that it would be the only way to avoid another plot to send me back to jail."

"Mukandoli?" I asked. "Do you trust her that much?"

"No, unfortunately, I don't. So hard to live with a wife I don't trust. But I know she can do anything to save herself from trouble. I have threatened to reveal what she did during the genocide against the Tutsi and talk about her involvement in the theft and falsification of your mother's house documents."

"Yeah," I said. "Mukandoli is your wife and I respect that.

But I would be happy to see her punished for having delivered our mother to the killers."

"She will be punished. If not by the world's courts, she will face God's judgment. She seems repentant. Whether she means it or is playing another game, I want to take advantage of her moments of weakness. I will now use her as my eyes and ears for whatever Kamara does and says. Please, tell me if you're okay with the plan."

"Yes, you may go ahead. But please make sure Kamara does not suspect I'm involved. Do not tell your wife how David was killed or that you want to seek his justice. Instead, pretend you have grudges against all members of our family, including myself."

"That's the plan," Habimana said. "I will tell her it's only for clearing our reputation and saving our marriage."

"Thank you. I guess I now have to go. Nobody should see us together."

As I was going back to my apartment, my phone rang. I took the call.

"Hey, Carlos," Linda said. "I wanted to thank you. Celine has called me. We will have our first meeting tomorrow. She wants to launch the modeling company next week. If you had not introduced me to her, I would not have gotten the biggest opportunity of my life."

"That's good news indeed," I said. "Now, you have many reasons to be more disciplined. I guess you understand what I mean. Celine is so strict with respecting time and commitments. So you need to be the soberest you can ever be."

"Don't worry about that. I have already decided. No more smoking or drinking. I'm starting another chapter of my life."

"That sounds good."

"Carlos, listen, please. I'm sorry for what I said to you about your sister, Celine, the other day. It's Fofo, my friend, who had told me everything. I hope you did not tell her I knew where she was. I have chosen to believe what she said on TV."

"Don't worry. I didn't tell Celine anything. My sister was not kidnapped. As she said on TV, she had taken some time away for meditation and rest."

"No need to talk about that, whether true or false. Celine is now my boss, and I have no business in what she does with her private life."

"Wow! I like the Linda I'm talking to. Where did you fetch all that wisdom from?"

"How do you mean? So, you did not love me before because you thought I wasn't wise enough?"

"Stop it," I said. "Linda, you know I like you. You're like a precious sister to me."

"A sister? I thought I was just a friend. Now a sister? I'm not sure if it's a promotion or a demotion. But if I had to choose between being a sister or a friend, I would choose to be your friend."

"All right. You're my best friend."

"That sounds much better. I have been promoted from a 'just friend' to a 'best friend.' How about celebrating it?"

"What do you mean?"

"I mean, if you're at your place, I can come and spend some time with you. Or we may go out and share a drink."

"A drink? Haven't you just said no more drinking?"

"Yes. No more alcoholic beverages. I will go for Fanta orange like a virgin."

We laughed before I said, "Let's plan it for tomorrow. Today, I want to spend time with only myself. I have a lot to ponder on."

"If you say so," Linda said with a lower voice. "I hope you won't come up with another excuse tomorrow."

"No, I won't."

After arriving at my apartment, I checked my messenger for any messages from James, a.k.a. Angelas Umutoni. There was a YouTube link. A new lyric song by Mr. D. the Badguy. The song was titled "Ubuhanuzi," which means "prophecy." Only ten minutes had elapsed since it was posted. Still, it already had hundreds of views and ten heart-touching comments. One of the comments read like this: "The king of hip-hop has risen from the dead. Pilato and his loyalists must be shaking of fear for the explosive miracles his spirit might do."

As I listened to the song and read the comments, my phone rang.

"Hi, Celine," I said. "How are you?"

"Are you at your place?" she asked. "We have to talk as soon as possible."

"Yes, I'm at home. What happened?"

"You know what happened. But we can't talk about it on the phone. I'm on my way."

She hung up.

Yes, I could guess what had happened. Our younger brother had resurrected, and I was enjoying his new prophecy.

Luckily he was now immortal, and nobody could kill him again.

Celine was already in Nyakabanda and knocking on my door in less than twenty minutes.

"Hi, sister," I said. "Welcome. Is it not your first time coming here?"

"No, it's not. But it's my first time entering your apartment. I once gave you a lift from your office and dropped you here. The day I had planned to come and share dinner with you, the devils had their own plan."

"Yeah, the good news is that you're here again. What may I offer you for a drink?"

"Not now. Please sit down. You know why I'm here. Who has uploaded David's song on YouTube? Everybody is calling me."

"Who is calling you? And why?"

"That's not my question. Tell me who has uploaded that damn song. Carlos, I hope you're not behind this. You can't do that to me, can you?"

"First, I don't know who has uploaded the song," I replied. "Second, I don't understand why you should be bothered by the fact that someone is perpetuating the legacy of our younger brother."

"What legacy? Why would his legacy live on at the stake of our lives? You have no idea how many people have been offended by that song's lyrics. That's not prophecy. He was singing politics. Go to social media, and see what that stupid old man who calls himself the opposition leader has posted."

"A stupid old man?" I asked, laughing. "Who is that?"

"There are names I can never mention, and that is one of them. All I know is that the man's name must have something to do with Mana or Mungu."

"Are you talking about Twizeramungu? What has he posted?"

"Yes, that ingrate enemy of his own country. Go and read what he has written on Twitter. I'm afraid that the fact that he is using our brother's songs for his dirty propaganda may put us in trouble. Carlos, we have to make sure that song is removed from YouTube. We are the only siblings to David, and nobody has more rights than we do on his so-called songs."

"No, sister. I won't do that. I was not there when David was writing and producing those songs. Our brother had his own circle of friends who proved to him family love more than we did. If he chose to entrust his legacy with those people, who am I to claim ownership of the most precious gift he offered to the world that rejected him?"

"Why did I think I could count on you?" Celine said, seemingly disappointed by my response. "You have always sided with David as if you agreed with everything he did and said. Maybe you are also … I mean, you probably have the same ideas as those in his songs, the so-called prophecy. If you can't help me remove that song from YouTube, do never attempt to preach to me about family love when I decide to deny David publicly. I have a lot at stake and won't allow him to ruin my plans."

"Sister, don't worry. David, our younger brother, won't ruin any of your plans because he is dead. They killed him. Have you forgotten?"

After saying that, I left Celine in the living room and walked to my bedroom to swallow back the tears that were already wetting my eyes. I did not know what to think of my sister. After the kidnap and torture she had experienced, I had thought that she would be more empathetic to what our younger brother had endured before he was murdered. But it seemed Celine had somehow adopted the same mindset as those she called devils. Like Uncle Kamara, my sister was ready to eliminate whatever would be in the way of her plans, and that scared me.

"Brother, please try to understand me," Celine said when I walked back to the living room. "This is not about David. It's about our survival in this Rwanda. If we are not careful, we might end our lives the same way our younger brother ended his."

"Celine, please, let's change the subject if you like. I don't want to ever talk to you again about our little brother. Whenever I want to talk about David, I will kneel down and call out our mother's name or God in heaven. Did you say David hated you? He never did. You hate yourself. Sister, why did you allow the world to make you who you were not raised to be? Please forgive me. I'm sorry. I don't mean to hurt your feelings. I just wanted to tell you that, now that David is no more, you should at least respect his memory."

She stood up and stared at me for seconds before saying,

"You're all the same. What did I expect?" Then, she walked out on me without saying bye.

As I watched my only sister stepping up to the gates, I wanted to cry but couldn't. I only leaned my head on the wall in an attempt to reflect on Celine's attitude. *Does she hate David only because he is the only one she can hate without consequences?* I wondered. I concluded that maybe my sister did not hate David but hated being a sister to a boy who was not among those celebrated by society for everything from beauty to character. I felt pity for my sister, Celine. Then I said to myself, *After all Celine experienced, the last person she should despise is her own brother, David, who wanted nothing but the best.* When Celine was declared the most beautiful girl in Rwanda, David, her younger brother, was being bullied for his looks. When the Government's Assistance Fund for Genocide survivors was taking care of Celine's school, David lost his way to school after his paternal uncle was assassinated. When Celine was making money as a model, David was in the streets living at the mercy of other street boys before he decided to make hip-hop music. The only people Celine should blame for what had happened to her were society's arrogant and violent people. Those who were praised for patriotism, despite how destructive their fight mentality was to our beloved country.

When I checked the internet and social media for more comments about my brother's new song, I was shocked to see that Badguy was trending everywhere. This included the social media pages of those who politicized everything.

On the one hand, those in the opposition groups called my brother their hero, even though most of them did not know any of his songs before he was jailed, accused of having a genocidal ideology. On the other hand, The propagandists and loyalists of the ruling political party were trying hard to tarnish his name and legacy. But many young people, especially those in the entertainment industry or those who identified themselves as free thinkers, only celebrated the fact that a Rwandan singer had refused to die the same way Bob Marley had not. Some of them did not shy away from reminding politicians, political activists, and propagandists that David was a fundi who did not care much about politics. To these young people, my brother was just expressing his anger at the world that had made him an orphan and later a street boy.

It was not only on social media where the news of my late brother's new song was trending. The publicity Mr. D., as he called himself, had not received when he was still alive, he was getting months after his death. Isaha.com, the online newspaper, often criticized for being a propaganda channel for the ruling party, had published an article titled, "Investigations have started on who released a song of Mr. D. In that song, the artist who called himself Badguy seems to incite people to rise against the government." In the body of that article, they wrote that David was a genocide ideologist who was shot dead trying to escape prison. The writer of that article encouraged the youth not to be fooled by that drug addict who was manipulated by the enemies of Rwanda.

On the other hand, another online newspaper, nduwirwanda.com, associated with the opposition groups, had also published an article about Mr. D's new song and stated that my younger brother's prophecy was addressed to those in power.

I wanted to also take it to social media and tell everybody that my brother's message was addressed to all members of society. To those associated with the killers of his mother in 1994 and to those associated with the postgenocide system that turned my brother into a street boy, accused him of having a genocidal ideology, jailed him, and assassinated him. In David's world, the villains had neither a particular color nor a particular name. His prophecy was addressed to all those who used their political, social, or economic power to oppress the powerless.

When I wrote to James, a.k.a. Angelas Umutoni, via Facebook messenger and told him that I wanted to write something on social media, he discommended the idea.

"No, if you write anything about the song," he said, "all you will be doing is shifting those extremists' attention from your brother to you. You may not be able to handle their verbal abuses."

"James, I think we made a mistake. We shouldn't have decided to release my brother's songs. Some people have started to harass my sister. She says we should ask YouTube to remove that song from the platform for copyright reasons. I have told her I have no right to claim ownership of David's songs. But after reading the newspapers, I feel somehow scared and wonder what I should do to calm the storm."

"Don't worry. Tell whoever asks you that you have no idea who has put out the song and whether or not they have the copyright to it."

"So far, nobody else has talked to me about it but my sister.

Even on social media, they are only talking about David and the song, but not Celine or me. It's all about the lyrics of his songs, some praising them for the truth they contain, others accusing them of inciting people for insurrection."

"Brother, I'm sorry to say, but one of the people you should be careful with is your sister. So please, don't tell her anything about David's songs."

"I won't," I said.

"I have an idea," James said, after a few seconds of reflection. "Is your sister still planning to open up a modeling company?"

"Yes."

"I will send you James's telephone number—"

"Do you mean your number?" I interrupted.

"Stop it. I'm not James. I'm Angelas Umutoni. The telephone number I'm sending to you can only be dialed or texted to communicate to James, not Angelas Umutoni. I believe you understand what I mean. Do never send to James messages that should be addressed to Angelas Umutoni."

"I get it," I said. "Sorry for that."

"That's all right. Please give James's number to your sister and tell her I asked you questions about the project you had told me about. Then, if she wants to contact him about photography or anything related to modeling, she can text or call him."

"And how shall that help us?"

"James shall do all he can to gain your sister's trust and become the ear she talks to whenever she feels like talking to someone outside her current circle of friends and acquaintances. Through James, we will keep an eye on her plans and moves, maybe not all but some."

"Do you think she will open up to you, knowing that you're my friend?"

"You've done it again," James wrote, and added a smile emoji. "I'm not James but Angelas Umutoni."

"Oh, sorry. I meant to ask if Celine shall open up to James, knowing that he is my friend."

"It will depend on how James shall approach her. Leave it to him. He knows what he will say to her to immediately gain her trust."

"Okay. I will give Celine James's number. James should take care of my sister and remind her that self-love is the only shield that protects us from harm."

"He will. Don't worry about that."

XVII

After my conversation with James, I decided to close my eyes to see if I could catch some sleep. But only a few minutes later, my phone rang.

"Hello," I said.

"Hello," the caller responded. "This is St. Luke Hospital. Are you Carlos, Celine's brother?"

"Yes. What happened to my sister? Where is she?"

"She had an accident. But don't worry. It wasn't serious. She is being taken care of. The doctor would like to speak to her close relative. Is it possible for you to come now?"

It was already six. I put on trousers and rushed immediately to that hospital.

After I arrived there, they showed me my sister lying on the hospital bed, with a bandage on her forehead and another one on her legs.

"How did it happen?" I asked the nurse.

"Go to door number 126; the therapist is waiting for you."

I knocked on the indicated door, and a light-skinned lady who seemed to be in her late fifties welcomed me in. She was not in the usual doctor's white coat. Her smile was so welcoming, as if she were inviting me to drop all my burdens in front of her.

"How are you, Carlos?" She greeted me by my first name after introducing herself to me as Dr. Mbabazi.

Though it was a standard greeting, it sounded like a question I could not respond to.

"Sorry for what happened to your sister. She will be fine. I have called you here because I wanted to help your sister. Is it the first time she has attempted to commit suicide?"

"What? Do you mean Celine tried to kill herself?"

"The police are investigating the circumstances of the accident. Your sister has told me that she decided to hit the electric pole in an attempt to kill herself. But it seems she had not taken enough time to evaluate the implications of her decision. Self-harm and suicidal thoughts are symptoms of mental unwellness. Have you spoken to her recently?"

"Yes," I replied, wondering if I should tell that therapist what I had discussed with my sister. "In fact, she was coming from my place," I added. "We did not have a good conversation. But I'm not sure I can tell you what it was about because I don't know if she would like it."

"That's all right. You don't have to tell me what you're not ready to say or what your sister may not like anybody to know. Do you have parents?"

"No, we don't. Our mother was killed during the genocide against the Tutsi. Celine had gone to pay a visit to her father. She was found unconscious, surrounded by the corpses of her entire paternal family, including her father. That's how she survived the genocide."

"That's sad," the therapist said. "Does she often talk about what happened on the day her family members were killed?"

"No, she never tells the entire story about what happened to her during the genocide. After July 1994, we found her together with other children who were treated by the Red Cross. Silence had become the only way she expressed her sadness. A few months later, she was taken to live with a maternal uncle and … I mean … I also left the country and went to France. When I returned, my younger brother was dead, and my sister had changed into another person."

Though I did not want to continue that conversation, I felt like staying in that all-white room, which smelled like a sanctuary and where I could hide from all the noise.

"You have said your mother was killed during the genocide. Were you with her? How about your younger brother?"

"Doctor, I'm sorry. I don't want to talk about what we endured during the genocide against the Tutsi. No, I will neither talk about my mother nor my younger brother. Please tell me, how is my sister? Why does she have bandages? Is she severely wounded?"

"She has mild injuries and is receiving the necessary care. They have also run x-rays and other tests, and all revealed she is okay. That's why I'm focusing on her mental well-being. The best start is to understand your family background. I understand and respect that you are not ready to discuss everything. That's okay. Please, have my business card. You can call me anytime you feel like talking to somebody."

"Thank you," I said. "How about my sister? When do you think she shall be released from the hospital?"

"I don't know. But I believe she will be released tomorrow or the day after tomorrow."

"Doctor, I'm sorry I have no energy to tell you more about our family now. But please help my sister. I am worried about her."

"I will. That's why I'm here. I also want to ask you for a favor. Please, be more patient with her. It's hard to tell what she is psychologically suffering from. But all indicators show that she needs therapy. I will talk to her. She may initially hesitate, but I believe, one day, she will accept help. Don't tell her about our conversation today."

"I won't," I said.

After my conversation with Dr. Mbabazi, I went back to the room where my sister was. She had woken up.

"Sorry for what happened to you," I said to her. "You will be fine."

She looked at me for a second and tried to turn her head to the other side, but she couldn't. She decided to close her eyes.

I had a lot to say to her but remembered that Dr. Mbabazi had advised me to be more patient with my sister.

I watched her for about five minutes before I walked to the nurse and asked her, "Please tell me. What should I bring for her?"

"A toothbrush and toothpaste. You can also bring toiletries and some undergarments if you can. She may be discharged tomorrow or the day after tomorrow."

I did not have the key to Celine's apartment and had never bought toiletries or undergarments for any woman before. So I decided to call Linda.

"Hello, Carlos," Linda said. "I hope you're not going to postpone our plan for tomorrow."

"Unfortunately, that's the reason I'm calling you. Where are you? Can we meet in town, please? I need your help."

"What happened?" she asked. "Where are you? I mean, where exactly?"

"Let's meet in front of Isoko supermarket."

"Okay. I'm taking a bike and will be there in ten minutes."

It did not take long before Linda was there.

"Carlos, don't tell me they are after you. Martin has come to see me. They want to know who has put out Badguy's song."

"It's okay," I said, without thinking about the meaning of what I was saying. "That's not why I have called you ... But wait, did you say Martin came to see you? Why? What did he say?"

"He only asked if I knew who published the new Badguy song. When I told him I didn't know, he said, 'It must be that muzungu.' I understood he was referring to you. Martin thinks you and I are in a relationship. Please, Carlos, be careful. Those people seem to have the right and the power to harm you."

"What do you mean by 'those people'?"

"Martin and whoever he works for. There are things I can't tell you. But just know that Martin is dangerous. He thinks I am an idiot and that I never understood his telephone conversations with some people."

"Conversations about what?" I asked.

"I won't tell you. Just know that they are looking for the

person who released that song, and they suspect it could be you. Anyway, tell me why you called me."

"My sister, Celine, is in a hospital. She has had an accident, but it's not serious."

"That can't be. Where is she? Please don't tell me she is … no … not when I was starting to think that my life was going to change. No. Please tell me Celine is okay."

"That's exactly what I just said. My sister is all right. I only wanted you to help me buy things she needs, like toiletries and clothes."

"Clothes? What kind of clothes?"

"At the hospital, they only give her the normal ugly blue dress. She needs what to wear underneath that dress."

Linda laughed and said, "I get it. We need to buy for her some unmentionables, right?"

"Yes. Please take my card and go and buy whatever you think fits Celine. I will be waiting for you here."

"No, come with me. Let's go and buy it together from Nana Lingerie Shop."

"Stop it. I can't go there with you. What shall people think?"

"They will think you are accompanying me to buy my secrets. How romantic, isn't it?"

"Linda, you should know the right timing for jokes. I'm serious. Please go and buy whatever you think my sister needs."

"Okay. Don't get angry if I also buy for myself," Linda said as she walked to the shop.

As I waited for her, I reflected on what she had told me

about Martin. *Is Linda still in a relationship with Martin?* I wondered. Then, why did she call him a dangerous person? I could not comprehend why the postmortem release of my brother's song was shaking some people. I wanted to ask James to stop releasing other songs but felt I should not do that to my brother's legacy.

"Here you are," Linda said, handing me what she had bought for Celine. "Take your card. I did not buy anything for myself because tomorrow you're buying me a drink."

"Thanks, Linda. But I'm sorry I won't make it tomorrow. I would not be able to give you my full attention, knowing that my sister is in a hospital bed."

"That's right," she said. "Can we go together to see her?"

"Yes. But now it's too late. They wouldn't allow us in her room. I will go there tomorrow morning. You can come along if you like."

"Thanks."

When we were walking to the road to stop bikes, Linda asked why I had not yet bought a car.

"Because I don't have money to buy it," I responded.

"Stop it," she said. "A muzungu who works in a big company like STC but doesn't have money to buy a car? Maybe you want to pretend like those bazungu who call themselves volunteers and walk around Kigali in flip-flops."

"Linda, please. I'm not a muzungu. I'm an African. I'm Rwandan."

"Yes. But it's really awkward to see a handsome muzungu like you always jumping on a motorbike. You should buy a car."

"I will when I will get money."

Two bikes stopped in front of us, then we jumped on them.

At 7:30 in the morning, Linda was at my place, ready to accompany me to the hospital to see my sister, Celine.

"I have had a bad night," Linda said. "I could not sleep. It was the nightmares of the genocide again. Shall you please accompany me somewhere after we visit the hospital?"

"Oh, sorry for that," I said, before asking her where she wanted me to accompany her.

"I want to go to the genocide memorial. It's the sanctuary I normally go to whenever I want to speak to my mother's spirit. There, I feel her presence. She listens to me and responds. I normally go there alone, but today I would love to go there with you. You're the only person I feel comfortable talking about my dreary life."

"Linda, do you remember the first time you spent a night in my room?"

"Yes, I do. Why are you asking?"

"You had nightmares of what you experienced during the genocide against the Tutsi. That's the time I developed a brotherly affection for you. I felt your pain, and it was as if we were linked by what both of us saw when we were too young to understand why human beings had turned into ferocious wild animals. I could see my sister in you. I could see my mother in you. I was in your world because I could also see the same killers you saw in that nightmare. My dear, may I reveal something to you?"

"Yes," Linda replied.

"I have never been to the genocide memorial," I said. "Since, apparently, everybody goes there, including foreign tourists, when people ask me, I lie that I have also been there. Because I don't want them to ask me why I haven't. To me, it feels like going back, not to the memorial but to the genocide. I feel as if I would see the corpses, the machetes, and the killers again. Maybe the whole place would smell death. It would probably make me hate living in this world. But, my dear, thank you for opening that door for me. I will not refuse. From the hospital, we will go to the genocide memorial. I believe I also need to talk to my mother. I have a lot to say to her. Maybe I will smell her perfume and hear her telling me that it will all be fine one day."

When I finished talking, Linda was in tears. I pulled her to my chest and hugged her tightly for about five minutes.

"Thank you," she said as she moved away from my arms. "Let's go to see Celine."

"Yes," I said. "We have to go. Let me get what we bought yesterday."

At the hospital, Celine was awake, and when we greeted her, she responded.

"Sister, how are you this morning?" I asked her. "Better than yesterday?"

"Yes," she responded. "They have calmed the pain and said that I will be discharged from the hospital tomorrow." Then, she turned and said to Linda, "Thank you for coming to see me. I have meant to call you and ask you if you went to see the person I recommended to you."

"Yes, I did," Linda responded to Celine.

"What are you talking about?" I asked.

"It's girl talk," Celine responded. "Linda has big plans for herself, and she has made big decisions to turn those plans into a reality. As soon as I recover from these self-inflicted injuries, you shall start to see Linda on TV, modeling for the most prominent fashion houses."

"If that's what you were talking about, you have my full support. I don't know much about modeling, but if it's about beauty, a company of you two shall catch the world's attention."

"Linda is not just pretty," Celine said, "she is also talented. Did she not tell you about our first informal casting? This girl has a lot to offer."

"Do you mean you already did an audition? I'm not sure if that's what you also call it in modeling."

"Yes, sort of. It was just me, the girls, and two photographers. We can't do anything bigger before I register the company."

When Celine was happily talking about her project, I wondered if she was the same person who had attempted to commit suicide two days earlier. But I decided I shouldn't ruin the mood by talking about why she was lying on the hospital bed.

When we said bye to her, Celine called me as if she wanted me to stay behind for a minute.

"Brother, I'm sorry. I don't know what came over me. The last thing I remember is that I decided to hit that electric pole and leave this world for good. It's not the first time I have attempted suicide, and whenever it happens, I feel even worse about myself."

"It's okay, sister. You shall be fine. I was shocked when the hospital called to tell me that you had had an accident. I blamed myself. But I guess what's more important now is your health."

"They have recommended for me to see a therapist," Celine said. "She is a wonderful lady. Her name is Dr. Mbabazi. She is like an older version of my friend Ingabire. They are both attentive listeners. I will have sessions with her once a week till the day I will feel much better. Though I don't know what she will do or say to heal me from those suicidal thoughts, so far, I feel good when talking to her."

"Yes, it's scary when a person decides to take her own life. But, sister, though I'm not a psychologist, I think you should tell the therapist about the hallucinations and the pain killers. I believe you know what I'm talking about."

"Yes, I will tell her. Carlos, please understand me. It's not that I'm a bad person. I'm afraid you may also turn against me or betray me like every other person I have met in my life. It is as if I cannot keep any healthy relationship. My mother left me in this world. My younger brother hated me till his death. My uncle abused me. No boyfriend has ever loved me as much as I loved him. Every person I meet comes into my life for their own interests, then abandons me as soon as they get what they want. Brother, I'm afraid that, probably, one day, you shall also hate me and abandon me."

"Don't worry. In this world, it's just two of us, Kayitesi's children. I have you, you have me, and it will remain like that forever, no matter what. So please don't also say nobody else loves you. How about Ingabire, your friend?"

"Yes, Ingabire loves me. But you have made me realize that I have not been empathetic toward her pains, which she does never talk about. One day, I shall invite her and lend her my ears so she may tell me more about her family and what she endured in life. Can you imagine she is on her way here? She is always available whenever I need help. I can't thank her enough. But sometimes, I'm afraid that, one day, she shall also give up and abandon me."

"No, dear, she won't. No need to think negatively about what people might do or shall do. You should always expect the positive."

"Thank you," she said.

"Sister, I have to go. Linda is waiting outside. I will pass by again in the evening."

"Okay. Have a nice day."

I rushed outside and apologized to Linda for keeping her waiting.

"It's okay," she said. "You needed to talk with your sister in private."

From the hospital, we headed to the bus stop. Then, we jumped on the one to Gisozi, where the Kigali Genocide Memorial was located.

"Linda," I said after we took seats on the bus, "shall you tell me the person Celine was talking about? The one she said she recommended you should meet?"

"Why do you want to know? Celine is now like my elder

sister, and we also have our secrets. Did I ask you what you were discussing with her a few minutes ago?"

"Linda, stop it. Aren't you my friend? Please tell me. I hope you're not meeting another guy."

"And if I were? Are we not just friends?"

"No, we are not. We are best friends. Have you forgotten? Best friends do never hide anything from each other."

"Okay, my best friend. It's nothing serious. Celine sent me to a lady she calls my personal coach. I thought coaches were only for sports, but it seems I have somebody who should teach me how to walk, talk, eat, basically everything."

"I don't get it," I said. "Is that person teaching you how to walk and talk? How?"

"Yes. She wants me to be like Celine. I shouldn't be too loud or too soft. I should walk like a cat, eat like a European, and wear neither too revealing nor too covering clothes. I didn't know it was that hard to be a model."

"Do you like it?" I asked. "I hope they don't change you into another person. I like you the way you are, so natural and unpredictable."

"Don't worry. I'm doing it for the modeling job. Off the stage, I will be myself."

"Are you sure? All models I know walk and talk as if their aim is to please photographers and videographers. Anyway, if you want to succeed in that career, maybe you have no other option but to listen to that personal coach."

"Yes. Since my childhood, I have always been fascinated by models, and I never thought I could one day get the chance to be one of them." After saying so, she added, "Hey, let's get out. We need to buy flowers from here, then walk to the memorial."

I felt bad that I had not even thought about flowers. Maybe I had refused my mind the permission to think about the genocide memorial. But I knew we were not going to the memorial to talk about modeling or any other common topic. Instead, we were going there to pay respect to hundreds of thousands of victims of the genocide against the Tutsi, whose remains were inhumed there.

Linda picked two tiny bouquets of flowers.

"Why don't we take these bigger ones?" I asked.

"I normally take the small ones because they are cheaper," she replied.

"Don't worry. I will pay."

"Okay," she replied, taking the bigger bouquets.

When we entered the memorial gate, the guides we met at the reception greeted Linda by her name. It was as if she were one of their regular visitors.

Looking at the white building surrounded by calm greenery, I felt as if I was at the only place I could consider home. I felt my mother's presence. I had a lot to say to her. I wanted to hug her tightly and finally allow myself to sob.

"Let's go to the graveyard first," Linda said. "If you want to do a tour of the memorial, you can do it after visiting our mothers."

Our mothers? I mused over it for seconds. Yes, my mother was also in one of the graves at the memorial. I thought about calling Celine and asking her the number of the grave Mama was in. But I had no words to tell her where I was and how I had come there. I wished I had told her that Linda and I were going to the memorial.

As we descended the stairs, Linda was also silent. I figured that that was the acceptable behavior at the genocide memorial.

"Both my parents and five siblings are buried in this grave together with two hundred Tutsis from Nyamirambo," she said after reaching the graveyard. "We exhumed them in 2004 from the same mass grave where the Hutus had thrown them, then we brought them here for a dignified burial."

I noted that she called the killers Hutus without adding a qualifier like extremists or militiamen to exclude those who did not participate in the genocide. But the time was not right for me to start preaching that the words *Hutus* and *killers* were not synonyms. When it's about another person's painful experience, it's important to speak more to their emotional brain than talking to their logical brain.

"In 1994, the day the Hutus attacked our house and killed my entire family," Linda continued to narrate her story, "what I experienced was shock or trauma, and that's something to do with the brain. But in 2004, when we exhumed the remains of my parents and siblings after realizing how they had become, my heart broke into pieces I shall never be able to rejoin. Whenever I come here, all I want is to think about my parents as they were before they died. I can see them walking in the corridor of our house. I hear the noise my younger brothers used to make jumping up and down on their beds. I can see my elder sisters painting their nails. Here, I can lay my head on my mother's lap and let her touch my hair. I see my dear father reading a newspaper with a glass of beer in front of him."

Linda continued to talk about her family as tears flew on her cheeks. She was weeping and smiling, and I did not know what that meant.

"I'm so sorry for your loss," I said. "I can't even imagine how it feels when your entire family is exterminated in one day. When I hear a story like yours, I feel guilty for being luckier. Maybe it's what they call survivor's guilt. It's as if I have no permission to be sad or broken. I have to be strong for all people like you ..."

My voice immediately failed me. My chest swelled as if I needed to burst. Tears in my eyes said more than I could say with words.

After calming myself, I said, "Yes, my mother is also here. But I was not there to provide her a dignified burial. I also wanted to visit her grave, talk to her, cry for her, and tell her I am sorry that I did not keep the family together. I was not even in Rwanda the day her remains were brought here. I failed her. I'm a coward."

"It's okay," Linda said. "Please take it easy on yourself. It's not your fault. If Hutus had not killed our people, we wouldn't have faced this world alone. Whenever I come here, I talk to my mother. We argue a lot. I remind her that she left me alone and lonely in this world and tell her she has no right to question my behavior today. I'm no longer her girl but an orphan who has lost both dreams and direction. I smoke, drink, and entertain men, and that's not who my parents wanted me to become. But that's who I am today. Whenever I am here, I talk to my parents and siblings in silence. Nobody hears what I say to them nor what they respond to me. So please, let's take some time to meditate and talk to our parents."

"How about the flowers?" I asked. "Aren't we supposed to lay them on the grave first?"

"No, we shall do that after the moment of silence."

We spent about ten minutes of quietness facing the grave. Though I was at the genocide memorial, I did not think about the genocide but about our loved ones. It was not about the killers but the killed. It was not about the guns but the bond. It was not about the machetes but the human beings. It was not about hatred but love. I could see my mother smiling. I remembered her hair chignon. I visualized her welcoming visitors to our house; many of them did not survive the genocide. My beautiful childhood. The memories. The warmth. The love. I could see the little Celine and the small David during those innocent years. In that moment of remembrance, Mama would interrupt my thoughts and tell me that she continued to watch over us from wherever she was. She would remind me that I needed to be strong for her daughter, Celine. She would weep for what happened to David and tell me that David was the son she birthed and mothered and not what the world wanted to call him.

After that moment of silence and talking to our loved ones, we laid the flowers on the grave, played a Kwibuka song from YouTube, then left the memorial. I told Linda that I would come back to do a tour of the inside.

From that day, the memorial became my sanctuary, a place I went to whenever I needed to speak to my mother.

XVIII

On Monday, I had to go to the office. I had a lot of pending tasks. I was lucky to have a supervisor who was so understanding. My sister, Celine, was also discharged from the hospital, though she had to continue the sessions with the therapist. I was happy she was looking forward to the psychological help.

During the week, on Wednesday, I received a call from a number I did not have in my contacts.

"Hello, Carlos, it's me, Rotty. I wanted to inform you that I'm back in Kigali. Sorry that I left without saying bye to you."

"Hey, Rotty. Where are you? Are you in Biryogo at the Inzuki boys' compound?"

"No. That's actually why I wanted to talk to you. I have nowhere else to go. I have been advised not to go back to places like those because it may lead to a relapse."

"Where are you now? How can I help you?"

"I have spent the night in the house of one of the rehab center workers. But I can't stay here because he and his family are all relocating to Butare not far from the center. So, I was wondering if you could let me stay in your house for a few days, during which I will be searching for a job and a place to live in."

"It's all right," I said, though I was reluctant to welcome another person to live in my tiny studio. "Let's meet at the club Rafiki at six this evening. From there, we will walk to my place."

"Thank you so much, Carlos. I have no words to express my gratitude."

After work, I took the bus to Nyamirambo and dropped at club Rafiki to wait for Rotty.

When he appeared, I could not recognize him. Though he had kept his dreadlocks, he had changed a lot, with smooth skin, clear eyes, and whitish teeth. He was in blue jeans and a gray T-shirt, carrying a big book that looked like a Bible in his hands.

"Praise the Lord," he said as he gave me a hug.

"Did you say praise the Lord?" I asked.

"Uh, I did not realize that's how I greeted you. Carlos, I'm now a changed person. I gave my life to Jesus, the only repairer of broken hearts and savior of sinners. Without his mercy, I would not have been set free from the chains of drug addiction."

From a fundi to a murokore, I did not know which of the two I was more comfortable with. It felt as if Rotty had been set free from the chains of drug addiction only to be bound in the chains of spiritual irrationality.

"It's good that you no longer take drugs," I said, not making any comment about the savior who healed him. "Let's take this way and cross to Nyakabanda."

On our way to my place, Rotty told me about life in the rehabilitation center and the treatment approaches they apply. I did not know that in addition to behavioral counseling, they also give addicts some medication to manage withdrawal symptoms and prevent relapse. They also offer them training in other life skills so they may become more productive in society.

"Luckily, they told me that I was only at the beginning of stage three, which is not yet full blown addiction," Rotty said. "At the center, there were other people who had gone somehow insane. I felt their pain and thanked God that I was being treated before getting to that level of addiction."

"That's good," I said. "Was the introduction to religion also part of the treatment?"

"Not really," he said. "But they told us it was helpful to have faith and used to call pastors and priests to preach to us. The caretaker to whom I was assigned is a born-again Christian. Though his job does not allow him to focus on religion, we later became friends, and I learned a lot from his faith in Jesus. Then, one day, when the pastor came for prayer time, I decided to repent my sins and give my life to the Savior."

"Okay, I get it."

"Carlos, I wanted to ask you something, if you don't mind."

"What is it? Please go ahead."

"Are you the one who released the new Badguy song?"

"Why?" I asked.

"I know all the songs on that album. I was in the studio with Badguy when he recorded them. They are loaded with language and the messages this world may not want to hear. Please listen to all of them before putting them out."

"I did," I said.

"What do you mean?" he asked.

"I listened to the songs, though I could not understand that figurative language."

"So, does that mean you're the one who is releasing the songs?"

When he asked that, I recalled that any person could be used to spy on me. *Maybe Rotty has been sent to get words out of my mouth,* I mused.

"No. I don't know who is releasing the songs. I guess it's done by David's friends or his producer."

"But a second ago, you said you listened to all the songs."

"I meant I listened to the one he titled 'Ubuhanuzi.' Did he leave other unpublished songs?"

"Yes," Rotty responded, but did not say any other word. I gathered he did not believe what I had just said.

After arriving at my place, I found Habimana by the gates, waiting for me.

"Hello," I said. "You did not tell me you were coming."

"Sorry. I did not want to use the phone. You never know. Maybe one of our phones is on their listening."

"Please meet Rotty," I said to Habimana, before turning to Rotty and saying, "Please meet Habimana." I did not want to add more introductions.

"Nice meeting you," Rotty said to Habimana.

"Please, let me show my visitor in," I said to Habimana. "I will be right back."

He understood I did not want Rotty to listen to our conversation.

"I remember a guy like that who used to visit David at the prison," Habimana said when I came back. "Is he the one who is publishing the songs?"

"Yes, he was a friend to David. But he is not the one who is releasing the songs. Though he is a good guy, I have learned to be suspicious of everybody in this Rwanda. He has asked to live in my apartment for a few days, and I suspect he could have been sent by somebody."

"Please be careful," Habimana said. "That's actually why I am here." Then, he handed me his phone and earphones and asked me to listen to a recorded conversation between him and his wife, Mukandoli.

In the audio, Mukandoli was telling her husband that Uncle Kamara suspected I was the one who had released my brother's song. Apparently, my uncle was planning to kidnap me so I may not put out more songs. The woman said that my uncle was even ready to make me vanish from the earth for the sake of his reputation.

"What?" I said. "That man is sick."

"Carlos," Habimana said. "I think you should tell the person to stop releasing more songs and let people first digest 'Ubuhanuzi.' I would never forgive myself if anything, God forbid, happens to you."

"Don't worry. I will speak to Uncle Kamara and tell him I don't know who released the song."

"Are you sure he shall believe you?"

"I am not sure. But I will give it a try. I will talk to him as if we are in the same camp."

The following Saturday, I went to see Uncle Kamara at his place. I brought him a bottle of whiskey and chocolates for his kids.

"This is a miracle," he said as he welcomed me into his living room. "To what do I owe this visit?"

"To family bond," I said as I handed him the polythene bag carrying the whiskey and the chocolates. "Don't I have the right to see my uncle whenever I miss him?" I asked.

"Have you realized that only today?"

"Uncle, I'm sorry," I said. "Please forgive me for everything."

"For what?" he asked.

"When Celine disappeared, I lost my mind and told you words I shouldn't have said. I'm sorry that I suspected you could have had a hand in the kidnapping. Now I know the whole truth."

"What truth?" he asked, as if he were ready to deny whatever I was about to say. "What did your sister tell you?"

"She said she had gone for meditation or reflection. I did not believe her. Maybe, as you had suspected, Celine was having a good time with some of her naughty angels."

"Please don't say that about your sister," Uncle Kamara said, after a big laugh.

I knew I had gotten him. I was speaking his language, though I hated to pretend to be who I was not. But deep in my heart, I wanted to burst and tell that evil man everything my sister had told me.

"Did you believe the story she told on TV?" I asked Uncle Kamara, somehow showing him that that story did not make much sense.

"Maybe she was telling the truth? Who knows?"

"Yeah, maybe. I was joking. My sister is a good girl. She did not need to lie about that. Uncle, as I said, a lot has happened in our family in a way that led to mistrust. But after that experience, I learned that suspicions can lead to many mistakes. Imagine if I had taken it to newspapers and told them that Celine had come to your place the day she disappeared. You know those so-called journalists, don't you? They would have put it on their cover page: Miss Rwanda 2000 has been kidnapped by her uncle, who happens to be a city tycoon."

"Were you planning to do that?" Uncle asked.

"It was one of the options I contemplated."

My aim was to convince Uncle that he should not also suspect me for anything he did not have proof I did. It was my way of getting him to the point where he would believe I had nothing to do with David's new songs.

As I had predicted, Uncle shifted to another topic and said, "Carlos, there is something else I wanted to ask you. If you're the one who is publishing the songs of that mugger you called your brother, David, please stop it. Have you seen the noise his song has made? Check what those enemies of Rwanda, the fake politicians in the opposition, are saying about it: all sorts of conspiracy theories. You should be careful exposing our family matters in the media. It won't be good for any of us."

"You're right about that," I said. "I was also shocked to hear the language in that song he titled 'Ubuhanuzi.' My brother had turned into a dangerously angry person. But, Uncle, weren't we talking about mistrust? How can you even suspect I could be the one releasing those songs? At what point in time would David have given me them? Did I not come back to Rwanda when he was already dead? David had many friends in this Kigali, including the drug addicts he spent his time with. You should have been there the day he was buried. I am sure those people he mingled with are the ones who released that song. Only God knows if there are more songs to be published."

"Sorry I mistrusted you. Please help me find the members of his gang. I have already started my intelligence. Somebody said to me they call themselves Inzuki boys. When I shall find them, I will dismantle their beehive and bury all of them alive."

"No, Uncle," I said. "Don't say that. You are not an assassin. Let's find who is putting out the songs and ask him to stop."

"There is something else you could do for me."

"Like what?"

"Claiming the copyright. Nobody else but you and Celine have the right to the intellectual property of your brother."

"That's a possibility," I said, "but maybe the songs are being released by a label or a producer who registered the copyright. So before we make any move, we need to gather more information first."

"I know someone who can tell us about that. His name is Martin. He was the music manager your sister had found for David so he could keep him on a watch."

When he mentioned the name Martin, I recalled that Linda had told me that he had gone to her place to ask her if I was the one releasing the songs. Habimana had also heard from his wife, Mukandoli, that Uncle suspected I was publishing the songs and that he was ready to kill me. *What if Martin is hired to make all my uncle's suspects, including myself, vanish?* I mused. Then, I decided to sow confusion between Uncle Kamara and Martin.

"Yes, that person should have more info about the deals David signed with his producers. He will tell us who has the copyright. Maybe he is the one who wants to continue earning from my brother's songs. I understand YouTube and other music streaming platforms pay good money."

"No, Martin cannot release that kind of song," Uncle said. "He was not hired to help the stupid David produce those songs but to prevent it from happening. He knows well the consequences of publishing songs that could potentially fuel the anger of the lower-class people in this Rwanda."

"I heard you saying that he was hired by Celine and thought it was because my sister wanted to help David. Anyway, Uncle, I think nothing tells us Martin cannot release the songs for money because he realized David, Mr. D., or Badguy as he is known to the public, had a wide fan base. So please, don't exclude him from the list of people who could have published the song."

"All right. I will talk to Martin. I'm sure he will lead me to your brother's network of gang members, drug addicts, and muggers. I will make sure all of them are destroyed."

After a few minutes, I concluded my visit. Uncle saw me off to the gate, praising me for having grown into a smart guy. He did not know how I felt so dirty and nasty to have played the game his way. It was as if I were some kind of imposter. So criminal, I should say.

At home, Rotty was waiting for me. He had cooked imvange, which is a mixture of beans, green veggies, small fish, and tomatoes, garnished with different condiments.

"Carlos, I have good news," he said. "The man from the rehab center has called me. Guess what? I have a new job and a new apartment to live in."

"Tell me more about it," I said. What's the job about? Where are you going to be staying?"

"I will be working in a carpentry workshop in Gakinjiro wood market. I will start as an apprentice and, later, a full carpenter. There are affordable compound studios in Gisozi, not far from the market. That's where I will be staying. I can't believe I'm finally going to live like a normal person."

"I am so happy for you," I said, as my phone rang.

Uncle Kamara was calling.

I took the call and said, "Hello, Uncle. I have arrived safely and am now taking dinner."

"That's good," he said. "But I was calling to tell you that we have got them."

"I'm sorry, I don't understand. Whom have you gotten?"

"Inzuki boys. The police are arresting them tomorrow or the day after tomorrow. You should know I have connections with powerful people who make things happen in this country. Those boys should have known before releasing that song. Now, the prophecy, or the so-called ubuhanuzi, has been fulfilled to them before it does to anybody else."

"Uncle, what are you talking about? Why are they arresting those innocent guys? Are you sure they are the ones that released that song? No, Uncle, you can't do that."

"You don't know what you're talking about. Sorry to say, but those thugs are like your younger brother, David. They are among the young Hutus who blame our leaders for their misery. Some of them are descendants of those who committed the genocide."

"Genocide?" I asked. "What does it have to do with those young boys who were babies or not alive in 1994? Uncle, we were talking about David's songs, and now you're bringing in ethnicity and the genocide. I don't get you. Please, don't harm those innocent boys. They were David's family when all of us had forsaken him. They sheltered him. They loved him. They shared whatever they had with them. I will not get over it if anything happens to them because of David."

"If you don't want them to disappear from the public, you should tell me who else may be releasing those songs. Check the screenshot I'm sending to you. A girl named Angelas Umutoni has posted on Facebook that a new song titled 'Marume' is about to be released. Did you get that? I have no time to waste. I have to stop this madness before the ghost of that pig you called your brother ruins my reputation."

When he mentioned Umutoni, I immediately understood that James was about to release another song. I could remember the words in that song and knew it would be devastating to Uncle Kamara. In that song, "Marume," David told our uncle that he would not have become a dead person if he had not sent him to the streets. It was as if he knew he was going to die. *I have to stop James,* I mused. *I won't forgive myself if Uncle hurts any of David's friends.*

"Uncle, you and I agree that those songs should not be

published. But please don't tell me you're capable of destroying those boys' lives just because you want to save your reputation. What if, after they are caught and jailed, whoever is releasing those songs continues to do so? Shall you go back to the police and say the boys should be freed?"

"Of course not. They won't be jailed because of the songs. It's easy to find other crimes for which they can be sent to prison. Don't they take drugs? Even if they didn't, it would not be difficult to make sure drugs are found in their house."

Finally, Uncle Kamara was revealing his true colors to me. Rotty was still next to me, listening to what I was saying on the phone. I could not go on with that conversation. I needed to quickly think about what to do.

"Uncle, may I suggest something? Tomorrow morning, I will go and confront those guys and tell them I will report them to the police because they are publishing the songs under my brother's name. I will scare them to the point of making them hate ever mentioning my brother's name or doing anything that could jeopardize our family. Please, leave it to me. I will deal with it without having to ruin the innocent boys' lives."

"Okay," Uncle said. "You have until the day after tomorrow. Please make sure that song about me is never released. Help me stop your brother's madness, which seems to have no end even after his death."

It was painful to listen to Uncle Kamara, but I had to pretend I was on his side.

After the telephone call with Uncle, I looked at Rotty but failed to get any words out because tears wet my eyes.

"Carlos, who were you talking to? Was he talking about

Inzuki boys? Please, tell him the fundis never do anything that could put them in trouble. Their sins are only drugs and girls, nothing related to politics. I told you, your brother, Badguy, was different. He wanted to tell the world his truth. He was angry. He was not like other fundis who had given up on this world. Those guys live as if tomorrow does not belong to them. All they want is to enjoy today's peace."

"I know. Rotty, I was speaking to Uncle Kamara. Do you remember him? He is the one you once heard Martin and Bosco plotting to kill. Though I pretended to be on his side for my own security on the phone, my uncle is evil. He thought he had finished my brother, and now that David's new songs are coming out, Uncle is afraid of facing revenge from a dead person."

"Badguy used to tell me about his atrocious uncle, who hated both his nose and noise. That man is dangerous. Please, don't let him harm the fundis."

"Please tell me what we should do. Maybe I should go to see Inzuki boys and advise them to leave the compound and run away. They should find a way out of the country."

"What? Why should they go into exile for a sin they have not committed? Simply tell your uncle those songs are not being released by Inzuki boys. Carlos, don't tell me you don't know who is putting out the songs. You told me you listened to all of them. How? When? Who gave them to you?"

I looked at Rotty for minutes, wondering if I should reveal the truth to him. I was afraid that in an attempt to save Inzuki boys, whom he considered his brothers, Rotty would tell Uncle Kamara that I knew who was releasing the songs.

"Yes, I listened to the songs," I said to him. "But I'm

not the one who is publishing them on YouTube and other song-streaming platforms. I gave them to a friend of mine who is in Europe. I will talk to him. Rotty, you and David were not only friends but brothers. Do you remember when I told you that his soul was crying for justice? If we cannot punish his assassins for what they did, we should at least let David do it his way. Those songs are his way of claiming justice. I won't stop whoever is releasing them. What you and I need to do now is think about what we should do to save Inzuki boys. Let's see them early in the morning and advise them to take cover."

"No, I wouldn't advise you to go there. I will go to see the fundis myself. I won't tell them it's about Badguy. I will simply tell them that reports have been slipped to the police that they do drugs and that the feds are about to burn the ghetto."

"Thank you. I also wanted to suggest that you should not immediately move to Gisozi. Please, stay here for a few more days."

"No, Carlos, I'm starting another chapter of my life. I want to leave all the drama. All I shall do is work, eat, pray, and sing. I will be living in this world as a guest, waiting for the day I will be called to live in heaven's bliss."

"Rotty, I won't hide it from you. I'm scared. My uncle is a true monster. Though I had heard a lot about him, it's only today that I have interacted with his criminal mind. That man is heartless. The worst of all is that he links his crimes to the ethnic conflicts that have torn Rwanda apart. People like my uncle are a danger to society and a disservice to the government."

"I heard you ask him why he was linking Inzuki boys to the genocide. What did he say that shocked you?"

"He called them Hutus and added that they could be descendants of genocide perpetrators. That's insane. We are in 2015. The genocide happened twenty-one years ago. How can Uncle Kamara link the genocide to the boys who were babies in 1994? Who told him Inzuki boys are all Hutus? Hasn't the country banned the so-called ethnic identities? Are we not adopting the Rwandan identity as we leave behind those so-called ethnic identities that led to the genocide against the Tutsi? What measures did Uncle apply to determine that all members of Inzuki are Hutus?"

"Don't even try to comprehend that," Rotty said. "Your uncle is probably like those who think all poor people can only be Hutu. He is wrong. Poverty has neither ethnicity nor history. All orphans of this nation, irrespective of their background and who their parents were, find themselves abandoned and rejected, first by their family members and then by society. Inzuki boys, like all fundis, are Rwandans and non-Rwandans from different backgrounds and so-called ethnicities. They share nothing else but the fact they are all trash eaters. Some of them might have lost their parents on the battlefield during the war. Others lost their parents during the genocide against the Tutsi, and the world did not understand they needed more than school fees. Some others lost their parents in the refu-gee camps before and after 1994. Many lost their parents to poverty-related diseases and others to AIDS. Academics and politicians may write separately about the different causes of death, but when it comes to the suffering of orphans, misery puts all of them in the same boat."

"That's wisdom, Rotty. I always like the analytical eye you use to comprehend even the incomprehensible."

"Thank you. Brother, let me go to sleep. In the morning, I will go to talk to the fundis, before moving to Gisozi."

"Yes, Rotty. Since I can't convince you to stay here, please let me beg you to keep in touch. You're the younger brother David left me with."

"Thanks for the honor."

The following day, on Sunday, Rotty left my house. In the evening, when I asked him what Inzuki boys had said after he talked to them, he simply responded that they had refused to go anywhere. He did not give me details because we were on the phone. He promised he would come to see me during the week.

On Monday, as soon as I arrived at work, I turned on Facebook and wrote a message to James, a.k.a. Angelas Umutoni. I asked him to delay the release of the next song. Unfortunately, he was not online, but I was sure he would see the message later.

At around eleven o'clock, my sister, Celine, called me and asked if we could share lunch at a restaurant not far from my office.

"What do you want us to discuss that cannot be said on the phone? I am curious."

"Don't worry. It's all wonderful news. I am organizing a launch ceremony for my modeling company. You are the only person who can help me plan it well. I also thought you could play piano publicly on that day. So please don't say no. We will discuss the details at lunchtime."

"All right, I will be waiting for you."

It was as if Celine never dwelled on any issue. She could be furious today and joyful tomorrow. I wished I could never do anything that would make her contemplate death again.

In one hour, she was already there. We drove to Isombe restaurant and served ourselves from the buffet.

"Last Saturday, I paid a visit to Uncle Kamara," I said. "Since I came back to Rwanda, it was my first time to have a seemingly calm conversation with him. Though I tried to pretend, I could not help but see the monster in him. He revealed all his true colors to me."

"Please, Carlos, I am here to share lunch with my dear brother. I don't want to talk about that criminal we call our uncle."

"Do you mean you never talk to him?" I asked.

"I do," Celine responded. "But with a purpose to make him not suspect I could be up to something. I already told you that I shall not rest before Kamara and Kananga pay for what they did to me. They have no idea they are under my watch."

"What do you mean? Sister, don't tell me you are spying on them."

"I cannot tell you anything now. I don't want to argue with you again, but I would have loved it if you had listened to me when I told you that you should be careful. Carlos, Uncle Kamara is dangerous and can do anything to anybody he would suspect to be in his way. I knew he was suspecting you. He told me you went to see him and managed to convince him you are not the one who is releasing David's songs. Brother, I also hope you are not. I don't want to lose you the same way I lost David."

"No, I am not the one who is putting out those songs. Uncle Kamara should investigate well before taking any action. What if none of the people in Rwanda has those songs? What if David sent them to somebody out of the country?"

"That's a possibility," Celine said. "Maybe our brother had links with those enemies of progress who jump on anything that may tarnish the image of our government. Why did you not say it to Uncle Kamara? You shouldn't have told him that you suspected the boys David used to live with. Now, that monster we call uncle will chase whoever was known as Badguy's fan or friend. Martin, who worked for Kananga, has a long list of people to hunt down. He showed it to me. You were number one on the list before you decided to go to Uncle Kamara's place."

"What? A list? How did you know? Do you speak to Martin? Does it mean Uncle Kamara was right when he said you hired Martin to keep David in control? Sister, I never understand why you keep ties with the people you call monsters. Please tell me what's going on."

"Stop it, brother," Celine replied. "Have I not told you that Martin was hired by Kananga to be David's music manager? Though he works for those criminals, I keep him close to me because I have found his weakness. The guy loses his rationality whenever he sees my teeth. I am a woman, and I know how to spot a man's vulnerability. He cannot shake off the few moments we spent together. He begs to work for me."

"That's scary. You should be careful. Maybe the guy was sent to keep his eyes and ears on you. If you hire him, bear in mind you will have a double agent. I am sure he has been sent to keep you on Kananga's watch."

"Don't worry about that. I don't tell Martin anything he should not know. All he gets are praises for his bosses and my fear that maybe they do not love me as much as I love them. Then, he tells me all their doings and plans, trying to convince me that it's just the imperatives of the survival game and not that they are bad people."

"Okay," I said, before asking Celine if she could help me convince Uncle Kamara not to harm Inzuki boys.

"The problem is that you don't want us to claim copyright of those songs as the only siblings of David. I will not insist because we already talked about it and you said to me you cannot do it. However, you must understand that Uncle Kamara will not sit and wait for his image to be tarnished by the upcoming song, which, I understand, is titled 'Marume.' Besides, it's not only Uncle who is worried; some politicians have also called me."

"Some politicians? Why?"

"Did you listen to the song 'Ubuhanuzi'? It was as if David were blaming the government for the misery of orphans and poor people. When I came to talk to you, it was because they were already calling me. I told them I had nothing to do with David when he was alive and that they shouldn't ask me about him after his death. Two of them have already asked about you. I said you were not in Rwanda when David was writing those songs and that you never supported his ideas. They did not believe me. Carlos, my brother, please do not hate me. You are the only person I have in this world. It is not easy to survive in this Kigali. I only tell you all this because I am afraid something bad may happen to you."

"My dear sister, I hear you. Let's leave that to fate. It's almost time to go back to the office, and you have not yet told me about the launch ceremony for your new company. By the way, what's the name of your company?"

"Yes. It's called Model Diverse. I want to underline that it's about the diversity of beauty. I registered it as a modeling agency. Our main business shall be to find models or Rwandans who have the potential to be models; train, coach, and groom them; then find deals for them. I will earn from getting a percentage, a commission, from those deals."

"So, you shall basically be selling the beauty of Rwandan girls?"

"No. I will be helping those girls commercialize not their beauty but their modeling skills the same way dancers or choreographers do."

"I like the way you explain it. I will be there. If there is anything else you want me to do for you, I will. But I don't think I will be able to play the piano. I am only in the mood to play a melancholy, and that's not what you need for that day."

"No, brother. Please accept to play the piano in the background. I want a class ceremony. Few colors for the decor. No loud music. Just a soft background piano harmony."

"Okay, I will do it for you, just because I cannot say no to my dear sister."

"Thank you, brother. Let's go before you're late for work."

When I got home from work in the evening and turned on the TV, the first news was about police showing drug users and dealers to the media. I could not believe my eyes when I saw the few Inzuki boys I had seen before among those people. When I looked for my phone, which was still in the back pocket of my laptop bag, I found five missed calls from Rotty. I called him back.

"Hi, Rotty. Sorry I have missed your calls. I am watching TV. I am so sorry for what has happened to Inzuki boys. But don't worry, I will go and talk to the police."

"You have nothing to say to the police," Rotty responded angrily. "The fundis have already pleaded guilty for using the herbs, though they have no idea where the brown sugar came from. Three of the people paraded on TV are known as the middlemen. Maybe they are the ones who were used to report the fundis, and tomorrow they will be out in the market and leave the fundis to perish in jail."

"Rotty, you're speaking again the language I don't understand. What herbs? Brown sugar? Middlemen? I don't understand. Anyway, if you don't want me to speak to the police, what else can we do?"

"Talk to your uncle. I am sure he is part of the big boys' network. Those from whom the middlemen get everything. I am sure he will get free of his pushers. But please, beg him to also let off the boys."

"I will talk to him," I said, though I had no idea what to do.

When I opened my Facebook account to check if James, a.k.a. Angelas Umutoni, had responded, I realized he hadn't. I decided to write a message and send it to the real James's telephone number: Hello brother, I miss you. I hope you're surviving the cold weather. He did not respond.

The whole night I could not sleep wondering about the innocent boys who were sent to jail for using drugs, which Rotty suspected were smuggled to Rwanda by people like Uncle Kamara, the same mastermind of their arrest for reasons that have nothing to do with drugs. I felt pity for the police institution and probably the entire justice system manipulated by criminals like my uncle.

XIX

I begged Uncle Kamara to do all he could do to get Inzuki boys out of police custody. But he did not agree to do it because I could not assure him that no more of David's songs would come out.

The week was not easy for me. I had to help my sister, Celine, organize the launch ceremony for her company. She did not understand why I cared much about the drug addicts our brother David considered to be his family. James had not yet responded to my messages, either on the phone or on Facebook. Rotty was begging me to do something about the situation. I could sense he had started to doubt my intentions.

On Saturday, when I was putting on a black suit and a red tie to go to her ceremony, Celine called me.

"They have decided to ruin my day," she said, whimpering. "This is not a mere coincidence. Whoever released that song wanted to deviate the public's attention from my modeling company to the drama in my family. So now, everybody will be talking about the fact that I had a brother who died trying to escape jail and who wrote a song that insinuates that our uncle caused that death. Some journalists are already call-ing me, and I am afraid to take their calls."

I could not find anything to say to my sister. I was per-plexed. *What game is James playing now?* I wondered. How did he decide to release that song on a day when my sister was launching her model agency?

"Sister, it's okay," I said to Celine. "Don't worry. Stop cry-ing. Nobody will link David's new song to the launch of your company. I am really sorry this is happening to us. I wish I knew what to do to stop it. I guess what's more important now is your happiness. Maybe I also need to go back to France, rebuild my life, and leave all of these tensions behind."

"Carlos, we have to do something about it. I thought no other song would come out after the arrest of those hood-lums, whom David called his friends, Inzuki boys. I was wrong. You were right that maybe everything is being done from outside the country. This issue is bigger than I thought. I wonder who is coordinating it. Now they are targeting me or want to use my day to gain more publicity for that song. I will not allow them to tarnish my image or the brand of my new company."

"To be honest with you," I said. "I am also short of ideas. It's now beyond my comprehension. I am afraid of what Uncle Kamara shall do after listening to the new song."

As I was still talking to Celine, Uncle Kamara called.

"Sister, speak of the devil, he calls."

"Please, Carlos, be careful. Don't argue with Uncle. Just accept whatever he instructs you to do."

"I am neither the author nor the publisher of those songs.

If Uncle Kamara has the power to stop whoever is releasing them, why does he not do it without involving me? He has already sent those innocent boys to jail, but another song is out. Who else is he going to destroy?"

"But the problem is that he suspects you."

"That's his problem, not mine," I said. "Please, let me take his call before he thinks I don't want to speak with him."

"Yes, go ahead," Celine said.

After I took his call, Uncle Kamara said, "Carlos, I am giving you only three hours. Before I call you again, that damn song should be nowhere to be found on the net. Do you hear me?"

"Yes, Uncle. But how can I remove something I have not put on the net? I am equally puzzled."

"I don't know how you will do it or who you should talk to. All I know is that if that song is not removed within three hours, the thunder shall hit someone."

That was a threat. I sat down on my bed feeling helpless. *If only I could turn back the clock,* I mused, *I would never have given those songs to James.*

A few minutes later, Celine sent me an SMS to inform me that she was already heading to Sunset Hotel. That's where the launching ceremony of her model agency would take place. I wanted to tell my sister that I would not make it to the ceremony because Uncle Kamara had given me a three-hour ultimatum. But I needed to be by her side. I needed to make sure she was okay. If anything happened to her, I would never forgive myself.

When I arrived at the venue, journalists came running to take photos and videos of me with their cameras. I wondered why I was given that attention, but I had nobody to ask.

"Hey, Carlos," Celine said. "Thanks for being on time. Do you already have the chords to play? The piano is over there. You may familiarize yourself with it. Other performers have been rehearsing while you were busy at work. You will play after the fashion show, during the cocktail hour. For the show, DJ Madinah shall do the music mix. She is a pro at that."

"Thanks," I said, before adding, "Sister, may I ask you something?"

"Yes, of course."

We moved a few steps away from the people testing the mikes.

"Have you been in touch with James?" I asked. "I mean my friend who is in the UK?"

"Of course, yes. We planned this together. James is the one who introduced to me the publicist who is boosting my brand awareness. But at the last minute, James decided to travel to Japan. Apparently, he cannot receive calls on his UK number. I have also been trying to reach him, in vain. If it's not urgent, he will be back in the UK next Wednesday."

"No, it's not urgent. I was only wondering why he did not respond to the SMS I sent to him a few days ago."

"What did you want to tell James?" Celine asked. "I hope you are not thinking about leaving the country."

"What are you talking about? Why would I have to call him for that? Don't I have my French passport? Why would I go to the UK instead of France? I only wanted to have a chat with him. But apparently, after I linked him up with you, he is now more your friend than mine."

"How did I forget you were French? I wish I also had another nationality. I would forget this country forever. Don't worry, your friend is all right. I wish I had known James before. He is not just a photographer. He understands this business I am in. Most of the foreigners you will see among the guests were invited by the publicist James found for me. Some are designers, and others are marketers who sometimes hire models for product advertising."

"That sounds good. I am glad James is helping you. But don't talk about leaving the country. Because when you shall achieve the success you aim for, the whole world shall be yours. You shall never forget Rwanda. Please also note that I am not French, as you said, but Rwandan. It does not matter what nationality people associate me with. What counts is my social and cultural bond with a country, and my soul is nowhere else but Rwanda."

"That's true. Hey, Carlos, we are left with only fifteen minutes before the guests start coming in. Let me go check on my models. Today, I have to sign at least three good deals."

"Good luck. I will be playing the piano."

After about twenty minutes, the ceremony started. I was absentminded during the fashion show, thinking about Uncle Kamara's ultimatum. The only person who could remove the songs from the net and end that drama was James, but according to my sister, he was in Japan and unreachable on the phone. I felt not just guilty but stupid. *Why did I ask James to put those songs out?* I mused. I should have realized that maybe my brother, David, was killed because some people wanted to shut him up and would not take it to hear him sing again.

By a tap on my shoulder, somebody interrupted my thoughts and said, "You must be Carlos. I saw you at the funeral of your late brother, David. May his soul rest in peace. I am Martin, Celine's friend."

"Nice meeting you," I said, wondering why Celine had invited him to the ceremony. The game my sister was playing was beyond my reach.

Before Martin responded, I recognized the old man seated at the same table as Celine. He was Kananga. I wondered if the lady on his left was his wife or another random woman. All the people in that room appeared rich and different from the ordinary Rwandans on Kigali streets. That's the bourgeoisie that my sister could never imagine not being a member of, the same clique of high-level criminals who had turned her into an object of beauty and a toy for their fleshly desires.

"Your uncle, Kamara, has not been able to come," Martin said to me, as if he were up to something. "He is distraught by your brother's new song, titled 'Marume.' Have you listened to it?"

"No, I haven't had a chance to," I said. "I was in a hurry to come to the ceremony when I was told the song was out."

"If you need my advice, please know that whoever is releasing Mr. D's songs is doing a disservice to you and your sister, Celine. Please check what people are writing on Twitter when you have a minute. Your family is trending. Some people suspect you could be the one releasing those songs. They also blame Celine for being on the side of an uncle who allegedly mistreated her brother. But that is not my biggest worry. The opposition groups are using your late brother's songs to tarnish the image of our country. I am not sure our government shall allow that to continue. I am saying this because I care for you and your sister. I was David's music manager, not because I earned a lot but because I liked his talent, though I disapproved of his ideas. So please, do all you can to make sure those songs vanish from the net."

"Thank you for caring," I said. I gathered the strength to add, "May I ask you a question?"

"Yes. Go ahead."

"How come, as David's music manager, you did not know about those songs? Who registered their copyright?"

"I suspect they are not registered. Your brother was not what you think he was. He lived in another world. Yes, I was his music manager, but sometimes he did things without my knowledge. I would not have allowed him to write those lyrics."

"Does it mean he did not trust you?" I asked.

"What are you insinuating?" Martin asked. "Maybe he did not. All I can tell you is that those he trusted and who may have helped him write those songs won't see the sunset tomorrow morning."

"What do you mean?" I asked.

"It's okay, man," Martin said, walking away. "Let's enjoy the ceremony. It was nice chatting with you."

It was painful to keep calm and continue watching pretty

girls cat-walking in front of the men, including Kananga and Martin, and probably some other head criminals disguised as businessmen. My sister's world could never be mine. It felt as if it was a punishment to be there. Every move any of those people made led my mind to think they could be up to something. I would run away and vanish from the scene if I could.

When the guests were about to walk to the garden for a cocktail, accompanied by my piano music, I received a telephone message. It was from Rotty and had only six words: They are going to kill me. When I tried to call him, the phone was already off. He had told me that he stayed in Gisozi, but I did not have the exact address.

"Sister, I am sorry. I have to go," I said to Celine when she came to remind me that it was time for me to start playing the piano.

"No, you can't go anywhere. What are you talking about?"

"A friend of mine is in danger. I have to go and see what's happening. Look at the message I have just received."

"The name Rotty again?" Celine asked, looking at my phone's screen. "This is the same person who called you another time and said he had been arrested. Brother, what is your business with the muggers David called his friends? I have no time for this. Please don't do this to me. You can't leave me at the time when you are supposed to play the piano. We cannot change the program."

Tears were already dancing in my sister's eyes. I recalled what her therapist had told me and decided to stay so she may not make another self-harming decision.

"It's okay, I will play the piano. Let me just call him to

check what is happening. If it's not serious, I will go to his place tomorrow."

I felt a quick heartbeat for fear that what he had written had happened. I had no name or number of anyone who could direct me to his place. My sister reminded me that it was the time for the piano. I must have played only touches of melancholy. Luckily, my sister's guests were too busy to pay attention to the music. The floor was taken by different people. Some of the speakers did not miss the opportunity to remind Celine that modeling was not about cat-walking but about beauty. One guy said that some girls were not tall enough. When Celine took the floor, she reminded the audience that modeling was not about height, weight, or facial features but about showcasing beauty, especially when dressed by talented designers. She explained why she chose to name her company Model Diverse. She told the audience that her company shall not teach Rwandan girls how to be beautiful but how to showcase their beauty.

In the night, when I was in my room trying to catch sleep, I received a call from a telephone number I did not have in my contacts.

"My name is Aphrodis. I work at the rehabilitation center where your friend Rotty spent months. I wanted to ask you if you know his whereabouts. Some unidentified people have taken him out of his house this afternoon. He is not back since then, and his phone is off."

"Thank you for calling me," I said. "Rotty has also sent me a message, but his phone was off when I tried to call him. I am afraid he could be in danger. We should search for him. Please, tell me where he stays. I have to see him as soon as possible."

"I have just told you I don't know his whereabouts. At what time did he send you the message? Please tell me everything you know. He told me he was scared, apparently because of your family. You must do all you can to save Rotty from whoever wants to harm him."

"I don't know where he is or what happened to him. We should report his disappearance to the police first thing tomorrow morning."

"Why wait for tomorrow morning? I have already reported it to the police. They said it was too early to think he could have been kidnapped. But at least they promised to search for him."

"That's good. Thank you. We should keep Rotty in our prayers and believe that the police will find him."

"Yes."

After that call, I decided to recite a rosary and pray for Rotty and Inzuki boys. Only the Virgin Mary could hear the cry of orphans, I believed. I fell asleep in those prayers.

I was woken up by Habimana's knock on my door in the morning.

"I am in trouble," he said. "Mukandoli has not spent the night at home. Now my children are saying that I should tell the police."

"Please don't say that," I said. "I can't chew more than I already have on my plate. Do you remember the guy you met here last time? Rotty? He has also disappeared. Yesterday, he sent me a message that he was about to be killed. When I tried to call him, his phone was already off. Till now, it is still unreachable."

"It's not a mere coincidence. I suspect this is all because of your brother's song released yesterday. Does your uncle think Mukandoli could be involved in the release of David's songs? Or maybe he is targeting me and thinks the only way to get me would be through my wife. He can do whatever he wants to that heartless wife. That's how Satan pays his servants."

"Please, don't say that about your wife," I said. "Even though I wish your wife should be punished for having delivered my mother to the killers in 1994, I don't think that Uncle Kamara should have any right to kidnap anybody. Now, as if jailing Inzuki boys was not enough, Rotty has also gone missing."

"What hurts me the most whenever a person disappears is that his corpse is never found by his family. It pains a lot to wait for somebody who shall never come back. I hope you shall find your friend, dead or alive."

"Please, don't talk about death already. We should not lose hope. I will find Rotty, and you will find your wife. But we need to do something. Why don't you report your wife's disappearance to the police?"

"No, I won't say anything to the police. I do not want to call any unnecessary attention to myself. Who cares about the wife of a genocide convict?"

"Stop it. This is not about the genocide. Mukandoli, like any other Rwandan, has the right to be safe and secure in her country, and the police are there to ensure she exercises that right."

"You don't know this country. If I report my wife's disappearance, I am sure the first person to be investigated shall be myself. Nobody can ever tell the outcome of any investigations, especially in this country, where being a suspect means being guilty until proven innocent."

"Why do you think they would suspect you?"

"I did not say they would suspect me. I just meant that you may never know. In this country, the police know everybody and everything. I am sure they know that I never participated in the genocide, though I was charged and convicted for it. They know that my wife, Mukandoli, is the one who delivered your mother to the killers during the genocide against the Tutsi. They also have information about how she connived with your uncle to punish me for the crime she committed. So if I report that she has mysteriously disappeared, they might think I have carried out an act of revenge."

"That's probable. But how shall you manage your kids alone without their mother? Soon, they shall start asking what you're doing to search for her."

"The eldest girl is asking me many questions, as if she thinks I have something to do with her mother's disappearance. Mukandoli has succeeded in turning my children against me. To them, I am the bad person who was jailed for having killed people in 1994."

"That's not easy for you, I can imagine."

"No, it's not easy at all. But I have experienced worse. Carlos, please tell the person to whom you gave the songs to slow down. If any other song goes out, we will be finished. Your uncle is dangerous, but it looks like this is even beyond him. On Isaha.com, they have published an article about the relationship between your brother, David, your sister, Celine and your uncle Kamara. As usual, they are looking at the issue only from one angle, politics. The more political it gets, the more dangerous this game shall be. We should be careful."

"I don't know what to do. The guy who has the songs is not reachable on his phone and has neither read my messages on social media nor via email."

"I hope he is safe," Habimana said. "Criminals have no borders. They can reach wherever they target their victim. You must not reveal his name to anybody."

"I won't. Now my biggest concern is Rotty. His disappearance has been reported to the police by another person. I guess I should wait, but I am not sure I will hold my breath for so long. I feel like shouting so loud, shouting to the world, shouting to Rwanda, and telling Rwandans that they have gone insane; yes, all of us have gone mad. Listen, go to your place. I am going to try to sleep before I go to my sister's this evening. She has invited me so we may take stock of what happened yesterday during her company launch ceremony. I will call you tomorrow."

"It's okay. I am also going to hide in my house, with kids crying for their mother."

"Take heart. Let's hope your wife shall reappear one day."

After Habimana left my house, I lay on my bed, closed my eyes, and begged my brain to shut down and sleep. I was so exhausted and somehow resigned. All I could think about was that I was not safe in my birth country and probably needed to pack my stuff and go back to France.

In the evening, I went to Kacyiru to my sister's place. She was not alone. Linda was also there. Their world did not smell like mine. They were in joy because of the deals Celine had signed the previous day at her company's launch ceremony.

"Carlos, drink whatever you want, beer, wine, whiskey, cognac, anything. Guess what, Linda is going to your country, France. She has been picked by a cosmetics company called Beauté Précision. Very soon, she will be on billboards in the city of Paris and on TV commercials in living rooms worldwide."

"What? That fast? You guys are in business. Congratulations!"

"That's not all. I have actually signed two deals. Did you see the short girl people laughed at?"

"Yes. Though I was not paying much attention, I turned to see what was happening when I heard the noise. Some people were clapping and others mocking one of the models. Even one musician next to me said that you had made a mistake to include that girl."

"Yes, her name is Mireille, but she goes by Mimi," Celine said. "Those who mocked her were wrong. I made a good decision to pick her over the tall and slender girls praised for beauty in this Rwanda. But to be honest, I was also surprised when a model agency based in Los Angeles decided not only to sign a contract with us but to take that girl completely. She will now live in the US and be groomed into an international model. They said their aim was to promote African beauty, and in their understanding, she is what they were looking for."

"Celine, you are my sister, but I never understand you. I

think you are a genius. When do you plan all those business moves? How did you connect with those companies from France and the US?"

"I guess it all started when I became Miss Rwanda in 2000. But because I did not understand the game's rules, my fame profited other people who had made me their cash cow. I had always thought I was the richest girl in this Kigali. But now I know I could have been richer if I was not a captive of some people. I enjoyed traveling to different countries, participating in fashion shows, and appearing on billboards. I accepted whatever amounts I was paid without knowing that some people had earned bigger sums from those deals. Linda is here because I don't want to be like those people. We have a contract. She knows how much my company is receiving and that we will only take thirty percent and give her the bigger share. For Mimi, it's different because she is leaving our company for good. They will pay her directly for the relocation and pay us our share for having recruited and coached her."

"I understand," I said, before turning to Linda and telling her, "Dear, congratulations on the opportunity. I wished I was in France to welcome you to my second home country. How long shall you be there for?"

"My contract is different from Mimi's," Linda said, as if she were not so happy. "I will not live in France. I will only be going there for a few weeks. But I am grateful. I have never dreamed even once that I would ever fly to Europe. It feels as if I am a character in a fantasy movie. All thanks to Celine."

"I am so happy for you and believe it's just the beginning," I said. "Celine has learned a lot in this modeling career. Please, listen to her. She will tell you the mistakes you should never make. And remember one thing always: you should stay the same Linda I like."

"May I say something to you both?" Linda asked.

"Of course," I said. "What is it?"

"I don't know how to say this … I wanted to say … Please, forgive me. I am sorry for what I did to your brother, David. He was a nice person. We were friends. I did not want him to be jailed. After the sessions I have had with my personal coach, I now understand that I was living a risky life in those years, and some people took advantage of me. The mastermind of the plan to send Badguy to jail was Martin. He was the one who reported him to the police and forced me to testify. David had indeed said bad words to me, but that's how we communicated. I also used to call him a Kambari, despite that he had told me everything he endured during the genocide against the Tutsi. Though I loved Badguy so much, I hated that he was a Hutu. I thought he understood why, and I did not realize I was hurting him. I hated Hutus, and maybe I still do because they killed my entire family. But after all the love you have proven to me, I can't help but feel bad for what happened to the brother you loved. To you, David was not just a Hutu but your sibling. I am really sorry."

"Linda, that's enough," Celine said. "Stop condemning yourself for something you had no control over. Our brother was jailed because he had said words punishable by the law. You should also not feel guilty for hating people who exterminated our families. I also hate Hutus as a group and shall never forgive them for what they did to our Tutsi families.

But that does not mean I hate everybody who identifies with the Hutu identity. I work with Hutus. I have Hutu friends. I like them and value our friendship. Though I hated that David had chosen to associate more with the Hutus than the Tutsis, he was my brother who was fed by the same chest that fed me. He experienced the genocide against the Tutsi. He was hiding together with Mama and Carlos. He saw the killers the day they came to take Mama. I did not understand him. I wished I had acknowledged that he was probably more confused than I was. Maybe he also hated Hutus and felt bad whenever people associated him with them. Whenever you called him a Kambari, he felt so bad because it was as if you were linking him to his mother's killers. Oh my God! What am I talking about now? Do you even understand what I am saying? I hate Hutus, but I don't hate them. David was a Hutu, but he was my brother, and I loved him. Total confusion ..."

"Please stop it, both of you," I said. "Let David continue to rest in peace. None of you should be blamed for what happened. We are all victims of this madness and the total stupidity of the generations before us. David was also a victim, and even in his death, he continues ... No, I shouldn't say more. Girls, focus on what you are doing, your modeling careers. Do never allow this world to drag you into its foolhardiness. Be who you are and forget those Hutu and Tutsi labels. Nobody is a good or bad person because of their so-called ethnicity. Those who exterminated our families thought they were killing enemies of their ethnic group. Maybe they believed they were hated and decided to be harsher haters, and that's how they turned themselves into murderers and genocidaires. Nothing justifies hate, whether toward an individual or a certain group. We should not hate anybody. Though we were hated, we should love even those who do not love us."

"What are you insinuating?" Celine asked. "I did not mean that I hate Hutus. No, I don't. I only hate that Hutus killed my family, and nobody can make me forget that."

"That's true," I said. "Our mother and other family members were killed because they were Tutsi, and those who killed them sang that the world belonged only to the Hutu. But we are all here because of the few Hutus who hid us and saved our lives. Isn't that true?"

"Yes," both Celine and Linda replied.

"But that does not mean—" Celine started.

"It does not mean the killers were not Hutus. All I wanted you to understand is that since some Hutus did not commit the genocide, the group identity was simply an illusion used by politicians to convince the killers' minds that they had the support of all Hutus. So, when we put all Hutus in the same camp with the genocidaires, we hurt innocent souls like that of our dear brother, David."

"Carlos, you said we should stop talking about Hutus and Tutsis," Celine said. "But you are the one who is now dwelling on the subject you do not want us to comment on. I am sure Linda understands me because both of us are the only survivors of our Tutsi families. At least me, I have you. She has nobody. I don't think what she needs to hear from the world now is that she is bad because she hates those who made her a lonely orphan. As you said, let's stop talking about this and

continue with the healing journey. Maybe on this life journey, we shall meet more Hutus who shall make us realize that
love and kindness can be found in any person, irrespective of
the group they are associated with."

"You are right," I said, without adding any word.

As usual, Celine insinuated that I could not understand
their pain because I was not fully Tutsi since my father was
French. I judged it was indeed time to end that conversation.
"Girls, I have to go. It's already late. Tomorrow, I will go to
work."

"Thanks, brother," Celine said. "Tomorrow my day is also
fully booked. At the launch ceremony, I took many commitments I have to fulfill."

"Let's go together," Linda said to me. "I also need to leave
now. Otherwise, I may not get the bus to Nyamirambo."

"Nyamirambo buses are available twenty-four/seven.
But I don't mind your company. So, please, let's go."

XX

After we got out of the compound, I said to Linda, "Once again, congratulations. I am so proud of you."

"Thank you," she replied. "When I heard that Inzuki boys had been arrested because the police found herbs in their ghetto, I trembled with fear, thinking I would also be in jail if I had not stopped smoking ganja. I really thank you and your sister for having shown me that there is more to life than misery."

"Tell me," I said. "Do you know Rotty? He was also a member of Inzuki boys and a friend of David's."

"Yes, I know him. They told me he went to the Iwawa center. I guess that's why I did not see his face among those arrested."

"No, he never went to Iwawa. He voluntarily sought support from a proper rehabilitation center. When he came back, I could not recognize him. He had a Bible in his hands, his dreadlocks were clean, and his nails were clean. And now ..."

"Now what? What happened to him? Why are you sad?"

"Look at this message," I said, showing Linda the SMS Rotty had sent to me the day before.

"Who was going to kill Rotty? Did you call him?"

"His phone was already off when I tried to call. He stays in Gisozi, but I have no idea where exactly."

"I know somebody who may help us," Linda said, after a few seconds of reflection. "His cousin, a moto rider. I must have taken his number when he once dropped me home. Let me call him."

Linda called the guy. All I could hear was that she was repeating no, no, no, no, before asking the guy to direct her to where he was.

"They have found him," Linda said to me after the call.

"Where? What happened to him?"

"Dead. Carlos, Rotty is gone. They have killed him."

I became emotionless, stood still like a tree, and words refused to come out of my mouth. I had never felt guilty before. It hurts. It actually kills. Rotty was dead because of me and his friendship with my younger brother.

"Let's go there," Linda said.

"Where?" I asked.

"His corpse has just been found a few minutes ago. They are taking him to the morgue. Let's go and pay him our last respects."

"Yes," I said. "Where are they taking him?"

"To the morgue of the Kigali General Hospital."

"Let's go. I can't believe this is happening. Why? God, why? No, not Rotty. Not after … I mean, he did not deserve to die."

"Nobody deserves to be killed," Linda responded.

I had not realized I was loud. I decided to button my lips as we jumped on the bus to the city center.

At the hospital, we were not allowed to approach Rotty's

body. I could remember sharing asusa beans with him in a Biryogo restaurant when he told me I should not attempt to seek justice for David. Rotty never wanted to create problems with anybody. He used to say to me that he was a fundi and that fundis play it cool. He was an orphan who never talked about how his parents died. But he was not a bitter person. He had found refuge in the fundi life of drugs and dreadlocks until he realized he was digging his grave and decided to seek therapy. When he returned from the rehabilitation center, he was an even better person, determined to embrace life and live instead of only surviving.

A lady who seemed to be in her early sixties came to the morgue, crying and shouting that they had killed the only survivor of her brother's family. Listening to what she was saying, I was scared that she could be put in prison because of the accusations she was making. She pointed to the policemen and said that they had killed Rotty the same way they killed his entire family in 1997. She must have been one of those Rwandans stuck in the tragedies of the '90s. Those who take anybody with a gun as the cause for all war-related deaths. As the lady continued to tell their family story, I learned that Rotty was from North West Rwanda. He had survived the Abacengezi insurgencies of the postgenocide era. I wanted to say to the woman that the mastermind of Rotty's assassination must have been nobody else but my maternal uncle, who was neither a soldier nor a policeman. But I had no proof Uncle Kamara had killed Rotty. Even if I did, I would not have said it to that angry woman in a fight mode. After minutes of shouting, the security guards came and took the poor woman to only God knows where.

"Carlos, whoever killed Rotty must be the same person who arranged for the Inzuki boys to be arrested," Linda said. "It's not a mere coincidence. I suspect it is because of Badguy's newly released songs. Do you remember I told you Martin came to ask me if you were the one releasing the songs? Maybe they found out that Badguy's friends were the ones publishing the songs, and that's why they want them to vanish. I don't want to think that Martin could have killed Rotty. I would never forgive him for that. Carlos, if you know the person who is releasing those songs, please tell him to stop before they kill all of us."

"Don't worry," I said. "They cannot kill everybody."

I was not sure about what I had just said. Though I could not reveal anything to Linda, I wanted to shout, call James and tell him he should remove all David's songs from the net.

"Carlos, this is beyond Martin. I have read what people are writing on social media about those songs. What relationship do you have with your uncle, Kamara? Badguy called him a devil, though he never told me why. Yesterday, when I was listening to the new song titled 'Marume,' I could feel Badguy's pain in the voice and the melody. But I couldn't help it to note that he called your uncle a spear in some verses and added that he could not understand that his sister could give birth to a Kambari. He was talking about ethnicities, and that's not acceptable in Rwanda. I am afraid many people might want to ensure no more songs come out."

"Linda, I don't want to talk about the so-called spears and kambaris, and whenever you are with me, please don't call David the name Badguy. I always want to think about them as two different people. David is my innocent little brother. Badguy is the product of this madness that has taken over our Rwandan society."

"I am sorry," she said, and did not utter any other word.

I guessed she was not happy with the tone of my reply. The truth was that I cared less about the ethnicities and the ethnic discrimination than about the criminals who seemed to have the power to shatter the life of anybody they did not want to see in our beloved Rwanda.

To change the topic or end that conversation, I said, "Apparently, the burial arrangements shall be decided after the police complete initial investigations. I guess we have nothing more to do here. We will keep in touch with Rotty's cousin so that he may inform us of the burial day and time."

"Yes, you are right. It's almost midnight. I need to go home.

"Let's take a taxi, first to your place, then my apartment."

After arriving at her place, I gave Linda a peck and said, "Good night. I will talk to you tomorrow morning."

"Good night," she replied, walking away in the darkness of the night.

I felt terrible to see her sad.

At the gate of my apartment, a guy in a black cardigan covering his head and a part of his face was waiting for me.

"Hello," he said. "Would you please allow me to sleep in

your house only tonight? My landlord has kicked me out of the house and kept all my possessions till I will be able to pay rent."

"Who are you? I mean … what's your name? Where do you stay? Why did you choose to come here?"

"I am your neighbor, on the street after this one. You and I take the same bus every morning. I came here because I believe you are a cool person who cannot send away a poor person in need of a shelter just for one night."

"Why did you not go to other neighbors, maybe those with bigger houses? I have only one bed and no space for any other person. So please forgive me for not helping you."

"Please, let me sleep at least in your kitchen or on the floor in your living room. I don't even need a mattress. If I continue to roam in this cold, I may be abused or killed by Kigali night criminals."

"Please don't insist," I said to the man. "I have no place for you."

"Please don't do this to me. If I get attacked by criminals, you will never forgive yourself for my death."

When he talked about death and being killed by Kigali criminals, I immediately thought he could be one of the young Rwandans who have no family members and decided that maybe I should consider letting him in just for the night. But before I responded to him, my phone rang. I did not want to get it out of my bag for fear that somebody could snatch it from me in that night's darkness.

"Give me a second," I said to the man. "I will be right back."

"Please, don't go … Listen …"

"I have just said I am coming back," I replied, locking the gate behind me.

"Hello," I said to Habimana, who was calling me on the phone.

"Hi, Carlos. I have been trying to reach you without success. I hope you are not in trouble."

"No, I am okay. I mean … I am sad and troubled but physically okay. I am coming from the mortuary. Rotty, the guy you met at my place the other day, my late brother's friend, has been murdered."

"What? All because of those songs? Carlos, maybe there is another reason why the guy was killed. This is too much."

"I don't want to think about it now. I couldn't believe the covered body was of Rotty. I wished somebody assured me that he was not killed because of his brotherly friendship with my late brother, David."

"Carlos, you need to be careful. You should have eyes that see front, back, left, and right. Now, all of us are under their watch, and any move can lead to more deaths. You should not trust anybody."

"You are scaring me," I said, thinking about the guy I had just left by the gate.

"Yes. Powerful criminals do not have to carry out executions themselves. They pay low-class executioners who have nothing to lose if caught and sent to prison. If not your favorite motor rider, it might be a handler at the market you like to shop from. It may also be a security guard in your neighborhood or anybody else who can easily monitor your movements."

"Do you mean even the guy I have just left at my gate may be up to something? I found him standing there, claiming to have been kicked out of the house by his landlord and begging me to shelter him at least for one night. I have told him to wait because the phone was ringing. I was about to go back and welcome him in."

"Please don't," Habimana said. "I have heard stories of people who have been found dead alone in their houses, and their deaths are often concluded as suicides. When I was still in prison, one inmate told me how he used to kill people. He would then leave a suicide note, poison pills, and a glass of water on their tables so that the police would believe it was suicide."

"Does the police in Rwanda conclude the cause of death without carrying out investigations? First of all, when the criminal gets out of the house, he either locks the door and takes the key or leaves the door open. That should be the first clue. Second, the body should be sent for autopsy. Third, forensics should find the DNA of the person who last touched on those things the criminal left to make the death look like a suicide."

"I don't know why they do not always conduct an autopsy or analyze the DNA," Habimana replied. "I guess when suicide seems obvious, the police decide not to spend more money and time on autopsy and forensics. About the keys, I heard from that inmate that he always entered his victims' houses with a spare key or took one from his victim's key holder. You know how many people keep all keys and their copies together? So, after the execution, the guy would put the victim's key holder on the table. When the police came, they would think the victim had locked the door from inside and placed the keys on the table."

"Oh my gosh, you are right. Even I still have all the three keys my landlord handed over to me. How stupid! If I lose them, I would not be able to enter the apartment, yet the spare key is normally meant for that purpose, to be used when the other is lost. I guess I should give you my key copies. You are the only person I trust in this Kigali."

"No, I am sorry, I won't take them. Don't give them to anybody. You may keep one hidden somewhere in your office and bury the other somewhere outside your house. But those criminals have many ways. You can never know when and how they make copies of your keys. I have heard that to take its measures, they lay the key on a wet soap bar, then take the soap to the blacksmiths so they may make for them a copy. So, somebody could enter your house, kill you, get out, and lock the door behind him, for people to find you dead days or weeks after."

"So scary," I said.

"Carlos, listen. Can you imagine that my daughter is not yet home? She has left the house early afternoon after accusing me that I am not doing anything to search for her mother. Something told me that she probably knew her mother's whereabouts and was being used to play her games. But now I am worried that she could be in danger. It's the first time

Uwimana is spending a night away from home. I hope she is all right. Mukandoli can vanish for good, but not my daughter. If Uwimana does not reappear tomorrow, I will have no choice but report her disappearance to the police."

"Sorry for that. I also hope your daughter is all right. Have you checked with her friends? Maybe she decided to get out of the house because she thought you did not care about her mother's disappearance. I understand how worried you must be as a parent. But I suggest you give yourself at least two days before reporting her disappearance to the police."

"I don't know what to do," Habimana said. "I am afraid the police will ask me why I had not reported the disappearance of my wife, Mukandoli. Carlos, let me go to bed and sleep on it. Tomorrow, I shall know what to do. Please lock your door and go to bed. Don't open to anybody. You should be careful."

"Yes. Thank you. Good night."

I woke up to a call from my sister, Celine, in the morning.

"Carlos, we need to do something about David's songs. It's now going too far. After the song titled 'Marume,' a few minutes ago, a new song titled 'Mama' was released."

"A new song?" I asked. "No, not again. What can I do to stop this? I am afraid they will kill another person. Please, God, help us."

"Yes, a new song in which David seems to be singing to Mama that all of us forsake her son after her death. He sings that the jungle tigers killed the lioness, and now the lions are killing the lioness's son because he looks like tigers. What was he talking about? I hope it's not what I am thinking. He calls you white and says that you decided to leave the black behind and boarded a plane to join the whites, forgetting that the blood was red everywhere. Anyway, take time to listen to it. If you cannot do anything about it, I will. Whoever is releasing these songs shall soon find himself dead or behind bars."

"What did you just say?" I asked my sister, shocked that she could threaten to kill people or send them behind bars. "Don't tell me you are the one behind these … no … Are you capable of killing or sending anybody to jail?"

"Of course not," she replied. "I meant that I shall report to the police whoever is releasing the songs."

"But you said the person shall find himself dead. Does the police kill people? Celine, you should never say those words. Do you remember the message I received last Saturday from Rotty, our late brother's best friend? It was not a joke. His body is now lying in a morgue. Only God knows who is next to be killed. Is this happening only because of mere songs? What can those songs of our poor brother David do to the powerful people of this country? If they want to punish anybody for those songs, they should bring back David to life, kill him again, and leave alone people who did neither write nor sing them."

"Sorry for the loss of your friend, Rotty," my sister said coldly. "But nothing tells you he was killed because of those songs. Maybe he was a thief or something similar and was killed by the criminals he mingled with. Carlos, the world our brother, David, had created around him is a dangerous zone. If you do not want to disappear like they often do, or end up in jail like them, stop mingling with those thugs and drug addicts."

"Sister, a human being is dead, and that's all you can say? You know what? You are right. I don't understand our late brother's world the same way I don't understand yours. It seems like many Rwandans have lost sense and shall never recover it. Let me take a shower and go to the office before I am late. We will talk in the evening."

After hanging up on my sister, I immediately searched for James on Facebook. But unfortunately, he had not yet read my messages.

I wrote, "If you don't delete all Badguy's songs from the net as soon as you receive this message, it may be too late. They are killing everybody suspected of releasing them, and I am afraid I may be the next."

When I arrived at the office, I failed to work on any projects or perform simple tasks. When I told my supervisor that I had a headache, he allowed me to go back home and rest. He must have thought I had had a busy weekend.

At the bus station, a motorbike stopped in front of me, and the moto rider suggested taking me home.

"Don't worry," I said to the guy. "I will wait for the bus."

"Why? A moto is faster. Aren't you going to Nyakabanda? That's where I am heading to. Let's go."

"How do you know I am going to Nyakabanda?" I asked. "And why are you going there?

"Uh? It's just that I know you. I guess everybody knows a

muzungu who stays in Nyakabanda. Your ponytail is a signature. I was going to get something I forgot there and thought that I would give you a ride."

"Thanks," I said, "but I am not going to Nyakabanda and would love to take a bus to my destination."

"Okay. If you say so."

After he rode off, I wondered if it was another trap like the one I had survived last night. *Maybe I am paranoiac for no reason,* I mused. Why would anybody want to kill me? Even though Uncle Kamara suspected I could be the one releasing the songs, I did not think he would kill me for that.

Before I reached home, I received a call from Linda.

"Hey, Carlos, I have one good news and another worrying news."

"Start with the bad news," I said. "Who else has died?"

"That's not what I wanted to talk about, but I am worried that somebody else may be killed because of the new song released this morning."

"And the good news?"

"Eh? I feel like you are not in a good mood to hear it out."

"No, it's all right. Tell me about it."

"It's just that … I have been selected to participate in the Miss Africa beauty pageant in Dakar, Senegal. Celine has told me that I will travel next week."

"So soon, so fast like that?" I asked.

"Aren't you happy for me? Try to imagine the possibility of being crowned the most beautiful girl in Africa. Me, Linda, the orphan who spent years wandering on the streets of Kigali, the drug addict, the naive girl mistreated by all sorts of men in this male-dominated country. Carlos, please tell me you are proud of me. I can never find words to thank you and your sister enough."

"Linda, you have never been all those things you said. I am actually afraid this world will change you and make you think and behave like some girls who have lost the vulnerability that connects all human souls. It's only after realizing how vulnerable we are that we shall start to appreciate the existence of other human beings."

"It seems I called at the wrong time," Linda said. "I was expecting congratulations and not a philosophical lecture about life."

"Oh, sorry for that. Indeed, I am happy for you. It's just that so many things are happening simultaneously, and I don't know how to react to them. Do you have any news about Rotty's funeral?"

"Oh, now I understand. You're still devastated by Rotty's death. Yes, his cousin has called me today to inform me that the police promised to give them the body next Saturday. So we still have a few days before we can pay Rotty our last respects."

"Saturday? What shall the police be doing with the body for five days?"

"Autopsy or maybe some other tests, I guess. What do I know about police investigations? Let them do their work. Hopefully, they will find the assassin."

"I doubt they will."

"Why?"

"I don't know. I have just lost hope in our institutions."

"No, we should not lose hope. Rotty's assassins shall be punished for what they did."

Fifty meters to my home, my heart jumped at the sight of three guys standing by the gate to my apartment.

"Linda, may I confide in you?" I said.

"Of course, yes," she replied.

"I am afraid I may be the next."

"The next to do what?"

"To die. Some people have been stalking me. It looks like they are up to something. May I ask you for a favor? Please come and stay with me in my apartment at least for today. I am just coming from my office because I cannot work. I am frightened by what may happen to me."

"No, please don't say so. Nothing is going to happen to you. Is it Martin you are afraid of?"

"We can't talk about it on the phone. Please come to my place."

"I am sorry, I have an appointment with my personal coach this afternoon. I will come as soon as I leave her office. Maybe around five o'clock. Is that okay?"

"All right," I said. "Listen, I am putting the phone in my pocket, but I will not hang up. I can see some guys standing by my gate. Please keep the line. If anything happens to me, you will hear me screaming, then call the police."

"Don't worry. Just walk in the gate, go to your apartment, and then lock the door. I will keep the line until you tell me you are in your room."

"Thanks."

When I arrived at the gate, one of the three guys said, "Hello Muzungu, how are you this morning?"

"I am fine, thanks," I responded.

"Do you have some tea in the house? We are hungry."

"Unfortunately not. Maybe next time."

After saying so, I rushed immediately into the compound and ran to my apartment. Nobody followed me. Apparently, they had no plan to even touch me or do me any harm.

At three o'clock, after hours of melancholic solitude, I heard a knock on my door and thought Linda was coming earlier than planned.

When I opened it, I was shocked to see that my visitor was not Linda, but Habimana's daughter, whom her father had told me had disappeared.

"You? What are you doing here?"

"I needed to talk to you. Please hear me out. I am sorry for all the words I said to you the last time you came to our house. My mother is missing, and I think you may help us find her."

"Why would you think I could know your mother's whereabouts?"

"Please, let me sit down. I will tell you everything."

"Does your father know you are here?"

"No, he does not, and he shouldn't know. He does not care about my mother. Maybe he is happy she disappeared."

After a quick minute, I decided to let her sit so I may inform Habimana that her daughter had come to see me.

"Would you like to drink something?" I asked. "I have apple juice."

"Not now. Maybe later."

"Okay. Please give me a minute; I was doing something in my room. I will be right back."

In my bedroom, I immediately dialed Habimana's number.

"Hi, Carlos," he said.

"Hello, you cannot believe who is in my apartment. Your daughter is here."

"Who? Do you mean Uwimana? What is she doing there? How did she know your place? I am coming right away."

Before I responded, Uwimana burst into my bedroom.

"What are you doing here?" I asked her. "You have no right to enter my bedroom. Please go back to the living room."

She tried to push me to my bed, but I was too strong to fall. Only the phone fell on the bed. I guess she did not realize her father was listening in.

"My mother has been kidnapped by your uncle, and the only thing that can save her is my body. So do whatever you want with it so my mother can be free."

"What are you talking about?" I asked. "The only thing I can do to your body now is to throw it out of my bedroom. Why are you unbuttoning your shirt? What are you up to? Who sent you here?"

"Your people sent me here. I grew up without a father because your people had sent him to jail. I will not allow them to take my mother away."

"Please stop it and get out of here," I said. "Don't make

me hit you. Instead of doing whatever you want me to do with your body, I will strangle you if you continue to push yourself on me."

The girl jumped on my bed, removed all her clothes, and called me to join her for a conversation. I rushed out of my bedroom and back to the living room.

Three minutes later, Uwimana came out with weeping red eyes, wrinkled skirts, and an unbuttoned shirt.

"Sorry for what I am doing to save my dear mother," the demon girl said. "You have just raped me, and the world will forever judge you for it."

"Me? Have I touched you? Please sit down. You cannot go out like that."

She started screaming and calling neighbors to come and help her.

"Please, don't do it again," she shouted, crying as if it were real. "Help! Help! Don't do it again." She opened the door and ran to the compound, screaming that I had raped her.

Some neighbors were already outside, saying they never knew I could do such a thing.

Five minutes later, Linda knocked on my door and pushed it before I could open it.

"Carlos, what happened?" Linda asked. "Outside, they are saying you have raped a young girl. Please tell me it's not true. What has come over you?"

"Linda, I don't know what has happened. I thought I was having a nightmare though I seemed to be awake. A demon was here. She removed her clothes, pushed herself to my bed, then screamed that I raped her."

"Who is she? Do you know her?"

"Yes. She is a daughter to the woman who delivered my mother to the killers in 1994."

Before Linda responded, Habimana walked in.

"Where is she? Where is my daughter? Carlos, I heard everything she said to you. The call was still on. Mukandoli turned my child into an evil woman like her."

"Who are you?" Linda asked Habimana, before turning to me. "Carlos, please tell me what is going on. Did you not just say the girl's parents committed the genocide? What is her father doing here? Please tell him to get out of here."

"Linda, calm down. I will explain everything to you. Habimana did not kill anybody. I have told you his wife is the one who delivered my mother to the killers. You should know that not all Hutus committed the genocide."

"Let's not go there," she replied. "Habimana is not just a Hutu but a husband to the woman who killed your mother and a father to the girl who is wrongly accusing you of having raped her. Carlos, you may think I am wet behind the ears, but you are probably naiver than I am. You should never trust these Hutus who killed our people in 1994 or anybody related to them."

"Linda, you know how much I care for you, don't you? I hear you and understand what you are saying. But please believe me when I tell you that Habimana is not a bad person. He is the one who hid us in his kitchen, and because of that, David and I survived the genocide. His wife is evil, but Habimana is not his wife."

"Please, let's focus on what has just happened," Habimana

said. "Carlos, I hope you did not do what Uwimana was pushing you to do. She must have been sent by some people to trap you so that, before you know it, you may be accused of raping a minor."

"Did you say we should focus on what just happened?" Linda asked Habimana. "Is that all you have to say about the fact that your wife delivered Carlos's mother to the killers, and as if that were not enough, you have sent your daughter to trap him so he may be sent to jail? I don't understand what you are doing here. Maybe I should leave Carlos to sort out whatever deals he has with people like you. I am disappointed."

"Apparently, you did not hear everything," I said to Habimana. "I have not touched even one of your daughter's hairs. But she went out of the house screaming that I had raped her. After that, neighbors were out, calling me all sorts of bad names."

"You should get out of here," Habimana said. "Maybe the police are already on their way to this place. Uwimana was probably sent by … But no. I mean, it was a trap to get you."

"Why should he run away?" Linda, who was still there, asked. "Do you want the police to catch Carlos trying to escape so they may conclude he is guilty? I know him very well and can testify to the police that he cannot touch any girl without her consent … In fact, Carlos never does … I am a witness to that. In fact, nobody can accuse Carlos of having done with that pig girl what he cannot do with normal girls."

"I believe Habimana is trying to help me," I said to Linda. "He does not mean to cause me more trouble."

"You should never trust anybody," she responded.

As I was reflecting on what Linda had said and wondering why I trusted Habimana so much, the police entered.

My time has come, I mused. I am going to die in jail like my brother, David.

They handcuffed me and took me to Nyamirambo Police for questioning. Linda and Habimana followed us, but they were not allowed to enter.

XXI

The questioning took about three hours. I had no answers to some questions, including those about my friendship with Habimana, the man who was convicted and jailed for having killed my mother in 1994. The interpretation was that I had stayed in touch with him so I could one day avenge my mother's death. According to the police, that was the motive for raping Habimana's daughter. They also asked where I was keeping Mukandoli, Habimana's wife.

"Please hear me out," I said. "I hate Mukandoli with all my heart. But I can never harm anybody from Habimana's family. Besides, I am not a criminal or a rapist."

"We have evidence that you once went to Habimana's house to threaten Mukandoli. Did you ever go to talk to Mukandoli when Habimana was still in jail? Why would anyone in his right mind talk to a woman he accuses of involvement in his mother's death?"

"I did not go there because I wanted to threaten Mukandoli. When I came back from France, I went to the same neighborhood where I grew up, only to find strangers in my mother's house. All the other neighbors were new and did not know who I was. The only person who could tell me what had happened to my family's home was that evil woman. It was painful to talk to her, but I had no option. I even went to the prison to ask the same questions to her husband, Habimana."

"Is it at that time that you and Habimana planned revenge against Mukandoli? Did you rape her daughter so she may never tell anybody how you threatened her mother and that you could be suspected of having kidnapped her?"

"Listen," I said to the police. "I respect you and believe you have the necessary skills and willingness to conduct investigations. But please allow me to say that your questions are beside the point. What evidence do you have that I raped that girl or know her mother's whereabouts?"

"The victim's DNA was all over your bedroom. The neighbors heard her screaming for help and saw her getting out with torn and wrinkled clothes. There is also forensic evidence that shows she had intercourse on that day."

"Did those forensic tests show anything to do with my semen or DNA?"

One policeman moved toward me, fixed me too closely, and said, "Good job! You must be an experienced criminal. Where did you put the condom you used so we may never find your semen? Did you throw it in the toilet? Did you bury it somewhere? Where is it?"

"What are you talking about?" I asked. "I never used any condom. I did not touch that evil girl."

At that point, I could not take it anymore. I burst into tears and did not pay attention to anything else that officer said.

Another policeman asked, "Do you want to inform your family members or your lawyer that you have been arrested?"

"No, I have nobody … But, I mean, yes, I would love to talk to my sister."

"The landline is over there," he said, pointing to the corner.

"Hello," Celine said, after I dialed her number.

"It's me. I have been arrested."

"Linda has told me. We are outside, but they told us we cannot speak to you. Brother, don't worry. Those pigs, or whoever they call themselves, have no power to send you to jail. Their time in this Rwanda is over. You will get out shortly. I am talking to some people. Please tell the police we are outside and would love to see you."

I hung up the phone and told the police, "My sister is outside. She would love to see me."

"Only for five minutes," Said the policeman who had asked if I wanted to talk to my family. "Then, I will show you the cell you will spend days in with other criminals like you till the day the court shall send you to prison."

Celine and Linda were not alone but with Uncle Kamara. I wanted to punch him for his apparent involvement in Rotty's assassination and the arrest of Inzuki boys. For what was happening to me, I was too confused and could not tell who between Uncle Kamara and Habimana was the master of the game.

"Brother, didn't I warn you?" Celine said. "You should never have trusted those genocidaires? How can you befriend the person who killed our mother? Look now, you, a genocide survivor, are accused by a free genocide perpetrator of having raped the nowhere girl he calls a daughter. What an insult! This is unacceptable. The police should understand that man's purpose is nothing else but to send you to the same prison he was in for years because of his involvement in our mother's death."

I was not in the mood to respond to what my sister had just said.

"What your sister is saying is true," Uncle Kamara said. "I also warned you. Those people still have the same plan they had in 1994: to exterminate all of us. We should keep our family bond and not allow anybody to turn us against each other."

Why is he talking about the family bond? I wondered. *Who is turning us against one another?*

"We will get time to talk about all that," I said. "Now, the police is doing its job. Please let them do what they are trained to do. We should trust our institutions, right? At the end of it all, I am sure my innocence shall be proven in courts or before going to court."

"No," Celine argued. "You should get out of jail tonight or no later than tomorrow."

"Your brother is right," Uncle Kamara said to Celine. "We should let the police do their job."

"Which job?" Celine asked. "Torturing my brother with interrogations for the crime he did not commit?"

"If they have evidence," Uncle Kamara said, "our words cannot convince them otherwise."

At that point, I was tired of that conversation and

wondered why the police were not telling us that the five minutes were over. Linda was there, with wet eyes, but without saying anything. I wondered if she doubted me or if she was sad I was wrongly accused.

I approached her and murmured to her, "I love you. I have never said it to you before, but whatever happens to me, please know that I love you. I have not touched that girl or any other girl in this Kigali. Please do never doubt me."

She burst into tears, and everybody turned to see what was happening.

"Linda," Celine called her name with a commanding voice. "What is it? Please control your emotions."

Linda quickly wiped her tears as if she had to obey Celine's commands, then she approached me again and asked what I wanted her to bring for me the following day. I took the key to my apartment out of my pocket and gave it to her.

"Toiletries, sweaters, and sheets to cover my legs at night," I said. "That's all. My debit and credit cards are in the drawer of my bed. Please keep them safe for me."

"See you tomorrow," Linda said to me before turning to Celine and Uncle Kamara and saying to them, "I have to go."

"We are all leaving," Celine responded. "Let's drop you at your home. That policeman is coming back to take Carlos to his cell."

"Okay."

"Bye, for now, brother," Celine said. "Take courage. As promised, you will get out of here shortly.

The policeman led me to the cell, I mean a shared room, where all arrested individuals were detained.

As soon as I appeared, one of the detainees said, "I didn't know we were in a VIP station where even bazungu are detained. This one won't only pay for the candles. He will buy for all of us bedsheets to cover ourselves in the cold of the night. Please go to the major and introduce yourself."

The word *major* was familiar; that is how even Inzuki boys called their leader. So, I assumed the giant guy with tattoos on almost his entire body was the self-proclaimed major of everybody in that detention room.

"What heroic act have you committed?" the major asked. "Have you killed a Babylonian? Have you moved a million from the privileged to the deserved? Or you have savored a Rwandan beauty?"

"None of those," I responded. "I have not committed any crime."

"Why are you here then?"

"I don't know."

"Don't worry; you shall soon know. The day you shall be forced to admit you did whatever you are accused of, you will know why you are here. Give me the money. We need candles, petrol, soaps, bedsheets, and since we are lucky to have a muzungu among us, you should care for all our needs."

"I have no money," I said.

"I get it. After the baptism, you will remember where you kept the money."

"How do you mean?"

"Remove all your clothes."

"Why should I?"

"For the baptism. Only those who buy candles are exempted from the baptism."

I immediately understood they were going to either beat me up or keep me in the cold without any clothes. Then, I took all the notes from my pocket and said, "This is all I have. If it's not enough, I will give you more when my friend shall come to visit me."

The major took the notes, counted, then laughed and shouted, "I told you! We are lucky to have a muzungu among us. He has paid seventeen thousand five hundred." He turned back to me and said, "You are good. We all take a bath from that corner and pee in that bucket. We hide nothing from each other. You are now a full family member. Welcome. But since you are a new member, you should be the one to pray for us tonight."

Then everybody hugged me and told me that I should take heart. They all narrated to me why they were in police custody. Most of them admitted they had committed the crimes they had been arrested for. But one detainee said he was innocent and had not embezzled any government money. I understood he was one of the government employees who were often jailed for embezzlement or corruption.

After the conversation with other detainees, I felt not relieved but less fearful. I was ready to wait for whatever fate had in store for me.

The following day, early in the morning, a policeman informed me that I had a visit.

Linda was there, in black leggings and a red and white top showing the elegance of her chest and neck.

"Good morning, Linda," I said. "I will never find words to thank you."

"It's okay. What have the police said? Are they releasing you today?"

"I don't know. But from yesterday's interrogation, I understood that my case shall not be resolved by the police but the courts."

"Don't say so. Celine promised to do something about it. She is well connected with powerful people in this country. I am sure she will get you out of here. Carlos, I do not doubt you. It's just that I did not like the fact that you interact with people who committed the genocide. That's worrying."

"You know well that I have nothing to do with the genocidaires. Habimana hid us in his kitchen during the genocide. But that's not the only reason I kept in contact with him. He has a lot of information about what happened to our brother, David, because of the house our mother was given by David's father. That's where it all started. The conflict between David and Uncle Kamara started when Uncle Kamara forged papers to claim the ownership of that house. After that, more crimes were committed, but I guess it's not yet the time to tell the police anything. Through Habimana, I am gathering more evidence. One day, my uncle shall be brought to justice."

"Carlos, I am afraid. Please let it go. David is gone and will not come back. But you are there, and I would love to see you alive forever. I love you … I mean, I love you too."

"Thank you, dear. I wished I had pronounced those three words to you before, and not the way I did it last night. I don't know how the words slipped on my tongue. Some situations make us braver than ever. Linda, I promise you that I will get out of here triumphantly."

"Let's hope," she said.

"Tell me, when are you going to Dakar for the Miss Africa beauty pageants? How about your trip to France?"

"I will go to Dakar next Saturday. My trip to France has been postponed until after the Miss Africa competition. But I feel like I should ask Celine to send another person. Knowing that I have left you in this place, I don't know how I will be able to cat-walk and pose for photos."

"I will probably have left this place. Other experienced detainees have told me that my case may be taken to the prosecution today or tomorrow. I wanted to ask Celine to stop talking to whoever she is talking to and instead find me a lawyer."

"I know a lawyer who can help. He was a friend of my late uncle. He used to check on how I was doing till he realized I was already in another world. So if it's okay with you, I can ask him if he can take your case."

"Please do," I said, before adding, "Apparently, that policeman is reminding me that time is over. If I don't see you before you leave for Dakar and Paris, I wish you a safe trip and success. I am sure you will be crowned Miss Africa."

"With your blessings, everything is possible. I will come to check on you before my trip. We will spend three weeks in Dakar before the grand finale and my trip to France."

"My dear, I have to go. Please don't worry about me. I will be fine."

"I will pray for you. But please take heart and keep that faith."

She hugged me, gave me a peck on the cheek, gave me what she had brought, and then walked away. I could not help but wonder why I had expressed my love to Linda. *Am I really committed to making her my girlfriend?* I mused. I should not have raised her expectations. My life was too unpredictable to think about any long-term love relationship.

In the evening, Celine came to see me. All the people she had talked to had not done anything to get me out of police custody. She had other plans.

"Carlos, our younger brother, David, is gone, and I am trying to accept that. But I will not allow this Rwanda to take the only sibling I am left with. We are taking it to the streets to protest your detention. There is no way a genocide survivor may be sent to prison, accused of having touched a child of a genocide perpetrator."

"Sister, why do you link everything to the genocide? What happened to me is not because I am a survivor or because that girl is a child of a man who was wrongly convicted for having committed the genocide. What if the mastermind of my arrest is Uncle Kamara? Haven't I told you how he connived with Habimana's wife to take ownership of our mother's house and send Habimana to jail? You may not believe it if I tell you what that girl said to me. She said she came to my apartment to do whatever she did because she wanted to free her mother, who was allegedly kidnapped by our uncle."

"That's a lie," Celine said. "Brother, don't be deceived by those people. Uncle Kamara may have used Mukandoli to get papers for our mother's house, but he has nothing to do with her now. Maybe you don't remember how our uncle despises Hutus."

"Did I say he is a friend to Mukandoli? No. All I am saying is that Uncle Kamara can do anything with anybody as long it serves his selfish interests. I am here because of my brother's songs. Whoever got me arrested believed that it would stop releasing David's songs."

"I don't agree with you," Celine said. "But talking about the songs, if any other song comes out, I will have no choice but to report the account to YouTube. If whoever is releasing them has the copyright, they will have to show it to YouTube."

"You may do whatever you want with the songs, but please don't organize the street protests you have just talked about. It's not acceptable in Rwanda and may put you into trouble. Let's not all of us perish like fools. David is gone, and I may not safely come out of this detention. Please don't make any mistake that could call the attention of this country's powerful criminals to you."

"Don't worry. Everybody knows about the protests. I have been advised to do it by the party leaders. The members of the association of youth survivors of the genocide are all mobilized. It will be a peaceful protest aimed at influencing the court judgment."

"You do as you please. But I would not want my case to be a public matter."

"Brother, you have to trust me. There is something else

I should tell you." She looked left and right, approached me closer, then said, "You know what? Kananga has already been arrested. The media doesn't know yet. You were shocked to see him at my company launch ceremony, weren't you? I knew what I was doing. Two days later, I had gathered all the evidence I needed to report him to the highest authorities in this country. I am sure he won't be released soon because he is accused of having links with the opposition outside the country. I reported his conversations with his cousin, who defected from the party. Don't worry about Uncle Kamara and any other person who hurt me. Their time shall also come."

Whenever my sister spoke about her connections with influential people and her ability to avenge her enemies, I hated the woman she had become. She resembled somehow those people she called criminals.

"I am not sure if I should rejoice to hear the news of Kananga's arrest. However, I don't like that you chose to report that he speaks to his cousin in the opposition instead of reporting what he did to you. Celine, that man should be in jail for having kidnapped you and sexually abused you and not for speaking to his family member who defected from the party in power. Why would you care about who he speaks to?"

"Carlos, I did not see that coming from you. Okay, maybe I should let you explain to the police how you raped a seventeen-year-old girl. Since you trust this country's courts, please tell them everything you know about Uncle Kamara and prove your innocence to them. We shall see. If you want to know, please understand that nobody would have cared to arrest Kananga for having made a girl crowned Miss Rwanda his sex toy. That's what powerful men do with beautiful girls, right? Though to whoever arrested him, Kananga is punished for political betrayal, to me, he is being punished for what he did to me. But what hurts the most is that you, my brother, do not see the unfair world we have to survive in. I am not a bad person. I just play the game of those who seemed to have figured out how to live in this Rwanda."

"Celine, my sister, I am sorry. I did not mean to hurt you. Please do whatever you can to get me out of here. You are a courageous woman. It's just that I want you to be safe both physically, emotionally, and spiritually. In this Rwanda, I am not only afraid that I could be hurt physically but that I might lose my soul and the meaning of what life is and should be. Celine, I feel as if I am lost in an unfamiliar world."

"I hear you," my sister responded. "Please understand this world has done so much harm to me. Maybe what you see in me is the product of what I received from the people who abused me day and night. Brother, you know well that I have finally decided to claim my life back. If this had not happened to you, everything would be going as I planned. Kananga is now behind bars, my modeling company has prematurely gained success, and Linda is participating in the Miss Africa competition. The day before yesterday, I finally managed to speak to James. He promised to recommend to me an experienced model of Rwandan descent who lives in the UK and would accept being sponsored by my company to participate in the Miss World competition. I have already talked to some authorities who promised to give her a Rwandan passport. Unfortunately, in the middle of all of that, you got arrested. Don't you understand how frustrating it is? If I don't do all I can to prove your innocence, some journalists may use your story to tarnish my company's image. There is no way I could be promoting girls when my brother is accused of assaulting a minor."

I had kept quiet to listen to that long speech from my sister. It seemed it always had to be about her and her plans. But the most crucial bit of information that caught my attention was that she had spoken to James, but I could not jump to that before showing interest in her modeling company and her plans.

"Sister, as I said before, you are a courageous and intelligent woman. Nobody should ever make you doubt that. I am glad for everything you are doing to stand on your feet and make life the way you want."

"Thanks," she replied, and added no other word.

"Did you say you spoke to James?" I asked.

"Yes, I did," Celine said. "He actually told me that he would send you a message, I guess, on your WhatsApp. He must have sent it yesterday when you were already with the police."

"Please tell him I have been arrested and ask him to read the messages I sent to him a few days ago."

"I will," Celine said, before looking at her watch and saying, "I have to go. I have spoken to Ingabire. Tomorrow, she will bring you a brush and toothpaste. I guess that's all we can bring now for the few days you will spend here."

"Thank you," I said. I did not want to reveal to my sister that Linda had already brought all I needed.

Two days later, a policeman entered our cell and called my name.

"You will go to court tomorrow morning at nine o'clock," he said as he walked around to inspect the cell.

I wondered if the protests Celine had told me about had taken place or not. The preliminary hearing was meant to determine whether there was enough evidence that Habimana's daughter was raped and that there was a high probability I could be the rapist. In Rwanda, whenever the judge confirmed enough evidence to suspect a person in police custody, the next step was always to send him to prison. Then, they would wait for months before the actual trial. That's what happened to my brother David. He was never convicted for the crime he was jailed for until he lost his life in prison.

I approached the policeman and said, "I don't have a lawyer. May I call my family and ask them to find me one?"

"Are you sure? How about the lawyer who has asked to come to talk to you tonight? He should be here in a few minutes."

"That I did not know. Okay, I will wait for him, then."

In about thirty minutes, the lawyer recommended by Linda came and asked me questions. I told him everything that was dancing in my mind. I narrated to him how Uwimana, the daughter of Habimana, broke into my room the day I was arrested. He advised me that, in court, I should only narrate what happened and leave the rest to him. He had read my file and was convinced there was insufficient evidence to inculpate me.

That morning, the sun rose earlier than usual. After other detainees hugged me to wish me good luck, I got out of the cell and walked to the parking lot, where I jumped in an all-covered police van.

Arrived at the court, I could not believe my eyes. There were many young people wearing T-shirts on which was written, I am Carlos. I figured they were the survivors of the genocide against the Tutsi, because Celine and Linda were among them. I could also see many white people, including those with cameras and microphones. I wondered why my case had attracted the attention of the international media and some other foreigners who were not journalists. I judged that it was Celine's doing but could not fathom how she could convince them to follow my case.

The courtroom was also full of people, apparently of all ages and walks of life. But I neither saw Habimana nor my uncle Kamara. So, once again, I wondered if Habimana was behind my arrest or conniving with Uncle Kamara. It was all confusing.

As soon as I took a seat, Celine approached and murmured, "Be courageous. It's almost over. Have you seen the French ambassador? The lady who is sitting on the fourth row is the ambassador. The judge will not make the mistake of sending a French citizen to jail without enough incriminating evidence."

"Thank you," I said, and did not add any other word. It

was as if I were an observer in a story where I also happened to be the main character. *Why would the ambassador come to my court hearing?* I mused. *I hope Celine is not making my case more political than it should be.*

When the prosecution was given the floor, they took a turn to present their evidence. It was basically the same thing the police had told. Forensics showed that Uwimana was raped, and her DNA was also found on my bedsheets. So, according to the prosecution, the evidence was enough to conclude that I had raped her.

The judge asked me if I pleaded guilty or not guilty.

"Not guilty," I said. "I did not touch that girl."

When he was given the floor, my lawyer said that his client should be granted bail because the prosecution did not have enough incriminating evidence. He added that I had no reason to escape justice should I be proven guilty. To substantiate his claims, my lawyer asked the prosecution if they had proof I invited Uwimana to my place. Almost everybody in the courtroom made a disapproving sound when he said so. His argument was not convincing. He continued his speech and asked if the evidence presented by the prosecution included the DNA details of the semen found in the victim. He concluded that evidence that the girl was raped does not imply she was raped by me and urged the prosecution to search for the actual rapist and free the innocent. At this time, some people in the courtroom seemed to agree with my lawyer.

The judge asked me if I had anything to say, and I accepted.

"On Monday afternoon," I said, "when I heard a knock

on my door, I thought it was my friend who had promised to pay me a visit, then I opened the door. Uwimana, whom I knew as the daughter of the people involved in my mother's death in 1994, broke into my house. She said she needed my help to find her missing mother, whom she believed had been kidnapped by my uncle. She did not tell me who that uncle of mine was and how he could have kidnapped her mother. I begged her to get out of my house because I did not understand what she was talking about. When she refused, I decided to allow her to sit, calm down, and tell me what she thought I could do to help her. After giving her a glass of water, I went to my bedroom to make a telephone call. A few seconds later, Uwimana entered my room, unbuttoned her clothes, and invited me to touch her. She pushed me to my bed, but I was too strong to fall. She jumped on the bed, naked, saying that my people had sent her to my place so I could do whatever I wanted with her body as a price for her mother's freedom. It was as if she were crazy and speaking a language I did not understand. I managed to get out of the bedroom and left her lying on my bed. That's when she came to the living room saying that she would tell the whole world that I had raped her. My Lord, the next thing I saw was the police who came to arrest me for a crime I had not committed."

People in the court were murmuring about what I had said, but I could not get a word of what they were saying.

When the prosecution was given the floor for their concluding remarks, they said that everything I had said was to shift the blame to the victim. They also said I should not try to implicate other people who had nothing to do with the rape crime.

My lawyer concluded by repeating that the judge should consider what I had said and request the prosecution to find more evidence.

The judge said that the verdict would be read the following Tuesday.

When I got out, I wanted to talk to my sister, Celine, and apologize for having mentioned our uncle in my statement. But the police rushed me to their van without giving me a minute to thank all the people who had come to prove their support to me.

On that evening, Linda came to say goodbye to me. Her flight to Dakar was the following morning. When I came out, the first thing she told me was that Celine was disappointed by what I had said in court.

"Why?" I asked. "What have I said that I shouldn't have said?"

"She thinks you should have not said that your uncle kidnapped that girl's mother and that he sent her to trap you to get her mother's freedom."

"Linda, all I did was narrate what I saw and heard on the day I was arrested. Wasn't I repeating what Uwimana said to me? Did I insinuate she was telling the truth? It's now up to the police or the prosecution to do whatever they want with that information. To be honest, I don't know what is going on. I have no idea who wants me to perish in jail or die. It could be Uncle Kamara or Habimana and his family. I don't know."

"Let's wait and see what happens on Tuesday," Linda responded. "I am sure the judge shall grant you bail. That's the most important, for now."

"I hope," I said. "I am no longer sure of anything in this country I call mine."

"Carlos, I won't stay for long. I just came to say goodbye to you. My flight is tomorrow morning."

"Please, go and get it. You have all it takes to be crowned Miss Africa: a different kind of beauty, kindness, sensibility, and awareness of your vulnerability. Do never change into a stony lady. Be beautiful and human. Good luck, my dear. Don't worry about me. I will get out of here very soon."

"Thank you for your encouragement. I hope I will be able to prove to Celine that I can. I did not like it when she told me that she was sending another girl to the Miss World competition. Some people are saying that she has found one of those diaspora people whose parents were involved in the genocide against the Tutsi."

"What are you talking about?" I asked. "I can understand if Celine chose to send a more experienced model to the Miss World competition. But I am sure my sister can never interact with anyone whose family members were involved in the genocide. Maybe she does not have that piece of information."

"I don't know. Celine only told me that she was sending another person to Miss World. It's my coach who told me that the girl is a daughter of a former minister in the government that planned and executed the genocide against the Tutsi."

"What's her name? I mean, what's the name of that girl?"

"Uwase, if I remember correctly."

"Do you have the names of her father?"

"No. My coach did not tell me his names."

"If it's true that that girl's father committed the genocide, I am sure my sister, Celine, is not aware of that. I should talk to her. She needs to make an informed decision."

"Please don't tell her you got the information from me."

"I won't."

"Let me go," Linda said. "Please send me a message when you shall be out of this place."

"I will tell you."

She kissed me goodbye and left.

I could not help but wonder if the girl Linda was talking about had been recommended to Celine by James. *Does he know she is a daughter to a genocidaire?* I wondered. Did he tell the truth to Celine? Unfortunately, all my phones had been taken away from me. I could neither call nor send a message to anybody. I only hoped that the judge's verdict would be to temporarily release me. I needed to find James and tell him to stop releasing David's songs. He would also have to confirm to me the identity of the Rwandan model he had recommended to Celine.

On Tuesday, I boarded the all-covered police van again and headed to the court. The young survivors of the genocide were there with the same T-shirts. My sister, Celine, was among them. Many journalists, including those of renowned international media, were there. I did not see the lady Celine had told me was the French ambassador, but there were other white men and women in official attire, suits, and ties. I guessed they could be diplomats. Unlike on the day of the trial, Habimana had come to hear the verdict.

After a verbose reading of everything that was said the previous Friday, the judge said there was enough evidence to suspect that I had committed the crime I was accused of. He added that taking into account the gravity of the crime, I should be in jail for a period not exceeding thirty days, during which my trial would take place. The young genocide survivors in the room made noise, some of them even tried to come forward to talk to the judge, but the police pushed them away.

Some journalists approached to ask me what I thought about the verdict, but all I managed to say to them was that I was innocent. The police told them they had no permission to interview me at that moment.

Habimana approached me but did not say a word. I could read blues in his face. Somehow I understood his look as if he meant to tell me to take heart.

Celine was in tears, and some of those young people tried to calm her. I was afraid she could have one of her depressive episodes. When I attempted to approach her, the police told me it was time to go. I entered the van and went back to the police custody area to take my stuff before being taken to the general prison of Kigali. That was the same place where my younger brother's life was shattered almost two years before.

XXII

Life in prison was the misery I shall never be able to describe. But I will always cherish the lessons I drew from fellow inmates' life stories, especially those told by the young prisoners. I felt like I would recommend to scholars who wanted to understand the diversity that makes up Rwanda's population to just ask the prisoners to write down their stories. Then, they would take time to read each story, paying attention to the particularities of each of their experiences. Initially, I thought most prisoners would be those convicted for their involvement in the genocide against the Tutsi. It was true that most of the older prisoners, those aged sixty years or older, had the word *genocide* in their judgments. But the young inmates were there because of other crimes, which they might have been pushed into by the harrowing experiences they lived in the aftermath.

Ndahayo was the first inmate who welcomed me and volunteered to show me a place where to put my bag. He also linked me with another inmate who sold me a mattress on credit. I don't know how I would have managed life in Kigali prison if I had not met Ndahayo there.

"I know who you are," he said to me after I settled and when other inmates had already been used to seeing a muzungu among them.

"How do you mean?" I asked. "Of course, I have told you my name. What else do you know about me?"

"In that corner where you have laid your mattress, that's the same place Mr. D. occupied. The day I came to this prison, he was the one who received me, and from that day, we became inseparable, till the day he was shot dead. I let him down and shall never forgive myself for that."

"Wait a minute," I said. "Do you mean you were a friend to my brother and were there when he was shot dead? Did you also want to escape jail?"

"No. Even Mr. D. never thought of escaping jail. In fact, he had had enough with the world that he wanted to spend the rest of his life in this place. I was tricked by the prison officer who asked me to call Mr. D. I thought they had a deal for him."

"What kind of a deal would that be?"

"You won't understand," he said. "Even in prison, life goes on. We have dealers and consumers."

"I don't understand. What deal was that prison officer going to sign with my brother?"

"He was going to make him a distributor."

"Of what?"

"Everything he could find—herbs, powder, water, basically whatever the consumers needed to calm themselves."

"Okay, I guess by herbs you mean weed. So then what happened that night?"

"I heard the gun sound and ran away. Another prisoner, named Habimana, now a free person, had followed us maybe because he wanted to ensure David was safe. He can also tell you what happened that night. Mr. D. did not come to sleep. In the morning, we were gathered to be told that he was shot dead trying to escape prison. Please don't make me give you more details. I will not say any name. But two weeks ago, the prison officer who took your brother's life was also found dead in the small forest next to the Kicukiro vocational school. He is also now a memory."

"What's the name of that prison officer?"

"I have said I cannot say any names. There were actually two officers, but I think only one of them had the plan to eliminate Mr. D."

"Why do you think so?"

"Because the other one is known as a good person."

I wanted to ask Ndahayo if the prison officer who had been found dead in a forest was named Bosco, but I did not want him to ask me how I knew that name. I decided to give him some days to trust me enough to tell me everything.

"That's life, brother," I said. "I am glad I have found a friend in the most unusual place. At what time do you eat?"

"At four o'clock, they will give us a cup full of dent corn and beans. If your teeth are not strong enough, you won't be able to chew the corn."

"I will manage with the beans. I have never eaten dent corn before."

"You cannot survive on beans here. Your cup will be filled with corn mixed with about only five beans. But don't worry, if nobody has sent you money yet, I will buy milk for you from the canteen."

"Do you mean you have money? Does your family pay you visits often?"

"No, I don't have parents. The only person I have in this world is my sister. But the poor woman does not have time for me but for her kids whom she raises alone after their father went into exile in Uganda."

"Sorry for that. In this Rwanda, many people have gone through the harshest life experiences. Please forgive me for the question. May I know what you were convicted of?"

"Murder," Ndahayo responded immediately, without hesitation. "I killed the wife of my former boss."

"You did what?" I asked with astonishment.

"I can imagine how it sounds. But I indeed killed the evil woman. I remember it as if it happened yesterday. I had never thought I would kill anybody, but I did, though I feel as if I were moved by some other force."

The way Ndahayo said it did not appear to me as regretful. It was as if he would kill her again if he had met that woman on the street. At that moment, I was scared of that anger force that could push a young guy like Ndahayo to kill a human being.

"Does it mean you are an assassin and don't regret having killed a poor, innocent woman?" I asked.

"When I think about what that woman had said to me, I feel like strangling her again. Please don't judge me because I am already judged by this wicked world. Yes, I was convicted of murder and sent to jail, but I am not an assassin."

Surprisingly, on Ndahayo's mattress, there was a big Bible. I picked it up and started to read what I did not even pay attention to. I did not know what to say or how to behave in that strange environment. Who was I to call Ndahayo an assassin when I was also accused of being a rapist? I wanted to think Ndahayo had not killed anybody but wondered why he admitted to having strangled that woman to death.

The following Friday, it was a visit day. I had two visits. The first person was Ingabire, who had been sent by my sister, Celine. To my surprise, the second person was Habimana. The prison officer gave me five minutes to speak to Ingabire and another five minutes to talk to Habimana.

"Hello," Ingabire said. "Celine has given me money to deposit at the canteen, so you may be ordering whatever you need. She has also tasked me to be coming to see you on each visit day. In this bag, you will find a few clothes and light shoes. You shall have to buy soaps, toothpaste, and lotion from the prison's boutique. They do not allow us to bring in liquids. Please let me know if there is anything else I should bring for you on the next visit day."

"Thank you, Ingabire," I said. "No need to come here every visit day. If Celine thought it was necessary, she would come herself instead of sending you."

"She cannot manage this place. It's complicated. The motorbike left me at the gate because bikes are not allowed to come up here. The climbing took me about fifteen minutes. That would have been so tiring for Celine. Then, the queuing as they checked what we had brought, waiting for you to come out. At least your sister has sent me. Other prisoners are often forgotten and rejected by their wealthy family members. Celine cares for you. But please understand coming to places like these is not for everybody."

"Why you and not her? Ingabire, it's you I thank for the visit. It's more important than the money my sister has sent to me. I will never forget your kindness. But don't say to my sister that I am not happy she did not come. Please, tell her I am grateful for the gesture. As I said, you don't have to come because Celine has asked you to. I will be happier when you shall come because you want to check on me and not because my sister has sent you."

"It's okay. I will see you next week."

Before I responded to Ingabire, the prison officer reminded us that five minutes were over and immediately asked Habimana to move forward.

I said bye to Ingabire and hello to Habimana.

"Carlos, I am sorry," Habimana said. "I am sorry for being a coward again. I am sorry for letting you down. My daughter told me everything. She cries day and night because your uncle did not release her mother as he had promised. When Uwimana went back to Kamara's place, she was told her mother had come home, but until now, we have not yet seen Mukandoli. I am afraid they might have killed her. However, that's not why I am here. I did not visit you at the police detention because I was afraid of being interrogated either by the police or the journalists. On the verdict day, I came because I believed you would be released. I was shocked to hear what the judge said and vanished from the scene immediately after they took you back in the van. I was afraid that the protesters could throw stones at me."

"It's all right," I said, before asking him what his daughter had said.

"She told me that your uncle wanted you to disappear because you were doing things that could put him in danger. Can you imagine that my wife is the one who told her own daughter that she could trap you? She is the one who gave that idea to your uncle. I am done with that woman. Whether dead or alive, she has finally ceased to be my wife. What makes me sad is that even the kids she raised in my absence developed the same manners and misbehaviors."

"Sorry for that," I said, and did not add another word. I couldn't have cared less for Habimana's family. At least he had them.

"Carlos, I am ready. Whatever may happen, I will accept."

"Ready to do what?" I asked.

"To testify in courts. I will say everything."

"Too late," I said. "Who knows when they will confirm the date for my trial? Apparently, thirty days the judge talked about can be extended to two years, even though they call it an extension of the thirty days provisional imprisonment."

"Are you not aware? I have read in the newspapers that your lawyer appealed. You will go back to the courts again for another hearing. I will tell the judge how Mukandoli connived with your uncle to send me to jail to be punished for the crime I did not commit. I will tell them everything your uncle did because he wanted to take over the house your mother left. I will say everything I know about your brother's death. But the prison officer at the gate has just told me that Bosco was recently found dead in a forest in Kicukiro."

"Thank you," I said. "But are you sure the judge shall believe you? Do you have evidence of what you will be saying? I don't think they will accept your testimony. Tell me, did you say Bosco was killed? An inmate told me that the officer who killed my brother was found dead in a forest two weeks ago. Now I know he was referring to Bosco. I have no doubt he was eliminated by whoever sent him to murder my brother. Wait a minute, I remember something. One day, Rotty told me that he once heard Bosco and Martin mentioning my uncle's name. Bosco was saying that he would kill Uncle Kamara. Maybe the information leaked to Uncle, and he decided to eliminate Bosco before he could execute his plan."

"I have no idea who killed Bosco or why he was killed," Habimana said. "But what I never doubt is your uncle's involvement in your brother's death. That man did not want David to live. He hated him with all his heart, only because ..."

"Because of what?" I asked.

"You know what I am talking about. I believe that if you or Celine were living in your mother's house, Kamara would not have wanted to take it from you. He did not want those he despised to live in a house he was convinced was his sister's."

"But uncle knew that the house legally belonged to David's father, though he had given it to Mama."

"That's the fact he did not like. To Kamara, David and his paternal uncle, Mukinzi, did not deserve to live in that beautiful house in the postgenocide Rwanda."

"I hear you. But knowing what I know today about Uncle Kamara, I think he would do anything to anybody as long as it served his desires and made him feel more secure. He taught me one thing: People who hurt other human beings in the name of ethnicism or racism would also do the same to those they call theirs if they are convinced those people are threats to their survival or are against them. That's how Uncle Kamara thinks. He is a wicked and selfish human being."

"The prison officer is coming to tell me time is up," Habimana said. "I will put something in his hands for having given us more minutes to discuss. That's how it goes here. Don't mind the publicity about zero tolerance for corruption. Bribing prison officers is one of the tricks to survive in this prison. Carlos, see you next time."

"Wait," I said. "Do you know Ndahayo? He is the inmate who told me about the death of Bosco. Can I trust him?"

"Yes, I know him. He is a good guy and was a friend to David. But don't fully trust anybody. People change. Bye for now."

"Bye."

He walked away after giving a handshake to the prison officer, who thanked him before checking the note and putting it quickly in his pocket.

That evening, I decided to approach Ndahayo and ask him more about my brother's death.

"I hope you are not planning to say it in courts," he said. "Let those people die one by one as karma takes justice. I told you the prison officer who killed David is now in hell. But he was just an agent. The person who should be punished is the principal, the mastermind, and we shall never know who he is."

"Was the prison officer you are talking about named Bosco?"

"How did you know?" Ndahayo asked.

"I once came here to ask the director how my brother was killed. On that day, he was with a prison officer named Bosco."

"Then, how did you know he was the one who killed your brother?"

"I don't know, actually. Maybe it's because the way he was looking at me that day and the questions he was asking made me think he could be hiding something."

"Yes, Bosco is the one who murdered David. The other prison officer is named Callixte. Let me bring something."

Ndahayo stood up to reach his bag and got a device that looked like a voice recorder out of it.

"Take a listen," he said.

I could hear somebody narrating to Ndahayo how and why David was killed. He said that Bosco was promised to be paid a lot of money, but the principal paid less than a third of what they had agreed upon. He added that when Bosco threatened the man who had given him the murder job that he would tell the world about it, the man responded that he had other boys who could put Bosco on their list of pending executions. In the recording, the prison officer did not reveal that man's name but said that Bosco told him that the man's sister was killed by David's father during the genocide against the Tutsi.

"That's not true. Our mother was not killed by David's father."

"Hmmm? What are you talking about?"

"Hmmm? Sorry. What did I just say? No, I meant David's father did not kill anybody. Whose sister was that?"

"Carlos, why do I have a feeling you are hiding something? Do you know the man who hired Bosco to kill your brother?"

"No, I don't know him. It's just that David and I were together during the genocide against the Tutsi. He was there when the killers abused our mother before they killed her. David saw what no other child should see. I can't imagine that David could have been killed by people who confounded him with those who killed our mother. Did you know why he was jailed?"

"Yes. Mr. D. was accused of genocide ideology. Don't mind the wickedness of this world. How can somebody be an ideologist of a genocide that was committed when he was still a child? I have told you Mr. D. was my friend. I know he was fathered by a Hutu and suffered a lot because of that. However, he hated nobody, and even if he did, it would not be because of who his father was or whatever people called him."

"Thanks," I said. "Tell me, where is that officer? The one who was with Bosco when he shot my brother. Do you think he could accept talking to me?"

"No. In fact, he should not even know you are related

to David. After Bosco was found dead in a forest, Callixte decided to keep his mouth shut. He no longer wants to talk about what happened that night. He does not know I recorded him."

"How about you? Would you accept to testify in courts if I had sought justice for my brother, David?"

"Yes, but I can only say what I saw and heard that night. I wouldn't say anything that would make my life in prison more miserable than it already is. I don't want to face retaliation from Callixte or other prison officers."

"How many more years do you have to be in prison? I mean, what was your sentence?"

"My entire life. I was sentenced to life imprisonment for having killed a woman who called me one of those who exterminated my entire family."

When Ndahayo said that, I understood why he was a friend to David.

"I see," I said. Were you also accused of having a genocide ideology?"

"No. There is no way they could have accused me of that. I am a Tutsi, and my entire family was exterminated during the genocide. I am here because I killed a Tutsi woman from a well-connected family. I am here because I am an orphan who dropped out of school to work as a house helper in the house of the woman who insulted me day and night and called me all sorts of bad names. She crossed the red line the day she dared compare me to my entire family's killers. I do not regret having sent her to hell."

"Sorry for what happened to you. May the souls of your

family members rest in peace. I can't judge you. Some people don't understand how it hurts to be called Interahamwe when the real Interahamwe made you an orphan. That's the same way this world had turned my brother David into a bitter person. He could not take being called bad names and being mistreated by those he considered his people."

"I know. Mr. D. told me everything, including what your maternal uncle did to him. Some people are cruel. Though I do not regret having killed the woman, I think sometimes it is better to let karma do its job. But who am I to say that? Listen, don't worry; when you shall manage to get to the courts, I will be ready to testify about David's life and death in this prison."

"Thank you," I said, and hugged Ndahayo.

The following Thursday, I was told my lawyer wanted to speak to me. So I joined him in the visitor's room designated for lawyers and their clients.

"Next Monday, we shall go back to court," he said. "I appealed against the judge's decision to send you provisionally to jail, pending your trial. There is no reason to keep you here."

"What else shall I say that I did not say the last time? What other evidence do I need to provide to prove my innocence?"

"That's where the judge got it wrong. It's not up to you to prove your innocence but up to the prosecution to prove you guilty. Up to now, they have no tangible evidence you had intercourse with that girl. But don't worry, I have other plans. I have a witness who forbade me from revealing their name to anybody. Though it will not be the actual trial, I do not want to lose the chance to let the bomb explode."

"What bomb? I believe if it's my trial we are talking about, I should know who that witness is and why he does not want me to know his name."

"The witness is not a man but a woman. Please trust me, you are my client, and I will do all I can to prove your innocence in court."

"A woman? I think I can guess who she is. It must be Linda, the girl I was expecting the afternoon the devil planned to trap me. But what shall Linda say that I have not said to the judge?"

"Just get ready for Monday. As I said, I cannot reveal the witness's name to you."

After getting ready and putting on my rose uniform Monday, a prison officer showed me a van to jump in. Then, we headed to the court of the second instance of Nyarugenge.

My sister, Celine, and the youth who used to manifest their support for me were not there. Most of the journalists there were from international media, but very few were from the local media. The French ambassador was there in the courtroom, accompanied by some people I could not identify. I wondered why they only came to the court when none of them had ever come to see me at the prison. Habimana was also there, seated in the back corner.

When the proceedings started, the judge gave the floor to my lawyer to explain why the first instance court's decision should be reversed.

"Your Honor," my lawyer said. "My client appealed the first instance court's decision because he is innocent. The prosecution did not present enough evidence to prove a prima facie case: that the crime was committed and that my client did it. My client's DNA did not match that of the semen found on the victim. Only the victim's testimony was considered, and no attention was paid to my client's statement. Your Honor, I have a crucial witness with credible information about how the whole set-up was planned. If you allow, I will call her in."

The judge did not respond. Instead, he gave the floor to the prosecution to respond to the arguments of my lawyer.

"Your Honor, we provided all the evidence we had. The defendant's semen was not found by the forensics because he used a condom and threw it away afterward. Your Honor, this is an appeal to the preliminary hearing and not the trial. Therefore, we do not see why the defendant should present a witness."

"Did you find any semen on the victim's body?" the judge asked the prosecution.

"Yes, we did."

"Did it correlate to the defendant's DNA?"

"No."

"Do you know whose semen it was?"

"No, Your Honor. The victim believed it was the defendant's semen, though forensics revealed a mismatch."

"So, you decided to believe the victim and not the forensics."

"Your Honor, in similar cases, the rapists used different

tactics to obscure evidence. That's why we tend to believe the victims."

The judge, without saying anything, turned to my lawyer and allowed him to bring in the witness.

To my surprise, the witness was no one else but Mukandori, the mother of the girl I was accused of having raped. Moreover, she was accompanied by Martin. That was so confusing to me. I could not fathom what business Martin had with Mukandoli and why they would be there to say something that would prove my innocence.

After my lawyer introduced the witness, with bruises on her face and arms, and a crutch in her right hand, Mukandoli limped to the witness corner. So many questions were dancing in my mind. *Nothing good can come out of this woman's mouth,* I mused.

"I am sorry for what I did," Mukandoli said. "I have now lost everything, my life, marriage, and children. I should be in jail and not this innocent young man. In fact, I do not deserve jail but hell for what I did to my own family and to Kayitesi and her children."

"Please tell us what you have to say about the crime the defendant is accused of," the judge interrupted. "Where were you the day Uwimana was allegedly raped? What do you know about what happened that day?"

"Nobody raped my daughter. All she wanted was to save me from the hands of Kamara, who had locked me in his house after he caught me audio recording him. Mr. Judge, my husband, Habimana, was sent to prison for a crime he did not commit. During the genocide, he hid Kayitesi in our kitchen. Because of jealousy and fear, I revealed it to Interahamwe, who came and took her to be killed. This young man, Carlos, and his younger brother, David, were there. I had no problem with them. I feel bad for having made them orphans. Though my husband was angry with me, he had decided to forgive me till the day Kamara came to our house in 1997. He told me that he knew that I was the person who delivered his sister to the killers. Then he added that he would kill me if I did not accept to help him get ownership of his sister's house."

"Madam," the judge said, "would you please keep that story for another day or tell us how it is related to what happened to your daughter?"

"Yes. I will summarize. When my husband came out of prison, he told me that he would only accept to reconcile with me if I managed to gather evidence about all the crimes Kamara committed in order to have ownership of Kayitesi's house. That's how Kamara caught me recording our conversation and decided to blackmail me again and use me to stop Carlos from releasing Mr. D's songs. That man seated there is the one who saved my life. But he should also be punished because of what he did to my daughter. The sperm you found in my daughter is of that man. He works for Kamara."

When Mukandoli pointed fingers at Martin, the guy tried to escape from the scene, but the policemen stopped him. It was as if the judge did not know how to handle the situation. What Mukandoli had revealed was beyond the testimony that the court needed.

After a few minutes of chaos, the judge stated that the court was adjourned for an hour.

"You are getting out of prison today," my lawyer said to me.

"To be honest, I don't know what's happening here. How did you get that woman?"

"If I tell you who called my telephone number, you will not believe it. I am equally surprised, or I should say, baffled. That guy, Martin, whom the woman has just accused of involvement in everything that happened to your family, is the one who called me. He told me his intention was to save you because he is a friend to your sister. When we met for the first time, he said to me that the person who should be in prison is your uncle, Kamara. So, it's surprising to learn that the guy is the actual rapist. Something is not entirely clear."

"I don't know Martin that much," I said. "But I want to believe his intentions. Maybe he did not know Mukandoli was going to say everything. I think both of them are victims of my devious uncle, Kamara."

"Yes, I also think so. Maybe by now the police have already gone to arrest your uncle."

"Listen, is it possible for me to speak to somebody in the courtroom?"

"I don't think the policemen would allow you. You are not yet a free person. Who did you want to speak to?"

"The man seated over there. He is the husband of Mukandoli. I wanted to ask if he knew his wife was going to testify."

"I don't think he did. After he rescued her from the

basement your uncle had kept her in, Martin kept Mukandoli in another safe place till today. Nobody else knew her whereabouts."

After a few minutes, the court resumed. We all sat down to listen to what the judge had to say. After reading the summary of what the prosecution and the defense had said, the judge said the court had not found any evidence that I could have committed the crime I was accused of. He concluded that for that reason, the case was dismissed.

Then, he stood up and walked back to the backroom.

"You are a free man," my lawyer said.

"I can't believe it," I replied, before running to Habimana.

He hugged me and said, "I am sorry you had to go through all this because of my wicked wife. They have arrested her."

"Already?" I asked.

"Yes, she and that man she was with. Let them go and experience the same jail they sent us to. I pray the police catch your uncle too. He is the real criminal."

"I believe they have gone for him."

The prison officers approached me and asked me to get into the van back to the prison for proper checkout.

Though I was happy, I could not help but wonder where my sister, Celine, was and if she had received the news about my freedom. Her absence worried me.

XXIII

I had given my apartment keys, bank cards, laptop, and everything of value to Linda and did not know if she was back in Kigali or not. That is why I decided that after checking out from the prison, I would ask to be taken to my sister's place in Kacyiru. I needed to check on her. I needed to understand why she had not shown up at the court.

At the prison, I rushed to talk to Ndahayo and remind him of his promise.

"Congratulations," Ndahayo said as soon as he saw me. "We have heard the news. You are now a free man."

"I am not sure yet," I said. "I am released but not acquitted. The trial shall have to take place."

"I know, but since the judge has stated that there is no evidence to incriminate you, I am sure the trial shall just be a formality to confirm your innocence."

"Let's see how it goes. The good thing is that what was said in the courtroom may help us seek justice for my brother, David. I hope you are still ready to testify, right?"

"Yes, I am ready to testify, though I do not see how it shall help us. The guy who killed Mr. D is no more. Karma killed him."

"No, Ndahayo," I said. "Bosco, though he was also a criminal, did not deserve to be killed. He equally needs justice. There is a high probability that his assassin could be the same person who hired him to kill my brother. He took so many lives of innocent people, including Rotty, who was also my brother's best friend. I will not rest until he is punished for all his crimes."

"Did you say Rotty was also killed?" Ndahayo asked. "Mr. D. used to talk about him. Why? What did the police say?"

"Nothing. The investigations are still underway. Ndahayo, I suspect Rotty was killed because somebody suspected he was the one who was releasing David's songs. My brother's assassin shall not stop if not stopped."

"Do you have suspects?"

"Yes. I cannot hide it from you. After what Habimana's wife has said in the courtroom, I have no doubt our maternal uncle is the criminal who should be punished."

"Mr. D. used to tell me about how wicked your uncle is. But I never thought he could be an assassin. Is the Habimana you are talking about the one who was in this prison? Mr. D. told me he saved you during the genocide. What if he and his wife are carrying out revenge against your uncle for having wrongly accused Habimana of involvement in the genocide against the Tutsi?"

"If they are, then the police shall find out. Habimana's evil wife has already been arrested, and I am sure the police are searching for Uncle Kamara. For now, it's about their conspiracy to send me to jail for a crime I never committed. All we have to do is make sure they are also charged for what they did to my late brother, David. Habimana promised to be on my side. He has nothing to do with that wife who has hurt him many times."

"I have lost confidence in this country's judicial system," Ndahayo said. "But as promised, I will say everything I know about the night your brother was killed, though I shall not reveal the name of the prison officer who was with Bosco that night."

"Thank you. You shall say what you can say. Then, we will leave it to the investigators to find out more. That prison officer is also not totally innocent. He may have not killed my brother but did not do anything to stop or report his assassin."

"Carlos, please! I do not want to suffer in this prison because of retaliation. Let me talk about Bosco, who is already dead, but not about any other officer who may make me live in hell alive."

"It's okay. I understand. Let's do whatever is possible. Listen, I have to go. I guess I will need to take a taxi."

"Why? Is your sister not coming to pick you up? She never paid a visit to Mr. D., and I thought it was because they did not get along well. I thought you had a better relationship with her."

"She is not coming. Her phone is off. I will actually go to her place immediately because I am worried. Celine cannot come to places like this one, but I wonder why I did not see her even at the court. I hope she is all right."

"Then, you will have to walk to the first gate. If a cab is not available, you will at least find a motorbike."

"Thank you, brother. Thanks for everything. I will never

forget how you made this place feel livable because of your friendship and support. We will keep in touch."

I hugged Ndahayo, went to the administration office for the prison checkout process, then walked thirty minutes to the first gate. I was lucky to find a taxi that took me to my sister's place in Kacyiru.

After arriving at Celine's place, I took the lift to the fifth floor and knocked on her apartment door. Nobody responded.

"It's me," I said. "Your brother, Carlos."

"Who?"

"Carlos."

She went silent for about three minutes, and when I was wondering what to do, she opened the door for me. She was already in tears.

"Brother, I did not know you had been released. How did it happen? Who helped you?"

"It's a long story. What's most important is that I am now free. Tell me, what happened to you? Your face. Your eyes. It looks like you have been crying and have not eaten for days. Sister, please tell me what happened."

"It's also a long story. Now that you are here, brother, if you want me to keep on living in this world, please help me get out of this country. Let's leave and never come back to this society of wicked people."

"Why? Does it have something to do with my imprisonment? Did anybody harass you or bully you because of that? The last time we talked, you were happy about your company's success and that the man who abused you for years was sent to jail. So what changed now?"

"Everything changed. First, Kananga escaped jail. He is now outside the country, speaking on the so-called radios of the opposition groups. I think some powerful people helped him escape. But that's the least of my worries. I am like this because some Rwandans are doing all they can to destroy me and my modeling business."

"How? Did Linda not win the Miss Africa competition, and people are blaming you for having sent an unqualified model?"

"That's actually the only good news. Linda won Miss Africa and is celebrated by many Kigalians. She is now their star. After a tour in France, she will be back to the country tomorrow."

"Then, why are you not celebrating? Isn't it the first and biggest achievement of your company?"

"Yes, but now it's about the Miss World competition. People are smearing me on social media. They are insulting me, saying that I decided to send a daughter of a genocide perpetrator to the Miss World Competition."

"What? Which girl? Didn't you tell me she was recommended to you by James? Did he know about her father?" I did not want to tell my sister that Linda had told me about that girl.

"I don't think James knew anything about the girl's family," Celine responded. "Her father is a free man who lives in the UK. There have never been any charges against him. His only sin is that he is a Hutu who was a minister in the former regimes. If I had known the girl's background, maybe I would not have sponsored her participation in the Miss World competition. When I learned about her father, I immediately called the modeling company with which I signed the deal for all the costs related to her participation in the Miss World competition. But they told me I would be making the biggest mistake of my life if I asked Uwase to withdraw from the competition. Apparently, she is doing wonders and has many chances of being the first sub-Saharan African to be crowned Miss World. Today, I am glad I sponsored her. The insults and death threats I have faced have made me look forward to seeing her win the competition. The people who have been verbally attacking me on social media are not any different from the Hutu militias who made me an orphan."

"No, sister. You cannot make that comparison. You should understand our society is not ready for certain realities. I think it's not about that girl but the fear that somebody with that background could be proclaimed beautiful, when other Rwandan girls, culturally accepted as most attractive, could not even be on the finalists' list in similar competitions."

"That's probably true. Nobody said anything about Uwase's parents and background when I was trying to get Uwase a Rwandan passport. It was only when the girl started to catch the attention of international media and social media influencers that some officials even started questioning me about her parents."

"What? Even the officials? I can understand those who use social media to throw all their bitterness and hate to others, but why would a government official be interested in who participates in the beauty pageants? Is it not like any other art, business, or sport? Do they ever check the ethnic and family background of football players or dancers, for example?"

"Maybe it's because no Rwandan footballer has caught the attention of international media so far. If one did, the haters would not have failed to find something to say about who he is and why he should not have been allowed to shine. But I cannot say the entire government made a statement about Uwase's participation in the Miss World competition. The individual officials who called me are simply as sick as the social media haters. They do not represent the Rwandans who have decided to move forward despite the wounds caused by our dark past. Uwase is a beautiful, innocent girl who should not be penalized because of who her parents are and the so-called ethnic group she is associated with."

"I like what you have just said, especially your last sentence."

"Yes, brother. The verbal attacks I have endured for the last few days have made me realize that hatred can make even the most reasonable people destroy other human beings. When I read what people were writing about me on social media, I attempted to commit suicide. But I was stopped by a friend who encouraged me to be strong."

"No, sister, you had no reason to take your own life because of people whose hearts are filled with hatred, bitterness, and insecurity. Nobody chooses her parents, and that girl is not defined by who her father is."

"Indeed," Celine responded, before adding, "Brother, I guess God wanted me to understand the pain our younger brother David endured. Some people are accusing me of having decided to associate myself with those who made me an orphan because of money. Can you imagine? Me, Celine? Brother, Rwandans are cruel. I am so scared of what they could do to me if I was indeed associated with those they hate. They are evil."

Celine was in tears again.

I pulled her to my chest and said, "Don't say that, sister. I am sure many Rwandans are silently happy that you did not discriminate against that innocent girl because of a history she did not participate in writing. Do you remember the goal you had? You wanted to show that beauty comes in different shapes and shades, right? The same applies to inner beauty. It's not our background or the names people call us that define who we truly are. Thank you for giving Uwase the chance to prove her individuality. I am sure she will not use her fame to tarnish our country's image or promote divisionism and violence."

"Yes, the girl has done everything she could to talk about the history of the genocide against the Tutsi, condemn its perpetrators and deniers, and preach about peace and respect for diversity. But whatever she does seems not to be enough for the haters unless she changes who she is. It's pathetic how some people can hate others just for the sake of hatred. Carlos, I guess I have achieved my goal. Whether Uwase wins or not, I have sent my message out. Now I can take a rest and wait for the day I will die."

"Die? Why do you like to talk about death? You are too young to even think about dying."

"Carlos, there is something I have not told you. I have been living with death for five years. Every night I am reminded that I am dying. I guess I am now ready to go. Nothing is left for me to see or do."

"What are you talking about? I don't understand. Please wipe your tears."

"Brother, I am HIV positive. The day I was kidnapped, I stopped taking my tablets. I did not want to live anymore. All I wanted was to do what I could to leave a legacy. After Kananga was arrested, at a time when my company was prematurely doing well, I sent Ingabire to bring me more tablets. But now, once again, I have no strength to take my tablets. I am done living. Please take me out of this country to breathe another air and enjoy another type of life, at least for the few months I am left with."

I looked at my sister but failed to say a word. I had a lot to say but did not know how to say it. I recalled when Ingabire had told me that Celine took a tablet every night. Though I had suspected HIV on that day, I had forced my brain to conclude that the medications could be for depression or other conditions.

With a touch of her hair, I said, "No, Celine, you are not going anywhere. You cannot leave me alone and lonely in this world. You are all I have. We need to see a doctor. If those in Rwanda cannot find a solution, we will go to Europe. I am sure some medications can give you the long life you deserve."

"Yes, I know. But it's more complicated than that. Which hospital can I go to where people will not recognize me? I cannot queue with other HIV-positive people. Before you know it, all tabloids would be talking about the fact that I have AIDS."

"No, Celine. Though I don't know much about HIV and AIDS, I have heard that they are different. The fact that you are HIV positive does not mean you have AIDS. Don't worry about going to the hospital. I will go there with you, and if anybody asks you, you will respond that you have accompanied your brother to see his doctor."

"As if that resolves the problem," Celine said, smiling at least. "Do you think I would love people to gossip that my brother is HIV positive? If you want me to get treatment, you should take me to France."

"If it were possible, we would go there tomorrow. But it seems I cannot get out of this country before my normal trial. I have to be finally acquitted."

"That's true," she said, before taking her ringing phone and walking to her bedroom to take the call.

As she talked to the person who called her, I turned on the TV. After the commercials, the news started. They talked about the usual: the visitors the president had received in his office and the development projects some ministers and senators had visited. Then, in other news, shockingly, they said that Uncle Kamara had shot himself dead when the police had gone to catch him. Before I could call Celine to come and hear the bad news, I heard her screaming behind me. I had not realized she was done with the call and was also watching TV. She immediately fell down and lost consciousness.

"Celine, please wake up. Oh God, sister, please."

When I was about to pick up the phone and call the

ambulance, my sister woke up. I asked her to lay down on the couch.

"No," she said. "No, don't tell me he is dead. That man is evil. He cannot just end it like that. He is the cause of everything we have endured. He is second to those who exterminated our families in 1994."

"Please don't think about it. Uncle Kamara committed suicide because he did not want to face justice. He has given himself the same death he gave to so many innocent people."

"Carlos, what are we going to do? Tell me how we shall go to the funeral of the uncle who was going to be arrested for what he did to our family. I do not want to face the eyes of his wife and our family members who never cared about our misery."

"Let's see how things develop. I think we should go to the funeral. Whatever he did, he was our uncle."

"Do you know how I feel now?" Celine asked.

"Tell me."

"It's over. Uncle Kamara, who sexually abused me day and night and led me to a lifestyle that made me HIV positive, is no more. Brother, you are right. I now have to live and see all the men who abused me die, one by one, miserably. Kananga escaped jail, but I am sure he is not happy where he is. He is being used by the opposition people to say anything bad he could think of about the country leadership he admired and liked to praise. He is doing that so they may help him get asylum in the countries they are in. That in itself is misery for him."

"Sister, it's true that you need to live. But please live for yourself and not for revenging what was done to you. You will not live free if you don't let go of the past. The good thing is that those people are no longer in your life. So, cherish that life you have today and forget about them. Before you had a telephone call, we were talking about your treatment. You need to continue taking your tablets. Yes, I guess we need to travel to France and breathe a different air for a few months. But you cannot wait for the visa application process before retaking the medicine. Let's go to see your doctor tomorrow."

"I will see. Tomorrow, I will pick up Linda from the airport at two o'clock, and I do not want to be in a bad mood. I am afraid those haters and paparazzi journalists shall also be at the airport to show their support for Linda. They have been saying that she should have been the one to participate in the Miss World competition, though they know she does not speak any foreign international language fluently."

"Don't mind those people. I will be there with you. The problem is that I can't go to my apartment because I gave the keys to Linda and do not know where she put them."

"What? Did you say you gave your apartment keys to Linda? Why? Brother, are you and Linda in a relationship?"

"No, we are not. It's just that … I mean, I had to give the keys to somebody."

"Why didn't you give them to me then?"

"Please don't ask more questions about that. Isn't Linda a beautiful girl? Why would you mind if I were dating her?"

"Because she is not wife material," Celine said. "Linda is like me. She was also abused by men. Girls like us are no longer wife material."

"Please, stop giving those men the victory they do not deserve. They did not take everything from you. You and Linda are beautiful, intelligent, and kind girls. In fact, your experiences made you stronger and better future wives than any other girls who have not seen the darker sides of this world. Please, don't allow the people who hurt you to have a hold on your future."

"If you say so! But you did not tell me whether you are dating Linda."

"Not yet," I said. "But I can't say I don't like her."

"I also like her. But when the group of young genocide survivors she had connected me with decided to cut contact, I concluded it was because Linda was angry I did not sponsor her for the Miss World competition. I hated her for that."

"Oh, is that the reason why I did not see you and those young Rwandans at my second hearing?"

"Yes. Some of them are also venting all their anger at me on social media."

"Too bad. Young people should support each other and aim at creating a future that is not shaped by our country's past tragedies. For God's sake, Uwase is competing in a beauty pageant. It has nothing to do with the genocide and the role her family members may have allegedly played in it. Sister, if you had not insisted, I would also not have allowed you to use the genocide survivor card to advocate for my release. No person, irrespective of their history, should be jailed for a crime they did not commit."

"You are right. Now I know how it feels when every action or word is interpreted within the context of our tragic history.

It's as if we have refused ourselves the right to live in the twenty-first century."

"Listen, I am hungry. We have been talking for three hours. If you are not ready to cook for me, let me see what you have in the fridge and prepare for us a quick meal."

"The only thing I have cooked is the beef stew. Feel free to boil rice or fry potatoes. That will be enough. I would suggest taking you out, but I don't feel like it because of the news about Uncle Kamara's death."

"I was also wondering who can tell us more about his death. But the only person who would is also paying for the crimes our uncle paid him to commit."

"I feel sorry for Martin," Celine responded.

"Why would you feel sorry for him?"

"I feel like he is a good guy who aimed at nothing but surviving in this jungle. He thought he could not make it if he had not agreed to carry out those dirty jobs for the big boys, as they call themselves."

"That's not an excuse. Do all of us make money by committing crimes? He should be punished for having hurt many people, including you and David. I have not forgotten that he was also involved in your kidnap. Let him serve a few years in jail and reflect on the bad choices he made."

"That's life. What goes around comes around, they say."

The following morning, I accompanied Celine to the hospital. After we entered the doctor's office, I left her in, then waited on the corridor bench.

As I was waiting for my sister, my phone rang. It was Linda.

"Hello," I said. "Are you back?"

"No. I am calling from Nairobi. I am landing in Kigali at two o'clock. I have just read on Isaha.com that you have been released, and I could not wait to call you."

"That's so nice of you. Congratulations on having been declared the most beautiful girl in the entirety of Africa. How was the tour in France?"

"France or heaven? Carlos, what are you doing in that Rwanda when as a French, you have the right to be walking on Champs-Élysées Avenue every evening? If it wasn't because I did not want to disappoint Celine, I would have escaped the people I was with and found a way to stay in Paris."

"That would have been a bad decision. Now that you are an international model, you will have many opportunities to visit even more beautiful cities."

"Yes. I shall never find words to thank your sister. I read what has been written about her on social media and in newspapers. Those people are so cruel. They have no idea where Celine found me and turned me into the person I don't even believe I am. Initially, I also wondered why she was sending me to Dakar and not to the Miss World competition. But now, if I was told to choose, I would still choose the Miss Africa competition. It's weird to claim to represent the world's beauty. But Miss Africa! I now feel like I am the prototype of African beauty."

I could hear Linda's laugh breaking my eardrums and was glad she was happy and grateful.

"Wow! I am happy for you, Linda."

"Thank you. I got to go. We are going to grab something to eat before checking in on the flight to Kigali."

"See you at two. I will be right there, at the airport."

XXIV

When Celine got out of the doctor's office, tears were flowing down her cheeks.

"Sister, why are you crying? What did the doctor say to you?"

"Nothing," she responded.

"What do you mean nothing? You have been in that room for hours, and you are saying the doctor said nothing to you?"

"I am not crying because of what the doctor said to me. It is rather because of what I said to him. I have told him everything as if he were a psychologist. It was as if I were narrating a sad story in which I happened to be the main character. Carlos, the decision is taken. I don't care anymore about what people think of me. I will live for myself, you, David, and my parents. Mama must have been weeping to see me suffering in this world. I am going to make her proud of me. The doctor has explained that taking the tablets consistently shall weaken the virus and give me more years to live, like any other person with no medical condition."

"Glad to hear that. Sister, I am so proud of you. Guess what? I have some other good news for you. Linda has called me from Nairobi. She is on her way. She said she shall make all those who bullied you understand that she would not have become who she is today without your support. Apparently, she prefers being crowned Miss Africa."

"That's good to know. Let's see how it goes at the airport."

So many journalists and young Rwandans were waiting for Linda at the airport. When she came out, the minister of culture handed her a bouquet of flowers before she was given a mike to make her speech.

Linda thanked the government and everyone who supported her. After talking about how the competition was challenging, she said, "I had one goal in mind: to make Miss Celine proud of me. You may not know what she means to me. Without her, I would probably be dead by now. You all know that my parents and siblings were killed during the genocide against the Tutsi, right? Like me, Celine is also the only survivor of her entire paternal family. Her mother was also tortured and murdered because she was a Tutsi. Before I met her, I was lost in this world of selfish people. I was a drug addict who had no hope for a brighter future. But when I talked to Celine for the first time, I knew I had found an elder sister in her. She understood me. She encouraged me to stop taking drugs. She paid a coach for me and introduced me to modeling. I am here today because of what Miss Celine did for me. When I saw what some of you wrote about her because she is giving another girl the same chance she gave me, I felt sad and angry at everybody who was abusing my hero. Let me tell you something, I don't want to be Miss

World. I am honored to represent African beauty. This is a miracle, and I still can't believe it happened to me. Uwase, the girl you call the daughter of a genocide perpetrator, is an experienced model who speaks French and English fluently. She has more chances of winning that competition. But there is another thing you do not know. During the competition for Miss Africa, Uwase called me every night to wish me good luck and give me the tips I needed. She is not defined by who her father is. She is a Rwandan girl carrying the Rwandan flag to the Miss World competition. If you are my fan, please give me the gift of supporting Uwase, shall you?"

After that long speech, the crowd applauded. I could see some people approaching to hug Celine as if they meant to apologize to her.

From the airport, we went to the Sunset Hotel to celebrate with employees and models in Celine's company and a few friends. Then, Linda took me to where she had left my keys and stuff. After that, she went to Celine's apartment, where she spent a few days searching for her own apartment in one of the chic neighborhoods of Kigali.

A few days later, my lawyer called to inform me that the charges against me had been dropped and that I was a totally free man.

"That's excellent news," Celine said, after I told her.

"Sister, it's not over yet," I said.

"How do you mean?"

"Though Uncle Kamara is dead, I want the whole world to know about our brother, David. I asked my lawyer, and he said we cannot sue a dead person. Now, I am wondering how I should seek justice for David."

"How about the prison officers who shot him?"

"Bosco was killed, I believe, by Uncle Kamara. But there is … I mean, maybe. Anyway, maybe a judicial justice is not possible now."

"Brother Carlos, though I do not want any more drama that would call more negative attention to us, I think it is not for us to think about whether suspects are alive or dead. If we can, all we need to prove is that our brother had no intention of escaping prison, then leave the task to the police to investigate why he was killed and who killed him."

"You are right. I have two witnesses who will talk about the night my brother was killed. Tomorrow, I will initiate the case."

"Just be careful," Celine said. "It should not be regarded as accusing the prison management."

"No. I am sure the prison management was also deceived by the criminals who infiltrated its system. But they should not have rushed to conclude that David was trying to escape. They will have to facilitate the investigations."

The next day, I went to the police and said I wanted them to investigate the murder of my younger brother, who was shot dead in prison.

After I told them whom I was talking about, one of the officers said, "That's a closed case. David Mukiga, known as Mr. D., was shot trying to escape jail. His death was an accident, not a homicide."

"Officer," I said, "don't our laws punish even involuntary homicide?"

"Of course they do. But in that situation, the prison officer was doing his job."

"That I understand. You said the intention was not to kill my brother. If that was the case, that officer should at least be charged with involuntary murder because he should have been careful, right? But how can it be confirmed without a doubt that it was involuntary?"

"What are you up to?" the policeman asked. "Are you here to teach us how to do our job?"

"I am sorry, sir. More than two years have elapsed since the death of my brother. I had not come here, because I wanted to believe he was indeed shot trying to escape prison. But after what happened to me and the testimonies of witnesses in my court proceedings, I have no doubt about who killed my brother. His death was masterminded by my uncle Kamara, who committed suicide a few days ago."

"So, if the suspect committed suicide, who else do you want to sue?" the policeman asked.

"Sir, what needs to be investigated is the circumstances of the death and everybody who was involved in it, either as the mastermind or the executor. I have not told you something else: even the prison officer who shot my brother is no more. He was found dead in a forest a few days before my uncle committed suicide. So maybe you may start by investigating that prison officer's death."

"What was his name?'

"I only know his first name: Bosco."

"That case is already under investigation. But we are not sure we can help you with your brother's death. The announcement of the prison directorate was final. He was shot trying to escape jail. Officers are administratively disciplined but not charged with any crime when that happens."

"That is not fair," I said. "I guess I have done my part. I will count on you to give justice to my brother, David."

"We shall see what we can do," another officer who had not uttered any word before said.

Then they gave me a paper on which I wrote my case report and signed.

The following Friday, I received a call from an unknown number.

"Hello, Carlos. It's me, James. I wanted to tell you that I am in Kigali. I came back yesterday. We need to meet and talk."

"What? Am I dreaming? James, where are you? How is Harumi?"

"I did not come with her. Brother, there is a lot we need to talk about. Sorry for everything you went through. When I read your messages on Facebook, I hated having let you down. I am so embarrassed."

"What if you come to my apartment?" I said. "There, we shall have our conversation without fear that somebody would be listening in."

"Perfect! See you at six o'clock."

As soon as I dropped the phone, I received another call. It was from Linda.

"Hi, Linda," I said. "You must have been too busy. I have

followed all your interviews. I did not know public speaking was one of your strengths."

"Thanks for the compliment," she said. "Carlos, I have something important and urgent to tell you."

"Please go ahead," I said.

"Not on the phone, please. Let me know if you are at your place. I would be there in twenty minutes."

"I am here, but I have an appointment with someone at six. What if we have the whole of tomorrow together? It will be a Saturday."

"That's also fine. I have another interview at Izuba TV early in the morning. As soon as I am done, I will immediately come to your place."

"Perfect."

When James came, we talked about everything—the songs, murders, jail, court proceedings.

"Brother, I am sorry you went through all that alone. I was also going through challenges. Harumi took me to Japan to introduce me to her family. I thought racism was only a thing of Europeans and not Asians. But what I experienced in Japan was at another level. Her parents called me bad names and threatened to disown Harumi. She was braver than me and ready to be disowned instead of breaking up with me. On the one hand, I did not want her to break ties with her family. But on the other hand, I did not see myself insisting on becoming part of that family that did not treat me as a human. That's how I decided to leave her in Japan, change my telephone number, and move to another apartment, so she may never find me again. It's over between us."

"Oh, sorry to hear that. You and Harumi made a wonderful couple. It's so sad you had to part ways like that. I pray for you to find another beauty like her."

"Another beauty? Yes, there is one who had been impressing me, and you know who she is."

"Who are you talking about? I hope you are not talking about my girl."

"Your girl? Or you mean your sister?"

"No, my girl, though I haven't told her officially how much I love her. Do you remember Linda?"

"Yes. But tell me, is the Linda who won Miss Africa the same girl we picked from the streets?"

"That's her. She was a hidden beauty, and I am madly in love."

"Wow! I am so happy for you."

"But you still haven't told me the beauty that lately caught your attention."

"Brother, don't take it in a bad way. I have feelings for your sister, Celine. She does not know anything. But that girl you call your sister has everything a man needs in a woman."

"Stop it," I said. "Forget about my sister."

"Why? Don't tell me you are that possessive. For God's sake, she is your sister, not your girlfriend."

"It's just that … I mean … Why would you fall in love with her when you know everything she went through? I remember telling you how she was … You know what Uncle Kamara did to her. Then, the old man, Kananga. Are you crazy? I don't want to think of you as one of those men who made her life miserable."

"Carlos, you are taking it too hard. Your sister may have been abused by different men. But that did not suck out of her all her outer and inner beauty. She is still worthy of true love. What I feel for her goes beyond what those men were up to. She is intelligent, caring, and captivating. She has what many girls cannot offer."

"Anyway, you better get those ideas or feelings out of your brain or heart. I am sure my sister is not searching. I have warned you."

"Warned me? About loving your sister? Carlos, I am sorry, I don't get you."

"One day, you will understand what I am talking about," I said.

"Let's wait and see," James said.

I could not tell James that my sister Celine was HIV positive.

"Let's change the topic," I said instead. "Please tell me, why did you recommend a daughter of a genocide perpetrator to Celine? Do you know what my sister went through because of that?"

"Brother, that girl lives with her parents in London, a noble family. I had no idea her father was involved in the genocide. But even today, I wonder why he is a free man."

"Don't you know many genocide perpetrators in the West escaped justice because those countries do not care about what happened to us?"

"I know, but since he was a minister in the former administration, if he indeed committed the genocide, he should have been taken to the international criminal court for

Rwanda in Tanzania. Maybe I would not have introduced Uwase to Celine if I had suspected anything. But now, when I think about it, I wonder if she should have been penalized for crimes that were committed before she was born. I am glad she is proving to be different. Next Saturday, we shall watch the grand finale, and I bet she wins Miss World."

After that conversation, I told James that I was finally seeking justice for my brother, David. Though he was pessimistic, he agreed with me that at least we will have tried.

He left my place at around nine o'clock.

The following morning, I cleaned my apartment and cooked a heavy breakfast in preparation for Linda's visit. It did not take long before she was there.

"Halloo," I said to her. "Finally, you are here."

She responded with a kiss on my cheek, then added, "Carlos, last time, I did not have a chance to tell you how happy I am that you are now a free man. This world's people can be wicked. You would still be in prison if it was not because of a strong judicial system."

"My dear, please have a seat and tell me more about the judicial system you are praising. So many people died, including my brother, David. I will fully rejoice the day they will also get the justice they deserve."

"Carlos, I am sorry to say, but you know well that the criminal behind everything was your uncle, Kamara. Karma caught up with him the day he did to himself what he had done to so many innocent people."

"Linda, Uncle Kamara's criminal acts would never have been possible without all the people who worked with him and a system that allowed them. Did Kamara shoot my brother, David? Did he kidnap my sister, Celine? Did he sentence to jail Habimana for a crime he never committed? Did he come to my room to seduce me so I may be accused of having raped that evil girl? I don't think he is also the one who shot our friend, Rotty. Yes, Uncle Kamara was the mastermind, but everybody who was involved in those crimes should pay for their actions."

"Listen," Linda said, "before we change the topic, I wanted to tell you that yesterday I was interrogated by the police. Apparently, they are already investigating the case of Badguy, I mean David."

"Are they?" I asked. "When I left the office of those in charge of investigations, I was pessimistic. They told me that the prison officer who shot dead my brother was executing his duty to prevent a prisoner from escaping. I am glad to know that they are finding out more about the circumstances of his death. What questions did they ask you?"

"Most of them were about Martin and my relationship with him. It seems he confessed to some crimes."

"What crimes?"

"I don't know. I only told the police what Martin used to say to me, like when he would have killed people or executed some kidnaps. I also told them that Martin and Bosco, the prison officer who shot dead Mr. D., were friends. But when they asked so many questions, I told them that I was not a reliable witness. They asked why and I said I was a drug addict who did not pay much attention to anything during those years."

"Have they asked about you and David?"

"They wanted to know why I cared about his death when he was jailed for what he had said to me. I told them how Martin pushed me to report David because he wanted him jailed, despite that what he had said to me was one of the bad jokes we used to throw at each other."

"Maybe we should not go back there. David shouldn't have said what he said to you, and he was punished for that. But he was not death-sentenced. Whoever was involved in his death should be accountable for that crime."

"Carlos, let's wait and see. Now that Martin is in their hands, I am sure he will tell them more. I know him. He is not a bad person but one of those guys who believes that nobody makes it in life if they are not brave enough to accept all sorts of dirt jobs. To Martin, the aim was to make money."

"Even by killing innocent people?" I asked.

"Yes, killing, kidnapping, and delivering young girls to their rapists. He used to tell me everything, sometimes tears flowing on his cheeks. It was as if he were possessed by those criminals and could not make a U-turn."

"Linda, listen. Come and have the breakfast prepared especially for you. You now have to tell me more about the Miss Africa competition and the Europe tour you did. I cannot believe my best friend is now a top international model."

"Your best friend? I thought I was …"

"Indeed, you are more than a best friend. I meant what I said to you the other day. I only hope you are still my Linda and not a top model I cannot afford."

After sharing breakfast, Linda spent the whole day with

me, talking, watching movies, and enjoying being together. She left in the evening after dinner.

My sister, Celine, came to my place on Thursday of the following week. I did not expect her to visit.

"Brother, tell me, what is wrong with your friend, James?" Celine asked, after I served her a drink.

"What happened to him?"

"I don't want to see him ever again."

"Why?"

"Who told him I am interested in love talks? Please tell him the only relationship I want to restore is with myself. Days when I was searching for love are long gone."

"I hear you. But why do you seem angry, as if James did anything wrong? Just tell him the truth: if he loves you, you don't love him back."

"The problem is that I would be lying if I said I am indifferent. Since the first day I heard James's voice, I knew something was different with him. But I did not think about it because he was with that Japanese girlfriend, and I was also going through my troubles. I only liked having a friend in him. Now, the guy says he loves me and wants to have a committed relationship with me. Is he mad? I understand there is a lot he does not know about me. But even what he knows is enough for him to understand I am not wife material."

"Stop it. Never again say that about yourself. My only worry would be that another man may break your heart if he decides to end the relationship after finding out your status.

You will have to tell James the truth if you want to build something solid with him."

"I have no problem telling him about my HIV status. In fact, one day, I will write my story, and the whole world shall know. However, I don't feel I am yet ready for a love relationship. In all the years of my adulthood, I have only been with men who wanted nothing but my body. I don't know how it feels to be in a relationship for love."

"If you have no problem with that, then the next time he talks about love, tell him you are HIV positive. I am sure that shall kick him off."

"Yes, that is what I will do. I wished I had met James before that monster I called my uncle abused me. I can confess he makes me feel a little weird."

"That means you are in love," I said, laughing.

Celine laughed back and said, "That is why I don't want to see him. I hate that I seem to lose control when he talks to me."

"Please allow yourself to feel that magic. They call it 'love.' My dear sister, I am sure, one day, you will find the happiness you so deserve."

"Thanks, brother. I just needed to talk to someone, then decided to come here. Now, I have to go. I am organizing a gathering on Saturday where everybody who supports Uwase, and the modeling industry in general, will be watching the grand finale of the Miss World competition. Linda has convinced many people to accept Uwase. I look forward to seeing her crowned Miss World."

"Where shall it be?"

"At my favorite, Sunset Hotel."

"I will be there."

"Thanks."

On Saturday, we gathered to watch the finale of the Miss World competition. On the big screen, we could see Uwase walking elegantly in the traditional Rwandan imikenyero to showcase her talents. She recited a musical poem in a mixture of Kinyarwanda, English, and French. The way she played with languages was remarkable. After that, she also appeared in a modern formal dress with a beautiful ponytail. To respond to a question on diversity, Uwase said, "Diversity is the mother of scientific and artistic inventions and adventures. Nothing could be measured, differentiated from another thing, appreciated, or recognized if everything had the same shape, shade, and features. The same applies to human beings. Nobody's beauty could be acknowledged if not in comparison with another person's beauty." Some people in the room applauded. The guys seated behind me murmured that Uwase was sending a message to those who did not want her to participate in the competition.

After many hours of the show, the masters of the ceremony announced the winners. Waiting was killing us when they were explaining how all girls did well. Finally, when I heard the name Uwase, joy strangled me, and I could not say a word but kiss Linda, who was seated next to me.

"That's not fair," Linda said. "Uwase deserves more than that.

I had not realized Uwase was called the first runner-up. The crown for Miss World was given to a British girl.

"Linda," I said. "I think we still have reasons to celebrate. No other Rwandan girl has ever received any prize from those competitions. They never even reached the finals.

"You are right. But Uwase is different. She is beautiful in and out."

"Don't worry. She has already opened doors to so many other Rwandan girls."

When I was talking with Linda, Celine approached. "Carlos, we did it! I am so proud of Uwase. Though she is not Miss World, I believe she has proven it is possible."

A week after, Uwase landed at Kigali International Airport. She was received by many dignitaries, led by the minister of culture. A party was organized in the Hotel Corner for Creatives. I could not believe my eyes. The room was filled with all Rwandan celebrities, journalists, Kigali tycoons, and some government officials.

When my sister, Celine, was given the floor to talk, I thought she would limit her speech to congratulating Uwase. I was not prepared for what she had planned to say.

"When I was crowned Miss Rwanda 2000, I thought it was a privilege to be declared the most beautiful girl in the country. Since then, I have met wonderful and powerful people and traveled to many beautiful places. I have also made good money, though some vanished into other people's hands. However, many of you do not know that my beauty or my looks have also been a source of trouble for me. I experienced both verbal and physical abuse because of beauty. Today, I do not intend to tell you my story but to celebrate Uwase. I want to encourage you to see beyond her outer beauty. Uwase was close to being crowned Miss World, not only because she is stunning, which she indeed is, but because she proved to be competent and confident. That's how we want Rwandan girls to carry our country's flag: walking with confidence, showcasing their talents, and speaking substance and ideas that may change the world we live in. Our girls are not symbols of beauty and objects of men's pleasure. They should be respected and valued. I believe all girls are beautiful, and what they need is a chance to showcase their outer and inner beauty to the world."

After Celine's speech, the master of the ceremony gave the floor to the minister of culture.

"Beauty pageants are normally not part of our culture," he said. "So, I guess I am not here because a Rwandan woman has been declared one of the most beautiful girls in the whole world. The president of our country has sent me here to deliver this message to you and to all Rwandans: Uwase is Uw'u Rwanda like any other Rwandan. When she expressed her interest in representing our country in the Miss World competition, we helped her with the papers she needed. Nobody cared to know who her father was. Do you know why? Because both Uwase and her father are Rwandans who have rights and obligations like any other citizen. You all know how some people did not support Uwase. Some said she did not represent Rwandan beauty. Others said she should be penalized for the crimes allegedly committed by her father. I am here to congratulate Uwase for having not allowed herself to be broken by those challenges. She knew that she was carrying the flag of Rwanda and was determined to make us all proud to be Rwandans. Today, in all international media outlets, Rwanda is being mentioned. Do you know why? Because in addition to having Linda as Miss Africa, another Rwandan girl is the first runner-up to Miss World 2016. This would not have happened if these girls were not mentored by Miss Celine, who also deserves our appreciation. That is why I would like to inform these three girls that the president himself has offered the most precious gifts in our culture: abahaye amagaju, ngo ajye abakamirwa."

When everybody applauded, I saw tears flowing down Celine's cheeks. Looking at all those officials, celebrities, and journalists in the room, I was so happy that my sister had finally achieved her goal: fame and money. But I wondered if that was the only source of happiness she needed.

After everybody left, Celine proposed an after-party for Uwase, Linda, James, Ingabire, and me. So we went to the rooftop of the Agaciro building, where there was a luxurious restaurant called All for Love.

After we ordered drinks, the spontaneous Linda said, "Guys, did you read the news?"

"No," I responded. "What are they saying about Uwase?"

"It's not about Uwase. Look." She showed me an article on the screen of her phone. Then she said, "A prison officer named Callixte has been arrested. He was involved in the death of Badguy, sorry, I mean David. Apparently, the same crime has also been added to the charges against Martin. Finally, it looks like we will get justice for your brother."

"That's good news indeed," Celine said. "Carlos, sorry I did not tell you because I was busy preparing for the function. Yesterday, somebody called me to break the news to me. It seems the police have connected all the dots. Bosco, the officer who shot dead our brother, was introduced to Uncle Kamara by Martin. The report is that David had met some powerful people in prison, those who are sometimes jailed for corruption, and told them his story. Those people had started questioning Uncle Kamara before he decided that the only way to silence them was to eliminate David."

"Do you know what I am thinking about?" James asked. "This is David's achievement. If it was not for those songs, your uncle would not have gone crazy enough to kill and eliminate everybody he thought was publishing the songs. His downfall started with what he staged to look like rape. Sadly, so many people, including Rotty, lost their lives because of Kamara's madness."

"To my brother," I said with a loud voice. "And to all young boys and girls of Rwanda who want nothing else but to be recognized and accepted as who they are and not what the world thinks they are. Though my brother's killers are not yet sentenced, please let's toast to his justice."

"Wait," James said. "Celine and I have another announcement to make."

"Hmmm?" I asked.

"James and I have decided to give it a try," Celine responded. "He is crazy enough to love me even after I told him everything, including my health status. I guess Linda is the only one who does not know I am HIV positive."

"Don't say that," James responded to Celine. The beauty of both your eyes and your soul is what attracted me to you, and I am blessed to call you my girlfriend. There is no challenge we shall not be able to overcome together."

Tears of joy were already flowing down Ingabire's cheeks.

"Guys, please allow me to express my gratitude to this angel," Celine said, holding Ingabire. "Without her love and friendship, I would be dead by now. My dear, I am sorry for all the years I was too busy to spend more time with you. From now on, you are not just a friend but a sister."

"Don't worry about that," Ingabire said. "I am happy for you. Please, do never forget that you are worthy of love and long life. You survived everything you went through because God wants you to live and continue to bless people like me. I am glad I found an elder sister in you."

It was as if Linda were still digesting the news about Celine's HIV serostatus. Then, I felt the need to interrupt her deep thoughts.

"Guys, do you want another announcement?" I shouted.

"Yes," they all replied.

"I told Linda that I love her, but she has not yet told me she loves me back."

"That's not true," Linda said. "I said I love you too."

"Do you?" I asked. "If you do, please give me a kiss on the cheek."

When she approached to give me the peck, I grabbed her lips for a long kiss after murmuring into her ear that I wanted her to be the love of my life.

When others were clapping for Linda and me, I could not help but think that I needed to get back to France for a break and that I would not leave Linda behind.

After seeking justice for my late brother and rescuing my sister from the captivity of Kigali men, I went back to France in November 2016, accompanied by Linda. We got married in the summer of 2017.

James convinced Celine to stay in Rwanda so they may continue to contribute to the fashion and modeling industry in the country and fight against any sort of beauty bias or discrimination. They decided to have a long courtship before marriage.